GW00503159

ISBN: 978-1-915819-04-8

3

Grandma

Incandescence

By

Mehreen Ahmed

OTHER TITLES BY IMPSPIRED

Rowan –
by Maggie Mackay

Pinnacles of Hope -
By Charlie Brice

The Eternals –
by Ryan Quinn Flanagan

Feathers and Bones-
by John L. Stanizzi

Hometown –
by Ken Cathers

The Kingdom –
by Mary Farrell

A Snowfall in Paris –
by Theresa C. Gaynord

INTRODUCTION

Incandescence was inspired by Rabindranath Tagore's
The Last Poem—Shesher Kobita. I read it three times at
different stages of my life. And each time, I construed a
new meaning. At the most mature stage of my life,
Shesher Kobita led me to reflect on the ethical aspects of
romance and marriage, out of which this book came—but
not entirely because Incandescence also reflects on
revolution that sheds light further on characters' nuanced
ethical values.

What's important in this book is the exploitation of the
characters to the extent of what to expect from life, in
general, both philosophically and materialistically? Is it
always possible to do the right thing? What are its
consequences in the event of failure and how do we make
compensation in a broader sense? For instance, if we
attribute the benchmark to Mila Chowdhury and her
grandmother, who are continuously trying to set
guidelines, then we notice flaws on their end, also—
different kinds of flaws but flaws nonetheless. Which
gives rise to a fresh set of problems? How does one
benchmark ethical behaviour? Can it be benchmarked at
all?

In attempting to tie these up, the book ends up not
pursuing an answer but leaving it open-ended. In the
end, it's left to the reader to reflect and find their own
solutions. While it is an entertaining and heartwarming
book absorbing a full depiction of culture, it is not a
morality play, so to speak. In contemplating such
realities, regarding the matters of the heart, it is not

always possible to condone the moral issues which are the heart of the matter. Either way, I hope my readers will find this enjoyable and not judge the characters too harshly. And take it all in their stride.

CONTENTS

12 – café

22 – lake

34 – interlude

52 – southbound

74 – nighthawk

92 – bibi-wife

117 – awakening

132 – waves

140 – love

166 – memory

175 – roof

183 – silence

190 – change

197 – meeting

211 – proposal

221 – peacock-dance

242 – homecoming

254 – beach

275 – chilies

295 – neighbour

307 – canary

325 – black tongue

336 – winds

348 – incandescence

café

At Raven's Edge, Mila Chowdhury sat at The Blue Café
sipping sparkling water. A weather beaten leather bound
diary was open before her. It belonged to her grandmother,
Daadi Amma. She was reading it and jotting down some of
her own thoughts. A wind picked up just outside the glassed
window. An intermittent twiggy knock on the pane diverted
her attention. A tall gum tree stood there and a sudden blast
tore off a branch and felled it on the sill.

She glanced at the branch and whispered to the winds,
"Let me write my story in the sky." She gazed at a placid
winter afternoon, silent like a still painting. Her face stood
out amongst the café crowd, but not like a sore thumb. There
were others like her but more appealing with sprightly
demeanours. It eluded her. Carefree, she thought. Something
tore at her gut. She conferred with her inner self and tried to
understand joy colluding with despair. Not known to her,
why had it always been like that? Why couldn't she separate
the clashing emotions fused within the unmarked
boundaries of the soul?

Her soul was never at peace. It oscillated between here
and there; between a temporary world of the body and
elsewhere, a limitless life of the mind, or of the spirit. Of the
mind, she noted with care. An inner self of being, became a
dream; more so in hibernation. Hibernation was the word.
For that was a long journey. It offered no reprieve from
dreaming on a continuum. In awakening, the tall green grass
had now turned into straw. Dehydration caused her to
hallucinate. The letter came way too late, her fate could have

turned. But no, that was not written in the stars. Written off. Love, written off. She couldn't break someone's heart by accepting. Accepting meant a defeat for Papri. Married, yes, Papri had already married him, while his love for Mila lived. It was too late for Mila. He had already married Papri. His insoluble dilemma of marriage which Papri never found out even to this day.

Papri had nowhere else to go. It was a marriage of convenience. Still, Mila received his love letters, one too many. An imminent affair loomed at her doorstep; it nearly knocked her over. She read the letters but never responded. A marriage of the heart very well could have been. But the grass had been dehydrated by then. The dehydrated grass had turned into straw. The brittle straw clung to the earth for dear life.

She quietly went into hibernation. Now there was a bed of straw whose tortured roots lay rooted into the soil. The sand caved in. The unnurtured soil lay hollow. There was a hole. A hole in the soil where she had slept. She dreamt of nothing else. Awakened, hunger acted as fuel. Hunger drove her to eat all day. She walked in a dream, a dream of life, and she listened to the birds of spring breaking the silence of the morn. There was silence in her heart. It whispered a dirge. It was spring. Love was in the air. The air was fresh, Mila sat under an apple tree. Fresh, red apples hung over her.

An apple tree burdened with fruit. Burdened. Her heavy heart was burdened; it hung on a precipice of memories. If one could paint them, then there would be that many shades of red. She buried herself deeper into the burrow. The hole which she clawed. She picked up the dirt

13

with her own two hands. The dirt slithered between the five fingers. It slithered right through. The waves of her thoughts flowed undulated. She wanted to see him now. After many seasons, she wanted to know what he looked like. She had given him up for Papri, because Papri was an orphan. She had given him away only to find him after all these years. Age and ageing broke her now.

Broken bones, but not bad bones. They were just fine bones in the end. Hard to know. Would it be immoral to want him back in her life? She didn't have a single bad bone, they said. Alas! It was the paradox that killed her. The poison ivy crushed her unduly. Creepers, the ivy crept up her spine. The love potion at its best worked like magic, and at its worst created delusion. Maybe, it was a delusion. She never really wanted him. She was better off without him, perhaps. Leave him to his nemesis, to his Papri, the one he'd married and had second thoughts about her and wished that he had not married her, for he loved Mila. That was what he thought. And his thoughts turned in a while he took Papri back. Papri, a Bengali word, meant petal in English. She was soft and sensitive. She used to say, "Look at me as I embrace death. This world is too harsh, far too harsh." Yes, it perhaps was for her who never tried to do much.

Mila Chowdhury dug deeper into her trench. She had dodged a bullet. It could have taken its toll. He, Rahim Ali, would never have understood her. He was far too engrossed with money, matter, and materialism. She, on the other hand, soared on the wings of poesy looking for truth in the arts. It would not have worked out for her. In the end, she realised that it was far better this way. She pulled herself up and out of the burrow. The leaves under the tree were crunchy and brown. Brown, not as a natural process of

14

decay, but brown because they paved the way to new life. The dehydrated grass had turned into straw when she went into hibernation.

The straw now turned back into green grass. She felt content. Shades of pink turned her reds around. She felt not just content, but she was young again. She was a sheaf of corn; the life-giving properties of the sun; sprinklings of water. Back to the waves where life had begun as did hope and optimism. Optimism and hope had replaced the drought of the soul and the nihilism of the thought.

Mila Chowdhury burst into Dhanmondi Lake. She was with him—Rahim Ali. Affairs were common here. Surreptitious meetings, often clandestine, took place in the dark alleys of Dewangonj, not far from this lake; lovers kissed at sunset when the evening's azan was heard from the tall minarets of the mosques; the muezzin's hoarse voice heard through the high-pitched microphones, stirred the believers—scurrying along for evening prayer. Maghrib was offered just before sunset; bats self-organized to fly towards an unknown destination. Like a black alien flying ship, down the ocean's skyline, the bats set off at dusk. Hence, the rush to perform Maghrib, because it had to be offered within that very short time of the pale evening light and full darkness.

Mila Chowdhury knew him, Rahim Ali, since the war. He was her first love. He sat down by her at the lake today. She viewed him in a new light. Her old emotions were a distant memory. She tried to meet him as an old friend. Rahim in Arabic means to bestow kindness. It was okay, as far as the meaning was concerned, but to think of the sound, what kind of a name was that? Well, it wouldn't be his fault, of course, that his parents thought the little boy would grow up to be kind.

Mila smiled thinking of how he, Rahim Ali, sat down so casually looking at her as if they were still in a relationship. But Rahim saw that she gulped with desire. He didn't say much but smiled. He also had a skullcap that mullahs usually wear regardless of prayer times. She suppressed an urge to tease him by telling him that she felt like smoking. Rahim would probably have a cardiac arrest and would perhaps leave her in peace in this tranquil moment by the Dhanmondi Lake, but she couldn't give him a heart attack because he was also betrothed to Papri, a soft petal as the name suggested.

Rahim, however, continued to look at her as though he was about to divulge something. It was getting embarrassing for Mila who was trying to avert her gaze. Averting her gaze was more effortless than acknowledging that something was not right in his relationship with Papri. Mila looked at his skullcap momentarily. He started a conversation about some house he owned. Gosh! How good was his new job? What else? He had a foreign degree, an MBA from the University of Urbana-Champaign. Now returned as a newly appointed professor at Dacca University he was an academic success, of course. It was just this, that the conversation was stifling.

He was good for Papri. Who else was going to marry her? Mila knew Papri through a mutual friend, Shreya, and had met her at Shreya's place. Papri was an orphan growing up in her sister's home who treated her no better than the strays down the alley deemed as permanent bingers, eating her out of house and home. Still, Papri's situation was better than many other orphans. She at least had a roof over her head with three healthy meals a day. In the marriage market, since it was difficult to find a suitable man for the uneducated, orphan women, Rahim Ali was a very good catch. However, her fair skin colour and delicate features were enchanting and marketable to any man.

"What if I never find a man?" Papri confided to Mila, once they had become close friends, at a tea party on Papri's sister's verandah.

"Well, if you never find anyone, you just never get married, I guess. You die an old maid," Mila had observed.

"Old maid? In this house? My sister couldn't wait to marry me off. "

Mila thought of Papri's many boyfriends, who dated her on a regular basis, but never proposed to her. She wondered why that had happened? Papri had many men at different stages of her life and of different ages too. Some were vastly older than her, while others were younger. Even as young as eighteen. Tender age always didn't mean immature. That eighteen-year-old boy wasn't. Papri was pretty, and she attracted boys and men of all ages. When she went to school with a bag-pack on her shoulders, she'd walk down the alley in black shoes and a white dress wrapped over her like a pinafore. Trying to walk steadily was something she never bothered to do, and she skipped lightly under the bowing bamboo bush.

17

When the somber cloud river sat high over the bamboo bush, she waited underneath to get drenched. Often soaked, fever or not, she cared less. Rather, she didn't care much at all whether or not she could take her exams on time on account of an illness. Yes, she'd failed quite a bit. Her progress report was mostly in the red. Green was a pass. Then with her parents' sudden death, she'd become an orphan overnight. She'd walked up to the bamboo bush and simply cried her heart out. The bush stooped, stooped like a bent spine never to be straightened. Never to understand the pangs of her lonely heart, it just listened. It listened stooping before grief and stirred in the winds.

Life, but lifelessness was more like it. Silent—the bamboo stalks said nothing, did nothing. Still, they were alive, but without a soul, unlike humans. The truth was revealed in their presence. Questions were asked, some more cosmic than the others. Papri howled, cried, and asked, Why? Why do we suffer? What do we do to suffer like this? God punished us for no reason or perhaps the reasons were off-limits to human comprehension. Would the bamboo know? Burdened with the heavy wisdom. Maybe that's why they stooped?

The bamboo bush really meant something to Papri, a friend, who would only just listen and not talk back, a unique friendship between two living creatures, a plant and a human—but a relationship of a kind. This bamboo bush had the perfunctory function of a counsellor. A trust it had earned in her young mind that she unburdened so completely crying to it and talking to it about a certain harshness of life. She didn't understand why her parents had to die. She was just ten. It caused her so much grief. Her elder sister, much older than her by about fifteen years, could become a surrogate mother, yes and loving too, but she was married and had a family of her own. Papri had become a burden on them at ten.

The bamboo bush listened without a word. Winds rustled sweet nothings through and around. Satisfied, yes, she was satisfied. Her heart was lighter. She had found her bearings here. This place had become a spot of solace for her, and she couldn't stay away or stray away. Summer or winter, fall or spring, the bamboo bush was an extension of herself and couldn't be parted with. The rainwater dripped down its leaves. Skies above, far above somewhere, the greyness matched. It matched not above nor below but at the core, not the core of the earth, it was all a connected cycle—a Dreamtime. It matched the colour of her mood, the greyness of her heart, and formed an organic interconnection. The rain, the bamboo bush, the grey skies, her heightened mood, all in one chain of cosmic order. Separate, yet connected. Connected through a natural network. She loved her life, she hated her life, she just didn't know what to do with her life. Her sufferings purpled like the blooming jacarandas under a silent grey sky.

Papri had sensed a gap in her relationship with her parents when they were alive. Now that they were dead, she realised she was a frightened little girl, stricken with grief, who hid under the bed when her father lapsed into one of his bloody moods, throwing things around, breaking them and then crushing them under his two feet. The cause of this raging madness was because someone in the house had done something wrong. Perhaps, her mother did something wrong. Who knew? Who knew? But she saw them all, the deep dents in the furniture, the torn up books all along the mosaic skirt board trim down the hallway. Words, from those crunched up balled pages, popping out and moaning before her; Papri thought for a moment how insane it all was; the trashing, this yelling, and more importantly the permanent scarring of the soul.

This frightened young girl needed protection. No, her mother, a weakling herself, needed protection. She was too weak to even attempt to protect her own daughter, Papri. She just didn't know how to protect either of them, but the mother felt chided every time her daughter was chided. A weakling, she'd become complicit for not protesting. Like a zipper to secure family relationships, the mother tried to zip up the violence. She thought in this way she would keep her family safe and intact, but it never zipped up. It slid midway from the intensity of the rage. The zipper burst at the seams from the sheer volume of grief spilling out no matter how many times she tried to zip up. The broken jagged lines of the zipper could not be mended. A new zipper had to be sewn in, a water-tight compartment for healthy emotions to be housed.

That too happened but not until the accident. Her parents were killed in the crash. She was ten and growing up in her sister's house. Once she had reached the sweet marriageable age, Rahim Ali's father proposed to Papri's uncle, a family friend, for their niece's hand to marry Rahim. Without even asking Rahim, the father had given them his word. Rahim, being the kind, obedient boy, agreed to his father's wishes. He put his love for Mila securely away. Time and time again, the sun had set within its halo brightness. It was only Rahim, of all the people in the world, with his fresh ideas and impeccable reputation who could save Papri from her inconsolable grief, orphaned at ten. Papri and Rahim Ali were betrothed, but Rahim had asked for this meeting by the

Dhanmondi Lake. Shreya told Mila that he wanted to see her for one last time.

lake

Here they were. The old lovers, Rahim Ali and Mila Chowdhury were meeting alone at the Dhanmondi Lake. Mila saw him walking towards her, and it struck a chord to see him again. He smiled at her and sat down by the translucent lake, a mirror on a windless summer's afternoon, a cut-glassed vision of self-reflection.

Mila felt strange sitting with Rahim Ali. The war. It happened some years ago. Mila could never forget their first meeting, but now she kept those emotions at bay. This new Rahim Ali was Papri's. It was awkward. Sitting abreast, they glanced straight ahead at a couple of white swans basking in the lake's water. From the corner of her eye, Mila noted Rahim Ali's reading rimless spectacles. She wasn't expecting it, but he abruptly took them off and turned his gaze towards her. She bit her lips under his gaze as she lowered her eyelids. She began to knot and unknot her fingers without making any eye contact.

A host of flying foxes were passing by. She looked up at them instead and pretended to be distracted. Rahim had continued to look at her. He was a professor now with a foreign degree, not the rebellious hero she had once fallen in love with in those carefree days. He must be preoccupied with money and materialism these days. Priorities changed with marriage.

The flying foxes were heading north in a natural choreographed movement. A crow came by and swooped low over the lake. It found a few measly bread pieces floating in its calm water, ducked, beaked up a soggy portion, and swallowed it rapidly. Watching this, Mila hid a smile and thought the food scraps must have been left overnight by people, perhaps even lovers, who had come by to feed the swans. She felt Rahim Ali's bare eyes all over her face. Fancy sitting here with him. What was he looking at? Why did he even ask for this meeting? she thought, inching away from him, but Rahim also inched in, to sit closer to her.

Yearnings of love also burned elsewhere at the far end of an alley. It was a disreputable site where scandalous affairs took place. It was a hotbed for runaway lovers. Mila's grandparent's house, famously known as the House of Chowdhury, an imposing two-storied brick building, also stood within a short distance. This respectable house, the House of Chowdhury, was juxtaposed to this site like a seated grand lion beside a slinking jungle skunk.

Mila's grandparents were old money, an aristocratic family of the fallen zamindar, or king of a principality. Although fallen, The House of Chowdhury was not a bleak house. In their own right they felt patrician for being one of the most influential families in all of East Pakistan, currently Bangladesh. They were also the proud patrons of art and culture who made sure there was never any dearth of culture in their house. The members of the family paid regular visits to the local cinema theatres nearly every week, streaming the dashing postmodern hero Waheed Murad's top hits of the 1960s.

Every evening singing performances were held in the front yard of this house. A huge straw mat was spread carpeting most of its grassy patch except for its surrounding gardens. A secret garden at the edge of the front yard boasted monsoonal tiger lilies and thorny roses growing within the foliage of juicy berries and tall neem trees, enchanting, a sort of oriental paradise like the garden of A Midsummer Night's Dream with an idle full moon and mad puck igniting sparks of tender romance.

The members of the House of Chowdhury jostled tonight on the mat to listen to their youngest son, Ashik's, rendering of love songs. His songs were heart melting and touched at least one particular woman for sure, the neighbour Raja Hashem's bibi, his wife Prema Hashen, in an unflinching desire. Prema Hashem, the young mother of three, found Ashik's company more pleasurable than her own husband's. This transpired into an unsavoury chain of events. She decided to slowly move away from her husband and form a stronger bond with Ashik as only this spirited youngest son from the House of Chowdhury could give her a thrill and a meaning to live. Prema Hashem was a young woman of great beauty, an enchantress by a long shot in the neighbourhood. She didn't think that any age difference mattered. Ashik was eight years younger than her. He was only twenty-two, and she was thirty.

In the evenings when the House of Chowdhury woke up to Ashik's songs, Prema Hashem could not restrain herself. Regardless of the various moods exuded from those songs, melancholic or lively, she felt he sang them only for her. His love songs touched the core of her beating heart. Those lyrics, "I love you so much that only the moon knew its full depth" could mean only her. Whether or not he sang them out of deference to her or out of actual love, no one could tell. But as time rolled by, time and time again those lyrics sung in her presence were like a nemesis call. They left her undone. Trying to stay confined in her own house became futile. Neither could she stop listening to the songs,

24

which could be heard any way, because of the close proximity between the two houses only separated by a flimsy gated wall, nor could she restrain herself.

Under a full moon, these secret gardens reshaped into the mango grove in her mind where the enchanted Krishna made love to his Gopis. Krishna and his Gopis appeared before her as mythical dancers, performing ritualistic Bharatnatyam, the Krishna alarippu to the ancient magical tunes. At the behest of her muses, she felt like a Gopi herself surrendering to her amorous god, Ashik, whose open invitations awaited a full romance to ensue.

Such unbridled thirst pulled her towards the house like a star to a black hole, and it behooved her to respond to her senses. Songs which had made her feel beautiful, she felt whole in all those jewellery and sarees. They made her forget about the mundane chores, her children, and the drudgery of a prosaic insipid husband, Raja Hashem, who lived in his own world of studies like a happy idiot, oblivious to romance.

Ashik in Bangla means lover. Ashik couldn't deny that he too desired the young mother, Prema Hashem, the forbidden fruit, a mother of three, and married to his neighbour. They both knew that love neither understood nor respected any boundaries. It was literally coveting the neighbour's wife. However, nothing could or ever would obliterate the feelings they harboured for each other, nor keep them away from their mischievous dates. The rendezvous? What other place but the shady end of the alley? Just as well, the alley offered lovers like them some kind of recognition, a panacea to the souls. A place where clandestine relationships thrived without anyone judging.

Some were simply romantic interludes, short-lived and casual others were more promising, leading to marriage. It was yet to be discerned Ashik Chowdhury and Prema Hashem's relationship.

Within the House of Chowdhury another couple was also in love. A rounded verandah encircled the house, in the privacy of which this other romance blossomed. Lovers, Mila knew their love had come to fruition. The heyday of their lives when the leaves of the guava trees trembled with joy at the slightest touch of a pecking bird. Its whistles whipped the core of young hearts, the agony of restive days and listless evenings. The sallow lantern didn't quite reach the far side of the verandah where in this dim obscurity this young couple would sit in two cane chairs with their fingers braided into each other.

Her name was Lutfun Azhar, and he was Sheri Chowdhury, Ashik's older brother. Lutfun had just turned twenty, and Sheri twenty-five. They dated here at sunset every evening. They didn't have to go to the alley, for theirs was a more legitimate relationship. The family's tacit support encouraged it.

Mila was Sheri and Ashik's eldest brother, Ekram's daughter. As a child, she often wandered around the verandah when her Uncle Sheri dated this girlfriend. Some things she could never forget like the sense of subtle sweetness tense in the air. She'd hear their spoken words describe a quiet adoration for each other and unspoken heavy sighs and soft murmurs. They had also known that Mila watched without a din, but they would smile at her curiosity, not remotely bitter nor concerned. There was no

26

place for such negativity in their hearts which oozed with the ripened juices of pure love.

They told magical stories to each other. Impossibly intense love stories, stories of Romeo and Juliet, and of Laila and Majnu, stories which only inspired hope and optimism. Such stories alluded to no profanity and remained in their hearts like invaluable tales, relics gathered in the repository of an entwined tragic romance.

Lutfun was a virtuous woman, kind and pious. She loved people unconditionally, and her guileless smiles said it all. They beguiled everyone. She possessed natural selflessness like the perfect Hyperborean land. Such innate endowments became stronger with every passing season. These were some of the qualities that made Sheri Chowdhury fall in love with her. The gentle lady bestowed her affections steadily upon Sheri. When little Mila eavesdropped on their conversations, they'd let her in on it. She stood there in the dark passageway and would listen away to every little story they told her. She observed how they kissed, held hands, and whispered nothings at blue twilights.

It all seemed like a fable to the adult Mila. That this sort of kindness should prevail in pursuance of love. Utopia, at best, was something so divine that even time didn't or wouldn't tarnish it. These were exemplary instances. However, they also provided a rare glimpse into the natural order of things, what should be but rarely is. Like the perfect sun or the moon, or precise forces of gravitational pull, such love was rare and could find itself a home in the celestial pantheon. Uncle Sheri could easily die for Aunty Lutfun, as did Romeo for his Juliet.

By the lake a patch of cloud had gathered and veiled the sunlight. She noticed that Rahim had also put his spectacles on by now. He looked out at the lake unmindfully and said, "Do you not want to know why?"

"There's going to be a storm soon." Mila said. "I think I already know why, Shreya told me about Papri's broken home and your father's marriage offer to her uncle."

Rahim Ali was prepared for this bluntness, but he said. "I don't think we can sit here anymore. Why not come over to my place? I've got my car. We could talk there."

"Thanks, I'll go home. Why did you want to meet? To torment me?" she asked.

Mila understood that he wanted her in his car somehow. She felt that he still loved her. What were they going to talk about though? Money? Investments? Certainly not romance when he was going to marry Papri.

She looked up at the layered clouds set against an autumn sky on the satin edge of a dull horizon. Rahim kept a close watch hoping that somehow she would change her mind, but Mila bade her passions to lay elsewhere. She decided to be the quintessential introvert who made herself a recluse. She pondered and observed the world around her and tried to avoid romantic advances. No one would understand, nor even care, why her love had increased lately for the incessant rainfall, the thunder, and the swishes of the gusty winds, or the mists of the opaque drizzles, the frolicking birds such as the crows with their measured picks off the lake's surface.

When Mila didn't respond, Rahim stood up and walked away. He got into his car and left. The car raged as it sped. She couldn't figure out why he would get upset. Apart from the fact that Papri Khandakar was a close friend of hers, there were no other ties with him anymore. It wouldn't be right to get into his car and then go home without her friend being present. Her role models, Uncle Sheri and the virtuous Aunty Lutfun, would not approve. However, Prema Hashem and Uncle Ashik may have, she wouldn't know.

Prema Hashem and Ashik Chowdhury were just as passionate in love as any other couple. However, unlike Sheri and Lutfun, they would never be allowed to date in the House of Chowdhury. Despite the fact that Ashik was Sheri's brother, Ashik and Prema Hashem dated far down by the alley with all other shady couples with equally shifty commitments. Prema Hashem had come out every night after putting her children to bed. When her husband sat flicking through the boring evening newspaper, she would sneak out to meet her lover over by the designated lovers' den.

The lovers' den was a cave in a small mountain, conveniently located out of sight. At nighttime lovers would enshrine the cave with glowing candles. This was the moment when the cave would become a sanctuary illuminated with impassioned dialogues. This wasn't the place for Sheri and Lutfun at all, but only for the strays of the alley. Although Ashik Chowdhury wasn't one, he belonged to the same House of Chowdhury, a house held in high esteem. This dungeon was not the most suitable place for a man of his stature, at all. But his circumstance decreed otherwise. His was an unsightly affair compared to the Lutfun-Sheri relationship.

What difference did it make anyway? An older Mila thought in circumspect. Why should the society be inclined to condemn the types of Lady Chatterley or Madame Bovary? Were they any different from the Laila-Majnu, and the Romeo-Juliet's as far as love's purity was concerned? All's fair in love and war, no? Clichéd, but it was true.

One was fairer than the other though. What was deemed as sacred love entailed Lutfun and Sheri, a celestial pair sanctioned by society, favored by their elders. Who could sit beside one another on the mat every evening listening to Ashik's rendering of the love songs under the watchful eyes of their elders and holding hands in perfect bliss, exchanging tiny coy smiles?

Whereas Prema Hashem would push herself in through the gate and hover at the fence darkly like a dithering shadow waiting for a welcome cry from someone to join the party on the mat. Although she and Ashik were Cupid blind as anyone else in love, the elders of the House of Chowdhury looked upon Prema as nothing other than the beautiful lush wife of their quiet neighbour. Clueless to their affair, however, the family would never have condoned if they knew so much as a word.

Her husband, Raja Hashem barely spoke to anyone, but commanded huge respect in the neighbourhood on account of it. A learned man, Raja Hashem, couldn't understand his wife's fantasies. He thought three healthy meals, clothes, and ornaments sufficiently satisfied a woman; from head to toe, Prema Hashem was covered in jewellery like a queen. But her insufferable ennui was hard to break. No one could, except Ashik. Not even her own children could break its bounds. Although she couldn't go even remotely close to Ashik in the House of Chowdhury where she found a full life in spite of it. This was still better away from the stifling atmosphere of her own. For, her husband wouldn't notice her great beauty, let alone compliment it. Deep in his studies, he lived a life of the mind, a scholar, and a hermit in seclusion.

One night, however, Raja Hashem decided not to read his newspaper but be with his wife. He looked for her in the house. She wasn't there. He thought, maybe, Prema Hashem was at the neighbours, but he wished her here tonight. As the night progressed, he gradually fell asleep. When he woke up in the morning, she was still not in bed. Her side of the bed had not been slept in all night, at all. Suspicion or cynicism didn't enter his mind because he was not the sort. But when he entered the dining room for breakfast, he found his children sitting glumly without a mother. As soon as they saw their father, they broke down in tears.

Raja Hashem now feared the worst. He walked over to the verandah and found a note pressed under the heavy volumes of War and Peace on a feeble cane table by the red rhododendrons. He saw it and swiftly pulled it out from under the two tomes. It read very clearly that he, Raja Hashem, must not try to look for her as she had run away with her man next door. Was this some sort of a joke or serious elopement? Indeed, but as Raja Hashem struggled to grapple with the reality of the situation, he read the note a few times.

His children had come around and stood on the verandah. He looked at their grim faces and teary eyes. They had no idea where their mother had gone, let alone why she had gone. He grabbed them in panic and in sorrow. They began to cry.

Ashik and Prema's affair was bold and tantalising. Raja Hashem's sanctimonious life, or at least how Prema Hashem would interpret it, had not kept her away from her lover, Ashik. Raja Hashem could not give her what Ashik could. The couple had settled at the far end of the alley, without the blessings of the House of Chowdhury. Their elopement did not make his family proud either. It caused such turmoil that Mrs Chowdhury, the mistress of the house, had to disown him. And Ashik, forced to part with the glory of the House of Chowdhury, thought this sacrifice had justified his love. If Romeo and Juliet, and Laila and Majnu could transcend to a metaphor for love, theirs could too, one day.

In the heart of it he felt that they were equal. They were the modern day Romeo and Juliet because in terms of society's rebuke, none found a sympathetic hearing from any quarters. Conversely, Lutfun and Sheri thought of themselves as the proper embodiment of Romeo-Juliet since they fared better in the eyes of the elders in finding true love. But the definition of the real McCoy of the world remained indeterminate because love machines like Lady Chatterley's always justified their affairs not as profane, but as sacred.

Mila thought about Rahim Ali's offer to take her for a ride in his car. It would be another scandal if she were to agree to his advances. However, did he really love her? Then it would be pure, since love in itself was alway honourable. She had crushed her rising passion for this man and had not griped. But why had Rahim not defied his father's choice to marry Papri? She wanted to know but not go to his house alone with him. Was this meeting a sign to apprise Mila of his undying love for her? It baffled her and put her off guard.

interlude

It was an unforgettable evening, Mila thought
retrospectively at the Blue Café.

The servants of the House of Chowdhury had prepared the
front yard as usual for a regular singing session. The family
had just finished dinner. The master and the mistress, Mr
and Mrs Chowdhury, noticed that Ashik's chair at the table's
far end was empty. After dinner the family gathered on the
mat in the front yard as they did every evening. However,
no singing would be performed because Ashik the singer
had disappeared since last night. Adjacent to the gardens
next to the front yard, several lanterns were placed around a
musical instrument. They shed light on a forlorn harmonium
sitting on the mat without a vocalist. The gate between the
neighbour Raja Hashem's cottage and the House of
Chowdhury was ajar. The Chowdhury house housed at least
fifty members and dwarfed the cottage next door.

Among those fifty residents, almost no one had any
clues to Ashik's sudden disappearance except for Ashik's
brother, Sheri, and his girlfriend, Lutfun. Only they had
some inkling. After the elders had gone to bed, curiosity
goaded the duo to watch. Sheri and Lutfun witnessed Ashik
taking hold of Prema Hashem's hand. He pulled her
towards him, and she showed no resistance. To the contrary,
she relented without hesitation. It was a dark moonless
night. The monsoon had covered all of the stars with
impending rain, but the lanterns had not been snuffed out
just yet. The telltale tall shadows were a sign that the pair

34

was in love. They held each other closely. He pulled her shoulder towards him and kissed her.

Lutfun was rooted to the verandah's mosaic floor. She blinked a few times and gripped Sheri's hand. Their gaze transfixed at the looming shadows, she sensed that this was all wrong. How deplorable an act to covet the neighbour's wife! One which would also hurt the reputation of the noble House of Chowdhury. They saw the two shadows move to make an egress through the main gate.

The following evening, people sat glumly outside on the mat. Lutfun and Sheri were there too. Somewhat statued on the mat, they realised that this uncomfortable secret of the elopement needed to be told, but their courage failed them. This could become fodder for gossip amongst the elite for days on end. Ashik's absence stirred the core of his parents' heart as it was. Their son, a talented singer, had gone missing, and the singing was disrupted tonight on account of it.

A stormy wind picked up and swept through the front yard. The elders, Mr and Mrs Chowdhury, quickly rose from the mat and went indoors with all other fifty members in tow including Lutfun and Sheri. The flowers in the garden trembled in the gust. A few even wilted instantly snapping off their dry branches in a matter of seconds.

This sprawling home, the House of Chowdhury, was a show of grandeur. It was an old two-story house. The verandah had wrought iron balustrades with floral-shaped ivory inlays. It had five massive bedrooms upstairs, four bedrooms downstairs, a rectangular shaped living room, and a dining room. The kitchen was detached from the main

house but was roomed independently across the vast front
yard by the tall lush azadirachta indica. The kitchen was one
of many isolated rooms situated around the precipice of the
yard.

The Chowdhury family may not have been particularly
inclined towards conservatism, but the mistress of the family
knew where to draw the line. She would not have condoned
Ashik's elopement with the neighbour's wife. That would
push her limits too far. However, everyone was still in the
dark regarding their disappearance. They knew that
something had gone wrong, that Ashik had not been home
since the last soirée. Raja Hashem reported his wife, Prema
Hashem, missing as well. The family suspected as much,
especially Mr Chowdhury who thought that the two were
up to no good. It was too much of a coincidence that these
disappearances occurred at the same time. His suspicion
nagged as it nagged in the others too. It was Lutfun and
Sheri's best-kept secret. They continued to observe the
family trepidations without so much as a word.

A dream within a dream, a plot within a plot, a cloud
over a cloud, a layer upon a layer, blues played out through
the monsoon pour. Servants rushed to close windows
around the house as the winds raged. The beautiful Lyra
bushes behind the wooden shutters made a desperate bid to
enter. When they couldn't enter, the drifts drove up fallen
branches of dead leaves and the discarded weeds. The rain
hammered on the open verandah. Lutfun lit a few candles
inside the house and placed them around the room's antique
furniture.

She sat down on a high-backed chair in an alcove with
Mrs Chowdhury. She looked at her demeanour in the

candlelight, sharp nose, high cheekbones, erect posture. Her hands were folded gently on her lap as she held her head high. Lutfun thought about Mrs Chowdhury's aristocratic lineage. The zamindars generally piqued her curiosity which was nothing more than fantasy tales, only in this case they were real.

These much touted zamindars Lutfun imagined were every inch royalty, and rightful landlords of their villages. They retained the title Chowdhury, a remnant, a whiff of a bygone era, a hedonistic lifestyle which entertained decadence. The zamindars could engage in practically anything they wanted. Womanizing topped the list. The heavy smell of alcohol and the unending tinkling of ankle bells of court dancers stifled the palace air. Their official wives had not much say about who the zamindars took as paramours. They were powerful men who rarely cared about anyone's feelings. They cared less how they squandered the wealth accumulated over many generations. Clearly, some attracted more disrepute than others. This was an era of no accountability, the soulless kings got away with the crimes against the soulful peasants. The cozy confluence of power and money made them untouchables. The cozy confluence of power and money made them untouchables. The sanctuary of nobility was their refuge.

However, the wheels of the overhaul were underway. It foretold the end of this sagging system with the slow but sure raid of colonisation. This was the fulfilment of destiny riddled with the sins of the fathers and the forefathers. An era had ended. This end meant that the crows and the bats went to sleep to wake up to a new rule of law. Although the class of zamindars as a whole faced a major blow, they could not be cleansed any time soon. Some kept their old money, jewellery, and their land assets. Next, they forged deals with the new governments with serious facelifts. Such makeovers replaced the old corruption with a crisp newness. Corruption could never be wiped off.

God finally took a shine to the oppressed. Divine retribution descended on them in full fury like molten lead. It compromised the fate of the zamindars from the House of Chowdhury too, which now hung in the balance for a devastating flood had occurred to boot the onslaught of colonisation. It drowned many of their villages, ousting them into the cold. Most thought of it as comeuppance. It drove them out of their opulent homes and forced them to make a choice between either leaving the village or dying in the flood. They chose the former and migrated to town. Their ancestral village remained submerged for many years to come, but they survived by entering into business and flourishing on the reputation of being a fallen aristocracy. They managed to remain safely within the circle of similar high-profile families.

However, the wheels of the overhaul were underway; it foretold the end of this sagging system, with the slow, but sure raid of colonisation. This was the fulfilment of destiny, riddled with the sins of fathers and the forefathers. An era had ended. This end meant that the crows and the bats went to sleep, to wake up to a new rule of law. Although the class of zamindars as a whole faced a major blow, they could not be cleansed any time soon. Some kept their old money, jewellery, and their land assets. Next, they forged deals with the new government, and were given a public relations facelift. Such makeovers replaced the old corruption with a crisp newness; corruption could never be wiped off.

God finally took a shine to the lost souls whom the zamindars had oppressed over the years. Divine retribution descended on them in full fury like molten lead. It compromised the fate of these zamindars from the House of Chowdhury too, which now hung in the balance, for a devastating flood had occurred to boot the onslaught of colonisation. It drowned many of their villages, ousting them into the cold. Most thought of it as comeuppance. It drove them out of their opulent homes and forced them to make a choice between either leaving the village or dying in the flood. They chose the former and migrated to town. Their ancestral village remained submerged for many years to come. But they survived by entering into business and flourishing on the reputation of being a fallen aristocratic family. They managed to remain safe and nestled among the circle of high-profile families and friends.

This night of the monsoon rainfall, the family sat grumbling over the disappearance of their beloved Ashik. Reporting this incident to the police was possible. Lutfun and Sheri could shed some light, too. But their mouths were sealed like vexed children assaulted by a relative, vowing never to divulge. The steady monsoon rain tapered off, like the gradual fading of anklet bells lost in time-dust before a maudlin Chowdhury, soaked in lust and foamy alcohol.

There was a knock on the door which the family couldn't hear at first. They thought the window rattled from the raging wind, but this rattle became louder until a servant opened the door. Ashik Chowdhury stood on the doorstep with Prema Hashem. It was puzzling, but the news they had was even more shocking. Prema Hashem dressed in a red bridal saree had her head covered in a veil. They walked over the threshold. Ashik entered at first, followed by a demure Prema. In the lime candlelight she looked soft and young. Her fair flawless beauty impressed everyone in the room as they looked at her speechlessly. She came forward and stood before the mistress of the house.

Lutfun and Sheri watched in awe. Mrs Chowdhury's face paled. She rose from a leggy rickety chair. It creaked then collapsed owing to its weak structure. She looked at Ashik with rage emanating through her eyes and spat out, "What have you done? Are you in your right mind? Have you gone mad?"

Ashik stood there. His head lowered in front of the revered Mr and Mrs Chowdhury and the rest of the family.

"We're in love," he said.

It hurt Sheri to see his suave talented brother slighted and diminished to this.

"You couldn't find anyone else to fall in love with? Of all people, it had to be her?" His mother retorted and then she declared to everyone's astonishment.

"Get out. Out! This very minute. I don't care where you go!"

Mr Chowdhury tried to calm her down by patting her on her back, but she was inconsolable. She was not prepared to give even an inch of leeway.

"Calm down. Where would they go in this rain?" he asked.

"Rain or sunshine, I don't care. I disown you. Just go."

She turned towards the family and said in a low tone but full fury. "Listen up, everyone, if I find anyone helping them, make no mistake you too will be kicked out."

Followed by a docile servant with a candle in hand, she left the room. Mr Chowdhury meekly went out with her. However, Sheri and Lutfun couldn't endure this anymore. They knew they were taking a risk, but they came forward to aid the newlyweds anyway. As soon as the elders left, they whispered to Ashik and Prema that they could sleep over in the guest room for one night on the roof, a room, with a view of the full sky and a hanging garden of enchanting monsoon blossoms, green tiger ferns, peace lilies, arundina pink, and orchids growing abundantly over the musty, brick walls.

Although they colluded with Ashik against Mrs Chowdhury's will, this pleased Lutfun as much as it pleased Ashik and his new wife. Ashik agreed to spend his wedding night with his wedded wife in his own house but like a thief in a hideout. The wake of a fresh rain triggered a keening of a muggy night's wind. Mila—Ekram's little daughter's apprehensions got the better of her.

At midnight, the windowpane mirrored a candle flame. It also mirrored four adults and a child huddled together on a double mattress bed inside the room. Their tall shadows reflected on the wall, showing their heads. That was just a fraction of reality. Anyone looking at this image, would think these were heads of hunter-gatherers overseeing a kill.

41

Those who sat on the bed were Ashik, Prema, Lutfun, Sheri, and little Mila. They had not slept all night. After Mr and Mrs Chowdhury retired to bed, the siblings came together like water bubbles on a scalding pan, drawn together in the middle. Rules were meant to be broken, prevailed in the minds of these young rebels.

"Tell us what happened?" asked Lutfun.

'Well, it's a long story,"said Ashik.

"Tell us anyway."

Mila listened, wide-eyed with curiosity. "Wow, what a wild bunch of romantics."

At that impressionable age, Mila jotted down every detail in her mind. She felt excited that she was in the company of such great rebels. The sound of the heavy rainfall on the corrugated red roof drowned much of the talks. The colour of the roof faded into white in certain places which needed new paint. At ten, Mila relished the atmosphere in which all this drama was unfolding.

At the alley's end, not far from the House of Chowdhury, a masjid also stood. It housed not just the daily prayers of the faithful five times a day, but the imam had to attend to some perfunctory duties in the community. Eloped lovers who had been discarded by society came here to wed. The faithful imam did these duties reluctantly because he didn't like to wed such couples, however, neither did he want unwed couples to live in sin. When he saw Prema Hashem and Ashik Chowdhury come to his door at sundown after the Maghrib prayer, he frowned at them. At first, he didn't want to marry them at all, because of Ashik's standing in the society, and second, because she was not officially divorced yet. But the adamant Prema was ready to divorce her husband, Raja Hashem, there and then without any compunctions.

Still, the imam could not wed them legally, until a divorce settlement had been finalised according to Islamic stipulations. A waiting time of at least three months had to be observed for the previous marriage to be annulled, or else the new marriage could not be sanctioned. The imam gave a lengthy sermon as to how the talaq or repudiation by repeating talaq three times was pre-Islamic, known as Talaq al bidah. Although many may still practice it, not knowing full well, it was frowned upon and denounced by prophet Mohammad. Then, there was a third option, the judicial divorce where either spouse could divorce at a Sharia court.

Commonly in an Arab desert, men would pay a mohr to marry a woman and leave a note of talaq for the women when they went away for the long haul. Men paid heavily sometimes to give talaq to a woman. But it was something both could put in a contract where each could give talaq to the other in the event of a marriage break-down due to violence or infidelity. Those were the solid Islamic laws. However, people's customs deviated far too much from such legalities and showed even less inclination to adhere to these laws when they could take short cuts by uttering talaq, talaq, talaq three times to divorce, over and easily done with. With Prema that was exactly what had happened. The imam accepted her repudiation upon hearing it, and rendered the couple talaq. He summoned Raja Hashem to the mosque that evening, who pronounced the word three times in presence of the couple after which the imam put an end to this charade.

An overwhelming shame touched Raja Hashem in the aftermath of the divorce. But his wife, or ex-wife now, had not shared his emotion. He hurriedly left the mosque. The imam sat down with his Quran and Qalema to marry the new couple on the same mat that they had divorced. After the wedding, the imam blessed the newlyweds. The newlyweds felt a strange kind of solidarity towards each other once they too left the mosque and thought about the next course of action. There was none. Ashik, Prema's new husband, bought her a red saree from a shop down the alley to doll her up at least like a bride.

No power in the world could have stopped this wedding, Ashik thought and looked at his beautiful bride in red. He realised that during the dying days of the zamindars, there were many party politics played to keep the tradition alive. Deals were made with the British, but none had worked out in favour of the zamindars. The British well and truly expunged the tradition in the end. However, some were allowed to keep the title and their assets, such as palaces. Although they were not the lords of their little kingdoms anymore, they were still influential families for being old and rich which they cashed in unfailingly. Their reputation hinged on social connections. Prema Hashem's frowned upon wedding with Ashik Chowdhury would zest up the gossip but hurt friendships.

The morning birds, the hungry crows, the cuckoo, and an odd old eagle, all came out of the woodwork as a new sun smiled upon the world. They flew onto the roof to feed themselves on the nectar of the fresh monsoon blooms.

Prema took her morning bath and stood out on the roof. Mila had fallen asleep on the mattress there the night before. Sheri and Lutfun left early in the morning. The azan from the mosque's minaret which the same imam sang brought them to their senses that it was time to go to bed. Lutfun felt a thrill through her sensing Ashik's chivalry of love. So much so that she began to make preparations to let her own desires to be wedded to Sheri known to the family, although hers and Sheri's matter was more or less settled.

Lutfun Azhar was not an orphan. She had lived in this house but was not related to the Chowdhury family in any way. Her own parents had left her on the doorstep of the House of Chowdhury as a baby when they had to flee for bankruptcy. Mrs Chowdhury, then a young mother herself, had brought Lutfun home and raised her like her own children. Once she was old enough, Mrs Chowdhury told her about her biological parents. Sheri and Lutfun started off as friends, but they eventually fell in love in their teens. A relationship everyone found sweet.

Ashik, maybe a renegade, but he took full responsibility for what he did. Sheri was more of a conformist. Even though the age of zamindari had died out, maintaining customary civility was paramount. Marrying the neighbour's wife was a violation of those unwritten rules. However, Prema and Ashik were in deep denial. Her defection didn't stir any sense of remorse for moral wrongdoing. Rather this emboldened them to embrace love and this new life. Ashik and Prema, both knew they had to leave soon, but they also knew that their life was southbound. Ashik would be disowned from his inheritance, but they were not worried.

Prema, in all her prettiness, sat on the floor of an empty corner of the roof in the morning. Her silky long hair shone in the lazy summer's sun as she left it out to dry in the breeze. She watched birds play out their antics. They pecked greedily at a fallen seed on the roof. Seeds were mostly gutted out of the pink core of the ripened guavas. Redhead woodcutters beaked and drilled through the russet poplar bark. Honeysuckle cups overflowed with juices and more from rainwater, nature's ultimate goodies from which crows and ravens sipped.

Mila, who had dozed off in bed, woke up. Rubbing her eyes, she stepped down and came out drowsily on the roof where she found Prema. She sat down by her side on the roof's musty floor. They watched the Mynas poking each other like a choreographed dance.

"Do you want to feed them?" Mila asked Prema as she rubbed her eyes.

Prema Chowdhury smiled and nodded. She hardly slept all night. Mila saw how red her swollen eyes were. She smiled back and then they saw Ashik come out on the roof to join them. It was a gathering, a gathering of birds and humans. A few hours later they heard footsteps on the stairs. Not sure whose they were, they braced themselves. To their relief they saw Lutfun appear with a breakfast tray in her hand.

"Good, you're all up," Lutfun said.

"Yes, I've been up for a while now," Prema smiled.

"Here, I brought you guys some breakfast."

Lutfun put the tray down on a rain-beaten table. She thought and felt trepidation. It was most unusual that the newlyweds tore down all the customs. Prema's ex lived just next door. Lutfun could almost hear Prema's children crying, "Mum, there's Mum on the roof of the House of Chowdhury."

"Well, you'd better finish breakfast and be off, I guess, before the house wakes up to find you guys here," said Lutfun.

Then she turned to look at Mila and said. "Shouldn't you be off, too? Go downstairs before your mother wakes up looking for you here. Go already. Hurry."

Mila gave her new aunty a hug and escaped down the flights of stairs. She was startled when she found her mother, Nazmun Banu, on the landing, who was coming up the stairs to the roof to look for her. She had been into her daughter's bedroom in the morning. Nazmun Banu looked at her sternly waiting for an acceptable explanation. When her daughter had none, she held her by the hand and dragged the ten-year-old to their bedrooms downstairs.

"Do you know that I nearly fainted this morning when I found out you hadn't slept in your own room? Do you even realise how much anxiety you've caused me? Now tell me where were you? Tell me this minute."

Mila thought if her mettle was to be tested, then this was the time. There was no pride in untested virtue. Once and for all, how she responded to her mother now would prove her loyalty to the greater family, her uncles. Whose side was she on?

Even at that tender age, Mila knew she couldn't betray her uncles, but neither could she betray her own mother. She kept quiet until her mother's anger dissipated. Then Nazmun Banu broke into tears and mumbled how her own life took a bad turn because of Mila's father, Ekram. He had remarried her best friend! Trust, by far, was the fastest depleting value of all. Her love was blighted, it felt like being trapped in an indeterminate state between the last hours of sunset and total darkness. Ekram's sensuous visitations on her doorsteps in the middle of the night often awakened Mila to remind her of her parents' togetherness, that Nazmun Banu after all was the first of his two wedded wives, and that he had come back at night to claim what was only kosher as he frequented between his two wives. Nazmun Banu had relented without much of a protest because these kinds of intimacies with her husband gave her relationship half a meaning, a reason to live in this House of Chowdhury as his wedded first wife.

It was an illegitimate second marriage as per the Islamic Law. Multiple marriages may have been allowed in Islam, true, but the first wife's permission was paramount as no second marriage was legal without it. By far Nazmun Banu had not even known of such an existence of a second wife, let alone permitted it. Whether or not it was moral was moot. Nazmun Banu lapsed periodically into deep depression. As often was the case, she broke down in tears in front of Mila and gave her a few tight slaps across her face for minor mischiefs, or none at all. She just needed an excuse to vent herself. She had become deceptive like pith of the citrus fruits' hidden underlining. On the surface all was smooth, smiles and laughter, but they were as short-lived as the mandala, smeared with fleeting joy and pride. The colourful sand paint was painstakingly removed the moment they were finished. When dusk fell and the family retired to their quarters with their partners, only Nazmun Banu sat alone on her high regal bed wondering who her husband chose to be with for the night?

Sometimes she heard Sheri and Lutfun, their tinkle of soft laughter sailing through the open shutters towards the rose garden below. They bloomed while she sat upright like a thorny anomaly. Did she not feel like romancing? Did she not want her husband to accompany her to the movies like all other couples in the house to watch the handsome chocolate hero of the time, Waheed Murad? No, she suppressed those desires. In silence those desires ate right through her soul like termites until it turned into the mandala sand to be deposited downstream in the aftermath. For that was what her life had become in the end, termite stricken.

Only no one saw this infestation. The poisonous resin ultimately ate away the core of her heart. Mila didn't realise it, neither did her mother, but this poison left them both depleted of values, particularly Mila who was turning into a sadist. For when Nazmun Banu cried out in pain, and in front of her sometimes, Mila had a slight smile hovering on her lips.

Despite everything, Nazmun Banu was loyal to her in-laws who in turn had deep respect for her. Sheri and Ashik, Lutfun, and Mr and Mrs Chowdhury had more respect for Nazmun Banu than their own brother and son, Ekram, or his second wife. The second wife could never step foot into this house, let alone be respected. She stayed away from everybody, not by choice but because she was completely walled out by the members of the family, out of their deference for Nazmun Banu.

This special place or status that she held in the house was ample compensation, but Mila sometimes wondered why her mother had not left and moved back with her own parents who lived not too far away and by the mosque. The answer was all too simple, because her parents wouldn't have her back.

Nazmun Banu and Ekram Chowdhury too had eloped just like Ashik and Prema. Under Mrs Chowdhury's strict moral codes, while she accepted Nazmun Banu, she had discarded Prema. Fair enough, Nazmun Banu was an innocent child of fifteen and Prema? She was a grown woman. She was someone's wife. Those were her rules. In accordance with those rules, Ashik and Prema had lost Mrs Chowdhury's support.

No big deal, risk-takers such as Ashik and Prema never really cared much about rules. This total disregard for morals gave them a strange kind of a high. What had happened to them later was unbelievable by any stretch of the imagination, and they bid farewell. Stealthily they came downstairs by the spiral back stairs.

Lutfun saw them through the narrow green wooden door by the kitchen wall. On the road, they held each other's hands. They had no money and certainly nowhere to go. Lutfun gave them her pocket money. It was about 200 rupees, which in those days of the 1960s was a decent amount. They embarked on this journey with only that much and a small sack of clothes and bric-a-brac which Lutfun stole from the kitchen. They headed out for the slum by the alley, behind the mosque. Here in the slums, they started a new life.

southbound

First off, Prema and Ashik had no idea where they were headed. With no specific destination in mind, they held their hands and walked aimlessly down the alley by the mosque. They saw a slum behind the mosque, makeshift homes of crumpled plastic roofs and dry flimsy bamboo walls. These thatched little places stood out because of the decrepitude of the human condition. The monsoon rains threatened, and winds ripped through the fragile roofs. The corners of some of the plastic roofs looked like half-turned pages of a book in haphazard winds. Prema and Ashik ran to take shelter under a banyan tree by the mosque. They viewed a few dimpled roofs and some pointed ones also. The dimpled roofs had shoddy workmanship nailed from one end to the other, as opposed to the pointed roofs that were nailed properly to a pointy middle pole. A woman saw them and invited them in. The zamindars of the great house of Chowdhury may have seen a decline of power and sometimes wealth, but they never saw a comedown as sharp as this of impoverished neglect. Yet, a phoenix-rise to achieving something more substantial kept the newlywed's dreams alive. They decided to rent a room here because it was cheap.

In the precinct of the mosque where the imam preached about giving alms to the poor as one of the basic tenets of Islam, this slum grew ironically like the resplendent monsoon crop. Filthy backwater drains were an overflowing germ factory. Children were born nearly every second in this mire of filth and dirt, grunge on the fringes of society as though to challenge death. Not all died, and diseases couldn't cripple a lot of them either. Those who survived, became strong and immune to the most dangerous diseases.

Ashik and Prema would not have survived here had it not been for Lutfun and Sheri who supplied them money on a daily basis, secretly, to Mrs Chowdhury's strict ordinance. They would come at sundown and sit in their hut to have a cup of tea down by the alley. After a little chit-chat, they'd offer them money which Ashik gladly took. Lutfun had often visited them with leftover foods from the Chowdhury kitchen, enough to last for a week, while Ashik looked for work. They were living on the cheap, but their hearts sang lyrics of love. Poverty didn't seem to debilitate their happiness.

Ashik-Prema's legendary rebellion became exemplary to those who felt stifled by society's norms decreed by people like Mrs Chowdhury. However, it was also because of people like Mrs Chowdhury who chose values over mother's love, society's moral equalizers. Sure, there was gossip around Prema, how could she have left her children as young as they were? But little did she care about the moral implications of her action, and neither did the innumerable lovers whom she inspired.

Ashik and Prema started a new life in the precinct of the mosque at the far end of the alley. Their shack was made of plastic roof and matted thatched walls, a far cry from the House of Chowdhury. Ashik finally found work. With a little help from Sheri and Lutfun he forgot about being a singer and became a peddler instead, buying and selling all kinds of things that he could find. Pots and pans, sarees, bed covers, just name it, his shop was on open pavement. He sold more goods than he ever expected. He became sought after, and every established company wanted to hire him. Every retailer wanted to employ him as a door-to-door seller of goods. At a time when online shopping couldn't even be imagined, such peddlers carried goods on their shoulders from brick and mortar warehouses to sell door-to-door. It was cheap labor, but Ashik swallowed his pride and continued with this trade. He went to every middle-class and wealthy home except his own, the House of Chowdhury.

One morning Prema realised she was pregnant, her fourth including the ones she had left behind. Here was a situation that was going to be challenging, to raise a Chowdhury in a slum. The child was going to be deprived of the opulent living the House of Chowdhury would have provided, and have to reckon with this slum which reeked of odours from open drains, grey waters of floating paper pieces, and gurgled cough spit down its breeding grounds.

Mrs Chowdhury knew about the pregnancy. A maid who had frequented Ashik's hut with leftover foods from the kitchen sometimes, told her about the living condition of her son and his wife. The maid's name was Shimul. Returning after one of her visits to the slum, Shimul told her about the pregnancy. Mrs Chowdhury was basking in the sun out in the front yard under the neem tree. She saw the maid entering through the walk-in main gate. She asked her to come forward. Shimul did as she was told. Mrs Chowdhury asked what she saw. Shimul told her the truth about the pregnancy, and Mrs Chowdhury bade her go.

Although Mrs Chowdury was firm in her decision, in the heart of it, Shimul thought she probably wished them well, but she could not have them live under the same roof because she had disowned them. She was right, Mrs Chowdhury did wish them well because she knew about the regular delivery of food to the slum, but she did nothing to stop it.

Thinking of her new grandchild about to be born in the slum down by the alley, she became grim. She was once a queen of her husband's village, Pretigram, by the mighty River Kali. She was a princess in her father's village along the same river, Phoolgao, another great house of the zamindars. Hers was one of those legendary weddings. The Chowdhurys of Pretigram had match-made this wedding. A marriage of convenience amongst the aristocrats, and romance had no place in it.

The zamindars of Pretigram, she thought, were not only zamindars of one village but many. They had many contenders with whom they often engaged in violent clashes over land claims. The winner took all, and they did, the Chowdhurys' of Pretigram, occupying vast stretches of land. Her flashbacks stirred a strange magic realism in her heart. Those were the mad old days. Her reminiscences linked her to her father's house in Phoolgao; like holograms, they weaved glimpses of a haunted place.

Villagers of Phoolgao had said, healthy children born in this house of zamindars had often died for no reason. But when Raiza was born she survived; not only that, she also thought she conquered this elusive angel of death. However, this came with a price. She realised, as she grew up, something monstrous had possessed her. She became a prisoner of visions—an old woman dunking herself repeatedly in the river. She never disclosed her visions to anyone. Even today, she feels she sees them sometimes. That place truly was haunted.

On her wedding day, Raiza Chowdhury was in her bedroom of her father's wooden palace, a bride of fifteen: she, the only surviving daughter among six of Chowdhury Hashmat Ali Beg's children. A mere child, she played with dolls even two days ago before she wedded: dressing them up in layers of real white pearls. Now a doll herself, she was a child bride dressed in an extraordinary gold embroidered kathan saree of rare silk, and pearl necklaces.

As she played with her dolls in the rumpus, two short days before her wedding, she had encountered an incident. The timber floorboard had a few weak, loose planks. One of her playmates had pulled out a plank. Much to their horror, they discovered a row of massive snake eggs sitting like brown pods. The rumpus was a breeding ground for snakes in summer. Brown snakes frequented this warm place to store their eggs. The girls had also found shredded snakeskin. They screamed out of that room to the attention of the elders. In the event of which, a village snake-charmer was summoned to clear the place.

Two days on, Raiza became a poised bride, sitting with her mates in her bedroom to be wedded. The snake eggs were a lingering memory on her mind; she cringed thinking about them. In a few hours, she was to be wedded to the current Chowdhury of Pretigram from the next village— banked on the powerful River Kali. This river flowed along Phoolgao, too, and several other villages. When the sun dropped over the far west, Raiza heard a commotion in the house that a bojra, a decorated boat, had been sighted on the shore of Phoolgao.

This boat had anchored, and by a maid's recount, Raiza pictured it as Cleopatra's famous barge. She had read in fantasy tales about a gilded stern barge in which the ancient queen of Mishor in the Bengali language or Egypt had seduced Marc Anthony. Cleopatra had drunk her famous crushed pearl wine to impress him at a banquet; an exaggeration, perhaps. But one way or the other, the dark Chowdhury of Pretigram had stepped out of the bejeweled boat, to marry this enchanting princess Raiza of Phoolgao.

Night had fallen. The main hall room of the zamindar's palace was illuminated by candelabra. Raiza was led here by her maids; the couple got married in grandeur before all the villagers and some high-profile dignitaries such as Deputy Magistrates. It was so grand that the legend was retold through many generations of the actual worth of Raiza Chowdhury and how her worth was measured before the wedding guests; that she was weighed on a wooden balance scale; an equal amount of gold was placed in the other, which she had received as a gift from her groom. The thought made Mrs Chowdhury smile to this day.

Well into midnight, the wedding was over. Raiza and the groom's party prepared to depart. The bride and her husband bade goodbyes to her parents and her relatives by touching their feet as was the custom of performing a salaam. There were lots of feet to touch. But they did it all. With her parent's help, they stepped into the wedding palanquin. Six sturdy young men from the village carried the bride and the groom to the bank of the river. The beautiful barge or the bojra waited here. As soon as the palanquin was parked on the shore, Raiza stepped out of it and stood quietly. The groom came around and carried her into the boat. He sat her down on a large bed inside a cabin. A maid, called Tahera, closed the doors behind them.

The groom's name was Mirza Chowdhury. He sat down by her on the edge of the same bed and gently took her hand. He gazed at her veiled face. Mesmerised, his gaze traveled down the silk kathan. It revealed the contours of her delicate body. The pearls and the diamonds glittering off the necklaces, resting on her bosom. Chowdhury stood up and sat down at her feet. He tried to look at her face through the thin veil, pulled well down to her bosom. Her eyes were closed, and Chowdhury did not know how to make them open. First, he decided to pull her shoes off. They were silk naagra studded with pearls, woven with gold thread on the soft vamp. Mirza looked at them, momentarily. Then an outcry diverted him.

A moonlit night, a full moon pinned the dark sky, a glossy bindi on a woman's forehead, a third eye, with the power to control the waves, the ebb, and the flow of the world's waters. Mirza realised that the anchored boat rose as the tides came in. The water's soft splashing sang a destiny. However, was it glad tidings which came in the high tide this midnight? Mirza Chowdhury heard the muffled voices of the boatmen.

"What is it?"

His young bride asked. Her voice rose to a nervous pitch. She had opened her eyes now and looked at him wide and sharp. There, Mirza thought, he finally got her to open them. He looked into them large, black; they were incisive enough to cut through his heart. He was in love. The couple tried not to get distracted by the noisy sailors waving through the small bojra windows. But the circumstance looked grave; it had to be heeded. He wrung himself from her dark gaze and proceeded towards the door. He pushed them open and walked out to the deck.

Another boat had closed in alongside this bojra. A group of gypsies was glaring at them from across the boat. Under a waxing moon the silver waves lapped against the two boats as the gypsies negotiated with the Chowdhury's accountants from the adjacent boat. They demanded the priceless jewellery straight from the bride's perfumed plume, a figure as delicate as an ornamental ostrich feather.

The snake charmers threatened to unleash the most poisonous vipers ever imagined. Chowdhury saw a woman pulling out a flute to play a tune for an imminent snake dance. A basket was at her feet, and the lid was taken off by now. Soon the snake would rear its head and let them know of its presence. They demanded that negotiations must be finalised before the snake danced out of the basket. If it failed the snake would be hurled upon the Chowdhury and his men.

The gypsies harangued at them. Raiza came out oblivious to everyone and stood like a shadow on the deck with her young maid, Tahera. The moment she heard the flute, Tahera rushed to stand before her mistress in a stride just in case a viper was thrown at her. It was such a bold act of loyalty that it even astounded the dark gypsies. They chanted something that only they understood. The snake charmer stopped playing the flute and pulled out a cotton pouch tucked into her skirt. She opened it by the slight pull of its frail thread. She took out a ribboned talisman and placed it on her palm. She tossed it across the boat towards the maid and yelled at her to tie it around her neck.

The frightened maid was just as confused as everyone else on the boat. She picked it up as told and tied the charmed collar around her neck. The snake charmer laughed aloud. Her laughter reverberated through the muggy night air. However, Raiza, the young bride of a mere fifteen, came forward under the lantern light. She faced the gypsies, who had by now stopped laughing and were looking at her curiously. Raiza did the most courageous act of all. She asked for the gypsy's permission to come onboard. Beyond anyone's imagination and before anyone could even blink an eyelid or wait for the gypsy's permission, she picked up her saree to the ankle showing her golden anklets shining in the dark.

She walked across to the deck's edge in one fluid motion and skipped over to the next board onto the gypsy boat. The two boats were touching each other on the side hull. In the most unladylike manner, she grabbed the snake basket from the gypsy's feet and flung it overboard straight into the river. The snake charmer and the gypsies around her stood in bare astonishment. They realised how Raiza catapulted the negotiation. Before the gypsies could say or do anything, Raiza jumped back into her own boat with alacrity, and panting severely she fainted on the deck.

With the bargaining chip gone indefinitely downstream, the gypsies were befuddled. Exchanging angry words they oared away the boat, pushing it as far as it would go. However, the snake charmer scowled at her and hoped her talismanic powers should still work on the young maid, the bride's loyal servant.

The viper swam away. As soon as the gypsies left, Raiza was taken into the cabin and laid back in the bed with all her other maids looking over her in great trepidation. Yes, what she did was most outrageous and also most courageous. No one expected the delicate daughter of the great Chowdhury of Phoolgao and the wife of another Chowdhury of Pretigram to behave in such a candid and outright heroic manner. Raiza had defied all social customs. No lady was ever groomed to match such mettle across a hundred villages.

But Raiza knew exactly what the gypsies were after, her family heirlooms. Under no circumstances was she going to surrender them. They were not after any cash. The bridal boat did not carry that much cash because river piracy was notorious around these parts. The Chowdhury coffer was fully cashed up otherwise and locked within the chest of Pritigraam's hidden palace walls.

Raiza lay on the bed with her eyes closed. Her maids who stood around her occasionally fanned her to bring her back to consciousness. If it wasn't for the relentless efforts of the maids, she probably would have slept longer. When she finally opened her eyes it was near dawn. Her lazy glance landed on none other but her husband. The maids clapped their hands that the mistress had regained consciousness, and then left the room.

Mirza was alone with his newly wedded wife once again. He sat down beside her and took her tiny hand into his palm and cast a hazy gaze into her large eyes. He held her hand. Chowdhury sat her up. He held her face by the chin with his index finger and bent his head over her lips in a tight kiss.

The boat had been sailing down the bend of the river for quite a while now. The morning sun removed the darkness, shedding new light. In about several hours of continuous sail the boat had reached the shores of Pretigram. A few boatmen jumped mechanically, a skill they'd honed over many years, into the shallow waters to pull up the boat to the wrinkled strand. The noise woke up everyone, including the newlyweds who had slept shortly towards the early hours, nestled into each other's arms. Her veil was cast away in a corner of the big bed.

No one knocked on their door to inform them they had arrived. The master and the mistress woke up by themselves and realised the boat had been moored. He pulled his disheveled shirt and pants in place. Raiza woke up and organised her sari down to her ankles. She picked up the veil and put it on her head to hide her unadorned face. Her makeup had mostly faded after last night's fiasco. Once Raiza was decently clothed, Mirza opened the door, and followed by her they stepped into the rays of the young sun.

The morning looked new like a baby's fresh face. They saw from the deck that a reception party awaited on the strand under a bright red and yellow marquee. Tea was brewed in a huge aluminium kettle on a large clay stove by the marquee. A rich spread of breakfast on a table filled the air with the fragrances of molasses and deep oil fries of a great many varieties of pithas or village cakes.

Raiza and the man of the hour, her husband, smiled at the preparations. They disembarked from the bojra and stepped into a palanquin waiting to take them across the muddy lowland of the strands. This distance was short; they were on the dry highland in seconds. They came out of the palanquin and entered the marquee to be seated on ornate high-backed chairs. The mistress, Raiza Chowdhury, viewed all these magnificent, labor-intensive, and time-consuming preparations with a lot of interest. She felt love for her new home and for her new subjects.

There were complex bhapa pithas, steamed rice cakes, stuffed with coconut and molasses served alongside meat or vegetable curries. They were steamed on hot vapours of terracotta urns or kolshi. The rice would have to be crushed first, and made into dry rice flour, then water added to moist. A dollop of flour would then have to be dropped into a muslin cloth, and the cloth was allowed to sit in the narrow neck opening of the urn and tied up around the top. The urn itself would have to be filled with water to sit over a firewood clay stove for the steaming process to ensue. One at a time, each pitha was steamed inside the muslin cloth. Once done, the cloth covering was taken out of the urn's mouth. This way the pitha was moulded round, slightly plumped up in the middle.

She ate with her veil folded back on her head. After breakfast she pulled it down. Mirza stood up and was whisked away by his men. He whispered to her very briefly that he would be back soon and that she will be taken home. She nodded. The same palanquin took her into her new palace. As the palanquin approached, she saw a gated two-story palatial house from a distance with a pointed roof and a rounded verandah. It sat on many acres of land. Much like her father's home, this too was another fenced house with a heavily crafted wooden gate at the entrance with the fence hidden under green foliage. The palanquin entered through the gates, and it was placed in the centre of a courtyard. Raiza's new maids helped her out. The young queen stood before a timber bungalow-style house. She gazed at the rows of rooms along a broad verandah downstairs and a few smaller detached rooms around the courtyard. Her maids led her into the main house.

She was led up a spiral marble staircase. She saw from the landing that a white terrace jutted out. As she walked towards the terrace, she realised that it had a mosaic floor depicting a blossoming rose, and the balustrade was possibly made of white marble also. This house should bring her much happiness with her loving, handsome Mirza Chowdhury by her side, she thought, and a smile appeared on her thin lips under the veil. The maids took her to the master bedroom. It was spacious with a great many pieces of furniture. She sat down on the edge of a high mahogany bed with a head crest of an embellished peacock wood carving.

Over the coming weeks she slowly settled down in her new home. Her loving husband would bring her a morning fresh flower every day. Sometimes she would be woken up by the distant singing of a solitary cuckoo bird at the early hours of the morning. Unable to go back to sleep, she would see her slumbering husband beside her. Her days were uneventful but without fret. Her parents sent her gifts and sweets every week. There would be several clay pots of sweets lined up on the terrace.

Six months into the marriage, Raiza became pregnant. One afternoon after about eight months, heavy with pregnancy,

Raiza went out for a walk through the village with a maid. Mirza was in his office. She walked as far as a village pond. This pond was sheltered within the shrubbery of banana plants. The broad ribbed leaves supplied privacy for the bathers, many of whom were women. Raiza overheard small talks and ringing laughter. Talks alluded to her husband, Mirza. All ears into the chats, Raiza stood spellbound as bathers frolicked within the folds of the waves.

"Say, is it really true?" said one girl.

Her companion replied. "What is?"

"That Chowdhury has bedded his wife's loyal maid, Tahera?" the girl asked.

"Really? Oh no. But that's all too common for the Chowdhurys, isn't it? Why are you surprised?" asked the other girl. "They did much worse, I know from my father and Grandfather. This Chowdhury is an angel compared to the others."

"How so?" asked the first.

"Well, Mirza Chowdhury's Grandfather, Mozaffar Ahmed Chowdhury, used to go to the market. He never paid a dime for anything he bought. He would go to the fish market at sunrise and choose the best and the freshest catch of the day. All he had to do was to point at them with his closed umbrella and expect his men to haul up the entire basket and land it in the zamindar's kitchen. Worse, I have also heard that if anyone came close to him, stepped even the slightest into his shadow by mistake when he went out for a walk and such, he would have him thrown alive into a fishpond and have him eaten by fish."

"Oh no, really? Or are you just making this up?" asked the first girl.

"These are stories I have heard. I don't know if they are true. I have also heard that no one dared to cross the road in front of the palace if he sat smoking his huqqah on that huge round verandah upstairs. If he saw a passerby, he would have them thrown in the palace dungeon underground."

"Oh yeah? How do you know?" the first asked.

"My uncle worked as a dungeon guard," she said.

"I don't know if I should believe you?"

"Don't, but those were the stories. They could be fantasy too. Who knows?"

"Anyway, it's none of our business," replied the first.

"No. Not yet."

With those ominous words the girl concluded the conversation, and they both came out of the pond in wet sarees that clung to their virgin bodies. They moved quickly through the bushes muttering and running towards their homes to avoid lecherous looks from the zamindar's men who often took nude girls right there. A tragedy had occurred not too long ago to young Moina. This scandal had compelled Moina to leave her village with an illegitimate pregnancy. Raiza heard the fading words, and they overwhelmed her. Perspiration broke out on her forehead.

She returned from her afternoon walk. In all of the six months since her arrival to the village and living in this palace, she had not heard anything like this. She entered her bedroom and saw Mirza. He was relaxing with his eyes closed on an inclining chair set by the picture window. Her most loyal maid, Tahera, upon whom the snake charmer had cast a spell by a talisman on that hapless night on the boat, was also in the romm sitting down at his feet massaging them. Raiza startled visibly at the sight, but she sat down quietly on the edge of her bed.

No one noticed her. The maid had her back towards her, and Mirza's eyes were closed, engrossed in this magic pleasure. Raiza stood up and opened the heavy ornate almirah with a jingle of her keys locked in a silver key-holder. The noise, no more than the soft rhythm of a dancer's anklet, did nothing to wake him up, although the maid now inclined her head to look at her. With a shy gaze she lowered her eyes before the mistress's glower and stopped her massage. She rose and was ready to leave.

Raiza took her jewellery box out from the cast iron chest and put it on her bed. By now Mirza saw her too. She began to rummage through her jewellery to check which one she was going to wear today. She took out a heavy gold necklace with jiggling little balls. Tahera looked at it with a glint of desire as she left the room. Raiza enjoyed looking at her with a smile of revenge to say that they were far from being equal.

From this day onwards, Raiza felt a change in the household. She appeared to notice Tahera more around her husband. In the early mornings when the cuckoo birds awakened her, she heard the soft footsteps of her husband disappearing out of the room. One night she even followed him and saw Mirza disappearing into the maid's quarters at the back of the house, but Raiza, a noble, did not have an outburst nor even sit down to talk with her husband. She tolerated it and decided to let it pass into obscurity, but it didn't pass into obscurity. It became regular. In her pregnancy she started to throw tempers and tantrums at everyone. She saw Tahera less. These days, even if she asked for her, other maids would return with the response that Tahera got held up elsewhere. Where else? Raiza wondered if it was not on her husband's loins.

One day she decided to confront her husband. In the early morning again, she woke up at the cuckoo's call to find that her husband wasn't by her side. However, as the morning advanced, he brought her a morning fresh flower as always, kissed her forehead, and left. She took the flower with a smile and climbed out of bed. She walked towards the northern picture window of the room. She saw him outside. He was sitting on a chair under a mango tree. She began to tremble with fury. How dare he sit there so peacefully and bring her flowers as though nothing had happened.

Her mind was made up. In her rage, she knew exactly what to say. Pan faced, she stared at him and felt a bout of nausea overwhelm her. Necking out of the window, she threw up right outside which Mirza saw. This interrupted his moment of peace, and he ran inside to aid her. He brought Tahera with him, and they both came running into the room. Raiza felt seriously sick. She lay in bed and asked her husband to sit by her side, gesturing to the maid to leave. She left hurriedly. Chowdhury sat down and looked at her rotund pregnancy. Anytime now, he thought, but he was appalled by what his good wife had to say to him.

"I have a proposition," she said.

"You do, regarding what?"

Chowdhury asked, raising his brows and shrugging. She nodded her head, too and said, "You should finish what you've started. "

"Like what? What have I done?" he asked.

"What do you do with Tahera every night? Don't tell me that you don't know anything."

"With Tahera? Men in this family have been doing this for many generations. It's tradition," he said.

"I know that, but Tahera is special. That's why she was sent with me, for her loyalty. She is even prepared to die for me."

Her voice rose to a pitch, and she started to perspire. Her heartbeat was also raised.

"I'm not sure what exactly you are trying to say?" he sniggered.

With bated breath, she finally said it. Tight-tipped and terse, she said."Marry her."

"What? No one marries a maid. They know it and so does society. Are you even in your senses what you ask of me? You know how it all works being a Chowdhury yourself!" Mirza spat out.

"I'm perfectly sane. I know what I'm asking of you. Break the tradition and marry her, or I shall divorce you."

Divorce? He thought and chortled. Yes, that was well within her rights, of course, but it was also scandalous. Not a single divorce had taken place in the last seven generations in this house. Impossible! Out of the question! Particularly, now that a new Chowdhury was going to be added soon. He stood up and paced through the room. Raiza calmed down and realised that divorce would be pushing it. One could tweak the tradition only so far at a time. She had already done a few. After a pause, she said, "If something is not kosher, then make it kosher. For my sake and for the sake of your name bearer, this child that I carry. That's all I ask."

Now, that was a huge "ask" to marry that maid, the companion who had come in the same tide with his bride. Chowdhury stood there speechlessly and listened in silence, then he stalked out of the room. Raiza closed her eyes and fought back angry tears. What did she lack? she thought. Raiza's social standing, her kindness, and love were not enough to keep Mirza from all this? How did she fail him? With her fawn-like delicate beauty she belonged here in the house as his wife without a contender.

She sat up in bed and stared out at the gardens. She felt no joy in her heart, even with the baby which was kicking hard and coming soon. The sky, the tranquil garden, none could bring her peace. The talks by the pond, that girl, what's her name? Moina had to leave the village in shame because the zamindar's men had assaulted her. She loved her Mirza, how was she going to share him with her loyal maid who was prepared to die for her on the boat just a few months ago. She saw the trees and found them bleak. Nothing made any sense. No, this was how she was going to punish him, make him break tradition.

It was her firm decision that her husband marry Tahera if he ever wanted to sleep with her again. Tahera didn't have a say, because she was a penniless pauper with no home or family to go back to. Should the Chowdhury marry her, Raiza thought, she would give her the dignity of a sister as the Chowdhury's second wife. She worked it out. All of that in mind, now she wanted to fix a wedding date. The heaving heart bound her in a snake bind around this decision and nearly choked her, but she saw a brighter side to it. On the flip side, what if a maudlin zamindar stopped preying on the innocent and the poor for fear of being wedded to them? Raiza threatened Mirza with divorce, maybe there will be others following suit with tougher measures?

In the heart of it, Raiza knew that it was too fanciful an idea which was never going to stick against powerful men. She would never, ever be able to put a stop to this long-standing dreadful tradition of womanising. The tightening of the chest continued, and she lay down in bed and closed her eyes, but she wasn't going to sit around idly either, someone had to be done.

It was settled then. Another marriage was underway in this house with Tahera, the maid, and the Chowdhury, bonded unwillingly in wedlock for fear of a scandalous divorce. Oh! Raiza thought, how was it all going to play out? It irked her to call her maid a sister, a second wife in the house, but she would have to bear it like a noble with her head held high. In all fairness to Tahera, it would behoove Raiza to take steps in the right direction. This wasn't unIslamic either, a husband may take a second wife if the first wife gave her permission.

Today however, Mrs Chowdhury sighed sitting under the neem tree thinking of lust which was in the blood. Her sacrifice was in vain. Her sacrifice could have at least blessed and cleansed her sons in some ways. The most talented of all her sons, Ashik, now lived in the slums and married a neighbour's wife, Prema. Ekram? Her first-born had an affair with his wife's best friend and married without her permission. Nevertheless, her daring moves, those decisions she took back in the day were all to correct this illness in the gene, and to reshape a tradition. She tried, she thought with a heavy sigh.

Tahera failed to give the Chowdhury any children for she was infertile, whereas Raiza and Mirza's bloodline bore three strong boys. Raiza commanded great respect because of all the healthy retainers of the title she had produced and also for being the person she was. Tahera gradually faded into oblivion as Chowdhury's desire for her plummeted like a bird's short expel of feces. He moved on as his passion diminished, but Tahera became a wife unlike all other past maids.

It was foretold however, that Tahera's existence depended on how well she treated those boys, and she made her affections clear by caring for them so much, especially Ashik, that the boys called her Maa. She even gave Ashik a second name to match her own, Taher. Hence, in the village she came to be known as Taher's Mother. Even to this day, Tahera cooked delicious meals for her Taher. She took them to their distressed shack in the slum. While Tahera gave generously, Raiza didn't even lift a finger to help Ashik.

Mrs Chowdhury pondered, all was going to change now since a grandchild was coming. The maids who frequented the slum informed her. Like a nocturnal owl, she watched everything, listened to everything, but she continued to live the haunted past of darkness of her mind often tormented by visions of snakeskin and dunking women. She had a permanent deep frown between her brows although she had been the one always to make all the serious decisions.

Today, she sat under the neem tree in the House of Chowdhury in Dewangonj. The distant clouds rumbled. She inclined her head to see them behind the thorny berry tree and how rumbustious they were at his moment? Layers of dark grey lay thin over the blue sky. A light drizzle fell softly touching her through the elongated leaves of the neem tree. She sat on her chair for a while. The drizzle intensified with the winds. She rose to go indoors, and the chair suffered the battering.

nighthawk

Prema gave birth in her little shack with the help of midwives. It was a healthy boy. After the midwives left, even though it wasn't the end of the world, Prema thought alone in the silence of her room. She looked at her newborn, picked it up and breast-fed it. She felt that this little boy should not be deprived of his family's status. Just like anyone else in that House of Chowdhury, this baby boy was also a deserving Chowdhury. But to get that recognition, he must first find his proper place in that house. He wasn't a stray and must not be treated as one. However, entry into the House of Chowdhury, required Mrs Chowdhury's permission. It wasn't enough that her in-laws brought them food and handouts—money in secrecy to which Mrs Chowdhury turned a blind eye. Prema was convinced that she hadn't done anything wrong at all. It was written in the heavens, this love, and the fairness of it all in love and war. She decided to speak to Ashik when he came back tonight. These days, Ashik wandered the streets from one slum to another, selling sarees, bedclothes, cheap cutlery, or crockeries, and whatever else he thought could bring in money.

They hadn't even named the baby yet. The mosque at the far end of the alley was selected to host this event, a naming ceremony, Aquiqah. The imam would preside over the ceremony. An animal, possibly, a goat would have to be butchered, and people would be invited. If this had been hosted in the House of the Chowdhury, then the event would have been sensational. For now, though, this would have to do. Prema walked down to the mosque one day with the baby in her arms, to fix a ceremony time and date. The imam told her that the most suitable time was after the Jummah prayers, this Friday. He penned down the date.

After the baby had gone to sleep at night, Prema waited for Ashik eagerly, Ashik was coming home really late these days. She sat on the edge of the bed, trying not to fall asleep. After about midnight, she heard the soft swish of the flimsy straw door open. Her husband entered, a tired dog, who had long lost the Chowdhury lustre. She sat him down on a low stool by the bed where the baby also slept. Under the hurricane lamp, she figured that he needed some water. She handed him some in a tin glass poured from a terracotta urn that stood on a wooden table in the corner of the hut. He took the glass of water and drank it in two large gulps. She looked at him expectantly, and he asked. "What's up?"

"Well, just this, that our boy needs to be named."

"Yeah, so?" he said calmly. "Let's just name him. The imam will help you choose a few Muslim names, won't he?"

"Yeah, but a proper ceremony and all, you know what I mean?"

"I do, my jaan," he said. "But you also need to know this, as well as I do, that under the circumstances we can't. We're still living on handouts from my siblings."

"Maybe, they could help us out."

"They could. But I wouldn't want to pressure them. They're already doing what they can."

"Why not?" This is for their nephew, no?" she claimed.

Ashik did not argue. He knew what his jaan, the beloved, wanted. And he also knew that he was incapable of providing for them. He yawned and wanted to rest. Prema left it at that. She pulled out a thin roll up mattress from under the table, and then laid it out to make a bed for herself and her husband. Ashik and Prema lay down side by side. Ashik stretched his arms across and over her slim, supple back. She clutched it into her palm. He massaged her upper arm up and down until she turned over on her side to face him. He lifted her face and kissed her plain lips. Then he turned over on his stomach to peer closely into her eyes in the slight streetlight imparted through the matted walls. His oval-shaped large eyes were fixed on hers, glistening in the glow. Prema smiled and nodded her head in negation. She whispered to him that it wasn't time yet, because forty days were not over. It was just a little over a week. It took forty days for the female body to heal after birth.

The baby also woke up for a feed. Her taut breasts were heavy with milk. Ashik's face was over hers. He rolled over awkwardly and back to his side of the bed. She pulled her saree down and organized herself. She rose and crawled towards the bed where the baby was tossing and turning. She got on the bed and pulled him towards her. She picked him up and gave him the breast. Glued to her breasts for the next half hour or so, the baby drank satisfactorily. She burped him and put him back and looked down at her husband's handsome face. He resembled the great hero, Waheed Murad, with his large, droopy eyes, and hair pasted to his forehead: broad and thick, Waheedi sideburns imitating Elvis Presley. Who imitated whom? That was hard to know. But in the end, the hairstyles had become the

76

hairdressers' most wanted special cuts by every good-looking and fashionable man in town.

That was the Waheed Murad era for the film industry in Pakistan of which East Pakistan was a dear part for better or for worse, later known as Bangladesh. Waheed was as popular in the East as Elvis was in the West. Nearly every intergenerational woman was in love with this charming hero. And nearly every man wanted to charm women by having the Waheed Murad hairstyle. Ashik was a wannabe, and Prema found that cute. She thought he actually looked a bit like him, too. Prema climbed down and sat by his side, and then slowly lay down. Her husband slept peacefully. She thought of a second income. She thought of buying a sewing machine and starting a tailoring business in the slum.

Two days later, on an afternoon, when Ashik was at work, Prema was sitting on the baby's bed. The baby was asleep. She had a perplexed and edgy look on her face, thinking of another source of income. How was she going to manage the money? She needed it both for the naming ceremony and for the sewing machine.

Prema hadn't realised that the shack door was opening with a soft rustle and Lutfun had appeared in the doorway. Startled, she looked at her. But she smiled mechanically and rose from the bed. She walked over to the urn in the corner and pushed the low stool towards her. Lutfun didn't sit on the stool; instead, she handed over a container covered in a towel to Prema. Then she walked across to the baby's bed; she looked at him, smilingly. Prema lit the stove to heat water in a pan to make some tea. Lutfun sat on the edge of the bed and now turned her head to look at her sister-in-law.

"What are you having for lunch?" she asked.

"Lunch?" she said. "Not sure, now let's see."

Prema opened the container which Lutfun had given her. It was a delicious roast beef curry. "Who cooked this?" she asked.

"Who else, Maa?"

Tahera cooked well and had been sending food for Ashik ever since they moved up here. Prema put the container away in a meat safe for her husband. Then she rummaged through a basket full of vegetables. She picked out a couple of eggplants.

"This, for lunch," she smiled at Lutfun. "Why don't we have lunch together?"

"Sure," Lutfun said.

The baby woke up and yawned. Lutfun picked him up and squeezed his two chubby cheeks.

"What a bubbly boy," she cried.

Prema smiled at that and said. "Oh, yes, yes absolutely. He is the best. He'll wake up once or twice for a feed at night and that would be it."

"That's good."

Lutfun looked at him and sighed.

"What's up?" asked Prema.

"Oh, nothing much. I don't know where we're going with our relationship with Sheri," Lutfun mused.

"Why? Why is that?" asked Prema.

"We need to wait a couple of years before we can marry, it seems," she said. "He needs to get his degree first and then a job and blah, blah, blah."

"Money is important. But I didn't think of money when I left the security of my home to be with Ashik. I simply fell in love, we fell in love, got married, and that was the end of it," Prema said.

"How can you say that? Did you not even think for a moment how life would have worked out without money and a home? Or were you expecting to be accepted in the house?" she asked.

Prema was quiet. She thought about it before answering. And then she said.

"I didn't marry Ashik because of his family wealth or position. No one can accuse me of that."

Saying so, she sat down on another low stool by the urn and began to cut the eggplants into little cubes. She picked them in her conjoined hands and dropped them in a pot. She poured a tad of dalda into the pan to grease it on a small kerosine stove; she had finished making tea first and had handed a cup over to Lutfun. She also took a cup for herself and sipped tea as she cooked the eggplant. She stirred it and covered it with a lid.

"Oh, we're not accusing you of anything. I'm only trying to understand how love can flourish in this kind of dismal poverty. Now that you have him!"

Lutfun tried to understand looking at the baby.

"Well, what's the true measure of love anyway?" Money, power, position, what? If this isn't the true measure, our small wishes, happiness, sighs and despairs. This, our squalid little hut, then what is? Money cannot buy affection, surely."

Prema said in earnest with a light frown and a twisted smile, looking at Lutfun and nodding her head to provoke an assertion from her.

"Hmm, maybe not, poverty can?" Lutfun asked.

They sat quietly, lost in thoughts. Prema opened the lid to give the eggplant curry another stir. A hand full of vapour escaped and filled up the cramped hut. The baby started to cough and so did the adults. Prema turned off the stove quickly, while Lutfun grabbed the baby and went outside. Prema sat thinking of how she could ask Lutfun for more money for the ceremony. Her pride stopped her. It would be begging to someone who clearly thought that love couldn't survive without wealth. She found Lutfun outside in the open yard cuddling the baby. She stood by her.

"Well," she said. "What kind of a wedding do you want?" Prema asked.

"Wedding? Ha-ha, an expensive one, for sure."

Lutfun's laughter rang in the air, as Prema looked at her perplexed. Was this another side of Lutfun that the world had not known? This, "good-natured Lutfun, kind-soft-hearted". What went wrong that she would suddenly think that marriages depended solely on wealth and that love could not flourish, rather wither, in poverty?

"Lutfun, are you unwell?" Prema asked.

"No, of course, not, I'm just thinking aloud. You have given me a perspective, which I hadn't seen from my fairytalish, rosy world."

"And you would think that we must fail because we got no money?" Prema asked.

"Oh! I don't think you would fail. But it is clearly not easy to be in such a penniless relationship either, or is it?" Lutfun frowned.

"What if I proved you wrong?" Prema asked.

"Wow, that would take ages to prove it too, wouldn't it?

"As long as it takes, I'll prove it to you that we have a successful relationship and poverty couldn't tarnish our love."

"We'll see about that. Can we eat now? I'm hungry," Lutfun said.

"Sure, you can come inside now, the smoke's gone."

Prema put out the food on an eating mat spread on the mud floor. Lutfun walked over to the bed and put the child down gently. She sat down on the floor facing Prema.

"What's love, after all?" Lutfun asked.

"I don't understand it any more than you do. But this much I do understand that when he is not with me, I miss him. I want to be close to him and I feel devastated just thinking that what if he left me one day?" Prema answered. "I am also saddened that he has been reduced to a mere peddler."

"That intense, huh?" Lutfun asked.

Prema nodded to her question and watched Lutfun scoop some rice from a bowl into her plate. Lutfun took a spoonful of eggplant curry, too. Before plonking it on her plate, she looked at the portion of the eggplant on the spoon, then reduced it, thinking that she must leave some for dinner. This was probably all the meal Prema was going to cook for both lunch and dinner. It was generous of Prema to ask Lutfun to stay for lunch. Both Prema and Lutfun mixed the rice with the eggplant and gravy. The squalid room reeked of sweat and smoke and heavy smells of eggplant curry.

"Are you even happy here?" Lutfun asked, sniffing the pungent, stale air.

"I'm happy with Ashik. Wherever that maybe; the place is irrelevant!" she sneered.

That was a conversation stopper. Prema said no more but looked across at the baby in the bed. Lutfun ate away in silence. She had come here before, but this was the first time they actually had a conversation. Ashik and Prema's relationship was exciting and romantic, but Lutfun thought it wasn't a level-headed decision. Many strange questions burned inside her mind. She loved Sheri of course. But would she come this far to materialise a dream?

Pure love was a burning desire like an Olympian torch, which never went out even in fierce winds. Earthly love, on the other hand, depended on matter and materialism. Lutfun would have to be more circumspect to find the real meaning of love. What kind of love did she feel for Sheri? She wondered. Prema's love for Ashik had been proven beyond the benefit of the doubt. Their love could survive without money. To Lutfun, Prema was a deity of mystifying love, like Juliet. But she continued with her questioning.

"Can I ask you something?" Lutfun asked.

"Yeah, sure."

"Do you think of your children at all? The ones you left behind?"

Prema sat quietly looking out. She got up and walked towards the bed. Lutfun eyed her with interest, noticing a veiled cloud over her face.

"It would be a lie if I said no. But I made a decision, drastic as it maybe, but a decision in favor of love," she said. "I love my children and always will. But I was not happy with my ex."

"Well, one could argue that a lot of people aren't happily married, but they continue to live for the sake of children. After all, he wasn't abusive," Lutfun said.

"Sure, that's them. And this is me," Prema concluded.

Lutfun thought Prema was a hard woman, but soft-hearted enough or perhaps soft in the head, who knew that she should decide to move out and live like this to honour her love. Seeing Prema so quiet, Lutfun thought she must have hit a chord. She got up and stood by her. Prema looked at her.

"I'm sorry," Lutfun said.

"Oh, don't feel sorry for me. At least I'm not a hypocrite like many out there. They marry pretending to be in love, but live with another in their head."

"That's true too, but there's society to consider. Not everyone is brave like you, sister. By the way, your ex got married, you must have heard. Also, hear this, that she is an angel. A dear angel, who is everything required in a wife. She is your children's darling mother now," Lutfun declared.

She picked up her handbag and opened it. She handed Prema some petty cash, asking her to buy toys for the baby. Prema took it, almost grabbing it from her hand, which Lutfun noted with a smile. She saw her out, said goodbye and returned to the baby with the cash in her hand. She counted and there were hundred rupees. That brightened her up. She pulled out a metal trunk from under her bed and opened it. Rummaging through it, she found a battered tin box. She pulled open a rusty lid, pressed the money in and pressed the lid back on the tin.

The afternoon rolled on. The sky looked dark with looming clouds. Prema sat in one corner of the room and buttoned a shirt. She sewed it back that had dropped off one of Ashik's tatty shirts. She lit a candle. Waiting for Ashik was the hardest. A thunder rumbled; the sound traveled across space. It startled the baby, and he began to cry. She walked over and picked him up, comforting him in her arms. She heard cries coming from her neighbour's house, and then muffled sounds. She heard something falling, followed by a scream. A couple was out in the front. Darkness had descended; she vaguely saw a man dragging a woman by the hair across the yard. The man screamed. "You can take the boy out of the village, but not the village out of the boy." What did that even mean? Prema tried to understand through muttered sounds of drunkenness. "Oh! You're drunk! You vile man." The wife screamed. "Now you want to sell me, pimp me for more money, to bear the cost of booze. Well, let me tell you, I'll leave you and go back to the village."

"Hahaha! Go back to your parents who sold you to me in the first place? You should be lucky that I had actually married you. Did you think I would change just because we live out here? No, the village rule stays. Go and get me money. This is what you were born to do."

The wife was quiet. Prema craned her neck. She saw in the streetlight that the girl stomped out on a wobbly pair of high heel shoes, looking not so much like a village girl anymore, but sold out to the night ravens; lips smeared with red lipstick over the upper lip line; a cheap shocking pink nylon saree through which her belly button peeped like a cat's eye shell.

This affected Prema in a strange way and she sunk deep into her fears. She was able to see the fortuitous turn her life took in the aftermath of leaving her first husband. She felt she was still Prema, a respectable bibi—wife, who had so far been able to keep her dignity intact. Just transplanted herself. Whether or not she had made the right choice, was never an issue. But her love for the child she had given birth today carried some meaning, surely, about being a virtuous mother.

She found motherhood challenging, as Lutfun had also alluded to. She thought sometimes of her other children too, whom she had selfishly abandoned. Her own, whom she had nursed, exactly the way she nursed this baby. She was still nursing her son when she had left them, her own. If her boredom struck again in her relationship with Ashik, and she hoped it didn't, what would she do? Resign from this, too? Was she even capable of being caring enough? To what lengths would she go to care for her children? She looked at her baby and froze.

Nevertheless, the child naming ceremony must take place, as planned. As she waited for Ashik, she went through a guest list in her mind. When the oil lamp nearly burnt out at midnight, Ashik appeared at her doorstep. Prema heard footsteps. She opened the door. A young man stood in the shadows with Ashik. Ashik said. "This is Lal Das, my business partner and a loyal friend."

Prema and Lal Das exchanged greetings by saying, salaam and he, nomoskar.

"Please come in," Prema said.

They entered. Almost immediately, the neighbour's wife had also returned from her nightly doom. She came in with a burst of resounding laughter cracking up the silence of midnight. The night was doused in darkness, and she was steeped in drunkenness. Prema didn't see her but heard her drawl, her words spilled out as she spoke to her husband.

She seemed to hand him over some money by saying. "Here. Go fuck yourself. Fuck. Fuck."

The sound gradually fainted. Prema unrolled the eating mat inside her hut on the floor again and they all sat down for dinner. She gave them the leftover eggplant curry from lunch and Maa's cooked beef. Lal Das and Ashik were famished. Ashik relished Maa's curry. Prema sometimes wondered if there was any hidden story behind Ashik's birth. Tahera had named him Taher after her, and she was subsequently known as Taher's Maa both in the village and in town. She continued to send him food and knew his taste so well that it surprised Prema sometimes.

No matter, Prema emptied the container on Ashik's plate, as Lal Das was prohibited from having any beef because of his religion. When they finished, she realised that there was no food left for her. Although Ashik had asked her a few times why she wasn't eating, she told him that she had already had dinner.

After dinner, Ashik and Lal Das had a smoke together, and Lal Das wanted to depart. Ashik saw him out. Prema gathered the soiled dishes. She bade Lal Das goodbye and went outside to the tube well to clean them. She used ash collected in a tin to give the pots a shiny metallic gleam. Ashik stood behind her and watched her downtrodden state, to this, maid-like status. All because she loved him. Prema had everything once—status, prestige, and social position by dint of her ex-husband. Ashik decided he had to make it. He had to bring back the glory in her life. He had to make her proud again. He knew his business was picking up slowly, but surely, he would succeed one day.

Prema realised that Ashik was standing by the tube well. Without looking back, she told him to go to bed, she'd be there shortly. She placed her pots haphazardly and noisily around the tube well.

"So much noise, how do you expect me to sleep?" he asked.

A lid fell out of her hand and spun resoundingly. "I'm nearly done," she said. "Go already."

Ashik left her to her dishes. In the limelight, he saw her hunch back of a beautiful sinewy, slim shape—an enchantress. Prema finished and came indoors. She put away the dishes on a nearby wooden rack. And snuffed out the oil lamp. The room was fluorescent from the glazed moonlights. She looked at her baby fast asleep in bed, as she took her saree off and dumped it in a corner. She slipped under the blanket in her petticoat and blouse with Ashik on their floor bed. Ashik moved slightly to the side to make room for her, and then he pulled her and held her against his chest.

Deep into the night, Prema had a dream. She dreamt of Waheed Murad. In strange classical Urdu, Waheed spoke to her—a reality juxtaposed against a surreal, ancient land of the dead. He came up to her. They looked at each other. He kissed her on the lips. Waheed's handsome face was lost in the masses of her dark hair. He bent down and locked his lips onto hers until the lips moistened and looked glossy and dark. She pulled away from him. Each pair of lips was deadly dark, shining with saliva. Then, Waheed was gone. Just like that! A glass screen fell between them. She saw him through it. Waheed danced in the luminous rainbow colours amongst the dead. He was cajoling her to give him her body—her vessel if she fancied him so much. Prema felt trepidation in the dream. That the dead actor wished to return to her body. She saw greed in those beautiful eyes of his—give it up for him. How astonishing that she should dream of him like that? Her favourite, he wished him well. She wished he lived forever but in his own vessel.

The stuff of life; life rejuvenated, and reincarnated. Even the dead had life. Like love and other abstract elements, life lived on in some form or the other. A blade of grass or a sprightly butterfly, a complex morphological process took place before it changed into something new: the caterpillar into a butterfly—Waheed Murad, what did he transform into? She woke up in the darkness. She saw a face adrift through space. She opened her eyes and tried to see it for real. A bearded face of a stranger moved quickly across the space of the dim room, with his eyes cast downwards as it vanished completely. Oh! What was that? Her baby slept as peacefully as did her husband. Only, she saw, what she saw in wakefulness as well as in her dream, something ethereal. It was gone at a glance and didn't mean any harm.

Prema sat up and rubbed her eyes. The fluorescent street lamps accentuated the dimness of the room. She heard a street dog bark. She got out of bed noiselessly and stood up to walk towards the water pitcher. It was bizarre and surreal. She took a few steps towards the baby's bed to check on the baby and unfurled a blanket to cover him. She crept out of the doors. She sat down on the gritty threshold. A rush of sudden memories flooded her mind; her other three children. Her's. How did they fare? She heard that her ex had remarried, a few months ago. She wondered how her

89

children fared with a stepmother in the house. She reckoned;
they must hate their biological mother by now. For she was
the real stepmother; the other their real mother, now.

She was cruel—'now, now just a minute—not so fast—
what about your boredom? Had it not nearly killed you?
Had it not been for Ashik, you would have perished by now.
Oh! Think no further.' The fluorescent streetlamp flickered,
and it turned off by itself. She heard the morning azan drift
through the microphone of the mosque's minaret. The sweet
esoteric tune worked like magic, as the morning breeze
touched the dusky sky at dawn. The muezzin's clear voice
awakened the faithful for the early morning prayer. Fajr.

In a way, she found comfort in the azan's esoteric
words. Somehow, the heavenly sprites came down to tell her
that she followed no path of deception. She clearly took the
path of truth and love. The half-trodden path with her ex-
husband was a silent path to misery. A hinge creaked at a
neighbour's building in the morning breeze. She may have
saved her soul from boredom, but the dark clouds of the
past hovered in the back of her mind, a castle full of bad
memories, the whisperings of the past. In the heart of it, she
fully justified her conduct, a million times over. Her stomach
coiled with affliction and gripe, every time the undeniable
truth looped back; that she had left her babies, especially, the
boy she was nursing, who needed her care.

Anyway, she wasn't that religious. But today, she found
solace in the sound of the muezzin's voice; it made her feel
spiritual. She felt like praying. She walked over to the
common bathroom across the front yard and completed an
ablution for the morning prayer. She went indoors and
heard the baby stir; she glanced at him. She stood on the
clean floor facing the west. As she prostrated before God,

her mind danced away in millions of disjointed thoughts. She tried hard to concentrate, but the more she tried, the more she strayed, the three children, Mrs Chowdhury, a sea of clouds. She finished and crawled back to her bed beside her husband. Ashik slept deeply. When the sun rose, its rays entered through the hut's crevices. The baby woke up for a feed. She looked at the baby and thought of a name, which both of his parents would approve of.

bibi—wife

Ashik was getting ready for work. He heard a clamour outside. He also heard a melodious, tuned female voice singing Tagore's song on harmonium, jete, jete akla pothe—traveling along a forlorn path.

Ashik craned his neck through his hut's ratty window to listen to the song. He couldn't discern where it aired from. Heavy clouds had gathered; rain was imminent. Prema, his bibi, was sitting at the community tap installed by the government recently. Ashik saw a queue of slum-dwellers waiting to use the tap. They were hurling at her and bullying her for taking so long to finish.

Low water pressure was causing the delay. What flowed was a trickle. However, impatience grew large. They too had to go to work. Many were rickshaw-pullers, betel leaf sellers, and peddlers. Others were vendors, selling vegetables on wheels. Owners of mobile tea stalls selling hot brewed tea from their carts. Women who earned a living by making and selling roadside chapatis to the innumerable non-descript multitudes on the street.

Over the Ramadan, lentil and eggplant frittatas sold well. Sellers sold them from pushcarts for iftar on the side roads. All of these sounded like a booming business. But at the end of the day, these sellers crawled right back into the rat-infested hovels making barely enough to keep a roof over their heads. It was a life of constant short-change. No matter how many hours they put in, no plumed peacocks danced in the offing of the slum's courtyard.

This morning, the slum dwellers, the neighbours, stood yelling at Prema to hurry up. The ropey line of people looking at the rat tail trickle of the water. People dropped their rickety pails off their sweaty palms at their feet, and sooty pots and pans on the ground with a clamour to give vent to their frustrations. Ashik heard and saw his beautiful Prema reduced to this and the more he saw it, the more determined he became to salvage his family from this decrepit hell.

"Jahannam!" Hell, he swore as he took a sharp breath. He went outside and stood out in the crowd like a shining prince for his well-groomed appearance, somewhat marred by poverty, off late. He pulled his Prema out of the tap-stand by hand. Prema clumsily collected her clattering utensils, and both came back together into the privacy of the room. Ashik shut the door behind them, and the window. He stood there looking at his bibi. Prema's eyes were downcast as she saw a raw rugged floor. A tremor ran through her. Ashik took her hand and held her in a deep embrace. He felt her hot tears run through his shirt making wet patches. He brought his face down to her head and nudged her ears gently. He whispered. "I will take you out of here. We will leave this place in one short year, I promise."

The far end of the alley had now lost all its charms it once had for the couple when they were dating here. The marbled, mystic mosque stood cold and aloof in the square. The day's work ensued as Ashik left for work. He disentangled the bibi from his chest and walked over to the bed to kiss the baby goodbye. Then he kissed the bibi's forehead, which pulled a smile on her lips. He looked at her eyes, bringing her face closer to his lips. She closed them for him. He kissed her eye-lids, turned around and left.

That much Prema also knew; how agonising each day was for him, too; his extraordinary comedown, a labourer on the street, selling whatever he could lay his hands on. Toiling, by the sweat of his brow and bringing home just enough money to tie them up for two days at the most. Then the rent money had to be saved. If Ashik's siblings hadn't helped them out, this survival would be too hard. How much Mrs Chowdhury knew about it was hard to tell, but Prema and Ashik's baby-naming ceremony was going to go ahead in the mosque.

At night when Ashik returned after a hectic run of salesmanship, the bibi spread his dinner out on the kitchen floor mat, as usual. At dinner, she told him. "I have selected a nice name for our son."

"Yeah, what is it?"

"Mohammad Qasim Chowdhury, nicknamed Quasu."

"Nice name. Where did you find it?"

"I knew that name from my student life. I read it in Islamiat."

"Islamiat? And you still remembered? That must have been ages ago."

"Yes, I remembered because of its significance. It was prophet Mohammad's son's name."

"He had a son, too. I always thought he only had a daughter with Ayesha, his youngest wife, Bibi Fatma."

"Yes, I had also thought so. Apparently, he had a son too, who died at infancy," she concluded.

"Hmm. Interesting."

"Indeed. There's something else that I also found interesting."

"What's that?"

"Regarding the prophet, of all the bad things we hear about his multiple marriages, or rather, promiscuity, he only just had one son and one daughter."

"So?"

"Shouldn't he be having more? Particularly, when birth control was scarce or nearly non-existent?"

"Hmm. That is interesting." Ashik said.

He yawned, and he was in no mood for this serious conversation about the prophet's life or the validity of the story. He agreed on the name. It was nice.

A Friday afternoon was chosen for the naming ceremony. It is called the Aquiqah. Within the long forty days of the baby's birth, it was the last week of the month, selected for the ceremony, after the Jumma prayer. Prema, excitedly, wrote a letter and gave it to Ashik to give to Lal Das. Lal Das must deliver it to Lutfun in the House of Chowdhury. This was an invitation to the ceremony. Ashik agreed and gave it to Lal Das at work. In a few hours, Lal Das promptly walked over to the gates of the House of Chowdhury and handed it over to a maid. Lutfun received it almost immediately.

The morning of the ceremony was muggy and stifling hot. When the duo, Ashik, and Prema, prepared themselves and the baby for the ceremony, Ashik was sweating profusely down his forehead. He was getting the baby dressed in a white pajama and panjabi suit, which he had bought a while back from a second-hand bazaar off the footpath near the mosque. Too hot to wear anything really, Prema thought she would just put on a plain cotton saree with a golden border running all along its twelve yards. There was a mugshot mirror hooked on the shack's eastern mated wall.

It was almost impossible to wear the saree without a proper long mirror; she had to get Ashik to arrange the pleats of the saree at her foot, while she tucked them inside the petticoat around the waist. Once the pleats fell in place, the idle drape hung casually over her arms from her bloused shoulder. She was sweating too, even though she went to a nearby well to bathe.

"Ready?"

Ashik asked, smiling at her beauty, radiating through the dismal clamminess of the hut.

She smiled back. "Yes, what about you? Aren't you going to change? You need another cleanup."

"Yes, I'll go under the tap, if it's free."

"No, take the mug and the pail and go to the well over by the banyan tree.

Prema went through her clunky pots and pans and handed him the pail with a rusty mug in it and a leftover bony soap and a clean towel. He took it, wiping up the steady drops of sweat off his forehead. His harassed looks spoke a million words of frustrations he battled every day. He walked across the dirt road down the path leading towards the well to find a quiet spot to bathe in peace.

Under the banyan tree today, he stood in the clammy heat for a while away from the slum's regular crowd jostling around the tap stand. He sang a song after many days. God alone knew what had happened to his harmonium. Let alone singing, even thinking about songs seemed like a luxury these days. Singing the song, he walked over to the well.

It was an old well. The bare bricks without a facade looked like a full toothed grin devoid of the lustre of enamel. He tied the pail with a rope hanging by a wooden pole over the well. He dropped it into the well. Pulling up a few buckets, he poured the water straight over his head without paying much attention to the skeletal soap or the mug or even where the towel had been laid on the ground. The soap dug deeper, flattening out, and slowly dissolving into the soil from the heavy bucketing. At some point, it disappeared. The towel too was drenched.

He frolicked. And totally immersed in this carefree reverie. The bibi came by and stood quietly without him noticing her with the child in her lap. She felt happy just looking at him. He finally saw them and smiled. He lowered his pail to the wet soil. Prema picked up the drenched towel and handed it to him. He squeezed it and dried himself with the damp towel.

They arrived at the mosque on time. At its entrance, Prema pulled a veil to cover her head as they both entered the main rooms. The imam was sitting on the floor in one corner of this rather large room, where the Jummah Prayers would also be held soon. He was reading from the Qur'an. He lifted his face when they appeared at the doorstep.

He greeted, "Assalamualaikum."

The couple replied, "Waalaikumussalam."

He gestured to them to sit down; they followed his instructions with the baby asleep in Prema's lap. They sat on the floor along the whitewashed wall, while the imam continued to chant from the Qur'an. The holy book was placed on a rehal wood holder.

He resumed the recitations. After a good half an hour of solid reading, he decided to take a break. He closed the holy book on its rehal and looked at the parents. With a calm and most saintly smile, he told them that two goats had been sacrificed for the occasion. Ashik told him that they agreed on the name—Mohammad Qasim Chowdhury, because it was an auspicious name. The imam approved. Indeed! The imam nodded his bearded face. He asked if they knew what it meant. The parents said they did. It meant "to share" or "to distribute" in Arabic. The imam smiled again and inclined his head towards the holy book. He opened it and gave his full attention back to the verses.

The imam stopped reading after a while. Without looking at anyone, he drawled. His voice slowly dipping, "I have arranged for women to sit in the next room. Please take the baby and proceed to the next room. Men would be gathering here soon for the Jummah Prayers."

Ashik looked at the imam and then at Prema, whose reluctance to move to the next room was evidenced by a grimace. Ashik was just as reluctant and showed his displeasure by avoiding eye contact with the imam. She paused, and then she heard the Jummah Azan loud from the minaret. Suddenly, an overwhelming number of men entered the room. She felt outnumbered and awkward; all these men were crowding into the room and taking over the space pushing Prema to the wall. Nervously, she stood up stumbling over the saree at her feet, she picked it up to its ankle and walked fast with the baby towards a connecting door, and through it to the next room.

She did not particularly enjoy this segregation. It barred her from being with her husband in the same room, and also who she really was. But a special Aquiqua Dua, a prayer was going to be held here. Being a Muslim woman that was expected of her, and she knew it. Whether or not she liked it, was another matter. For Prema, never wore the hijab. She thought of herself as a free-thinking woman, pretty much like the prophet's first wife, Bibi Khadijah.

Bibi Khadijah was a woman of the world, a widow marrying the prophet, fifteen years younger. At the same time running her own business, with the assistance of her second husband, the prophet himself. She was a progressive woman for her time who had followed her own instincts. But she also believed in the existence of an omnipotent God, and the five pillars of Islam founded by the prophet. Although, unlike Bibi Rabeya Basri, who had fought alongside the men in religious wars, Bibi Khadijah, wasn't a warrior, but she considered herself equal to any men.

Prema was not shy. Socialising with men came naturally to her. The community that she mingled with before her slum life, was liberal enough to allow this

99

intermingling—attending mixed parties and hobnobbing with both men and women. This lifestyle was not viewed as decadent, neither anyone compelled her to wear the hijab. In the early days of the 1950s, and the 1960s in East Pakistan, the prevalence of the hijab and the burqa was scarce. Fashionable women, particularly, women of her standing didn't wear one. Those who did were small in numbers, confined only to a few renowned Sufi or religious families. Even they had the choice of not wearing them.

If she were to have a naming ceremony her way, Prema thought, it would have been far less stressful, without the interference of the imam. She would have organised a get-together at her place without letting the imam be privy to the colourful lifestyle of her inner circle of friends. If she had it her way, she would have had a religious ceremony first in the mosque, then at home, and a proper party with dance and hard drinks to boot.

Prema could still have a party in her dinghy slum room. But her circumstances decided otherwise. It would look almost farcical. Certainly, no woman would walk through those doors of her present abode in perfumed silken sarees, or sequinned chiffon. However, she still planned to do something, even though it may not be remotely posh. She kept that a secret from her husband. Only her husband's trusted partner, Lal Das knew whom she had engaged to organise a slum party. Who wasn't allowed to come even close to the mosque on account of being a Hindu?

The Jummah Prayers were over. Men and women prayed separately in their respective rooms. Lutfun, their niece Mila and Mila's mother, Nazmun Banu and Sheri attended. The women accompanied Prema on the praying mat, except Mila who couldn't pray today, because of a predisposition. She held the baby as they prayed. Greetings ensued after the prayer followed by humorous banter, as they sat down on the matted floor. Whether or not Mrs Chowdhury's blessings imbued this holy occasion was unknown.

"Oh that smells so good," Mila said, inhaling the fragrant biryani wafting in the air.

"Yes, they have slaughtered two goats today," replied Prema.

"Why did you wear white? Do you not have a red saree? Lutfun asked.

"Are you crazy? In this heat, I couldn't even bring myself to look at one."

"The heat is pretty stifling," Nazmun Banu replied. "Here give him to me."

Nazmun Banu indicated that she wanted to carry Quasu. She extended her arms with a smile to pull the baby off Mila and cuddle him. Mila handed Quasu over to her mother. Looking at the emerald silk Nazmun Banu was wearing, Prema asked. "Say, is this a new saree our brother bought for you?"

"And when was the last time you think he bought me anything nice? He isn't quite the lover that your Ashik is. How did our mother-in-law even know that he was going to be a lover, when she named him Ashik?" Nazmun Banu teased.

"Oh, I'm quite sure it was a mere coincidence that Ashik turned out to be the way he is," Prema laughed.

"A befitting name, all right," Nazmun Banu smiled. "Yes, names do influence characters, I believe. That's why meaningful names are so important. Ashik means lover, and Qasim means to share. I wonder what he would be distributing, I hope not squandering. And even if he did, I wouldn't be surprised. After all, it is in the blood."

"Oh, we don't know that. What's in a name, anyway? Maa calls Ashik, Taher. If he were given that name he would still be an Ashik, no?

Lutfun added to this friendly banter. In her mind, however, she was curious about the actual relationship between Tahera and Ashik. Why was she so close to him and not to the others? Nazmun Banu's reply cut through her thought.

"Hmm sister, now here's a thought. The thing is, it's a mystery, just as it is hard to discern why Maa loves Ashik so much. Only Amma would know, right?" Nazmun Banu added.

She looked obliquely at the playful baby in her lap, who in that instance revealed his baby pink gum with a sage smile.

The family knew that Nazmun Banu's bitterness developed over time as a result of her husband's infidelity. But her strength came from the support she received from her in-laws which was unheard of that any family would favor the daughter-in-law over the son. But Mrs Chowdhury did not condone his misconduct.

Inwardly, a thorny side grew within Nazmun Banu, despite all the love she had received from the family. A rose without its thorns would be quite bizarre. For she was just that, a rose, when she had eloped with her boyfriend, a restless teen, now her husband. Her seventeen-year-old body had just blossomed. And he was fifteen years older, bordering on thirty. It was a summer evening. The setting sun had splashed a rare blood-red hue over the sky. Her father had rolled out the praying mat for the Maghrib at the sound of the azan, her boyfriend, Ekram Chowdhury and Nazmun Banu chose to elope.

Ekram had stood under the verandah, like Romeo, and had whistled a familiar tune that only Nazmun Banu knew. She promptly appeared on the verandah. He had climbed up the guava tree and rested on a branch which was snaking into the verandah. They gazed at one another without a word. Like thunder in a clear blue sky, he had said. "Come with me now. Come away."

"Come away?" You mean, elope?"

"Yes, your father would never agree to our marriage?"

"And why not?"

"Because he hates us. The fallen zamindars, he was never one of us. He was never a zaminder. He hates us because he was never an aristocrat."

"And how do you know that?" she asked.

"Trust me, I do," he said.

103

"Now, look, Ekram, this is really a huge step. I'm not sure. This seems like a really bad plan."

"There is no such thing as a bad plan in love," Ekram said. "Besides, as soon as we are out of here, we will get married."

"And where would we go?"

"I'll take you to Calcutta. We shall stay at a friend's house. Now don't just stand there. C'mon, take that leap."

Without thinking, the seventeen-year-old had leaped. She crossed over the verandah's rail, latched onto the offering branch, and took Ekram's hand until they safely landed on the ground. First, they kissed and embraced and then took off for an unknown destination.

No one witnessed this, except for the setting sun. After the prayer, when her father called out for her, servants couldn't find her anywhere. They went into her room, and she was not there. Customarily, after these prayers, Nazmun Banu and her father would join on the verandah for snacks. When the servants couldn't find Naznum Banu anywhere, the father went to the police with a missing complaint. Her absence in the house was commemorated with a heavy silence.

Nazmun Banu never returned. However, a letter did arrive to her father that Nazmun Banu had done a runner with her boyfriend, who was the eldest son from the House of Chowdhury. Her father became furious. Because, their nobility never impressed him. They were a despicable lot, loathsome characters as far as he was concerned, whose lechery and loutish behavior knew no bounds. Stewing in anger, the father disowned Nazmun Banu, another evening of the setting sun, upon the arrival of the letter.

At Maghrib, the ominous words came to his lips. "I disown you as my daughter. I disown you from my property. You are never to return here. Your wishes will never be fulfilled."

Nazmun Banu's mother had begged him not to curse her in this manner at such an auspicious hour. But once the words were spat out, they had become the law of the house. And this was how it had transpired. Nazmun Banu, now bitterly aggrieved and resentful of her decision, after about two years of marriage, found no solace whatsoever; Ekram had moved on and found new love in her best friend. Harsh, she thought. The reality was harsh and yet it wasn't meant to be like this. Because, when they eloped, he had taken her straight to a railway station to catch the night train to Calcutta. Calcutta, now Kolkata was under British India at the time. These were the days when communal riots and blood baths were rampant.

Oblivious to such volatility, the lovebirds frisked in the thrill of the chosen path of adventure. On the train, they sat on a plastic seat side by side, holding hands at the prospect of getting married soon; the scorching simmering day of clammy summer's evening. The smell of sweat reeked through the air of the crowded, dingy train compartment.

The atmosphere was thick with social unrest too. A clear look of distrust and disgust was apparent in the eyes of the passengers. Women wearing the shindur, a red line along the middle parting of their head, clutched their slumbering children close to their heaving chests. Men stood haphazardly in the stifling heat of the grisly compartment in deadpan expressions. The train had suddenly stopped, and a group of men walked through the crowded place. Men looking at one of the women with the shindur, asked her name. She replied Shagorika. Then they turned towards her husband seated next to her, who was not in a dhoti. They looked at him suspiciously and asked his name. Before he could answer, Shagorika declared in a loud voice; her eyes widening so much that Nazmun Banu thought they were going to pop out. 'His name is Chakraborty, Sunil'. The men were not convinced; they gauged him up and down. He didn't look the part. Sunil went pale. He turned his face towards the window, away from the men's glare. The men left. Sunil let out a sigh so heavy that Nazmun Banu could hear it cutting through the space across to her and Ekram's seats. For the rest of the journey he was sullen. He looked at his wife only when she asked him to fetch a bottle from the overhead luggage. Nazmun Banu read a name on the bag he took the bottle out—Shahid Hussain. Her heart began to pound.

What a trip! She thought. Ekram couldn't have chosen a better time to elope, exposing her to this! Because, she had always led a protected life within her father's opulent home. A two-storied house on an acreage of a flourishing garden. Her mother was an aristocrat and married to her father only because they had fallen, too, just like the zamindars elsewhere. Whereas, the father, who was from a peasant class, rose by dint of his merit. Being a good student and skilful, he rapidly prospered. He earned his fortune from a cushy job in the far east. He worked very hard at school and secured a scholarship to go abroad to become an engineer.

He made enough money, returned and married into aristocracy. But he bore an eternal grudge against them. He could never change his family roots. He became even wealthier than the zamindars. Still, it was not enough for him. He'd never had a chance to bask in eminence and class. His glory and success would always be marred as being a nouveau riche. Something, not scandalous, but a rude reminder of his marked place in the social hierarchy. However, he married an aristocratic lady because he was a social climber. At least, his wife was an aristocrat, even though he would never walk in their shoes.

The train stopped at Hoogley Station in Calcutta. Ekram and Nazmun Banu disembarked. He gripped her hand so they wouldn't get separated in the crowd. They found a quieter place where they sat down and took a breath of relief.

"What now?" she asked.

"Trying to figure it out," he replied.

He looked into her guileless eyes and said. "Get married?"

She asked. "Here? You mean right here and now?"

He said. "Yes, right now. Stay here while I grab a mullah. Don't move from here, I'll be back soon."

She sat on a bench of a busy platform filled with the humming rhythm exuded by passengers' foot traffic. They walked alongside dhoti-wrapped panting boys, carrying luggage on their small heads—a meal ticket. Screeching noises of hauling boxes and suitcases. Children, as small as seven, ran alongside the train, shouting 'hard-boiled eggs,' and selling them to passengers through carriage windows. People were either saying goodbye or greeting loved ones. It was hot and humid. She needed to go to the toilet. In this strange place, with these complete strangers, she felt lost amongst a crowd of swarming little ants. When she stood up for the toilet, she saw him—a dark head of wavy thick hair pushing through a bobbing crowd.

"Finally," she smiled with a sigh of relief. "I was about to find the women's toilet."

He signalled to the mullah to wait on the platform while he grabbed her by the arm to take her into the women's. He was impassioned—impressive. She leaned against his chest momentarily to support herself. He squeezed her arms and then released her. She ran into the toilet. In the toilet, she stopped in her tracks. It reeked of human feces from the non-flushable squat toilets. She puked on the squalid mosaic floor filled with black water. But she had to go. She tiptoed through the murky water, balancing herself precariously on the squat. She finished, came out, and ran straight into Ekram's loving arms. She smiled and thought of the many beautiful days ahead. This sickening toilet was behind her now.

The mullah married them on the platform. Let alone, expensive jewellery and gaudy clothes, she didn't even have any clean ones on, when she signed the contract. Now that they were officially married, Ekram took her to his friend's house. Outside the station, they stopped a rickshaw and got on. The rickshaw-puller hauled them through the dusty roads to Shyam-Bazaar. The seventeen-year-old looked around in awe at a great many buildings, without any proper knowledge of which was what. But she liked what she saw. At the entrance of the alley of the Shyam-Bazaar, the rickshaw stopped. They got off and Ekram paid the fare. Nazmun Banu suddenly clutched Ekram's hand.

"What is it?" he asked.

"Oh I don't know. I have cold feet. I don't even know if this was such a great idea."

"You're telling me now. Now that we are married, everything is done. Trust me, it's all going to be fine. All will make sense in the end. Trust me, okay?"

He gave her a peck on her smooth, young cheek. Her modest eyes downcast, she looked tender and demure. However, when Ekram held her hand and gave it a squeeze, she brightened up and flashed a smile at him. They stood at the door to his friend's house. Ekram rang the bell. A maid opened it and let them in. She felt it was maddening.

At the start, Ekram and Nazmun Banu's life was adventurous until it took a tumble through the many ups and downs. Nazmun Banu was still his first wife and earned the respect of her in-laws for being so. She performed her duties and suppressed her bitterness. Her husband now took a second wife, her best friend. 'Oh! How could he?' she had fumed. 'This was just as insane as it was inexcusable after all we had gone through. It sounded romantic and it felt romantic at the time—an eloped wedding at a train station. What excuse was there to fall in love again and marry my best friend? There had to be something more insidious—something in the blood, the same blood of womanising which flowed through all his ancestors. Father hated them for a good reason.'

Nonetheless, he continued to come back to her some nights. Nazmun Banu would not resist. She had resigned. She too had her own physical needs. The next morning, he would be gone again like a desert wanderer.

Mrs Chowdhury had accepted her after they had returned from Calcutta. Married, and also because she was a mere child of seventeen. Mrs Chowdhury heard that Nazmun Banu's father had disowned her from all his properties. According to Mrs Chowdhury, Nazmun Banu's father clearly had no class, and despised the Chowdhurys for being aristocrats. No matter, she would not lay her eyes upon Ekram's second wife, ever; she gave Prema the same treatment. Mrs Chowdhury's logic was simple—no seconds or thirds were admissible. Only Tahera, who continued to live with them, was an isolated exception for being poor and an orphan.

Nazmun Banu, fell pregnant with Mila. She was born on a stormy evening in the House of Chowdhury. Mila entered the world with a thunderclap of a baby cry, as the winds had gushed outside the window. Ekram, a doctor, delivered his own child. However, by then, Ekram was already in a relationship with Nazmun Banu's best friend. A deep secret which eluded Nazmun Banu. When he started coming home really late at night, one night, she had asked him, and he was forced to tell her the truth.

"When did all this happen?" she demanded to know.

"Look, she has always been your best friend, now you can both be sisters."

"Sisters?" her fury knew no bounds. "I shall not lay my eyes on her again. That back-stabbing, home-wrecking bitch. Get out of my sight! Get out this minute!"

Soon, it had come to light and Mrs Chowdhury knew about it. She had ordained no one to contact Ekram's second wife. However, Ekram, her firstborn, had a special place in the mother's heart. Mrs Chowdhury could not bring herself to abandon him as she readily abandoned Ashik. Therefore, Ekram came and went as he pleased and when he pleased.

Nazmun Banu learned to live with an apparition of her best friend as her sister now, but never spoke to her again. She accepted Ekram with frozen congeniality, but couldn't ignore him completely because they shared Mila. Also, she had no place to go.

Prema had secretly befriended Ekram's second wife— Fatima, now Mrs Fatima Chowdhury; the two ill-disposed sisters-in-law. It wasn't that Nazmun Banu didn't suspect, because she'd also heard from the neighbours that they saw Fatima visit the bibi more than once in the slum. While Nazmun Banu didn't confront her, she often asked herself a million questions, wallowing in repentance, that she shouldn't have eloped at Maghrib. This suffering was her atonement on account of disobeying her father; this was her father's scourge.

After the Aquiqua, the family gathered out in the masjid's courtyard. Nazmun Banu carried the child, and Prema stood next to her. Ashik invited everyone to come home with them. He and Prema went up to the imam to say farewell. Afterward, they headed on foot to Ashik's humble abode. As they left the masjid, they queued up on the narrow dirt path towards the slum. They nattered like the sprightly spring birds, livening up the short walk as slight winds waved through their hair. They were on the periphery of the slums where they could hear a loud band party. Ashik looked at Prema in surprise. It was of course Lal Das's doing. She had asked Lal Das to organise another party in the slum and this was what he had done. It had to be loud to be in tune with their current situation in life—a life without any style. No one could even dream of cocktail/mocktail parties being held here. Mila began to laugh immediately out of joy. "What a pleasant surprise?" she clapped.

Nazmun Banu frowned thinking how crude and loud this was all. They proceeded straight into the heart of the party and into the blaring noise. Lal Das greeted them with open arms and a huge smile. The space was filled up with joy with all the slum-dwellers, the everyday peddlers, the rickshaw-wallahs, and the street merchants, alike. In the front yard, where they squabbled at the tap just that other morning, they were here too, squatted in a circle on the courtyard's grounds. The band party drummed up cheap but cheerful music in the shade of a mango tree. Two men played the drums. A red cotton belt tied the drums on both ends, which the men hung down their necks. Another man played the clarinet. The baby was sound asleep. He woke up startled from all the off tune blare.

"Come in, come in, hello," Lal Das said.

He screamed at the top of his voice. Ashik smiled and gave him a short, tight hug. His relatives smiled at him too and walked around him to sit on the hired, wooden chairs.

Much of the talks drowned in the cacophony. But they sat quietly and tried to look content.

Prema Chowdhury was radiant both from the heat and the joy. She took her little boy inside for a feed, while the party continued at full blast. Lal Das had done a wonderful job organising this. He had also ordered sweets to be distributed amongst the slum people: the brown elongated kalojamans; the rounded rosogollas; and the blotchy orange luddoo. Prema could smell the butter from here. 'When was it the last time I had actually had them?' she thought. She heard a knock on her door and saw someone pushing through. Who else? But her own Ashik.

"Here, have some?"

He had brought her the pricey sweets to her mouth and pushed one in. Her cheeks balled out from their sheer size.

The music continued for another quarter of an hour. The lazy, late afternoon moved along into an evening of calm meditation. The party broke, as the band stopped. They bid farewell one by one, the slum-dwellers left first, then the relatives. Mila, Lutfun, Sheri and Nazmun Banu, all bade goodbyes. Lal Das was the last to depart.

Prema and Ashik saw the relatives out at the entrance of the slum. Bats flew across like inkblots on a reddening sky. Ashik smiled and pulled his bibi closer to him. The bibi didn't mind. They stood close at the entrance with Ashik's arms wrapped in a tight grip around her slim waist. She smiled and hid her face into his distending chest.

"Quasu is asleep," she said.

"Yes, I know," he replied.

"But he could wake up anytime," she whispered.

"I know that too," he whispered. Enjoy this moment of quietness, you and I. And the evening, at our feet."

"I love you," she said.

He closed his eyes, listening, and rubbing his face on her head, kissing it at the same time. For a moment, standing here in an embrace in this very public space, they lost the sense of time and place. They heard a cough from someone passing by and alerting them. Ashik turned around but held his bibi close to walk the small yard back into their room. Quasu slept peacefully in bed. Ashik and the bibi sat down on the floorbed. He held up her chin with his index finger and looked at her in the shadowy streetlamp. She heard him take a sharp breath.

"Gosh! You're beautiful," he uttered.

She smiled and said nothing, her eyes meeting his.

"Will you always love me like this?" she asked. "Even when I am old?"

"Always. That's a promise, I don't want to be like brother Ekram—never. I don't understand why Amma didn't kick him out too."

"Amma has a weakness for her firstborn just as Maa has a weakness for you. She calls you her Taher, remember? She is still known as Taher's Maa—Mother in the village," Prema said. "Are you sure she was infertile? Are you sure she didn't have you?" Prema inclined her head with a glint of dark humor in her wide eyes.

"I don't know, and I couldn't care less."

His voice was hoarse, and he sighed heavily. Prema recognised a new emotion in this sound. Ashik made her mad enough to leave her first husband and her children. This madness had better last. The sincerity of his words rang through the stale, humid air like a cool breath. She closed her eyes and felt his lips pressing down on hers, holding her tighter and making her feel lighter. Oh! These tight pressures of his lips were precious; they left no emotions undone. In its heaviness, it carried every message of nuanced passion, desire, affection, respect and romance to a full brim. The kisses hardened. He kissed her on the soft flesh of the nape of her neck and up the delicate jawline. She moaned and felt pricks of tears gather in the corners of her eyes. The night deepened and Quasu slept right through.

The azan drifted shortly at the pale hours of the morning. Prema woke up and found her head nestled on his bare, hairy chest. Her clothes and his were on the side of the floor bed in a pile. Ashik was fast asleep. She stood up and tried to wrap her saree over her cold, dried up sweat. Quasu needed his morning feed. She rushed quietly towards the tap outdoors to get washed.

Thoughts of last night flooded her mind as her lips curved into a shy smile. Of course, there was no shame in making love to her own husband. Her love for him defied every scandal. This thrill of romance made her coy, like a blushing teenager on a first date.

That was a profound sense; the joy of love she experienced in her heart, which heaved every time when Ashik touched her with a kiss or an embrace. Nothing triggered any flutter nor trepidation in her hopelessly unromantic ex-husband. She defended her decision on account of this, not once but a hundred times. She believed that in time everyone would accept them, even her other children including their father. They will be welcomed in the House of Chowdhury, too. However, it wasn't a prediction, but a wish.

Prema didn't speculate, but she already knew why Ashik had chosen slum-life over an office job. Ashik hadn't completed his studies in Business Management when they had eloped. This new occupation in the slum's throes was a decision made for them, but this had also taught them resilience. What he desired to do in the end? He had become self-employed with the hope of becoming an entrepreneur one day. He was gathering valuable, bottom-up experience. Someday he would have the whole gamut of it under his belt.

awakening

One idyllic spring morning, Mila woke up with a yawn. Gibberish talks drifted from uncertain directions. She squinted to check the time. It was hardly 10 'o'clock—a lazy Sunday. But people had already dropped in. She got out of bed, walked up to the window, and gazed downstairs. She saw men in the orchard. These were her uncles and their friends, coming over for a Sunday midmorning tea. She heard them talk, often breaking into passionate outbursts, but could not understand the reason.

Mila's sixteenth birthday was last month. This tender age rendered her vulnerable. But she grew up feeling privileged in the House of Chowdhury. Her bedroom window lent a clear view of the orchard. The wooden, green, shutters of the window splayed wide this morning; she didn't close them the night before, to let some spring breeze seep through. She fell asleep in the wafted air of citrus fruit profusion. Standing by the window, a few words that she overheard from the heated debate eluded her. These were big words, such as revolution, change of government, and empowerment. Whatever those words meant, Mila had to run along. Her friends were coming over. They had planned a picnic under an Indian jujube tree at the far end of the orchard.

Mila saw their black bobbing heads through the window. She got dressed, picked up a matchbox from an ornate dresser-drawer, and ran downstairs. Pots and pans lay haphazard on the grassy patch. One friend picked up a rock and hurled it at a bunch of russet jujubes, hanging down its stringy bark. A few luscious fruits plopped on the ground. They bent over to pick a small hand full each. They giggled without a reason, as they chewed them, casually spitting the pits around.

Most of them lived locally—Shreya Mukherjee, a mutual friend of Papri Khandakar. When Shreya saw Mila come through the orchard, she went halfway to meet her. They greeted and hugged. Other friends, Shelly, and Lima, smiled at Mila. Shelly sat down by the pots as Lima dug out a hole in the ground to make a stove bowered by the tall orchard trees. They were four beautiful teenagers. Wrapped in curvy, silky scarves around their chests, and short, floral frocks, they wore them over long, stripe pants. They planned to make long khichuri this afternoon—a sumptuous gruel of rice, dal, salt, and a pinch of turmeric, some oil, cooked in a pot of water.

They shoved twigs and dry leaves into the stove-hole. Mila took a stick out of the matchbox and struck a flame. She held it to the stuffing of dry, leafy twigs in the stove-hole to light a fire. The four girls lifted the heavy pot of the khichuri mix and put it over the stove. Luminous embers emanated like fireflies around the orchard.

The girls cut out a long plantain leaf and spread it along, next to the jujube tree, to use as a shared plate. In about half an hour, the khichuri was ready. Lima opened the pot's lid. Charcoal smell pervaded the air; the remaining fire dwindled.

Shreya and Lima held the gruel pot off the stove and used this momentum to bring it over to the leaf, where the two other girls were sitting. They took the lid off and placed it on the grass. They scooped up the gruel and splashed it along on the banana leaf. Their laughter said it all. Whether or not it was tasty with a tinge of a smokey BBQ burnt flavor, they couldn't care less, but they ate it up with gusto. The twigs in the stove-hole burnt gradually to a cinder. The picnic was over.

"Where do we dispose of the banana leaf?" Shreya asked.

"Hmm, good question, I guess just leave it here under the tree," Mila answered.

"Under the tree? Just like that?" Shreya asked.

"Yeah."

"Okay. But it's hardly a clean leaf."

"Doesn't matter. It would eventually go into the soil. Where do you think all the fallen leaves go?" asked Mila.

"Into the soil, but—"

"Well?" Shelly asked, eagerly.

"You know, how the leaf is all filthy and everything. Besides, it would take some time for this to mix into the soil, too. It's still so green," said Shreya.

"Don't worry, just leave it. It will all be done, trust me," Mila said.

"Okay, if you say so."

Even for a sixteen year old, Shreya knew better. She knew that the soiled plantation leaf shouldn't be exposed to the elements like this.

"Why do you care so much about being tidy?" Mila asked, suddenly.

"Why not? What a crazy question is that? Why? You don't care about it at all?"

"No need, because nature takes care of it for us."

"Still, you just don't drop things like that and keep them lying around, just because it is going to biodegrade 'eventually.'

Mila kept quiet but Shreya discerned a dark, new dimension in Mila's character. She had a point though. However, sloth seemed more like a reason to Shreya. Mila went up to the main gate with her friends and saw them out. As she walked back, she saw Mrs Chowdhury's retinue of maids cleaning up the orchard. They shoveled dirt into the stove fire pit and levelled it up along with all the other litters. The orchard was back to its pristine, most magical state, in no time.

Mila and Shreya had a special bond. Mrs Chowdhury knew that. While back, she had discovered a secret hideout, a cubby house in the orchard's old jackfruit tree. Inside the little cubby house, there were copies of English Mills and Boon romance books, and Bangla spy series, Dashyu Bonhur, a carom board, biscuit crumbs, and pieces of torn chapati. She had also found a few cigarette butts on the floor next to an old blanket, which Mila had taken from a rusty, antique trunk in the attic. But how did these cigarette butts get here? Surely, it must be Shreya's idea. Her own granddaughter wouldn't dare, Mrs Chowdhury thought.

It was definitely Shreya who coughed the first smoke, Mrs Chowdhury imagined. It had to be her idea—that Shreya, who planted this in her granddaughter's head to pinch a cigarette packet from her uncles, which Mila did surreptitiously one afternoon when everyone had gone for a siesta. At least, they were careful not to burn this blanket. But Tahera knew better. She was nearby, doing laundry by the pond. She had overheard Mila propose that they smoked and that she would steal a packet of cigarettes from her uncles. Shreya had opposed the idea, in fact; it was Mila's all along.

Mila sat on the old blanket and looked for the hidden, cigarette pack under it. She pulled it out; it had dented by then. She drew a cigarette and ignited it. She took a couple of easy puffs; just then, she heard a sound. It distracted her. It was the sound of a rally passing through her alley. She stood up on her toes and looked through the cubby window. Over the short orchard fence, she saw a massive demonstration. Her cigarette burnt out; the heat touched, the tip of her index finger. She dropped it, stood up and crushed the smoking butt under her heels. She came out of the cubby house and jumped on her red bike, which was leaning against the cubby's wall. She rode it through the front yard out to the alley. She saw the rally. Along the way, she read slogans written largely in black on white placards. They demanded equality. Equal pay; freedom from oppression and exploitation. The rally went as far as the mosque, right to the end of the alley where the slum was; where uncle Ashik also lived?

Revolution sounded romantic, but notional to her. The likelihood of her participating in these protests was nearly nil. She would sit in the orchard a few evenings by herself wrapped in the enchantment, inspiring her to think big. She thought of the words she had eavesdropped on her uncles' conversation with friends. She could even drag Shreya into it. But she would have to hide it from her relatives. Every evening when this rally passed through, it aroused her revolutionary curiosity. She rode out to the meetings at the mosque square. It had become a hotbed for free speeches. Mila listened to them mesmerised. She began to attend them regularly. Her mother and Mrs Chowdhury noted her absence; they thought she was with friends.

However, one spring night of 1971, the alley was unnaturally calm. None of the demands had been met. Exploitation was at its peak. Leaders of this movement had declared war against the government and proposed that every household became a fortress. The government was given an ultimatum to resign, to make way for new leadership.

On such a night, Mila was returning from the mosque square. In the passing, she heard a terrible wail from Shreya's house. She saw Shreya, running haphazardly into the open street, followed by soldiers in Khaki uniforms. These were soldiers cracking down, not only on protestors but civilians as well. Mila hid behind a streetlamp and saw those hyenas chasing her.

A military truck stood at the entrance of the alley, and Mila heard girls and women crying. A truckload of women was picked up. Mila blinked a few times. A cold sweat ran down her spine. She saw the truck drive away. Shreya disappeared into the darkness on the road too. Mila rode home and entered the room of her grandparents; they sat grimly at the dining table listening to radio news.

Mrs Chowdhury looked up and said. "From now on, you're not allowed to go anywhere, except school. Do you understand?"

Mila nodded, with a frown. She told them what she had seen on the road and what she had heard at the rally meetings. Shreya, where was Shreya, anyway? She asked herself. Mrs Chowdhury sat Mila down. She explained to her that they were at war. The government had declared war on its own citizens. It was a civil war. The military ruthlessly tried to squash this rebellion. These absurdities, shameful, and merciless crimes against humanity broke out like blisters.

Suddenly, Shreya burst into the room. Her long hair was untied and disheveled; a mass of netted bird's nest. She flopped down on the floor.

"Shreya? What happened?" Mila asked. "I saw you running on the street a while back."

"They took Boro Didi!"

"They did what?" Mila asked.

"They took her."

Mila tried to understand the situation. Shreya's elder sister, Krishna, was on that truck. Why though? Mila was young, but her heart whispered its fears of why the military had taken young girls and women. This was how they were going to squash the movement, by taking the women away and making them pay for it. Mrs Chowdhury asked Shreya to sit on a chair at the table. She tried to calm her.

"If your mother is still at home, go now, go already to help her find out where the army may have taken your sister," Mrs Chowdhury said, urgently.

"But that's nearly impossible — Baba could never find out."

"Why not?" Mrs Chowdhury asked.

"Because he doesn't even know anyone in the army who could tell him."

"Could she stay the night here?" asked Mila.

"Yes, she could, but you must ask her mother."

Shreya rose to leave. She had a sense of foreboding that perhaps she would never see Mila again. She walked under the pale lamps; desultory darkness had enveloped the lane. Just two houses away from Mila's house. She reached home. She walked through the open door and saw her father and her twin brother, Shuvo, sitting glumly in the drawing room. Her mother performed puja at the altar of Vishnu — the great god of preserver, in a corner carved out for prayers.

Shreya stood at the door, feeling restive. She saw her mother was in deep meditation. This unparalleled devotion — could this change the course of history? What was it? What gave her this strength to be so calm at a moment like this? To be able to give Lord Vishnu her undivided attention. Even Vishnu himself would be perturbed. Or perhaps not, or else, he would have descended from heaven to rescue the drowning world. But he remained cold like this marble statue at the altar, as someone who only watched moving cinemas of human destiny, played out on earth on its axis of destruction and preservation. It was hard to know his hand in this. Shuvo came and stood beside her. She looked at his tear-stained eyes.

"I need to tell you something," he said.

"What?" Shreya asked.

"I am leaving home."

"Leaving home? At a time like this? What do you mean?"

"Yes, leaving. Now or never. Just tell them that. Tell Maa and Baba that I have joined the revolution."

"Are you crazy? At sixteen, you want to be a revolutionary? You have not even seen a gun yet, let alone used one."

"Don't be silly, Shreya. It has been going on for a while. Most young boys, my friends, have already joined. I have even seen Mila at the mosque square. Why do you think the military was here? Why do you think they came to our house?"

"Why?

"Because they want to arrest boys and men. They think they're the ones fanning the movement. And they are. Do you understand now? Young boys, men, are leaving in droves to join this fight."

"That is so foolish."

"Foolish? What's foolish is your naivety! The army is targeting every young person they can lay their hands on. They think other countries maybe behind this too. This army will find us and kill us one by one. Today, they couldn't. But they will come back looking for me since I am one of the eligible 'young boys.' Also, to take you and Didi to their pleasure house. You were lucky, you got away. I was at the corner shop lighting a cigarette. By the time I came home, it was too late. They had already taken her. They kept Maa and Baba alive because of me. The military is using them as bait to catch me. Someone must have tipped them off."

"Oh no! Even if all this were true, how were we going to win this? Our boys are no match for them."

"That maybe. But our enemy is clueless. They have no idea, and neither do you. Anyway, I've got to go. Tell Maa to pray for me."

"Wait, Shuvo."

But Shuvo had walked away; Shreya went after him to the door. He closed it behind him to brave a revolution. All this was so quick. What could have happened overnight to bring this on? It happened, all too bitter a revelation, at least for Shreya. Mila had known for a while now, sneaking out to attend those rallies at the mosque square. But Shreya had no idea. She was not political, nor an activist. She returned to the puja corner. It smelled of burned incense. At the altar, Vishnu stood with a conch shell amongst all its fruit offerings and sweets in return to the third eye that he had bestowed to its devotees. Except for the flicker of candles in the wind, there were no cosmic lights.

126

Lord Vishu's imposing presence created a strange aura. Shreya felt that the Lord would keep his promise and save the world for his devotees who remembered him with such loving, elaborate pujas. He would blow into the conch shell any time now to summon his demi-gods to carry out the commands. While her mother continued, Shreya felt she actually heard the ancient callings of preservation.

A desperate knock on the front door broke her spell. She saw Mila push herself in.

"What's up?" Shreya asked.

"We need to go."

"What do you mean?"

"I said, we need to go. Where's Aunty?" Mila asked.

"She's in puja."

"Pack a suitcase and come to our house with your Baba and Maa, as soon as you can."

"Why?"

"Seriously? Don't you listen to the BBC?"

Shreya kept quiet. Mila could be irritating sometimes.

"Tell me, do you or do you not know that there's a war upon us?" Mila asked.

"I didn't until Didi was abducted and Shuvo left home."

"Just as well, I heard that our place was going to be attacked soon. They're coming after us. They'll soon start a door-to-door search for every young boy and man in the vicinity, without fail. Our house is next. They will kill, plunder, and rape anyway they can. We are planning to flee to our ancestral home in the village. Daadi Amma said to get you, so you could escape with us."

"Okay, okay. Enough said. I'll see you at your place soon. Go now. It's not safe for you to be out and about either."

Shreya saw Mila out. Mila mounted her bike and peddled it along into the night. The suddenness of it made her dizzy; she began to throw up. The revolution had been brewing for a while. Yet, it just hadn't descended on her until now.

It was decided then. The two families would leave town and move to the village. Maids had whispered something in the orchard earlier, which had alerted Mrs Chowdhury.

"What is it?" she had asked them.

A maid looked at her. She was so pale that she startled Mrs Chowdhury. "Well, when I took Shreya Didi to the gate this evening, I saw things and overheard something."

"What did you hear and what did you see?"

"Two men were whispering, talking about the imam of the mosque," she said.

"What were they saying?" Mrs Chowdhury asked.

"That the imam is a military spy. He often tells the military about our neighbourhood kids, about how many young people live on this block; which homes have young girls, boys, and revolutionaries. He also tells them which house belongs to whom."

"The imam is a collaborator? An informant?" Mrs Chowdhury asked. "Quickly pack your bags and tell the other maids to do the same. We're leaving town."

The maids left. Meanwhile, she shouted out to Mila to gather Shreya and her family. The imam must have collaborated. He was the one to tip off the military about Shuvo, Krishna, and Shreya. How else would they know about these young people living in that house? The House of Chowdhury was next. The military had found out about them by now, she was certain of it.

She had two sons of her own, and lots of young girls in the house. The imam knew this neighbourhood better than any residents living here. They must leave at once. The Chowdhury family began packing little suitcases with clothes, hard molasses, and dried rice. It took them until midnight to finish. Mila's uncles and aunties were ready. They waited for Shreya and her family. As soon as they appeared in the doorway, they rose to leave. There would be at least twenty of them including the maids. The one car in the garage would not be nearly enough. Shreya's father also brought his own car. As they were ready to leave, Ashik appeared on the doorway with Prema, Quasu and Lal Das. All eyes were on Mrs Chowdhury. She looked at them and stood still. Her eyes were on her grandson. There was no time to waste. She had to make a quick decision. She smiled and waved at them to come inside.

The two cars set off in the cover of darkness towards the river, where they had planned to take boats across to their village. On the road, there was the reek of decomposed flesh; mangled distorted bodies, dumped callously in the drains. The killers, the army, called themselves humans but even the dead seemed more human. Expressions of horror and confusion were frozen on their cold faces. The soldiers had nothing. They were robotic creatures of the night. The two cars sped through the graveyard shift. Mila sitting in one of them, saw abandoned rickshaws lined up on the lane. The bodies of the pullers were still, like statues—arms and legs trailing. The mosque square was ground zero. Only vultures and crows flew at night in the full moon that shed light in the crematorium of this desolated place. This had become a wasteland of stark trees, tall and short pointy branches. They stood out like crooked, uneven fingers of a banshee, posed for a ritualistic dance of death and doom. Mila rolled-up the car window and covered her ears and eyes. Shreya, who sat next to her, held her close.

It was witnessed by some of the neighbours who stayed behind. That the army had looted every house and had ransacked the fruit-laden orchard of the House of Chowdhury. It was spring, but the deathly shadow was cast over the season's new bloom. They went after almost every citizen; murdered them or took them away at gunpoint; relentlessly, not sparing any young boys or girls. Children witnessed horrendous murders of parents. Their sharp cries rang through caged ribs within their bodies. Shuvo and his friends had already fled and joined the movement. The streets and dirt paths were packed with never-ending processions of men, women, children, and babies in their mothers' laps; babies never stopped crying. Hunger pains were greatest at a time like this, but they must all make it to the river.

Mila and Shreya's family cars were full. One of Mila's uncles even had to sit in a half-opened boot. And the suitcases were tied up on the bonnet. Closer to the river, Mila peered through the darkness. She could see boats in the offing. They would be needing a few of them at least. Mrs Chowdhury did not leave anyone behind. Everyone in the house came with them, including the orphan, Rabeya, whom her adopted daughter, Lutfun, had picked up from the dustbin two years ago. The distant gunshots reminded them of the orchard. Only birds pecked at its sullied fruits. Shreya mused, no one knew where her sister was, or Shuvo? Would they come home any time soon?

waves

On the bank of the River Kali, the two cars pulled up. The passengers sitting in them squeezed, came out of the cars jostled by each other. Looking out into the murky waves, they waited for the lifelines in the offing. Staring at uncertainty, these boats were lifelines that Providence threw at them. Fortuitously, they had fared so much better than those who couldn't make it.

It was well beyond midnight. The boats were sailing towards them under the sprinkled moonlight. Mila noticed something else in the moonlight and also in the dim lights of the lanterns carried by the boatmen. She saw swollen bodies. They were floating like rootless tree trunks on the water surface; dumped and abandoned in callous haste. Carcasses were soaked and looked larger than life in death. Curiously, some bodies were in police uniforms. Police who died, perhaps, defending this land—the valiant, brave soldiers. Mila looked without a blink. Totally aghast, there were far too many floating bodies piled up in a heap, much like blighted autumn leaves.

The boats arrived. The boatmen tethered them to the short bollards on the riverbank. People slowly stepped onto them in a queue. It took them at least five boats to make space for everyone. Thank God for Shreya's father's big microbus to fit everyone in. The boats swerved as they got on. Mila sat with Shreya. It was pitch dark everywhere, except for the slight light; a lantern stood in the middle of the boats to impart some light at the helm. The boatmen oared them off. Mila could see some villages alongside the

132

river, illuminated by fireflies. The surroundings looked blue, a blue-night, rendered by illumination. In the silent night, a few stars blinked and stirred a foreboding. Lutfun began to throw up into the river. The oars splashed one lap after another. A distant sound of gun fires sent trepidations across a smoky atmosphere. Mila, sitting on the edge of the boat, occasionally dunked her hand into the water.

Her mind wandered. She walked the streets of an alley back in the city; the roadside tea shacks were bustling with men wearing army pants and boots, laughing over how many kills they made that afternoon. The imam from the mosque joined them and whispered vile information about where all the freedom fighters hid.

The orchard smelled of fragrant and ripe pomegranate. Roses tossed in the winds hung over the verandah's roof walls. Birds in the orchard, surely that wouldn't be the end of it all. This couldn't be the end. She walked as far as the mosque—a silent alley, without any frolicking birds, cats, or stray dogs. Where was Papri? Has she gone missing? Dirge swept through the alley. Dust and dry leaves cobwebbed the murky drains filled with dirt, grit and green grime, purple and black filth where life germinated, creepy, hundreds and thousands of germs crawling.

A red alley—bloodbath—men, women, and children, over which another kind of germs grew. A red door—Mila entered. She heard laughter and tortured cries of pain, mingled. A nightingale shrieked. She saw men's nails being pulled out. Men hung from the gallows with broken necks. Gushing blood from their clenched teeth; eyes gouged out. Hollow. Face. Raw marks of whiplash. One too many— brown lashing backs—bloody streaks and violence marred

133

the torsos. A desert of rising sand, scruffy men scuffling though in the arid air. Sands—the satin dances of waves, swelling and falling glibly in autumnal winds. Both good and bad were like night and day, entwined.

War and peace, but where was no peace? Mila's restive mind rose and fell like an oscillating ocean, she walked the desert night. Under the starry sky, she watched a fiery comet; fireworks; Mila walked this journey alone, of happiness and unhappiness. Her delible footsteps of indelible experience of dreaming. On the sands—those were actually time. Layer upon layer of undulated sand dunes, time stood like a tower of carcasses, built on piled up bodies of once talking, laughing people. With all its invisible grit, pressing them down now under the carcass. Sands pressed down. Death fed on. Time wrinkled life, blighted it with age and decrepitude. Mila was growing old; her skin had tarnished as time sucked it dry. As if she had never existed; as if life had never existed. Time sucked out the essence from the hourglass of limpid youth, with all its freshness, dance, and tune.

A war was upon them. Who was to blame? The Government, the imam? God? Who worshipped God on planet Mars? What happened to God without people's worship? Where no life ever existed and no one lived or died, for whom did God exist there? Was God meant to exist only on planet Earth? Surely, God would die there, because there were no worshippers to keep Him alive, from Mila's perspective at least.

An uncertain journey of refugee life began. A new beginning would surely lead the way when the revolution ended. The boats sailed unhindered in the nightly breeze.

The river spoke of journeys; it gurgled a tale of mystery. That life was surrealistic, death was not. Because it was life which was characterised by impermanence; where relationships—father or mother, love dissipated into thin air. Without any signs, never to be found again anywhere—a void created by death—as though the loved ones never even existed. Taking life seriously was an indulgence—making it meaningful was an indulgence. Wisdom came only when people learned to communicate with the river; the river knew life's true essence—its beginnings and its endings; a silent witness of both the journey and the destination: births—ageing—deaths.

She ran her fingers through the murky water; her heart sank, her visions were stark. They were at a juncture of an unwieldy life; the boat sailed; the oars slid in and out of the satin, sloshing water. Then there was a sudden ripple, a splash in the dark. She looked around and sensed another boat. When she looked closer, she saw boys being lowered from it. Rifles over their heads, they walked through the river's shallow lowland—a storm picked up. Another storm in the orchard, the dragonfly got away like a far-off helicopter, up and up and up, airborne. Dizzy from chasing it far off, they spotted a coloured helicopter, delicate, now gone. How was she to know whether or not she was happy? Perhaps, the illusory happiness, that dragonfly, which was well within reach, she had chased it away. Happiness was like those delicate wings of the dragonfly. It broke easily. But it could make the soul soar, too. That was the nature of happiness to be ever elusive.

The river took many lives; it also aided in giving lives. Bountiful fishes from this very river fed the villagers; as the river also saw floating bodies and rifled boys—a repository of untold little stories of everyday men and women. One too many stories to write on its wet shores. The boats reached the muddy shores of Pretigram. This was the same Pretigram, where many boats of the past had also tethered. Mr and Mrs Chowdhury had started life. But then a flood had galvanised the village, and new lands after many years were beginning to resurface.

The boats stopped but swerved gently in the waters. The boatmen leaped out and tied them in short bollards on the riverbank. Mila, Shreya, and everyone got off awkwardly and stepped on the ground. Some tried to imitate the boatmen in attempting to jump with some alacrity but fell down heavily in the wetness. Their feet dug holes into the bank's soft soil.

They started walking through the paddy fields. Amongst the tall grass, few uniformed bodies lay scattered. Forlorn whips of rice grass lashed in the breeze; the bloody drama staged in red waters reeked of decapitated bodies. People fled in droves wherever they could. Across the border, to the next state. They moaned. A woman wailed in these fields, tonight, as she told her tales that cut through the space. How she was working the fields one morning, while her baby slept in the hut; the pitiless army hounded them. She ran with all the others in a frenzy and panic. By the time she remembered her baby, it was too late. Her hut had already been torched. In raging madness, this woman sat here, mornings, afternoons, and evenings, moaning and telling her little tale—the river knew better.

She howled. Her hollering reverberated in the hollow winds. The statue God watched, but did not take pity, only looked the other way. Mila's thoughts swam like satin; she heard this woman cry. Mila saw the dragonfly, again. Her floral short frock danced in the youthful days of favourable winds, then. The dragonfly got away. She had chased another through the orchard. Its flimsy netted wings flapped. Too quick through the wind; Mila's nimble feet couldn't keep up. Ah! This one too, got away. Just as well, she sat down in the orchard's wet grass and hurled a rock in the air. Her father came home that night. Her parents had an argument in the House of Chowdhury.

At dawn, during these uncertain moments in the village, Mila woke up, half asleep. She felt sad. In the early mornings, temporary depression set in; it played weird tricks on her mind. She felt death was closing in on her. She felt reality slipping away. Nothing. Nothing. Early mornings reminded her of all those dead people—an orchard full of dead leaves—dragonflies were gone—Shreya's sister, taken—a river full of Khaki uniformed floating bodies.

Raven's Edge was a completely different scenario. Mila was physically distanced from these scenes in her mind. Here she had one coffee after another, reading her grandmother's folder, and jotting down her own. The tranquil winds blew outside the café, but Mila continued to write about the past, when they had stepped on the mud of a war ravaged Pretigram, digging deep footprints into its soils, and dragging their feet through the wetness—making history. History was in the making. History, of torture, persecution, and civil war.

It was a long journey into the night and the night's journey had only just begun in Pretigram. The members of the Chowdhury family returned to their ancestral land after many decades of living in the city, Dewangonj. Some parts of the land had resurfaced from the river. They were northbound to Mr Chowdhury's uncle's house. The flood had not engulfed this portion of the village.

A long walk. People still used the old method of palanquin for transportation, but there didn't seem to be any around. The village was quiet at night. The afternoon bazaar was the best place for the villagers to gather for tea in tiny tea shacks where they gossiped and talked about politics. Walking in the light of ubiquitous fireflies, they heard a gunshot. What was that? The army? The freedom fighters? They kept on walking. It was arduous. This war was far from over.

Mila and Shreya stayed close to Nazmun Banu. The long line of people walked through the paddy fields, which could become a battle ground any time. In the starlight, Mila vaguely saw something. The men and boys were lying straight on the ground. They were covered in mud camouflage in the dark. Someone whistled. Mila's relatives stopped walking. Shreya struggled to breathe. Mila felt Nazmun Banu pull her hand. She and Shreya did what everyone was doing. Lie low. They lay down on the ground. Mila felt sweat beads on her forehead. Her breathing was restricted. She heard a whisper. She saw a man running through the paddy fields into the dark. There were two more whistles, and Mila saw quite a few men rise out of the paddy fields like ghosts who melted into the night.

Mila let out a sigh of relief. Shreya began to tremble. She felt privileged to be alive. But Mila felt unsure about who these people were. They had to be the freedom fighters, not the enemy. Surely, the enemy wouldn't spare them. Whoever they were, Mila and Shreya were pleased that they didn't end up in the cross hairs.

The next afternoon, talks in the bazaar confirmed that those men from last night were the freedom fighters. There was information of an imminent attack. But the enemy had lost its way upstream. They ended up somewhere else, instead.

love

Rahim Ali. This was where Mila had first met him. He wasn't betrothed to Papri Khandakar then. During the war, he was on the most wanted list for committing treason against the ruling enemy government. Rahim Ali was a revolutionary and a leader of the freedom fighters.

In Pretigram, the Chowdhury family did what they do best—sing. Here too, every evening, all sat in a matted courtyard under the waxing moonlight singing, joking, and trying to make the best of the situation. Ashik started singing again, love songs, songs of bereavement and separation.

This evening, someone was at the door. He had come to speak to the head of the family. Mr Chowdhury was sitting on the verandah, reading a newspaper in the lantern light. Two people had come in and wanted to speak to the most senior member of the family. Ashik and Ekram rose from the mat and walked over to see the visitors. Lutfun whispered on the mat that these were freedom fighters. It started to drizzle. Everyone jostled to go inside.

Mila stood leaning against the verandah wall, listening to the conversations. One of them introduced himself as Rahim Ali and the other was his cohort, Topon Chokroborty. Her uncles told them that they could speak to them. They handed something to Ekram. It was a parcel wrapped up in a checked cloth, a red gamcha—washcloth. They wanted them hidden in this house for their next operation. The next thing Mila heard was Mr Chowdhury asking them to sit. They sat on the verandah floor. Ekram came inside the

140

house and asked Naznum Banu to bring them something to eat.

Lutfun brought out two plates of cooked rice, dal, and curried fish. The family sat around them on the open verandah. A breeze blew through the drizzle, and lightly spat onto them. Fish curry, rice and dal was a princely meal under the present circumstances. Mila didn't come out. She stood behind the wall and continued to watch. Rahim Ali. She wanted to know him better. Ali didn't even notice her — a mere girl of sixteen, and he was a charismatic revolutionary — the Che Guevara of the day. The more she saw him, the more drawn she felt towards him.

Ali and Chokroborty finished eating. They are leaving now. Her uncles walked them across the courtyard. At the entrance, Rahim Ali lit a cigarette. Shreya called Mila to come out and sit down back on the singing mat. Once they departed, the singing would resume. Mila did that. She came out and sat with Shreya on the mat. Mila saw that Rahim Ali's lips were dark, as he exhaled a smoke ring into the air. A few spitting raindrops fell on her shoulders through the plantain leaves. After the smoke, the two freedom fighters bade goodbyes and covered themselves in big black shawls and disappeared into the dark. Lutfun came back to the mat.

A few weeks on, Mila noticed some covert activities in the house. She realised that her family was participating in the revolution. The family had begun to assist them with clothes, food, shelter, and medicine. Overnight, a hall room in the house had turned into an undercover, impromptu hospital for the wounded guerrilla fighters.

141

Night after night, Mila observed how these wounded men, hounded by the enemy, appeared on their doorstep — numbers increasing by the day. They carried cold messages of the war. Of the millions that took refuge in India, and the other millions who died. Lutfun, Nazmun Banu, Prema, and all the others nursed them through those injuries. They appeared in twos and threes. A village doctor visited the house frequently. The singing sessions camouflaged the covert activities. The talks in the bazaar described the Chowdhury family as the past hedonistic zamindars, who for many generations had been steeped in the pleasures of the flesh. The revolution wouldn't interest them.

One night, Quasu fell ill. He had a high fever. Prema sat by his head, sponge bathing him through the night. At one stage, he convulsed and went blue in the face and black in the lips. The family began to howl. Mrs Chowdhury came running and took him in her lap. She sprinkled water on his face, and he stopped convulsing. Towards early morning, his fever came down.

A village doctor was brought in, Quasu was diagnosed with a viral fever. On his way out, the doctor peeked into the hospital room. He entered and found Ekram examining two critically injured boys from bullet shots. A shoot-out had taken place across the river. The boys were brought in by boatmen. Ekram prepared himself to take the bullets out. He asked for assistance. Mila and Shreya volunteered. The doctor decided to assist Ekram. He asked Mila to hold up a lantern, and Shreya helped Ekram with hot water and medicines.

The doctor's medical bag held all the paraphernalia — surgical instruments, antibiotics, bandage, Dettol, and saline bags. Unlike Ekram, he was the practicing doctor in the village and had full access to the pharmacy which Ekram did not. Ekram, hence, used his supplies to treat the boys. He cut open the wound in the lower belly of one of the boys and pulled out a bullet with surgical scissors. He dropped the bullet in a kidney bowl. Shreya pressed the blood flow with gauze until he stitched it up. The other boy had a more serious injury. He was hurt in the shoulder. The same procedure was applied to him too. The bullet was taken out and the shoulder was bandaged heavily.

Ekram and the village doctor, both were suspicious of the village pharmacy. The doctor heard gossip and whispers about a mole in the pharmacy. Although he was never confronted, suspicions had risen among the chemists because of the sudden escalation in the demand for antibiotics and bandages. The doctor told them that the number of patients in the village had risen.

No one knew exactly how long this war was going to last. People were stopped and harassed on city streets, nearly every day. The military asked the civilians to read the kalema or verses from the Qur'an to check who was a Muslim and who wasn't. Even Muslims would forget to utter the kalema under duress. And non-Muslims couldn't recite any at all. Regardless, all those who couldn't would inevitably get shot unless they were very lucky. Such senseless killings would continue without a reprieve. The wounded freedom fighters also told the family how the seventh fleet from the USA had arrived and was anchored on the Bay of Bengal. Any day, they too could march in to squash this rebellion. Any day, the capital Dacca under East Pakistan, renamed Dhaka under Bangladesh, could be flattened to ground zero.

143

At Raven's Edge, Mila rose from her chair to fetch a glass of water for herself. She closed the diary and ran her fingers tentatively on its leather-bound cover. She walked over to the counter, bought yet another bottle of sparkling mineral water and came back to her table. She poured herself another glass.

She had poured Rahim Ali a glass of water. One evening, she lit a candle and placed it beside his bed on a stool; Rahim had been a patient in the safe house after an injury. She had handed him some letters and said, "I cannot get you out of my mind."

"I'm a freedom fighter. I could get killed any day."

" I know. This is a mistake," she said.

"How so?" he asked.

"I don't know. Oh! I don't know, I ought to take my words back, I suppose," she said.

"Why? Do you not love me?" he asked.

Mila had lowered her head. Her eyes glistened with tears.

"Come now," he whispered.

Mila kept quiet. She felt a surge of excitement. Rahim Ali's gaze was all over her. He quietly looked at her lips and her eyes. There was a blush on her cheeks in the candlelight which Rahim Ali noted with a smile. She was about to get up when he held her soft hands in his fist.

"Look at me," he said huskily.

Mila raised her head and looked at him. She felt a sob rise to her throat. Her hand was in his iron grips. " I think—" she said.

"Yes? What is it? You love me, right," he insisted.

Mila looked at his bandaged head; his dry lips, and his pale face. She started to sob.

"Don't cry. Please don't. You're breaking my resolve," he said.

Shreya stood in the doorway. She missed much of the conversation, but she had come in to find out if anything was needed. She startled them. They unlocked their hands quickly and looked at her. Their eyes gave away much, but Shreya pretended not to notice.

"Oh, I didn't mean to scare you or anything."

"You didn't," Rahim said with a smile. "How's Shuvo?"

"Yeah, he's all right, I think. He has joined the freedom fighters, too," Shreya replied.

"Yeah. How old is he?"

"My age, sixteen. He's my twin brother," Shreya said.

"Yes, boys as young as fourteen have joined our regiment," Rahim Ali said absentmindedly.

Mila got up and walked over to the door. He looked at her and smiled as she left. Mila smiled back. Shreya was there, but she had other issues on her mind. She had not seen Shuvo in all these months. Had he become a freedom fighter? Was he even alive? Did Rahim Ali know his whereabouts? Shreya also left with Mila, thinking that she must come back and ask him later. Rahim closed his eyes to rest.

They went into the kitchen. The kitchen was in the backyard, disjointed from the main house. It had a thatched roof, and clay walls pasted over green bamboo shafts; the floor was the same too. At a corner, several wood-fire stoves were built.

"What do you say?" Shreya asked.

"What do you mean?" Mila asked.

" Did Shuvo become a freedom fighter or not?"

"Ask him. Ask Rahim Ali. You must, especially after what had happened to Didi. Your sister was the sweetest person I know," Mila said.

Mila looked up at the sky, and beyond towards the river. She saw her uncles returning from the river, where they had gone to bathe. They also caught enough fish for lunch. The men were dressed as farmers in village lungi, folded up to the waist like a short sarong. Shuvo, was a muscular boy of sixteen. His voice was just cracking when he had left to join the freedom fighters. Mila didn't want him exposed to the dangers of the war, either. Shuvu was a friend too, like Shreya.

146

Both Shreya and Mila knew that orphan children came here as wounded fighters; some died on these makeshift hospital beds from lack of proper treatment and deep wounds. Many bodies were also found on the riverbanks rolled up in the mud. No, no this couldn't be Shuvo's fate. The hospital beds were full of teenage and orphaned boys. The brutal war took many lives—hundreds and thousands of boys, men, and women.

Mellow Autumn days of sparkled sunshine; a garden full of red berries, Mila burst into a park by the Dhanmondi Lake; her scarf flew in the careless winds; she ran after it. But the dancing scarf had already landed on the satin folds of the lake. She craved peace; she craved for those carefree days to return. The idea of Shuvo ever joining the freedom fighters was a nightmare.

At night, sleep came late. She stayed up thinking of the many unspoken words. Rahim Ali slept alone in the hall room, next door. It was early morning, and Mila woke up. It was a world she didn't know. It felt surrealistic to see so many dead faces everywhere. She heard her mother faintly. Nazmun Banu was calling, that breakfast was ready. Nazmun Banu asked her as always to cover her face when she went out into the sun because the sunlight was damaging to the skin. Her father, Ekram gave away all the money he had to Mrs Chowdhury to feed the family out here in the village. Time traveled only in one direction. Mila swam upstream on this tide. She woke up. Nazmun Banu was actually calling her for breakfast. It was nothing much.

These were crisis breakfasts; molasses and flaked rice with chai.

At the Raven's Edge café, Mila wiped her eyes as she wrote. Rahim Ali's confessions had an effect on her. Not only was he her valiant hero, but she realised that he too was falling in love with her. Rahim Ali was pleased to see that Mila visited him every night. He would, too, write letters to her when his arms healed. They sat together on Rahim's bed. Rahim would take her hand in his and say softly to her that she was beautiful.

.

One night, she brought him dinner. It was a soupy fish curry. But she had also brought him an omelette tonight. When no one was looking, she stole an egg from the kitchen and made an omelette—a luxury denied to everyone. She put the egg under a pile of rice on a plate and hid it. In the makeshift hospital bed, Rahim was reading a book in the dim light of a hurricane, by his bedside. Rahim put his book down and looked at Mila in the soft lantern. He looked at her, her neck, and at her eyes—head to toe. Mila was aware. She felt shy and quickly dropped her gaze. Her sixteen-year-old heart was fluttering with romance.

"Come here, sit with me," he asked.

Mila didn't move—the plate in her hands.

"I still can't walk. If I could, I would have carried you here, already," he sighed.

"You must not speak to me like that," she whispered.

148

"Why not? Why can't I express how I feel for you," he said. "Can you deny your feelings for me?"

Mila was quiet. Her silence spoke the words she couldn't utter.

"Oh, why must we torture ourselves, like this?" he asked.

"Do you think this would last?" she asked him.

"I don't know, please come—come now. Sit by me."

Mila walked over and handed him the plate. He took the plate with one hand and held her arm with the other. She sat on the edge of the bed. He pulled her head to rest on his chest. His arms, healing steadily. He bent his head and found her lips.

She smiled at Rahim. She had given him a rare treat; omelette on rice. Rahim took a scoop of rice and cut the egg in half. He had half and offered her the other. She nodded her head to say, no. He did the same. But he brought the spoon to her lips anyway, and he held it there, nudging and teasing her young lips, so she would open them. When she did, he gently pushed it into her mouth. She took a mouthful. Then she inclined her head.

"What is it?" Rahim asked.

"No, nothing, just checking something."

"What are you checking?" he asked.

"Say, did you hide a gun under the blanket, there?" she asked.

149

"Yes. Always. I always have a gun."

"Has anyone seen it?"

"No, I don't think so."

"Will you train me to use one, just in case?"

Rahim looked at her. He finished eating the last scoop of rice on his plate. He put it down by his side. Then he pulled her towards him and planted a kiss on her forehead. They looked at each other in a lingering gaze. He pulled a slow smile on his lips.

"No, not in a million years."

She sighed, and then said. "I must go now. I have to go".

"Go now and sleep well."

Mila took the empty plate, and stood up. Rahim took her other hand in his and gave it a squeeze. She looked at him and smiled.

"Will you come tomorrow morning? I want to see your face first thing," he whispered.

"I'll try. If I can wake up that early."

"Try, and goodnight, my love."

"Goodnight."

She whispered and picked up the lantern, slowly pulling her hand away from his grip. She walked out of the room and into the kitchen and dumped the empty plate under a foot tap by the stove. Mila found her place in bed between Shreya and Nazmun Banu.

It was late. She struggled to sleep.There was a tiger. She saw its burning eyes just outside the   window. What if the tiger came for her? She wondered and got out of bed and locked the bedroom door. She looked outside. The tiger was fearsome. It sat in the bedroom. She saw the tiger's glare through the darkness. She woke up with a sweat.

At least she didn't dream of the tiger tearing her apart, suffering the reality of the pain of the tiger gutting her in this outer reality—this otherness was just as real while people dreamt. Oh! Thank God, she woke up. What would Shreya, the wise one say if she knew of this romance between Rahim Ali and herself? How would she react? Would she think it was the right thing to do when her own brother and sister were missing? Mila wondered. 'No, no this was all wrong. These kisses, the soft touches, the whispers, and the passions, all a mistake.'

She shouldn't follow her father's footsteps or her uncles.' She closed her eyes, as tightly as she could. But her mind meandered to Rahim Ali anyway. She tried to block him, break away from him, blow him out of existence as she blew candlelights everyday. This was torturous. This was like having the tiger inside of her head. Rahim Ali's words, whispers, touches, and even his soft breathing were indelibly seared into her memory.

The next morning, she sensed some trepidations around the house. People were discussing something in the courtyard. She heard that Lutfun was to be married soon. The local imam was to marry Lutfun and Sheri in a small informal village gathering. This was good news. Mila felt elated. She went up to Lutfun and asked her.

"I just heard the good news," Mila said.

"Yes, the elders decided," Lutfun smiled.

"How do you feel though, getting married in such extraordinary circumstances?" Mila asked.

Lutfun shrugged and said nothing much. Mila guessed that they had been living under the same roof forever.

"The local imam is coming over to marry us," Lutfun said.

"It's going to be a really quiet wedding, yeah?" Mila said.

"Yes, it doesn't matter as long as we're together, I guess. However, I would have preferred a big wedding."

"Am I invited?" Mila asked.

Lutfun laughed and said. "Of course, silly!"

A wedding date was fixed about five days in. On the morning of the wedding day, Mila and Lutfun both woke up early. Lutfun looked cheerful. Nazmun Banu and Prema returned from the village bazaar, with garlands and a red bridal saree. They spent all morning shopping for Lutfun's wedding. Mila and Shreya took Lutfun to bathe in the river. After a few dips into the river, their saris were drenched. They sat down on the bank to dry the cascading hair in the sun. Mila and Shreya wrung the water out of Lutfun's hair with a cotton wipe cloth. The four of them relaxed on a grassy patch by the bank.

Lutfun lay longer. Her smooth, fair skin was soaking up the warm morning glow. A few hours passed. They rose to return. Just when a boat also sailed towards them. Shreya looked at it. She thought she saw someone familiar. When the boat reached the bank, a young boy jumped out into the river. Was it believable? Shreya pinched herself for a reality check. She screamed when all the others also turned around. No less, it was—Shuvo. Shreya dropped down in the mud. She stared blankly without a word.

The others stood up too in a moment of shock. It was Mila, who first ran forward and embraced Shuvo to say, 'welcome.' Shuvo came home! He was home! But he looked much older, and his face looked worn out and thin. He had lost weight, but that was to be expected. What an auspicious day too, for Shuvo to return home. Right on a wedding day! Shreya began to cry with joy. Everyone hugged him, kissed him, and brought home a prized wedding gift.

Everyone in the house had naturally focussed attention on Shuvo. The wedding seemed less important. He was made to sit in the center of the courtyard under the deluge of questions; about the war, his whereabouts, and how did he find out that they were here. Most importantly, though, if he traced Didi—their elder sister. Their mother sat here wiping her eyes. In great detail, Shuvo told them what he had heard from his mates. Some of those mates were here. That was how he knew about them—the fabulous Pretigram Chowdhury refuge.

Shuvo told them that he heard about innumerable rape victims. How they were locked up in warehouses around the country which were the enemy's pleasure houses. These women cried and stamped the soldiers with their feet, but they kept coming back, more and more to gang rape women and girls, and children. In her head, Mila imagined the worst possible scenarios, a living nightmare. The youngest rape victim died on the cold hard floor from forced intercourse and torture, Shuvo recounted. She was only ten.

Albeit, Shuvo had no specific information about Didi. But Mila imagined, she must have fallen pregnant by now, a miscarriage must have happened. She must have been tortured without a reprieve. Then her body would lay somewhere on the floor from all this brutality. Torn and bloody—no one cared. But Mila cared enough. She thought about her—Diva Didi. Her fertile imagination left out no details of the pains Diva must have endured. The thoughts gave her the shivers. Shuvo told his stories and wanted to meet the wounded fighters in the hospital hall. Mila said she would take him. He could also meet Rahim Ali here.

It was time to get Lutfun dressed for the wedding. Nazmun Banu and Prema took Lutfun straight into a room. It had been decorated by Nazmun Banu and Prema at dawn with wild mustard flowers and jasmine spread out on the bed for the bridal night. They sat Lutfun down on the hard floor. Then they dressed her up as best as they could. She was dressed in the red saree which they had bought from the village bazaar, and a garland.

It was a plain sari and a plain wedding—the war was upon them. No one knew when the war would end, hence the elders decided on this wedding. The local imam came over from the mosque, and the family gathered in the courtyard. Sheri sat outside with his brothers. Mr and Mrs Chowdhury sat with the imam. The ceremony started. The imam asked for Sheri's consent first outside, then took with him three witnesses indoors to get Lutfun's consent to the marriage. The shy Lutfun said 'yes' three times softly to the questions and agreed to marry Sheri. When they both said yes, the imam declared them married and came outside to sit with the family.

A few hours later Prema and Nazmun Banu came out into the courtyard with Lutfun dressed as a bride. She would have looked glamorous under a different circumstance, dressed up in expensive and proper bridal attire and all. But for now, this would have to do. Everyone in the house, including Shreya and her family with Shuvo was there.

The bride and the groom exchange garlands. Nazmun Banu dropped a dollop of firni, the rice pudding on the veiled Lutfun's hand to feed the groom, and the groom did the same. Then a small mirror was brought and held up in front of Sheri so he could see his bride—the beautiful Lutfun under the veil. Everyone clamoured to know what he had seen in the mirror, to which he replied—'star'. Lutfun lowered her head, shy, like a Bengali bride. After the ceremony, the couple was taken indoors to the same room where Lutfun had been dressed in bridal attire. They held hands and crossed over the threshold.

On the night of the wedding, Mila went to see Rahim Ali. She took him wedding dinner. He knew about the wedding already from Shuvo, when he and Mila had come earlier on for a chat with him.

"Was I invited to the wedding?" Rahim asked.

Mila laughed. "Everyone was invited."

"How was it?"

"Different," Mila answered.

"What did you wear?"

"Home clothes. Nothing fancy."

"Hmm, I can't wait to see you in a bridal sari," Rahim said.

He looked at Mila and searched for a reaction. Mila's expression confused him. There was an earnest frown and a smile at the same time. He took her in his arms and said, "One day, soon. That's a promise." He heard Mila sigh and felt it on his bare chest. He held her close quietly for a few moments of peace. Their eyes were closed. Someone coughed at the door, and Rahim and Mila opened their eyes to find Shuvo standing on the threshold. Mila rose and left. Shuvo winked at her as she walked past. She bantered with him and lightly slapped his arm—"save your winks for your girlfriend, dear."

A few days passed. Rahim Ali made a full recovery. Both Ekram and the doctor removed the bandage. One morning, Mila was hanging around the bog, waiting to use it. She was going to take Rahim Ali breakfast. As she waited, Lal Das came out of the bog. He smiled at her. She smiled back. Lal Das, her Uncle Ashik's bosom friend, and a business partner appeared anxious this morning. She saw him talking to Uncle Ashik. She overheard them talking. "What's wrong?" Ashik asked.

"I may have to leave tonight," he said.

"And where? Is there any place at all that's safe?" he asked.

"Well, the enemy is marching in, looking for Hindus in any hideouts. If I stay, I'll jeopardise everyone's safety."

"Is Rahim Ali still here?" Ashik asked.

"He is. Ekram Bhai and the doctor have taken his bandage off."

"How do you know you're not safe here?" Ashik asked.

"The doctor said that word has leaked from the pharmacy that this house is a camouflaged refuge. He was harangued at the pharmacy over the supplies he had been buying regularly. They were always suspicious, but now they are sure. There is a spy amongst them at the pharmacy, according to the doctor."

"Yeah, and how does the doc know that?"

"He heard whispers when he went to buy more bandages," Lal Das said. "Rahim is also not safe. Our front may have blown."

"You're not going anywhere," Ashik said. "We need a better hideout, for everyone, the sick, the women, and particularly for you and Shreya's family."

"The doctor already has a plan," Lal Das sounded perplexed.

"He does?" Ashik asked.

"The river," Lal Das replied.

"Yes, of course," Ashik nodded.

157

Mila quietly walked away. She felt a mad rush to see
Rahim. She ran up to the hospital hall, and found an empty
bed. Under the pillow, a bunch of letters were tied up in a
string with her name written on the back of a letter on top of
the bunch. She took them and hid them under her scarf. Not
knowing what to do next, she wandered towards the river.
She had a desire. What was the time? Was this the proper
time for Rahim's safe passage? There could be so many
pitfalls. Perhaps, her Uncle Ashik would know of a safer
route? No? Then she saw two boats passing by. She saw
Rahim Ali and Lal Das on one of them. Rahim Ali also saw
her, as she saw him. He waved at her, she waved back. That
was the end of it. She never saw him again. The other boat
was a mystery. How her uncle Ashik managed to do all this
in such a short time was a mystery too. Later on, Mila came
to know that the doctor had tipped off Rahim Ali when he
had come to take his bandage off. He had already organised
this escape.

A humming noise rose in the café. Mila looked around and
saw a crowd of people jostle through the narrow entrance.
The diary was open before her. She tried to pen down a few
more reminiscences. Her love for Rahim Ali was complex
and rich; war romances were almost too hard to
comprehend or forget. What kind of love was it? Who was
best suited for whom? Who knew? Rahim Ali, she didn't
know where he went that day on the boat. The whereabouts
of these people were a secret, as was also the revolution.
Mila didn't know much about how the revolution had
progressed. She only heard whispers from the moon shadow
under the plantain trees.

After she had returned from the river and bid goodbyes to Rahim and Lal Das on the boat, she went in search of Shreya and Shuvo. They were nowhere. When she asked her mother, she blinked and said that a spy had been spotted in the pharmacy; he was watching the doctor's movements. A man had followed him one day to the house. The doctor had picked up the supplies and this man volunteered to carry his bag. When the doctor refused and set off for this house alone, the man followed him there. At the entrance of the house, the doctor heard the rustling of someone stepping on dry leaves. When he turned his head, he saw someone's shadow. He suspected that he was being followed.

The second boat, then? Mila thought, could that have carried Shreya's family? Since this place was not safe anymore? She had heard, of course, how the enemy would line up people randomly, asking them to recite the Kalema, and ask many questions about Islam to suss out the true believers of Islam. Even Mila wouldn't know how to recite a kalema under the gun, being a Muslim herself, let alone a Hindu. Where had Shreya and Shuvo, Mashima and Mesho gone? Mila wrecked her brain for an answer. Would they meet again, if at all?

The news had traveled that some boats sailing to the North had been apprehended. Whose boats? On the brink of these terrible times, anxieties seemed to hang like a never ending nightmare. Mila couldn't think anymore. Who was this informant from the pharmacy?

In the aftermath of the war, Mila knew that the two boats had sailed unhindered. Thanks to the doctor who knew the timing for the safe passage. The doctor had alerted them. He knew from various places such as the bazaar that the enemy was planning a crackdown on the hideouts.

Both Rahim Ali and Shreya's family made it safely to India. Although boats brought back glad tidings, dangers lurked everywhere in East Pakistan. The Chowdhury refuge closed down immediately after they had left. The doctor had stopped coming. The enemy's heavy surveillance of the river, also, rampant river piracy didn't make the river a safe place. Mila knew of one such family, at least, who had fallen victim not to the enemy, but to the river piracy. Their boat was turned into a slaughterhouse, which went adrift over scarlet waters. Every single person was brutally murdered. Neighbours carried such bad news into their homes on a regular basis. Mila's family on edge, once the great zamindars of this land, now dwelled on the fringes, paralysed by fear and crippling poverty.

There would have to be an end to the war someday. After nine months of brutality, the enemy surrendered to India, and East Pakistan had become independent. In this interlude, many damages occurred, however, those who survived, lived another day to enjoy the fruits of freedom.

Serendipitously, one morning, someone shouted, "Joy Bangla," in the fields. Mila had gone for one of her lonely walks by the river. On her way back, she heard a scream. The tides had turned, and the new winds had brought good news of the independence. Mila didn't want to be reminded of the war anymore. She didn't want to live in the dark, grisly, world of horror. She wanted to escape it, she wanted to breathe the perfumed air of fresh jasmine back in her orchard. After the war, she heard that Rahim Ali returned as a hero, he could even become the next Prime Minister of this young country, now renamed Bangladesh. However, the country would have to fall many times before it started to walk again.

Mila imagined Rahim Ali as the new Prime Minister, and she as the first lady. The romance, although short-lived, was real. Mila could not forget him. He had written many heart melting romantic letters to her from India. She slept with them under her pillow, which she read every night. Everything fell right in place. But there were some things she could not foresee. She did not see it coming, how Rahim Ali betrayed her. News thus traveled; Shreya told her one day that Rahim Ali was getting married. It was arranged through a friend of Rahim's father. He was to be betrothed to Papri Khandakar. And that Rahim Ali was going away to study abroad. He was to marry her after he returned with a degree. Papri? Oh! Why her? Mila had screamed inwardly. But Mila couldn't be unhappy for her either because she knew how helpless Papri was. Mila was never going to stand in the way of her happiness.

Mila's family returned to the city and back into the House of Chowdhury, now that the war was over. Lal Das, Shreya's family, had all returned, one by one. Business slowly turned from the war-ravaged bust to the post-war boom. Her Uncle Ashik didn't live at the far end of the alley anymore. Neither did the collaborator imam of the mosque preside over prayers. He was pulled out by the freedom fighters one day and brutally murdered. His severed head and body was given literally to the dogs. The tide had turned. Power changed hands. But atrocities were still rampant, committed by different people now. The days of killings, murders, and kidnappings had not ended. It was now the turn of the winning party to play politics and commit fearsome sins in the name of revenge.

A few years had passed. Summer had descended with full seasonal monsoons. The gardens burst with the freshness of greenery and monsoon flowers. Mila stood at the bus stand on her way to the university. Shuvo came around and stood by her. It had started to rain by then.

"How long has it been since the last bus left?" he asked.

"I don't know. I just got here," Mila answered.

"Hmm, I have been waiting a while, having a cup of tea over by the tea stall."

Mila looked over her shoulder and saw a motley crowd there, sitting morosely and drinking tea.

"Why do they look so glum?"

"Oh! Have you not heard yet?" he asked.

"Hear what?"

"That the new government has reduced everyone's salary?"

"Oh, no, is that right?'

"Yep, that's why they're so sad."

Some time had passed. Still, there was no sign of the bus.

"You know what? Let's take a rickshaw. I think the bus may have broken down. One really can't depend on the university bus."

"Okay, then, we'll split the fare."

"Sure, no problems."

They called a rickshaw and Shuvo and Mila got on. They sat squashed next to each other in a snug fit on the seat. The rickshaw took off steadily on the wet roads, and through the winds lashing. They had covered themselves with a thick plastic sheet all the way to the chin. The man paddling away, exposed to the blinding rain. One wondered how he could even see where he was going.

"What terrible rain?" Shuvo commented.

"I like it though—the more the merrier. I love the little droplets— the hissing wind sounds— the heavy poundings on ponds, and on the little alley ruts. I just love it all."

"Wow, that was quite a poetic outburst. Are you turning into a poet now?" Shuvo asked.

"Ha-ha to the contrary. Trying to be a doctor come poet combo," Mila said.

"There's a puja at home this evening. Are you coming?" he asked. "It's a small get-together. Shreya may have forgotten to tell you, please do come."

"Okay," Mila agreed.

By now the rickshaw stopped at the university courtyard. They split the fare as promised, fifty-fifty. The rickshaw pulled over. The wrap was taken off and they jumped down. Shuvo got off first followed by Mila. The puller then folded the wrap neatly and put it out of sight under the passenger seat. As Shuvo and Mila walked abreast to the same university, Shuvo said suddenly. "Rahim bhai will be married to Papri, soon. Have you seen him lately?"

"No, umm, I haven't," Mila said.

"They will be at the puja too."

" Oh, really? Good, you told me. I'll catch you soon. I have to be in the Trauma Victim Counselling all day, today."

"Okay," Shuvo's face became somber suddenly. His jaw dropped and his mouth drooped. They parted ways. Mila was now in her final year of Medicine. And Shuvo was starting his third year.

The Trauma Victim Counselling within the Medical College was the Government's initiative to look at the case histories of each rape victim. They were encouraged to appear before a counselling body in special counselling sessions to talk about their horrific experiences. It was traumatic not just for the victims, but also for the counsellors present.

Mila entered one of the rooms. It was a spacious room with a panel of counsellors seated at a long table. Mila sat down in a chair as a student volunteer. Diva—Shreya and Shuvo's sister was today's patient. This was her story. Shuvo probably didn't know about it. Diva was horrifically mutilated when she was released from the enemy camp and was admitted to this hospital for many months now. Mila came to this session because she wanted to hear Diva's story.

"Tell us about your experience in the warehouse," the panel asked.

"I was taken from the courtyard of my house. I was helping my mother with cooking that evening—then—and then—"

"Yes, what happened after that?"

"And then they came—the enemy—the monsters—oh! My! My! A—a—a—a, no, no let me go. Maa, Baba, let me go, let me go. Help—"

Diva shrieked and cried and kicked and thumped her arms on the chair. "No, no, let me go. They tied me up to a bamboo pole, me, then they came, They took their pants off, and they did it to me, in broad daylight. There was light everywhere." She stopped and cried. "Maa, Maa. I cried. Why didn't I die? Oh! Why? Why? Why?"

She nodded her head and cried her guts out. "In the warehouse, there were hundreds of girls like me, women, and some were children. The brutes came back every night. They spared no one. Some fell pregnant, some bled to death—monthly periods. But they were all mostly virgins. I was gang-raped—every night. Why didn't I die? Why couldn't I die? The horror! Oh! the horror. How will I live with this? I can't go on. Get me some poison, I want to end it all."

She stopped, and then she collapsed. The nurses came and gave her an injection. Then they took her away. Mila sat petrified.

memory

Mila felt a chill. She had visualised something similar to Diva's report of rape in Pretigram. She had started to cry and rose from her chair at Raven's Edge and headed for the café washroom. She washed her face and returned. She thought of the beach at the Bay of Bengal. Sitting there on the calm beach and watching the great waves. She reflected on how this journey of life flowed not straight but braided through calm and turbulence, twists, and turns, upstream and down, troubled waters ebbing and flowing entwined towards a destination of a much deeper meaning.

The beach—a silent witness to a great many dreams—lovers entwined on the sinking sand in full moonlight—of the mandala of human dramas, a beautiful beginning but perhaps an imperfect ending, the ocean cleaned it away in its eternal ebb and flow. These mandalas had been done and redone until time had given up, a part of resurrection in the hours when all had become sand. The sand was indestructible, quintessentially minuscule. An atom of waves. H2O. Her thoughts threaded in and out weaved a tapestry on those very sands—the zamindari era was gone. Like the sand, its traceable history remained eternal, just not in the archives, but also in the repository of Mrs Chowdhury's memory, often told to friends. Mila listened to her narrative one evening.

It was dusk, a summer of the last great storm; the summer of discontent. Mangled mangoes fell in the wild winds, and people were dispossessed and lost as the storm took everything they loved. A summer in monsoon's grips; the monsoon had swept through, nipping buds, snapping bird nests perched on high branches of deep forests; ants ran amok, drains clogged up in decrepit disorder. Heightened with muggy drunkenness, the rain couldn't clear up this hot night's infusion of rain and mugginess. The dying sun imparted a reddish-darkish light into the room.

Mila lay in Mrs Chowdhury's room, reading Doshyu Banhour, by a Bangladeshi writer, Romena Afaz. Mrs Chowdhury, sat on a reclining chair with her eyes closed. A maid entered her room to tell her that she had a visitor. Her name was Halima. She asked the maid to bring her in. Halima, a stocky, dark, middle-aged woman entered in a red checked cotton saree. Mrs Chowdhury looked at her and smiled and asked her to pull up a chair. Halima sat down.

"How are you, Halima?" she asked.

"I am very well, how are you, my Lady?" Halima asked.

"I'm okay."

"You seem engrossed in thoughts. What are you thinking about at a darkish time like this?" Halima asked.

"Halima, do you want to know? Do you really want to know what happened to us, the zamindars?" Mrs Chowdhury asked in earnest.

"I do. I heard a lot about it from my father who was a loyal subject in your father's zamindari. I wish you would tell me more. What really happened?"

"What did your father do for a living?" Mrs Chowdhury asked.

"He was the village jeweller. He said he made exquisite jewellery for the women of the zamindar's household."

"Ah yes, those were the bygone days of glory."

"But how did they lose it all?" Halima asked.

"My father and his forefathers' land were all auctioned by their vile sycophants."

"How so, my Lady?" Halima asked.

"They had a great many villages, and parganas. They had—"

Mila visualized her family's great heritage. The great Chowdhury Hashmat Ali Beg, the noble zamindar, king of many villages and parganas or districts. He conducted his daily duties from his palace office. He sat smoking his hookah, as he listened to what his subjects came here to say, like his forefathers—listening and viewing through the smoke screen of the whiff.

His subjects came in droves to pay respect. Some were troubled who had come here to resolve issues, which he adjudicated to the best of his ability. Others came to pay taxes. Gold coins poured into his coffers.

Other days, when he wasn't in his office, he sailed on his bojra. His bojra was decorated with a Persian rug, a handcrafted bed, and a leather easy chair. He sailed to inspect his parganas. He traveled from one pargana to the next on the bojra, sailing up and down the open river and stopping at all the districts under his jurisdiction. He would sit out on the upper deck and oversee his subjects from here. An occasional gazelle would run along the river shore.

After these tours ended, he returned home to his own village at blue midnights. The fireflies and a silver moon illuminated his path to homecoming. A palanquin caddy chair would be lowered on the muddy shore which he climbed on the palms of the people to avoid touching dirt with his feet. The caddy would then be carried off in the arms of weighty men towards his palace into the village.

"This was my father," Mrs Chowdhury affirmed. "But the story didn't end here."

Mila pictured the scenario in her mind, as her grandmother continued. At Midnight, the zamindar arrived at the gated palace. His caddy passed through the heavily guarded entry and then placed in the center of the spacious palace courtyard. In the silent white stone palace, everyone slept, except the guards. In a minute, the palace woke up. Sounds of running footsteps and shuffling of sarees were heard through the dark passageways. His wife, Mrs Chowdhury's young stepmother, came out of her room and stood upstairs on the wide, long veranda which enveloped nearly the entire house. Hurricanes and lanterns were lit and held before the zamindar by his male servants.

He alighted from his caddy chair with a yawn. People stood in two rows with lanterns in their hands, as he walked through to his private chambers. There were no signs of dying days at this point in time, Mila thought. The zamindars were at the pinnacle of basking days. Whispers rose amongst the residents in dim passageways if he had

169

married this time as well; since this was what he did in all his previous tours to the pargonas—marry a virgin. However, he gave the brides back to their fathers, with sufficient money for one night's pleasure—fathers were too afraid to refuse.

Many of them fell pregnant, but nobody had the courage to inform him. That he had fathered innumerable children across his estates. As revenues kept coming, the zamindars rose to new heights of power and wealth. Blinded by these idle pleasures, they didn't notice that sycophants were scheming to steal their land and wealth.

"How did they lose everything, though?" Halima asked Mrs Chowdhury.

Mila was now sitting upright against a pillow on Mrs Chowdhury's bed. A muggy evening's sun was setting in the backdrop of spitting rains. Halima sat by Mrs Chowdhury listening to this unforgiving tale—mystified and terrified. Both of them looked at her in the dusky dimness. She smiled at them.

"Do you want to know our family history? And how, all their great wealth had fallen. How did the zamindari fall? Mrs Chowdhury asked Mila, and then kept quiet for a while.

"It was all stolen by sycophants. They had all the wealth and land sold and transferred in their names— auctioned, piece by piece. Until the British came along and abolished the system. That too was a tradeoff, the zamindars could keep their land as long as they portioned out revenues to the crown. But for us, a lot of the huge land had already been auctioned by my great grandfather's managers, accountants, and overseers. It was a huge conspiracy over many years which eluded great Grandfather, Grandfather, and my father—this slow bleed of their estates by their trusted treasures and bankers. It took them three generations to completely bleed us dry."

"What happened when all was lost? Exactly, how was it lost?" Mila asked.

She couldn't hold back her curiosity. She looked up at her grandmother's pensive expression, an inheritor of a great tradition, who was able to keep only the title and this house.

"I'm not sure. There were lots of forgeries and fake documents. Great Grandfather often signed on blank papers. When he asked why he was signing them, he was told by his treasurers and accountants that funds needed to be released for village schools or businesses such as fish farming and little things such as the bojra needed to be repaired or for the maintenance of the palace. Which Great Grandfather and his successors, unsuspectingly signed off actual land on blank papers, thinking that these were costs and maintenance?

"This didn't happen in one generation." Mrs Chowdhury blinked a tear. "Conspiracies were hatched; bit by bit they pinched away land over many generations so they couldn't be caught. Small loss of land often escaped the zamindars because they had so much that they didn't even care to notice—they were negligent and mostly misguided. I still remember their offices. These were the outer courts where Father and great grandfathers officiated the daily businesses.

Inside these courts, there were designated chairs to seat people from all walks of life. Small stools seated peasants;

high-backed chairs, and various hierarchical seating arrangements for people with ranks such as deputy magistrates. My ancestors sat or rather lay in long cushioned sofas when the office was in session. Their hookahs had such long hoses that they couldn't even be viewed from miles.

Mila listened in awe, as she continued with the story of her golden days. "A family history, which would never come back, even if all the wealth came back someday through modern-day trade," she said.

"Family background was all important in those days. A zamindar's family must marry an aristocrat. Even if a proposal came from a wealthy, high-ranking deputy magistrate, it could be refused if he wasn't from another zamindari background."

"Why though?" Mila asked.

"Our old family of seven generations housed many poor students. They gave them free lodging and food. When such students, who stayed in the zamindari homestead while they studied, later became high-ranking officers, sometimes sent marriage proposals to a zamindar's daughter or sister; only to be refused straightaway."

Mrs Chowdhury stopped to breathe.

"There was once a high-ranking government officer, a deputy magistrate who wanted to marry Uncle's daughter. Grandfather sat him down and interrogated him so severely about his fathers and forefathers, that after about three questions, it was revealed that he had come from a family of uneducated peasants. He was the first of his generation to receive an education. His proposal was denied, because he was a lowly jaigir, meaning, a homestay student whom the zamindars had housed and education funded.

"It still doesn't add up," Mila said. "How did they lose all this wealth? Where are all the palaces that you grew up in? Is this a fairy tale? No documentation, nothing?"

"Documentation?" Mrs Chowdhury, sat up on the chair and peered at Mila through the darkness. The window curtains had not been drawn yet, although the sun had dropped a while now.

"Do we document everything we do, or say? Can we document life and lifestyles? Yes, there will be documents of revenues paid to the government, but land lease? I'm not sure. They didn't need a lease, since they owned it all. But there will be files and evidence somewhere in the Governmental offices under a solid crust of dust. I dare say, a lot of them may even have been destroyed or burned, or eaten by moths. However, I remember as clear as daylight, both my father's and my husband's ancestral palaces. Unfortunately, my husband's palaces had been destroyed in the great flood. Much of their village still remains submerged in the riverbed. Someday, that land should resurface. But it would all be Government land then, which would have to be bought back—not ours. My father-in-law's name was Abdul Goni Chowdhury."

She trailed off and then added. "My father's house, however, is still there, but has fallen into disrepair and neglect, because of lack of maintenance funds. My brothers have moved out of the village with jobs, and there's no one to look after it now. They have neither the finances nor the intent to preserve the ancestral palace."

Mila kept quiet. She lifted her eyes to view some family pictures on the wall. There was one Mr and Mrs Chowdhury, with their daughter, Begum, of about five years who was born after Ekram but had subsequently passed away in a childhood illness. These pictures had captured a defining moment of a classy heyday—all three were wearing attires made of brocade fabrics, sitting on satin sofas and satin slippers with a studded pearl in the middle. Mila thought these pictures were all she had as evidence of this grand oral epic of seven generations.

The enchanting tales sounded like fairy tales. Mrs Chowdhury yawned and rested against the chair's back. She closed her eyes. A maid brought a lantern in and placed it on a shelf carved out of a wall.

Mrs Chowdhury liked handheld lanterns. Electric lights hurt her eyes. She signalled to Mila and Halima to leave. These re-visits into her past drained her. But Mrs Chowdhury did not sleep straight away. She closed her eyes and thought of something else. She thought of her grandson, Quasu, and how through Quasu, she reconciled with Prema. Anything could happen at wartimes.

roof

Mila left Mrs Chowdhury's bedroom and stepped into the corridor. Lutfun was walking by. They stopped to have a chat.

"Let's go to the roof, Aunty Lutfun," Mila suggested. "There's a full moon tonight."

"Sure, you go ahead, I'll join you in a bit. Let me grab a hand fan. Evenings, as muggy as they're, can be very uncomfortable on the roof, too."

"Okay, don't be late."

"I'll be there with you in a minute."

Lutfun disappeared. Mila walked towards the stairs and up. She stood under the open sky and waited. The night was muggy. She looked around and her gaze rested on Raja Hashem's house. She saw him sitting in a lantern-lit verandah with his new wife. They looked happy and peaceful together. Her gaze fell on their rain drenched roof. It had falling creepers cascading down its musty parapet wall. Leaf clusters of potting plants and rhododendrons hedged over it well. Water ponded in a rut on the roof.

Lutfun came by and stood behind her silently. Mila felt her presence and turned around to smile at her.

"Look at them," Mila said, pointing at the Hashem couple next door. "Without a care in the world, what do you think?"

175

"Is that what you think? That children don't think about their mother?" Lutfun asked.

"Pretty much, why, do they?"

"Prema is not a virtuous woman, Mila," Lutfun said looking at the neighbour's house. Sweat had glued to their skin like sticky date pudding. Lutfun flick-opened the hand fan and started to fan herself and Mila.

"Do you not think that the new mother could make the children happy?" Mila asked.

"I don't know about that. I guess they get their daily ration of meals."

"Hmm."

"Before the elopement, Ashik used to leave his bedroom door unlocked for Prema. So, she could sneak into his room at night. That inner fence wall between the two houses also remained unlocked."

"Really? How do you know?" Mila asked.

"I heard a woman's voice giggle one night. I couldn't sleep, so I sat alone on the verandah for fresh air. It came from Ashik's room."

"Oh my! I wonder if her ex knew about it. However, how did she enter the house, though? The mains would have been locked, no?"

"I wouldn't think so. Ashik would see to it that the main door to the house was unbolted. I'm sure. As for her ex, he wasn't the suspicious kind and slept heavily. Prema and Ashik were very quiet about it. The whole house would

176

be asleep when they made it out. The lamp in Ashik's bedroom would light up, when all the other rooms were dark. And there she was, the night pixie, entering Ashik's room—staying and leaving at dawn."

"Wow! How many nights did you see them together? And how would you know it was her? You only heard a giggle or two."

"It had to be her. Who else? At the time, of course, I hadn't recognised her in the dark. I had only seen a woman's back coming out of the room, arranging her disheveled clothes. Her hair was a knotted nest, from being rubbed up against the pillow. A few days later, I saw them—shadows kissing on the evening of the elopement."

"How did you know it was them, then? "Mila asked.

"Their faces were revealed in the street lamps."

"Oh! I see," Mila said.

"I've also heard from Rabeya that Prema's children want to move in with her. The children were discussing one day, which their maid overheard and told our Rabeya," Lutfun said.

"All three of them? Even the little boy?"

"It hasn't been decided just yet, who would and who wouldn't. But I have seen her talking to her three children near the tea stall down by the road."

"I wonder what Daadi Amma or Uncle Ashik have to say, now?"

"That would be interesting."

177

"To say the least. I can understand her angst. But Daadi Amma is also very strong, isn't she?" Mila asked.

"Yes, she is. What about you, Mila? Do you have a boyfriend?"

Mila kept quiet. She wasn't sure if her brief relationship with Rahim Ali counted. Could she perhaps call Rahim, her ex-boyfriend?

"Isn't it about time that you were in a relationship?" Lutfun asked.

"Yes, probably, but it'll have to wait, I guess, I haven't found anyone, yet."

They kept quiet after that. The full moon moved up, casting a platinum glow.

"What's more important?" Mila asked. "To follow one's heart, or lead a loveless life of doom?"

"Interesting question, I don't know, but when I think about those children and their painful childhood, because of Prema's infidelity, I struggle to find a correct answer, " Lutfun answered.

There was silence. Mila thought of her own predicament—was she going to die a spinster?

"Say, do you think Uncle Ashik could get a share of the property, if and when it gets sold?" Mila asked.

"Oh! That's such an odd question. Why would you even ask that?" Lutfun asked.

"No, I was just wondering. A time will come soon, I'm guessing when Daadi Amma and Dada Bhai get really old. And they may decide to sell this place. What will then happen to this beautiful place? Will it fall into disrepair and neglect, like all the zamindari palaces?"

"True. They'll get a share, I'm guessing unless someone doesn't want it. Or someone thinks that they have more claim over the other, for being in this house, maintaining it, and taking care of the elderly parents."

"Do you think that's fair, though?" Mila asked.

"What is?"

"That someone should be denied shares of ancestral property because they didn't care enough?"

"It's not our place to make that decision. But I've overheard Ashik saying to your Daadi Amma, that he'll write off his share to Sheri."

"Wow, really? When did you hear that?"

"Just, two days ago," Lutfun said.

Mila kept quiet and kept wondering if her father, Ekram would also be denied for marrying two times. Mrs Chowdhury had strict principles. What about her mother and herself? Where would they go if they didn't get a share? But she kept those apprehensions to herself. She wondered where her Aunty Lutfun's stance was in the affairs of the property. However, Lutfun wondered, why would Mila even raise such an issue about property? What was on her mind?

"Is there anything I need to know, Mila?" Lutfun asked.

Mila looked at her sheepishly and kept her gaze down at the cracks on the roof floor. A blast blew through the roof garden in the wake of another rain.

"Well?" Lutfun asked.

She was insistent. Mila looked at her and murmured. "I heard Maa speak to Mejo Khala, last night."

"What about?" Lutfun asked.

"About my marriage, Maa asked her to fix a match for me, I think. She sounded really concerned. Mejo Khala told Maa that it would be difficult to marry me off. Where would she find a decent boy for me? It isn't me, she said. It's how our culture is—harsh.

"Really? And why is that?" Lutfun asked.

"Because of my skin colour. For the dark-coloured girls, this is a harsh society."

"I don't think that would be a problem at all. Your mother's second sister is wrong. Besides, you're almost a doctor. Why would you even bother about these things? You'll soon have a job and a nice home of your own. You don't need to worry about properties or the skin colour," Lutfun concluded.

"What if? What if I don't get a decent job?" she asked.

"Even if you don't. You can't fall back on marriage, anyway." Lutfun assured.

Mila nodded, kept quiet, and felt silly. But she had to get those cruel words out of her system. Last evening, she had heard the conversation between her aunt and her mother as she was carrying a lantern to their bedroom following a load shedding, where Nazmun Banu was chatting with her second sister. They were having tea when the power outage occurred. Mila was chatting with them too in the bed. Laughing away as her Aunt Khairun told old jokes, which cracked them up. The electricity was gone and the room was dark. Nazmun Banu had asked Mila to fetch a lantern from the kitchen.

Mila was coming back up through the long hallway with the lantern. She heard the words spoken. She also heard a suppressed whisper, and a shh, from Nazmun Banu. "She's coming, don't say this to her face, she'll get hurt."

Hurt, she was. For the first time, she realised that she was a dark-skinned girl. In a country divided between light-coloured or "fair" and various shades of dark colour, complexion was a big deal, where marriages were concerned. Most young boys preferred to marry paler or fairer-skinned girls, as would their parents. Qualifications, or merit, wit, or the goodness of heart didn't really count as much as the complexion did.

"Oh! That's both woeful and awful." Lutfun broke the silence.

Mila shrugged. "It isn't my fault that I'm dark. As Mejo also said."

"No, of course not. But I wouldn't worry too much. You're smart, a doctor. Any eligible bachelor in town should be proud to have you as a wife."

181

However, she also looked at Mila from the corner of her eyes. In the heart of it, both knew the society only too well. They both knew how society condemned dark-coloured girls. It was far worse than the caste system or any racial discrimination. It was discrimination against one's own people. But Mila felt proud of her mother's family, anyway. She was proud because her mother and all her mother's siblings were such beautiful, fair creatures, whose delicate skin shone brightly in the golden sunlight.

Mila looked up at the moon.

"Do you still remember the moon lore?" Mila asked

"Yes?" Lutfun laughed. "That an old woman sat on her spinning throne, and spun silver threads."

"Yet, the solid moon rocks had no semblance to the old woman, by any long shot."

Lutfun laughed. "Thank God for those fairy tales of dream escapes. This reality was as hard as those moon rocks," she paused. "Should we go downstairs?" she asked.

Mila nodded and said. "yes."

silence

Mrs Chowdhury's reminiscences of the ghosts of the past, made her no more recluse than Mila' s lost love. The more Mrs Chowdhury thought about them, the more lost she became. Her sons had not become entirely dysfunctional, but she hoped they had better morals. Some evenings, she sat by herself on the verandah by the bougainvillea sighing and looking into oblivion.

Her mind was restive. But she was silent. She accepted Prema because of her grandchild Quasu. He was a retainer of the family name, Chowdhury. She would never let this opportunity as a torch bearer in the eighth generation pass. She sat in a void; the acceptance of Prema into the family and her son's disreputable behaviour had filled up to the brim—sins of her father, her husband, and her forbearers, revisited.

Quasu was born in a slum. She was already thinking of inviting them back into the house, just when the war had also broken out. Her grandchild had mellowed her heart towards them. She could not let the child grow up in the slum.

Her profound silence resulted in grief descending into the house. It affected Mr Chowdhury, and the rest of the family, particularly, Lutfun and Mila. Mila felt something needed to be done to make her talk again. Dinnertimes were unusually quiet, ghastly, like the deadly shadows of the zoroastrian towers of silence, where only vultures feed on carcasses. The dinner table chaired fewer and fewer people. Some nights, it was just Lutfun, Nazmun Banu, and Mila.

Mr and Mrs Chowdhury sat at the long table's both ends. They appeared frail; apart from a few words, such as 'pass me this' or 'pass me that,' be it rice or chicken curry, or sounds of the metallic tinkle of the golden kansa thali, and gurgling water being poured from kansa jugs into drinking glasses, the tower of babel had fallen, otherwise. The Chowdhury sons were never around to eat with them.

Elopement with a married woman by one son, Ashik and multiple marriages by another, Ekram, promiscuity, set in squarely even in this generation as well. In the war of the libido, even brave hearts like Mrs Chowdhury felt she was in a losing battle. Mila knew the cause of her grandmother's sadness. As she was growing up, she saw how the entire family would sit together for all three meals.

In the typical zamindari tradition, a wall-to-wall eating mat carpeted the floor. Ashik hadn't married then. Little Mila would sit with the family, and be fed out of love, either by her uncles, Lutfun, or her grandmother. Those were also Ashik's singing days in the front yard. Her uncles cracked jokes at each other, brothers chatting away, cousins dropping by for lunch or dinner and joining in occasionally. Ekram too, although he was in his other relationship, by then.

Those good times were etched in Mila's memory — magical and nostalgic. Prema was still the neighbour's wife. It didn't matter even if the food wasn't plentiful some days. But Mila knew that they were happy. Mrs Chowdhury often came around to supervise, and sometimes tell Tahera to cook some more for her nieces and nephews. While the cousins chatted silly, and told an odd joke or poked at each other, Mrs Chowdhury smiled at them, stuffing a paan or betel leaf jovially into her cheeks.

Contrarily, these days, nights mostly, her sons would dine out. Ashik couldn't step into the house for the first few years, not until Quasu was born anyway. But these post-war times, although they lived under the same roof, his presence was virtually non-existent. Not even any singing was performed, anymore. Whether or not Mrs Chowdhury had actually forgiven them was little known to anyone. Ashik and Prema, were not fully convinced that she did. They knew that Mrs Chowdhury made this concession for Quasu. Distancing Quasu was not possible. And he needed his parents living under the same roof. Tonight, however, it was Mrs Chowdhury who broke the silence at dinnertime.

"Has your father been home, Mila?" she asked, and gulped some water.

"No, I haven't seen him, of late," Mila answered.

And Nazmun Banu nodded to affirm.

"God knows what keeps him out these days," Mrs Chowdhury mumbled.

Lutfun and Prema listened but they said nothing. They continued to eat. Suddenly, Mr Chowdhury rose from his seat. But he sat down again and put a hand on the left side of his chest. Beads of sweat on his forehead. Mrs Chowdhury looked at him and asked sharply. "What's wrong?"

"I don't feel too well," he said.

Mila, Nazmun Banu, and Lutfun, quickly stood up leaving their unfinished meals on the thalis. They walked over to his chair, and held him, to bring him to his room. Mila and Lutfun held him by his two arms, while Nazmun Banu stood by them. Mrs Chowdhury looked at him frowning. The ladies took him into his bedroom along the passage. Mr Chowdhury complained that he couldn't breathe. He was quickly laid on his bed. Nazmun Banu ran out of the house to call a doctor from the nearest pharmacy which chambered his clinic.

The pharmacy was close by. However, by the time she arrived, the doctor was already packing up to leave. The collapsible gate was being pulled down by a tea boy, while the doctor waited until a padlock was secure. Nazmun Banu saw him in the dim streetlights. She called out. The doctor was startled to see her like this, at this hour. Her hands were still unwashed and were yellow from spices which had dried by now.

"What is it?" he asked.

"Please, come at once, Abba is unwell."

"Oh! What happened? Let's just quickly go," the doctor suggested.

They rushed towards the house. The doctor was in the front, followed by Nazmun Banu; her heart pounding from anxiety. When they neared the house, they heard a sonorous wailing wafting through the winds. Thinking of the worst, the duo burst into the house and into Mr and Mrs Chowdhury's bedroom. From the threshold, they saw the most poignant drama of all. Mr Chowdhury laying in bed;

foamy splatter all over his mouth. Mila sitting by him, his wrist on her lap, her finger on his once throbbing vein.

There were no tears in Mila's eyes; not yet. Lutfun howled, banging her head against the footrest of the bed like summer's wild winds, slamming on closed wooden shutters. Mrs Chowdhury sat erect and somber on a chair. Nazmun Banu, began to wail too. The doctor sat down by Mrs Chowdhury and held her hands in his. Mrs Chowdhury looked at him, and tear drops rolled down her wrinkled cheeks.

The news of this demise slowly spread through the night. Mila sent her friend Shreya a message through Rabeya, the maid. The neighbours, and the relatives, all knew eventually. The wailing became louder as the night progressed. Crows and vultures scoured the monsoon skies. Some even swooped low in the orchard and sat on the branch of the Indian jujube; an ogling night owl hooting, occasionally.

The night slowly turned into a grey dawn. Another imam from the mosque was summoned. People poured into the House of Chowdhury. They brought with them their Qur'ans and tazbih, the holy beads. They sat down wherever they could. Some sat down on chairs, while others on the floor to recite from the Holy Qu'ran. Mila had the good sense to blanket the floors, wall to wall, with bed covers by pushing the sofas far against the four walls to make more room, so relatives could sit on the floor, too as well as on the sofas. The Chowdhury sons arrived. Ashik and Prema with Quasu. Ekram and Sheri, all stood with their heads bowed in respect and sorrow at the foot of the departed father's bed.

Mr Chowdhury was not a person anymore. Overnight, he began to be referred to as the "body." The House of Chowdhury, was full now, teeming with people. People poured in from the villages to pay respect to this great zamindar, after the zamindari tradition. Even though they had fallen a long time ago, the family was still held in high esteem both in the city and in the villages. Mila dozed off for a bit, sitting in the chair. Suddenly, she opened her eyes for no reason. She saw Mr Chowdhury's happy, young face. He was standing there, before her, a smiling entity. The entity was him, except he was a wavering image of curvy colours like a malfunctioning hologram.

He was directing her with his index finger, to go somewhere. His index pointed towards Mrs Chowdhury, to say—'be with your Daadi Amma now.' Mila was fully conscious. She did not believe what she just saw. How was this even possible? She saw across the room, her grandmother embrace Quasu, and was now crying like a baby.

By now the sun had risen, and had streamed into the room through the parted curtains. As clear as this day, in the same light of August, she had seen her grandfather's face and had understood his full intentions. He was communicating with her and was instructing her to be there for Grandmother. Mila walked over to her side and sat down with Mrs Chowdhury. Her wrinkly hands were in hers. Mila tried to understand this game of the ephemera, as much as Mrs Chowdhury struggled to grasp the meaning of life.

Mrs Chowdhury looked at Mila. She murmured something to her, and Mila listened; she too had a dream last night. She saw that she tried to lock doors—two doors on the opposite sides of the room. There was a knock. She saw Mr Chowdhury, young and vibrant. He stood outside with a suitcase in his hands, wanting to come inside. Mrs Chowdhury looked at the other door. There was another man at that door—Mr Chowdhury's travel companion. He too asked to come inside. They were both looking at her and smiling. She smiled back. She didn't welcome them in. She woke up.

Mr Chowdhury had become an outsider now—a stranger, a vision. Once a living member of the community, now a creature of the night, standing outside the door—a transparent wall of separation—a suitcase sitting on the ground beside him—wanting to come inside—a dream. He was traveling a parallel world or perhaps even a string world. Who knows? However, he had fallen through time rip and had appeared to be in a young vessel, a full-blooded man looping back. He could even be as young as Mila, or even younger. Age was not a concern for him anymore. Mortal time had stopped ticking for Grandfather, Mila introspected, listening to Grandmother's dream.

change

Seasons came around a full circle. Mila noted a change in the house—a strange transformation around Mrs Chowdhury. She was increasingly becoming drawn towards a certain man, her father, Ekram. It was her, Mrs Chowdhury, who had reprimanded him in the first place for marrying Nazmun Banu's best friend, whom Mrs Chowdhury had never befriended, let alone spoken to or even seen her. But as days passed, she became more and more affectionate towards Ekram, which Mila found both odd and amusing.

At nights Daadi Amma would stay awake, waiting to serve Ekram late dinners herself. One night, Ekram came, but he was really late. As his key turned in the door; the hinge creaked. Nazmun Banu couldn't hear it from her room upstairs. But voices coming from the bottom of the staircase woke her up. Mila woke up too and saw her mother stepping out of doors; she heard her pussy-footing across the verandah. Mila climbed down from her bed and came out to the landing. She heard Grandma at the bottom of the dark stairs.

"Oh! Amma! It's you?" Ekram asked.

"Yes, you're finally home, Ekram. I saved you the best pieces of the meat, dear. It's in the meat safe."

"You didn't have to stay up for this, Amma," Ekram said.

"Why do you need to make everything so special for Ekram, Amma? There's Sheri and Ashik too, you know," Nazmun Banu said.

"Ekram is special. He was my firstborn."

"Okay, please go back to bed. I'll serve him the best meat pieces you saved for him," Nazmun Banu said.

"Okay."

Mrs Chowdhury resigned to bed. Ekram went upstairs for a wash. Mila went back to her room. She didn't understand her grandmother's newfound affection for her father. She thought, maybe grandma was losing it. These midnight sagas continued over many nights. One evening at teatime, she heard Uncle Sheri gripe.

Lutfun was with him in the orchard, and Nazmun Banu, too. Mila breezed along, for a biscuit. This evening, the orchard looked melancholy, in spite of the warmth from all the autumn colours. The bananas, the lime, and the pomegranate were fine specimens of what could be produced in this soil. Mila watched the gardener working hard in the orchard to produce some of the finest fruits. She looked up at the sky; such a serene evening. At the far end, the gardener pulled nettled palm fronds. He looked and nodded with a smile. Mila smiled back. The orchard looked deliciously luxurious this time of the year. It burst into all sorts of nature's vibrancy; the colours of the leaves changed to warm scarlet, deep magenta, sea turtle emerald, and saffron pouring onto the orchard. Impeccable was the word that summed it up. However, the gardener's intrepid work at cleaning the fallen, decrepit leaves, could not be ignored.

He brought the orchard to a full bloom every spring and cleaned the grounds throughout.

In winter, the colours faded. However, it all replenished and the orchard became resplendent the next monsoon. He cared for the garden. It showed, how tirelessly, he kept at it, sprucing it up, fertilising every priceless tree, and watering them diligently. He worked seamlessly with the laws of nature.

Lutfun seemed particularly chirpy this evening. She poured tea into the cups, humming a tune from a movie she had watched recently.

"Aina (The Mirror) was a great movie, yeah?" she said.

Her laughter rang in the air.

"Yes, it was going quite well until the mirror fell off the wall, and broke, it couldn't be mended of course, but it reflected a distorted reality," Nazmun Banu tuned in.

"Hmm, that's true. In hindsight, That's what the broken aina proved, I think."

"Distortion is a part of reality, too," Sheri said.

"Yes, the intentions of the protagonist could not be understood clearly enough until the mirror broke and his black soul was reflected in it," Lutfun said.

"Yeah!" Sheri sighed.

"What's with you today, Sheri?" Nazmun Banu asked.

"Well, I don't really know. Do you not see how Amma dotes on Ekram Bhai, these days? How she pines away for him, yet it was I, who was her most moral child. She doesn't even look at me these days. Let alone show appreciation for my better judgments."

"Are you saying that Amma loves Ekram more than she ever loved you?" Nazmun Banu asked.

"I don't know. It seems to me that way since our father passed away. While Abba was alive, she wasn't this lonely. Now that she is, she's trying to tie a tighter knot with Ekram Bhai, which I would have thought she would have done with me. This is terrifying even to think."

Nazmun Banu and Lutfun exchanged glances, as they perceived a wound in Sheri—a coiled up water pipe left leaking in an abandoned soil—his gripe.

"But she hasn't abandoned you," Nazmun Banu said.

"No, she hasn't. But she hasn't rewarded me either for being his ideal son, when that's what she wanted us to be. Why is it everything about him, these days? Ekram this and Ekram that —his first word, his first baby step, his first baby tooth. Why? Does she not see me, at all? Or Ashik Bhai? Yet, it was Ekram Bhai who hurt her the most. His firstborn— didn't he, Nazmun Bhabi, you tell me, sister?"

Nazmun Banu sighed and looked away. What was there to say? Ekram took everything she had to offer him and then selfishly moved on. She felt just as abandoned by him as Sheri felt abandoned by his mother. She was a child at the time of elopement. Her parents had abandoned her. She had risked her father's wrath at Maghrib, because she had followed her heart. Now, she had grown bitter like the

193

bitter gourd covered under the thick skin. No one could tell her bitterness from the outside.

Sheri had no idea, of course, why Nazmun Banu became quiet. But he looked at her somber face. He knew she was not in the moment. She gazed into a void. Sheri shook his head and felt that he couldn't defend a brother or a mother for their behavior. They were his family after all. He could rise above them but not rise against them.

Mila felt a drop in the temperature, both in the atmosphere, as well as in her relatives' moods. Just as well, she thought she would cheer them up. She walked to a nearby guava tree and picked a few luscious fruits and brought them back.

"Handpicked from our orchard. Here, try some," Mila said.

Sheri smiled at her efforts and took one from her hand. He rubbed it against his shirt and took a crunchy bite.

"Good?" Mila asked.

"Hmm, very juicy."

"Listen up everyone. I need to tell you something," Mila said.

When she got their attention, all three of them looked at her. She cowed before their questioning glance. She dropped her gaze.

'Well, what is it?" Lutfun asked. "Tell us, I'm dying to know."

"I'm in love."

Mila uttered shyly, and took a guava bite herself to avoid them gazing all over her face. After a few minutes of shock silence, Lutfun stood up. With some alacrity, she was by her side in a moment. Mila had by now inclined her head towards the guavas on her lap. Lutfun held her arm and made her stand up in one jolt.

"What? When did all this happen? Who is he? When are we going to meet him?" Lutfun asked.

There were all these questions gushing out of Aunt Lutfun. Her mother, Nazmun Banu opened her mouth, but said nothing.

"Are you serious? If you are, then maybe it's time to see him," Lutfun added.

"Yes, absolutely, yes," Sheri jumped with joy.

When everyone calmed down, Mila had a moment of recapitulation. She said."He's a psychiatrist."

"There you go!" Lutfun said. "We wouldn't expect any less."

Mila smiled. And looked at Nazmun Banu. Nazmun Banu appeared normal. Not too excited. 'Was she even happy?' Mila thought. 'Or is it just a shock?'

It was getting dark. Mosquitoes had descended on them. They stood up and walked indoors. Lutfun zapping a few on her arm. Mila sauntered inside behind everyone. She saw Nazmun Banu proceed towards her bedroom. Mila followed her quietly. Once they were inside, Mila closed the bedroom doors behind her.

"Say something, Maa," she cried.

"Say something? What do you want me to say that I'm happy for you? When were you going to tell me? That you humiliate me in front of them with your bombshell news?"

"Humiliate you? No, Never. That was never my intent. I just didn't get the time to tell you."

"You didn't get the time to tell your own mother? I hope you'll get the time to invite me."

Mila felt disconsolate. She came forward and hugged her mother despite her protests. In a while, Nazmun Banu surrendered and embraced Mila. Tears of joy and sorrow fell on each other's shoulders. Nazmun Banu was now middle-aged and so was her friend—her husband's second wife. The latest gossip was that he had taken a third, a much younger girl about his daughter, Mila's age. Yet, Nazmun Banu was beyond caring. Her only concern was Mila's happiness.

A wedding date needed to be fixed. But before that the family had to know the boy. The boy was marrying not just with Mila, but the family too, in a way. Lutfun came up to Nazmun Banu's door and knocked. Mila opened it.

"Take a walk with me?" Lutfun asked.

"Sure," Mila answered.

They walked towards the roof. On the roof, Lutfun and Mila sat down in a corner by a parapet. "Tell me, everything," Lutfun said.

meeting

Mila had taken a shine to a man. She had met him not at the university, but in a corner bookstore on University Drive. She had bumped into him as she was entering the store and he was exiting. She was saying goodbye to a friend. When she turned around, they collided with each other.

"So sorry," she had said in passing. But he stood still in the middle of the bookstore and watched her. She had no idea that he was watching. She attentively browsed through the shelves. Then she selected a book, Tagore's Shesher Kabita, (The Last Poem). She went up to pay for it and didn't even notice him. She came out of the store, and he had followed her to the street. She called a rickshaw, and when it pulled up, they were standing abreast. She shot him a sidelong glance and climbed up. The rickshaw puller smiled at him and pedalled off. However, not until much later, after about a week, she had met him again in the public library courtyard. She was sitting down, and reading with a cup of tea at a corner table, when he had walked over.

"What're the chances of meeting you, again?" he had smiled at Mila.

What a cute smile, Mila thought. "Why? What do you mean? We go to the same university. I think the chances are fairly high."

"Hahaha, may I sit down?" he asked.

"Of course."

"I see that you've started to read your new book."

"Oh! This book, Tagore's Shesher Kobita, I have read at least three times, at three different stages of my life. The first time at sixteen, then two years later, and again."

"Wow! You must really love that book," he said.

"There is a lot to love in this. You marry the one you don't love. You love the one you don't marry. That way, you don't get the love juices sullied. The heart will swim in the ocean of love and romance once in a while. And Marriage? Everyday water— collected in a bucket for everyday use."

"Hmm, that's pretty harsh. He says that?" he asked.

"According to this character, yes," Mila laughed and waved the book at him.

"Oh well! That's him, then. What about you? What're your thoughts about love and marriage?"

Mila inclined her head at the question to look away. She thought of her interlude with Rahim Ali; she just couldn't get him out of her head.

"Hello there?" he asked.

He looked deeply into her big, brown eyes, as they drifted. They were an enigma, those swimming eyes of hers.

"I really need to go, please excuse me," she said.

"I'll wait for your reply."

"Sure, if we meet again," she said.

"Oh, I'll find you."

Mila rushed to get out of his gaze. She even blushed. He noticed that and smiled. Mila left, but they didn't get introduced; they didn't know each other's names. But then, 'what's in a name?' If something were to happen, then it would. Happenings occurred regardless of plans, seemingly within a plan. Who knew they would bump into one another in the bookstore? Marriages were made in heaven.

Very well, then. Every time Mila went to the library, he was there. In the canteen and by the rickshaw stand. As if he knew her schedule. One day, as she stood in a queue to order tea in the canteen, she felt a breath on her shoulder. She had moved forward, but the heavy breathing fanned her shoulder. 'What the heck?' She turned around. It was him.

"You?" Mila had asked.

"Yep! I have been following you since we met in the bookstore."

"How come? What did you do?"

"Well, for a starter, I followed you to your building the very same day behind the rickshaw. I saw which department you went into, and to which class. I hung around on the verandah with your mates, before class started while you were in class already, sitting studiously at the desk. I chatted up one of your mates and asked your name. After that day, I waited for you every afternoon at this precise moment and followed you around. Easy."

"Why didn't you come and talk to me, then? Like you're doing now?"

"Oh! I had my classes too. I was off for my class afterwards."

"Right," Mila said.

"Right? Is that all you can think of? Come out of the queue, I need to take you somewhere."

"Where?"

"Just come, will you? For God's sake—come."

He took her hand and pulled her towards him. All the students found this amusing, smiling, and looking at them. His insistence embarrassed her. She stumbled and saved herself from falling on his chest. He smiled at that and whispered. "Not long now." Once they walked abreast, he continued to hold her hand. And Mila found a strange thrill running through her. She blushed and lowered her head. He saw her face paint a shade of red, and he tightened his grip around her hand at that.

They walked to the car park and towards a car. He stood by the door and opened it for her. She hesitated. He nudged her in. She entered. She saw him coming around and sitting next to her at the steering wheel. Mila thought to herself. Why? How was all this happening? She didn't even know who she was going out with? Why would she even give him so much control? No, no—stop. This must not be allowed to go further. She had to put a stop to it right now. Questions would arise, eventually, regarding who her parents were. Was she going to tell him that she was a daughter of a man married three times? How many step-siblings, half-brothers, and half-sisters, only God knows? They were these faceless numbers, she was forbidden to see, or meet even or know their names. That, a mandatory unwritten order, her mother Nazmun Banu issued; ground rules in the House of Chowdhury that no one must ever,

ever see the faces of her husband's other wives, let alone know the children. No. No. She must ask him to stop. She couldn't go out with him. Suddenly, his hands were on hers, again. He looked at her and flashed a smile.

"You think a lot don't you?" he asked.

"Hmm, I guess. I need to tell you something, now," she said.

Now or never, she willed.

"What's the urgency? We have a whole lifetime," he said.

"No, no, you don't understand. There's someone else in my life," she lied.

"Someone else?" he looked serious. "Who is this someone else", any names? he asked.

"Can't tell you. I have to go. You must let me go," she begged.

"Here? You have to walk miles for a rickshaw," he said.

"I'll walk and catch one, eventually," she said.

"Aha! Not until you tell me the name of your boyfriend."

"Name? What would you do with a name? What difference would it make?" she asked.

"Still, tell me," he insisted.

"Shuvo."

"Shuvo?" he asked

"You know him? I mean, them?" she asked him.

"No," he said.

She let out a sigh of relief thinking that her story might just stick. He said nothing for a while. Then he asked her a strange question.

"Where did you hide during the war?"

"Oh, we went to our village, Pretigram," she said.

"Did the army enter?"

"Yes, I heard they did, we were really concerned about Shuvo's family who were with us at that time," she said.

"I see," he said. "Tell me more about this Shuvo, and his family."

"What's there to tell? They are our old neighbours and friends. The enemy took his sister. We invited them to come with us to the village."

"How old were you?" he asked.

"I was pretty young, and so was Shuvo and his twin sister Shreya, my best friend. I was really sad how Didi was taken like that."

"Yes, they were brutal," he paused. "I had once compiled a case study on the rape victims. It was an unforgettably horrendous experience those women suffered."

"Then you may have come across Didi too."

202

"Yes—I may have."

Mila had stepped into the car as they chatted. She felt a little relaxed, now that he knew about her being in a relationship—she was safer with him now, as far as romance was concerned. They drove around in silence for a while. And then he took Mila to a riverfront resort. He switched off the ignition and they sat quietly inside the car. He inclined his head at her and asked. "Is Shuvo, Shyeya's twin brother?"

"Yes," Mila said.

For some reason, Mila felt like an idiot. That she was selling Shuvo like this. But now that she had resorted to this charade, she felt she had to keep it going.

"You don't mind dating boys of your age, then?"

Mila kept quiet and looked out at the river.

"By the way, my name is Irfaan Khan."

Mila suppressed a smile at her ruse to subterfuge. She looked at Irfaan and said in a low voice. "You already know my name," she said.

"Yeah, I do. So, Mila tell me, have you always been like this?"

Mila looked at him wide-eyed and asked, "Like what?"

"I don't know. You always seem a bit lost. This is the second time I've noticed this."

Mila didn't say much. She looked at him calmly.

"Don't you think Shuvo would mind if he knew we had come out for a drive? Shouldn't you take me home?" she asked.

"Yes, thanks for reminding me. My apologies if I brought you here against your will. That wasn't the intent."

"I know, that's okay. Please let me out at the university bus stand."

Irfaan Khan looked ahead at the river. He paused before he started the car. On their way back, Irfaan didn't talk much. He looked almost morose. His lips pouted and he had an earnest frown. She felt a pang of guilt for misleading him. But Mila was too afraid. At the university square, Irfaan made a hard turn to the right where the bus stop was. He braked and brought his car to a halt. He turned at Mila and flashed a smile. Mila smiled back and said thank you for the ride.

She opened the door and stepped out on the hot concrete of the tar road. He waited in the car until the bus arrived. The sky turned a patch of grey in the corner. The bus was late as usual, and gusty wind had also picked up. Irfaan honked and signalled Mila to return to the car. Her saree went everywhere in the wind. She struggled to keep it in place. Irfaan couldn't take his eyes off her. She, in this spectacular situation of finding her saree in these wavering winds. This, this lost look, yet acutely conscious of her present whereabouts.

Irfaan got out of the car and walked up to her. He held her hand tight again and kept her close, as though he had rescued a distressed damsel fighting a demonic gale. Mila, on the other hand, loved this sudden change of weather. The menacing clouds and the wiry winds always made her day, regardless of the circumstances. In Irfaan's resolute hands, she felt strangely secured. Irfaan brought her back into the car.

"There, now tell me where home is?" Irfaan asked.

"Dewangonj, thank you."

Irfaan took her in the car and drove swiftly. Once they were in the lane, he slowed down. It was a narrow lane in old Dacca: Dacca under East Pakistan, now changed to Dhaka after the independence. When they arrived near the House of Chowdhury, Mila directed him to stop in front of the house. The slightly ajar gate lent a view to the orchard. It was in disarray because of the ferocity of the winds. The day had dimmed by now; an evening was closing in.

Mila looked at Irfaan and said. "I think you need to come inside until the storm clears up." Irfaan laughed and said with a glint in his eyes. "What if it doesn't clear up? Will he, this Shuvo, come with a bow and arrow to fight me?"

Mila laughed and said nothing. Irfaan grimaced. He let Mila out and parked ahead of the house near the tea stall. He saw that the car was parked in a gutter. He shrugged and locked it. He met up with Mila at the main gate.

He said. "I wish I was there first."

Mila looked away. She led him through the spiral back stairs straight to the roof, which had roomed the one night stay for her renegade Uncle Ashik and Aunty Prema. Irfaan and Mila couldn't walk fast enough through the gust. Its

205

sharp keening could be heard across the bamboo bush in the orchard's far side.

Mila gripped the circuitous railing of the staircase, as Irfaan stood right behind her. She could smell his body odor. She struggled to keep her garment about her. They were soon near the rusty roof door. It banged hard in the air as though it was making an atonement. Irfaan struggled to hold the door open, so the duo could walk through. They brushed against each other rushing towards the bedroom across the short roof space between that rusty door and the bedroom. Once they were in, Mila had to shut the door. The duo let out a sigh of relief and sat down on the bed.

"Wouldn't it be great to have some strong tea with samosa?" Irfaan said.

"Hmm, let's see. I think it can be arranged. I just have to go downstairs to the kitchen."

"Never mind—stay here."

"Hang on, there is an old stove in that small kitchenette, just there. Let me check if there's some tea in the storage. For samosa, though, I'll have to go downstairs."

Mila stood up and walked across to the tiny kitchenette. They were in luck. There were some dried tea leaves which Aunty Lutfun must have left. She often made tea here for Uncle Sheri and whoever wished to accompany her to the roof. Mila boiled some water in the kettle, as the winds raged on. Tea was made and she brought it over. Irfaan looked at her and smiled; he took a cup from Mila's extended hand.

"What would Shuvo say if he saw this?"

206

"Nothing. What's there to say? What person would ask another to leave in this dangerous storm? I think Shuvo would understand."

"I would've been really jealous. Sorry, I'm not that liberal."

"What's liberalism got to do with it? It's all about being sentient," Mila said.

"Still, there are certain human traits that are beyond reasoning. They happen spontaneously—jealousy is one of them. How would you feel, if Shuvo did this?" he asked her.

"I'd try to understand."

"Strong love goes hand in hand with jealousy. You've not loved him deeply enough, I am guessing. I wouldn't be happy at all if I knew you were with another man in our current situation. I don't know about Shuvo, though."

They sipped tea in silence. Mila's thoughts raged just as much as the winds. She tried to understand Irfaan. He spoke about love. What did he know about it? He met her only three days ago and knew her a little better just today. He thought he was deeply in love with her, already. And how was she ever going to tell him about her father's three wives?

Her thoughts got the better of her. She thought it would upset Nazmun Banu to find Irfaan sitting here in such close proximity, regardless of the circumstance.

"Why? Have you lost yourself, again?" he asked.

"I have?" Mila asked.

Irfaan looked at her big brown eyes. His gaze softened. He said in a whisper.

"Please tell me you don't have a boyfriend, please."

"I ... I don't." Mila stammered.

"Oh! I knew it! I knew it!" he sighed.

He pulled her by her arm against his chest and she tried to resist. This was just the first meeting and not even officially a date. He pulled her again, gently nudging her to come closer. This time she surrendered. She lay there in the musky warmth of his chest's hair. He rubbed his lips on her nape. He inhaled her perfumed hair. He held her chin and lifted it to his mouth. He nodded and said that he was going to kiss her now.

He kissed her lightly first, barely a touch on her curved lips, then he pressed hard and then harder. She pushed him back a little—whispering. " Let me go." He held her tighter at that and uttered softly. "Why must you go? I don't want to let you go, ever, anywhere. What's the problem?" His hands roamed down her spine and explored her body over her blouse. His hands groped for more, and still more until finally, they found her breasts. He squeezed them gently. It was irresistible. Mila moaned. He lay her down on the bed and gently pulled up her saree. He unzipped his pants as well. They lay on the bed on top of each other. The penetration was bloody. It was divine. The wild winds suppressed the sounds.

"I want to marry you, Mila."

He groaned. His head on her chest. Mila kept quiet.

"Say something, anything. Were you disappointed?" he demanded.

"No. It was just, just so sudden, it happened too fast. We hardly know one another," she smiled and blushed.

He gazed at her. He smiled, then played with her locks.

"How could you be so cruel as to say you had a boyfriend?" he asked.

"I, I have something to tell you."

"What another cock and bull story to get me out of the way?" he chuckled.

"No, no there's something else."

"Tell me, what is it? What is it that keeps you awake at night and makes you lose yourself in thoughts? Where do you go?" Tell me about it now. I want to know."

"I got issues," she said at last after a pause, while Irfaan continued to gaze at her. Her shaded downcast eyes, her thick long lashes; her sharp nose down her smooth dark forehead. Her dark silky hair fell like water streaming down a mountain fall. He gazed, and she blushed. He brushed his index over the cheeks.

"I don't care," he said. "I don't need to know. I don't want to know."

He held her chin up and made her look at him. She looked into his eyes calmly and found sincerity there. She found love in those tender brown eyes. Maybe, she thought, he won't betray her after all as her father did to her mother or as her Aunt Prema did to her first husband, even Rahim

Ali. Maybe, she will be okay to take chances with him. But did she love him, the way she loved Rahim Ali? There were no answers, there.

"Okay," she said shyly. "Let's marry then."

Irfaan couldn't or wouldn't restrain himself after that. He pulled her towards him. He embraced her tightly and they remained like that for some time, until she disengaged herself to say that he should really go home now because it was late. Irfaan kissed her on the forehead. He looked deep into her unguarded eyes and smiled. He brought his mouth to her ears to whisper—"everything will be okay—I promise you."

Lutfun had heard everything now. She thought it was a great love story. She took Mila's face in her hand and kissed her cheeks. They both came downstairs afterwards.

proposal

Mila cleared her head at the Raven's Edge Blue Café. She put her pen down and looked up—far too heavy emotions to deal with. Fancy, Rahim Ali, sitting at one of those tables and spying on her. She giggled and ran a finger through her salt and pepper hair. She cut it short now, to be able to better manage it. She had little time for herself now that she was an obstetrician and held a position at the Medical College Hospital. Off duty, today.

Her wedding plans were underway. In an outpouring rain, one afternoon, at the House of Chowdhury, her wedding was arranged in the early days of February in 1983. Irfaan's parents had visited Mila's guardians at the House of Chowdhury with a formal marriage proposal. The news had spread like musk through the neighbourhood—another wedding, but it was the first, in the second generation. A tea party was organized for this special occasion. At the dot of five, 2nd of February, Mila heard a car pulling up under the porch of the house. She and Lutfun ran up the stairs to be on the roof—glowing with excitement, and breathing rapidly. Mila must not be seen around during the talks.

Ducking below the short roof wall, Mila and Lutfun sat with bated breath. Lutfun craned her neck just enough to see what was happening in the front yard. She whispered to Mila. "A lady has just stepped out of a car. She looks elegant in a beige-coloured silk saree with dancing girls in batik prints on the paar: the saree's border. Must be the mother.

An elderly man has also made an egress, the father, I'm guessing. Now two other men have come out of the backseats—cousins, maybe? Or uncles."

"Who is driving?" Mila asked.

"The father, I, umm, don't see a chauffeur. Say, have you been to their house?" Lutfun asked.

"No. No. Never," Mila whispered. "It happened too fast. Just one date and that was it!"

"Sometimes that's all you need. Look at us, we have dated forever. We would still be dating today if that war hadn't happened."

Lutfun and Mila, both giggled. The groom's party had now gone inside.

Shimul met them at the entrance of the house and let them through. Nazmun Banu, who stood behind Shimul, came forward. They exchanged salaam. Shimul stood behind the door, while Nazmun Banu led them down the passage into the formal living room. The guests sat down. The lady caressed the upholstery of the aged chair's Mahogany armrests to get a feel of the antique. Nazmun Banu smiled politely and excused herself to call the family. Mrs Chowdhury, the most important member, was followed by her two sons Ashik, and Sheri.

In the meantime, Mila and Lutfun came downstairs and stood on the adjacent verandah to eavesdrop. They remained out of sight but could hear everything. After the round of introduction, the groom's mother, Mrs Rehana Khan proposed that they wait until the son found suitable employment since they were still students. To which

Nazmun Banu tuned in that their daughter was also in the same situation. However, it wasn't until Mrs Chowdhury spoke that it all began to make sense.

"So what? What if they're still students, does it mean that they would stop seeing each other until they get degrees and employment?" she asked.

"No, of course not, they can still see one another, except that a wedding wouldn't be likely to take place until later," said Mr Khan.

"But, of course, if they're allowed to see each other, in the same vein, a wedding is also possible and must not be postponed," Mrs Chowdhury proposed.

While the talks continued, the doors opened, and Prema walked in with a wheeled trolley full of snacks and tea. She looked beautiful in a red cotton saree and her fair face framed in a perfect veil. She handed them plates, cutlery, and cotton napkins. They took them, as the pleasantries continued. In a few minutes, Mrs Chowdhury gestured to them to help themselves; they were gourmet homemade snacks—rice cakes, meat kebabs and vegetable samosas, onion pakoras, potato, and mutton chops, and chicken patisse. Prema sat down demurely on a highchair and parked the trolley by her side. She poured freshly brewed creamy tea from an ornate silver teapot into each cup.

"Where's the girl's father?" Mr Khan asked.

He took his cup of tea from Prema's hand and placed it on a tea table beside him, while he held the snacks on a plate.

213

Mila and Lutfun stiffened. The Chowdhurys knew that this question would arise at some point; they were ready for an answer too. The father's absence was awkward. But he was uncontactable at the time when Nazmun Banu tried to call him.

Sheri quickly said. "I apologize for his absence. I know, we uncles can never fill the father's place. But as you know he is a renowned surgeon. He had to go to our village to perform an emergency operation on our village butcher. He couldn't travel to the city because of the illness."

"Hmm, very strange that a renowned surgeon should go into a village. Usually, they don't. He must care about his patients a lot that he couldn't send his colleagues instead. This was after all an auspicious event of his daughter's wedding," concluded Mr Khan.

"Quiet right? As you said, most doctors wouldn't do what he does—travel to the village. But I'm the daughter's mother. And my mother-in-law here, Amma, is the head of this family, not my husband. Of course, it goes without saying that her we—Mila's uncles and aunties—her elders are also present." Nazmun Banu said.

"Fair enough, we have decided on an alimony of one lakh taka, if that's agreeable," Mr Khan said.

"Certainly," Mrs Chowdhury said. "Alimony is for rainy days, should there be a divorce. Today's one lakh may have no value at all in the future. What do you think? Should this calculation be based on the market value of the time?"

A silence dropped in the room. No one thought of this. Speculation was neither Ashik nor Sheri's forte. But Mrs Chowdhury knew exactly what she was saying.

"Sure, sure, if it comes to that I'm sure our son would take the market value into consideration," Mr Khan coughed.

Mila thought to herself, in the event of a fallout, an ugly divorce, why would she even want a divorce settlement? If she hated the man, shouldn't she also hate his money? That was only logical. However, her opinions didn't matter on marriage laws. If it had to happen, it happened. Alimony was settled at one lakh, in a binding deed in the event of a divorce.

A wedding day was fixed. The talks ended. The tea was much appreciated. The party broke at dusk. They bid goodbyes but did not want to see Mila. However, just before they left, the boy's mother, Mrs Khan, peaked towards the verandah, where Mila and Lutfun had been hiding in the dark. She sensed a shadow behind a pillar.

"Where's Mila? Is it possible to meet her?" Mrs Khan broached.

"Umm, I don't know, maybe she's on the roof," Prema said. " Do you want to meet her before you go?"

"Yes, if that's possible," Mrs Khan said.

Mila and Lutfun shot one another a quick glance, and ran softly down the verandah like a pair of fawns and up the stairs onto the roof. They were sitting on one corner of the short fence wall enclosing this large roof. They heard several footsteps coming up the stairs. They turned around

215

and looked innocuously at them. Prema, Nazmun Banu, and Mrs Khan came to the roof. Mrs Khan smiled at Mila, and Mila smiled back coyly, dropping her gaze like a blushing bride. Mrs Khan came forward a few steps and gave Mila a hug.

"How're you?" she asked.

"I'm well, thanks," Mila answered.

"Not long now, you'll be our family, soon."

Mila said nothing. Mrs Khan looked at her demure expression on the face. She patted her head and slid her palm down her face.

"See you soon, take care," she said.

"You too."

Nazmun Banu, Prema and Lutfun, stood quietly until Mrs Khan finished. She looked around the roof and commented. "A huge roof. When was this house built?"

"Oh! When the river took Pretigram, our village, in the great flood. My father-in-law built this. They had to move to the city," Nazmun Banu answered.

"Nice, really nice. I love the roof garden, too. Who does gardening?" Mrs Khan asked.

"I do," Lutfun said."But the rain takes care of it, mostly. However, we also have a gardener."

"Hmm, you have a large orchard too, I can see. A front yard and a backyard—valuable property."

216

The women listened silently. They were not sure what she was alluding to. But Mrs Khan walked up and down, and finally turned around to face them.

"It's time we left. My husband must be getting impatient."

"Sure, we'll take you downstairs," Prema said.

Mila looked at her and uttered a small goodbye, as they walked towards the door. They descended the stairs; their footsteps slowly faded.

An engagement date was fixed. In one short month, it was held on the 14th of March. That was the second time her in-laws came to the House of Chowdhury. An engagement ceremony with a few close relatives took place. They arrived in the evening and were taken into the formal living room, where Mila appeared in an expensive new saree, a kathan, decked in family jewellery. She sat down on a chair, next to her grandmother. This time, her father was present. The guests were milling about in the drawing room. Her father seemed to be getting along well with Mr Khan, Mila noted through her veil. As the evening rolled by, her mother-in-law walked towards her and sat down beside her. Everyone was quiet by now and observed the solemn ceremony. Mrs Khan placed a diamond ring on Mila's wedding finger. She was now officially engaged, and Irfaan Khan's fiancé.

This wedding was not a war wedding or a wedding out of elopement, but noteworthy—befitting the House of Chowdhury. It had yet to have witnessed a wedding of such grandeur. Mila and Irfaan restrained themselves from meeting before the wedding. But the phone calls throughout the day, was a sign of lovers' getting impatient. Not long now, Mila consoled Irfaan one day, when he had called. His deep sighs through the phone's mouthpiece revealed how much he missed her. If she would come out stealthily one afternoon when everyone had a siesta. She wouldn't have to do this stealthily anymore, she reminded him as they were officially betrothed. But there was sweetness in this. These sighs and non-committal giggles on the phone, not to meet until the wedding day, which was just a few days away now. But Irfaan was restless, and he asked her to come to the roof. Mila couldn't understand, why the roof? But upon Irfaan's insistence, and with the phone hot against her ears, she had agreed. At the roof's entrance, Irfaan grabbed her by the neck like a rake.

"What the … ?"

Before Mila could finish, he took her in his arms.

"Oh! The sweet smell of you, I miss it, I miss it all," he proclaimed.

Mila loved the gesture, and she buried her head deeper into his chest and realised that his shirt buttons might carve a hole in her forehead. She giggled.

"I'm dying here and you're giggling. Do you realise how long it has been? I missed you, I missed you. I called you today from the pharmacy down the alley, so I could come here nearly as soon as you dropped the handset on its cradle."

He moaned, his face was in the masses of her dark hair. He kissed them.

"Now, you must go, before anyone sees us like this," Mila whispered.

"Why? Why do you have to be so cruel?" he asked her.

His face was still in her hair. He was inhaling its fragrance.

"We cannot appear in front of our elders as a couple today," she said.

"We could always appear in front of our elders as a couple. No one in this house would ever mind, at all. This house should be called the House of Liberals, not the House of Chowdhury."

"Okay, okay, enough said," she said.

She giggled, fingering a button on his shirt that came undone.

"Aha, coy! Are we? I wanted to see those looks in your eyes."

He lifted her face, and Mila actually felt shy, so she dropped her eyelids looking at the loose button pressed between her fingers.

"Now look at me," he whispered. "Mila, look at me, my jaan—my love.

Mila could feel his hot breath over her forehead as he insisted. Mila looked into his eyes—her long lashes curling on the edge of her large eyelids. She saw them twinkle and soften.

"I can't wait even a minute. I want you now. This minute ..."

"This button, it's— it's—."

She couldn't finish the sentence.

"Are you trying to distract me with a button?" he laughed.

"Wait, just a few days now—"

He stopped her. His mouth brushed her lips, her eyelids, her forehead and then her two hot cheeks as they dimpled.

"Okay, I'll let you go. On the wedding night though— well, not even God can stop me."

He looked at her soft and delicate dark features as though he couldn't have enough of her. His tender gaze wooed across her face.

"Go already—" she whispered.

She said it lovingly and shoved him gently towards the roof's door. Gossip would spread like weed if anyone saw them in this embrace. He pulled her in for one last embrace. Then he extricated himself and left quickly down the backstairs. He sped down the twisty stairs like a bolt, as Mila watched him go. Mila stood here regaining her composure, before she too went downstairs. No one saw Irfaan. This was the only hidden way Irfaan knew. Come to think of it, Mila had never brought him into the house. And she never really introduced him formally to anyone, although the family would have approved free-mixing.

peacock-dance

On the wedding day, a few hired men came into the house to do the final touches. Early in the morning, they brought multi-coloured fairy lights and soft coverings, linen for chairs and tables, and streamers. The chairs and the tables had already been laid over the week. The ceremony was to be held in the evening. Mila's wedding with Irfaan Khan had to be, to Mrs Chowdhury's full satisfaction. It had to be done properly. Mrs Chowdhury asked her sons to hire a good decorator for the wedding. It was her intention to have a grand wedding for a change. Her sons hired CM and Company decorators. They provided chairs, tables, tarp, fairy lights, and speakers to play recorded songs—full on decorations.

The fairy lights lay in a braided jumble all over the grounds. While some men untied the jumble, others used a ladder to haul the wires to hang the lights across the entrance gate and over the rooftop of the big house. The House of Chowdhury would stand in the backdrop of a massive illumination in the evening. A makeshift wooden gate was temporarily raised before the fixed gated entrance. The double gates were framed within multi-coloured lights. This artificial gate served a decorative purpose only; rainbow-coloured cotton streamers were wrapped over it crisscrossed.

A tarpaulin was hoisted to cover the entire front yard over the wooden chairs. The chairs were placed next to each other. In the orchard, several new clay stoves were carved out to cook a wedding feast. The wedding menu was

221

biriyani, mutton kabab, and murag musallam and a yoghurt drink called the lassi. A chef was appointed along with a retinue of assistants; a DJ, to play continuous recorded songs.

The rain dripped continuously through a few cracks and crevices of the tarp all day long. Wet chairs sat on wet grounds. There was nothing much anyone could do to keep the rain away. Except, perhaps hire more people to keep the chairs plastic-covered, then uncover them just before the guests arrived. Or hire more expensive tarp. But the bride, Mila, knew how difficult it was for her mother, Nazmun Banu, to fight the wedding funds out of her father. Had it not been for her uncles, Sheri, and Ashik, who chipped in and supported this wedding, it would not have even come close. The bride's aunts, Aunty Prema, and Aunty Lutfun, went out shopping each Sunday morning with her mother Nazmun Banu for two entire weeks. They bought wedding sarees, and gold jewellery. The jewellery was studded with semi-precious stones of red ruby, green emerald, and white sapphire of cloudy hue. An old family jeweller was summoned, who was only too eager to help. He had found the best craftsmen in town.

Mila had just come out of the bath and was getting dressed in an everyday cotton saree, to go to the hairdresser when she peered through her bedroom window, to see her father, Ekram enter; sauntering through the outer gate. Mila quickly put her saree on and rushed out to greet him. Her grandmother was sitting at the dining table; Mila calmed down, and sat next to her, waiting for Ekram. In a moment, he breezed in through the door, humming a little tune.

"Where are you these days?" Mrs Chowdhury asked. "Am I glad to see you, today."

"Sorry, Amma. I'm sorry to disappoint you."

"Regardless, and thank God for your brothers, this wedding would have been a disaster."

"My brothers have saved yet another day, then?" he asked.

"As usual," Mila chimed in.

"Anyway, I'm here now and that makes a difference, no?" he said.

"Should it?"

A shrill voice wavered through the doorway.

Nazmun Banu and Prema walked in with jewellery boxes and sarees.

"Typical! How typical of you to disappear like this. Days on end you were gone. Not involved in anything. Then you appear suddenly, like a rare comet. Are you even the father or what? A guest, come by to sneak a peek?"

"Mum, please," Mila said. "Not today."

"No? What is he going to do? Walk out? Has he even paid a dime?" Nazmun Banu spat out.

"How much? How much do you need? Here, take it. There's all the money, right here."

He pushed a large A4 size brown envelope before them on the table.

"Huh? Stuff you."

Nazmun Banu turned on her heels and walked away.

"Here, Amma, you keep the money, then."

He, Dr. Ekram Chowdhury, had a flourishing medical practice in town. Money wasn't an issue. His bohemian nature was. Ekram insisted that his mother take the envelope. In fact, he forced it into her hand. Mrs Chowdhury took it. But she scowled deeply. She looked at Mila and gave it to her. Mila's father stood up and walked towards the orchard where her uncles were seated with a large pot of chai under the wet tarp. As soon as he appeared, they greeted him with smiles and asked him to sit down. He took a chair and sat by them.

The day advanced. Lutfun asked a pageboy to call a rickshaw. She was taking Mila to the hairdresser. The boy did as he was told. The vehicle arrived, and it waited for them outside the decorative gates. Lutfun and Mila came out of the house and managed somehow, they walked through the front yard's turmoil to the vehicle. The afternoon was quiet and grey. The rickshaw puller cycled slowly down the narrow alley and headed off for the salon down by the mosque square. Mila put her head on Lutfun's shoulder. Lutfun cruxed it into her elbow, caressing it with her other idle palm.

"Everything will be fine," Lutfun said, stressing on the letter 'e'. "I'm going to get my hair done too. I'm doing a french knot."

"Yeah, you'll look really good. What're you wearing, Aunty?" Mila asked.

"Glad that you sound a little upbeat now. It's your wedding for God's sake. Cheer up, girl! Yes, I'll wear my pink kathan with my pink diamonds. But we did discuss it the other day, remember?"

"Oh, yeah. I remember now."

The slow-paced rickshaw reached the salon. The puller stopped the vehicle by pressing hard on the hand brakes. They disembarked awkwardly from its caddy seat and stepped onto a sodden path. Mila followed Lutfun, tiptoeing through a rainwater puddle into a shop that had SALON written large on a billboard down the parapet. The outer wall looked moldy. The paint has peeled-off in various places, through which a set of horizontal bare bricks grinned like a Cheshire. The parlor was upstairs. After climbing two flights of stairs, Lutfun and Mila entered a crowded parlor. There was only one empty, corner chair left. Lutfun nudged Mila to take it, as Mila did the same to Lutfun. She pushed Mila right up to the chair and sat her down.

While Lutfun stood by Mila, they watched the other young brides-to-be, sitting in a row before their respective mirrors; still little dolls in the process of a full bridal makeover. Mila's turn came as soon as one finished. She sat down before a mirror; her reflection was clear. Lutfun was next when another chair became available. Mila and Lutfun sat close by, but they didn't speak much during the session. Only occasionally, they made eye contact through the mirror. Mila sat straight-faced like a dummy. She looked at her cobweb mass of long hair arranged by the expert hands of the hairdresser. It took a while to get it right. Lutfun's neat french knot was done before Mila had finished. She waited, as the dresser fine-tuned Mila's bridal bun. Pleased, Lutfun walked over and paid at the counter by the entrance. As soon as Mila finished, both left through the nearby front door.

The rain had not abated. They stood under the shop's parapet wall, looking for a rickshaw to take them home. One came along. They hailed it and dashed in the blinding rain in its direction, pulling the saree's fallen drape as half a veil, to cover the hair arrangements. Getting up on its slippery footboard was challenging; once they stepped on, they dropped themselves on the seat immediately, with a sigh, and rushed to pull the collapsible hood over their heads. The rickshaw puller gave them a long plastic sheet to cover themselves. They pulled it up to the chin, trying to hold it tightly about them, struggling in the blustery winds.

"I hope you won't get a chill today," Lutfun said.

"I hope not. I think I'll be fine," Mila answered.

After a pause, Mila asked, "Are you happy, Aunty Lutfun?"

Lutfun inclined her head towards her. "Yes, of course, I'm happy, dear. Do you not see it?"

"I do, but who knows what's going on deep down inside your heart?" Mila asked, then regretted it. "Never mind. You don't need to answer that."

"No, I will since you asked. Happiness is elusive. Money can't always make people happy. Material objects can't either. Even if they did, it would be short-lived.

Happiness is something else. It's much more complex. It's almost like a shooting star which we see, but we cannot really house it."

"I don't understand. When you feel happy that usually means you have housed the emotion permanently within your heart. Although, I do agree, material objects cannot always make one happy. Those who are happy, they're happy regardless. If one really searched for the meaning of happiness, they would find it among slum-dwellers, even."

"Yes, I meant, it's not a steady emotion. One cannot be consistently happy. It comes and goes. You know what I mean? An interplay, of sorrow and happiness, if you like."

"Yes, like the flashing lights of a shooting star in the night's sky, couldn't be pinned down."

They were quiet after that. The rickshaw soon stopped at the entrance of the House of Chowdhury. The puller got off his seat in the front and stepped into a puddle. He stood there as he removed the plastic sheet with one hand and took the fare on the palm of the other. Lutfun had been carrying a purse within her palm; she placed the money on his. Mila sprang out of the vehicle from her side; Lutfun followed. They ran indoors in the bucketing rain. They pulled the anchals' by the corners, and veiled the heads, again, to protect the expensive buns.

"Now, go to your room and get some rest, dear, I'll bring you lunch in a bit."

Having said so, Lutfun walked towards her mother-in-law, Mrs Chowdhury's room, and disappeared in the passageway. Mila entered her bedroom. It was empty.

Through the windows she saw her mother, her aunts, and uncles outside under the umbrella of the neem tree, giving instructions to the decorators and supervising the wedding dinner. Just this once, her father was also with them; it was a fine gathering of siblings and loved ones in the front yard.

She smiled to herself and looked at a rotund, mosaic table by the window. It stood on its curved antique legs by an easy chair, set at an angle. A radio sat on the table. She reached out for the radio and peered through the long, horizontal window grills. A dense rain splattered over trembling leaves. She picked up the radio, and tuned it to Dhaka Station, popular movie songs; Abdul Jabbar singing, Ore neel doriya, from the movie Sareng Bou. She spaced out for a while into the dazzling rain. She walked towards her bed and sat down on its edge, listening.

Oddly enough, she thought of her old fling. He should have become a relic by now. But he didn't. He still reminded her, remotely maybe, of a lost relationship. Rahim Ali had married Papri. Were they happy? Oh! Stop! Stop it! She screamed inside her head. Not now, not ever. She could hear her relatives' squeals of laughter, chiming in the winds. She lay down on one end of the bed, the song was enchanting—an ephemera—how fragile was this existence? Her journey had only just begun, and a sense of an ending was already closing in. This house, her relatives, where would they all be in fifty years' time? Where would she be on this bumpy road to posterity? Her eyes were closed. She opened them and saw that Lutfun had entered with a meal. She stood before her, smiling. She coughed lightly to awaken her from a reverie.

"Oh! It's you?" Mila said, opening her eyes.

228

"I hope you haven't ruined your hair," Lutfun said. "Let me see; no, it's okay, I think. Here take this and eat up. You'll need a lot of energy today."

"I don't think I have much appetite."

"Still, eat just a little," Lutfun insisted.

Mila took the plate and ate a few mouthfuls of rice and fried fish. Then she gave the plate back to her.

"Are you okay? What's bothering you, love? If I may ask?" Lutfun asked, touching her smooth forehead.

"No, it's just, just that I'm suddenly all philosophical today, thinking of life and death and the journey itself."

"Now, now! This is not the time to have such profound thoughts, is it?" Lutfun said.

"I know—I know," Mila said.

"Don't think of these things. Where is your trousseau?"

Lutfun looked under the bed and pulled out a heavy trunk. She opened it and found a few sarees, bed linens, and blankets. She took them out and glanced over them. Decidedly, more clothes needed to be trunked. Lutfun rose and zipped out of the room into her own and opened her wardrobe to find some new sarees sitting in their virgin folds. She pulled out the bunch and retraced her steps to Mila's room.

Mila looked at her surprised. "But these are all yours."

"So? They're yours now. What would your in-laws think if they knew you have a near-empty trousseau?"

"Who cares?" Mila pounced. "I don't want your sarees, Aunty Lutfun."

"Don't worry, you can buy me heaps later," she said, smiling, as she dropped them in the trunk and ironed the creases with her palm, leveling the clothes neatly. She closed the metal lid with both hands.

"Are you sure?" Mila asked.

"A hundred percent."

Lutfun reached for the lunch plate. As she exited, she crossed her path with Mila's other aunt, Prema on the threshold. Aunt Prema entered with a cosmetic case. She was doing bridal makeup. She left the case on Mila's bed and sped out of the room, mumbling that she had forgotten something. She closed the bedroom door behind her and caught up with Lutfun in the passage.

Mila climbed down her bed and sat on an easy chair, by the window. She felt trepidation. An ink doused, monsoon afternoon; she couldn't tell if it was evening already because the sky had never cleared. She sat absorbed, listening to the rain's sound. She heard a knock. She turned off the radio and looked at the door. It opened and in came her friends, Shreya and Shuvo with their mother, Shri Devi Mukherjee. Shri Devi came straight up and pulled her out of the easy chair. She gave Mila a tight hug and a deep kiss on her forehead.

"Why do you look so morose, dear?" she asked.

Mila smiled and stood aside. She offered her the chair. Shuvo and Shreya looked at her, who had by now settled themselves cozily on the edge of the bed. Mila walked across and sat alongside them, facing Shri Devi. Their feet dangled off the cold floor. Mila's bed was a unique antique of a leaf-shaped headrest of surreal light blue waves. This bed was a one off.

"How's everything coming along?" asked Shri Devi.

"So far so good, I guess. But the rain could spoil it," Mila said.

"You know what? There's a saying that wedding rains are not a harbinger of bad luck. On the contrary, they are a sign of peace. You're a peacemaker, love."

"I hope so, Mashima," Mila mumbled.

She thought of her rather angst-ridden childhood with her parents. Had it not been for her grandparents, uncles, and aunts, a street life was a near possibility. Where would her mother had taken her, today if kicked-out? Shreya peeked at her metal trousseau under the bed.

"Are you taking that with you?" she asked.

"Yes, that's my bridal trousseau," Mila said. "It has some sarees and bed linen."

"Well, it's all written in the stars, I believe," Shuvo began, suddenly.

"What do you mean? Don't you start already?" Shreya snapped.

"Start? What have I said? All I wanted to say is this, that we were born from elements of the stars which, when showered upon us, made us. Humans are born out of stars. They give us the essential building blocks, but in unique sort

231

of ways, not make clones out of us, but like the many Rubik's Cube patterns. Stars govern us. They give us our individual characteristics. Our destinies are made in Heaven, including marriages."

"How astonishing! I wonder which star made you. Must be something totally out of our visible orbit. However, I do know which star governs you for saying such nonsense! Saturn!"

"Hmm! You're insanely critical," Shuvo reflected, calmly.

They all laughed. Mila laughed the most. Shuvo sure brightened up this dull day for her.

The evening had now well and truly set in. The ceremony will start soon. Prema and Lutfun flitted in and out of the room. Cars' incessant honking at the entrance had begun. Chatter rose and became louder; peals of laughter like glass tapping and greetings enlivened the house. Shri Devi rose from the easy chair and excused herself, saying that she must meet with Mila's mother and grandmother. She had stepped out just when Prema also returned, gasping, nearly colliding with Shri Devi at the door. She entered the room and stood before Mila and her friends under the ceiling fan. She gauged the situation for a few seconds and asked Mila to move to the middle of the bed. In the meantime, more people poured in, causing a jam almost in the doorway. Decked in expensive sarees and jewellery, her friends entered, crowding into the room. Some sat around Mila, on the bed. Prema walked up to bolt the doors. It was now time to begin the bridal make-up.

232

Prema was a natural. She knew exactly what to do. She started with a facial foundation, then rubbed some of it down her neck and then to her arms and forearms. Her kit was fully equipped and she, a skilful makeup artist, applied the rouge, the powder, and lipsticks diligently—a detailed makeup was underway; the eye makeup was performed with great precision, with eyeliner, eyeshade, and long brushes of mascara strokes. Not until each nail was painted and perfected painstakingly with nail polish—nails sparkling like Murano glass.

The bed was strewn with stained cotton buds, ripped clothes, little pieces of chucks to wipe off the extra colours. By the time Prema finished, Mila had transformed into a princess. All that was left now was to put her bridal attire on.

A ruckus outside alerted them. Someone just screamed that the groom's party had arrived. Mila's friends who were seated calmly over the make-up session rose with sudden alacrity. They rushed towards the door to greet the groom; a perfumed trail of sweetness lingered in the air, as they left. Mila felt her heartbeat increase; it was stifling hot on this muggy evening. The ceiling fan was in full swing, but the steaminess wouldn't dissipate.

Shouts and cheers at the gate, the groom's party had been held up here by a queue of pretty girls. They'd barred them from entering unless he paid a certain amount of toll— a custom of good-natured banter.

"How much?" the groom's party shouted.

"Not less than a thousand rupees," one of Mila's cousins screamed back.

"Wow! That's too much."

"No, it isn't. Our sister doesn't come cheap."

"How about five-hundred?" a friend negotiated on behalf of the groom.

"No. Eight hundred," the girls cried.

"Deal."

A clear win for the girls; the deal closed after about fifteen minutes of haggling. They let them in. Some of the groom's friends winked at them, too; eligible bachelors trying to gate crash, pushing through the young beauties. The girls led the groom and his friends to the bridal podium.

The podium, built out of wide, wooden floor plank, was decorated with the same multi-coloured streamers as the outer gates were. It had a supporting back wall and was covered with a thick Persian rug. Rolled bolsters of glittery velvet were thrown over the rug as soft cushioning. Irfaan Khan, the groom, climbed up with his friends and sat on the rugged plank in his new white sequinned Sherwani suit and plain russet silk turban. He had a sharp nose and chiseled cheeks. His dark, thin lips showed determination. His hair was black and wavy in the front with long sideburns. He parted it sideways which befitted his long face. His eyes were sharp and had a devilish glint in them.

Irfaan sat in the middle of the podium, flanked by his friends. They leaned against the bolsters like a king with his knights in a king's court. He cracked jokes and laughed with friends tonight. One night's king; Mila, his queen would soon be by his side.

"Still there's time to escape, before signing on the dotted line," a friend joked.

They laughed and they knew that this was it. Irfaan's bachelor days were over.

Prema thickened the bride's lashes with an extra layer of mascara, as she did a finishing touch up. The room had quietened because the girls had gone to greet the groom's party. She put her index finger under Mila's chin to lift her face to a small mirror that she held in front of her. Mila looked into the mirror. She sure looked a dark beauty. It was time to put on the wedding saree. Prema and Mila both climbed down the bed.

Prema asked Mila to wear the matching blouse and the petticoat. Mila obeyed. The saree was expensive. It was a red sequinned kathan, heavy with gold-threaded gems. In her slim fitted blouse and the petticoat, Mila stood in the middle of the room. Prema took the saree and unfolded the nine-meter drape to wrap around Mila. Not a rushed job, deliberately, and artfully making sure that every single pleat of the unstitched drape fell evenly in place. She secured the pleats midway down the fall with a safety pin which had pierced through a small piece of paper to protect the fabric. The pleats had fallen uniformly at Mila's feet. Prema drew the rest of the drape to wrap it around her tender, curved waist and threw it over her full breasts. She pleated it again over the left shoulder and pinned the pleats through the blouse on that shoulder. A trail dangled elegantly at the hip.

Prema stepped back and appraised Mila. She thought the saree looked tight and tucked around Mila's taut body. Prema now turned her attention to jewellery. They were in boxes inside her almirah in one corner of the room. She opened it with a key, kept in the drawer of the mosaic table by the window. She pulled a few crisp, new boxes out of a hidden safe inside the almirah; a diamond necklace and several other semi-precious gilded necklaces studded in stone. She helped Mila wear them one after another. They adorned her long, unwrinkled neck. Prema took Chanel No.9 perfume out of her make-up box and sprayed some, lightly, over Mila's saree. Prema thought her beauty was fawn-like, delicate.

"How do you feel?" Prema asked.

"Nervous."

"You'll be fine. Before going to bed, take off your jewellery and put them in the box. If he'll give you the time, that is."

Prema smiled slyly, giving her a slight nudge. Mila nodded and lowered her eyes with a slight coining smile on her painted lips.

"It will hurt the first time."

Aunt Prema continued, oblivious that her niece wasn't little anymore, and that she was nearly a doctor. That's what the elders did, Mila thought. Love had blinded them in many ways. That was how her family was. Love was paramount over hardships. The same love to blanket distant relatives too, as far back as it could go, in a close-knit family. Whatever had happened in their lives, nothing came between relationships. Credit be to Mr and Mrs Chowdhury for raising such a devoted family.

The door burst open. Giggling girls jostled through the doorway. Mila, a demure bride, sat in the easy chair under the full speed of a ceiling fan. Prema left her to the girls. Their oohs and the aahs put a delicate smile on Mila's lips. The room had now begun to reek of light sweat and perfume. There was a knock on the door, the moulavi seeking permission to come inside. He had brought with him two elders, her two uncles, Sheri, and Ashik, as witnesses, to ask for Mila's permission to this wedding. If she said no, then the groom's party must depart without a marriage.

He recited, while her uncles gave a patient hearing.

"Mila Chowdhury—Do you of your own accord take Irfaan Khan to be your wedded husband?"

Mila was silent the first time. This silence, however, wasn't to be misconstrued as anything foreboding; it was uncivil and too forward to reply straight away. She said, 'yes,' 'yes' and 'yes,' to the questions asked three times but paused a few seconds between each. A contract was now handed to her with a pen. She held it tightly between her sweaty fingers, while her uncles held the contract paper on her lap to keep it steady. She signed. The most important moment of her life, her maiden life given away; this free life she had until now was over. An ugly cramp slowly rose within her belly. The moulavi and her uncles departed.

The same happened outside on the podium. Irfaan Khan signed the same contract. The wedding was now properly sealed and declared official. The guests held their hands up, like half-opened pistachio shells, to pray. When prayers finished, they vocalised Ameen together.

237

The pageboys served hot food. They spread them out on dining tables, in the makeshift dining area, not far from the guests, where they had been seated on the semi wet chairs, all this time and praying before the bridal podium. Those boys also poured lassi in each glass. However, the lassi drink had turned into a cocktail mix of leaking rainwater; sloppy management as no one oversaw that the lassi jugs were uncovered under a thick tarp tear over the table. A special banquet was prepared for the groom and his friends. The groom's table was served with several whole chickens, roasted in almond and ghee; whole smoked hilsa fish on silver platters.

The formalities out of the way, Nazmun Banu could relax. She was still worried about the lassi being too watery from the rainwater, but the constant presence of her two brothers-in-law by her side gave her some courage. They made sure that the food did not fall short in supply. The guests enjoyed the meal. In the end, they were entertained by the lassi fiasco, rather than offended.

Prema and Lutfun ate fast. They hurried back to Mila's bedroom. Mila sat, looking sedated in a queen's attire. Her silken veil trembled under the ceiling fan. It was time. She had to be moved to the bridal podium outside. The guests had by now sat down and settled in their chairs after dinner. The rain had abated. The groom reverted to the dais with his friends, enjoying an occasional witty joke; it sometimes fell short of wit, but they elicited a hiccup of laughter anyway.

Lutfun and Prema stood on both sides of the bride. They held her arms and slowly walked her out of the door, down the passageway towards the podium. Her shaded eyes were downcast inside her transparent sequin veil. She had the most surrealistic feeling of being semi-suspended. Off the floor through the air, in her aunt's good hands, she felt she didn't know her own house; where she was born and raised all these years, running along this passageway? The yard had transformed too. The house looked unrecognisable through this prism of a heavy makeover. Just as the bride was all dolled up herself.

There she was. Prema lifted her saree a little bit at her feet. She climbed the two low steps and sat down gently next to her dashing groom. Mila blinked. The groom too exuded unfamiliar newness. He smelled fresh, perfumed, and bathed. She could smell his understated cologne, as he could smell hers. But they hadn't looked at each other even once.

By now other people, Mila's friends, her cousins had all climbed the small podium. They kneeled behind the bridal couple to watch the ritual. A flimsy, transparent red scarf was laid over the couple's heads. An assortment of two traditional sweets, firni, and zarda, were placed in small silver-spooned bowls on a tray before the wedded couple. Lutfun performed the ritual. She took Mila's hand and planted a dollop of rice pudding, or the firni, in the middle of her palm. She stretched Mila's hand across towards the groom's mouth. He swiped it with the tongue. The groom now returned the courtesy to Mila, whom Prema assisted; the first time that the family had actually met the groom.

Irfaan stole a sly look at Mila. He saw her downcast eyes covered in layers of brown shades. A careless lip touch on Irfaan's soiled palm marked a red lipstick on it, as Mila licked her share of sweets off his palm. This faded red bore testament of a secret kiss in full public view; in the moment, he wished the stain would never erase.

Mila's friends and cousins noted this and found an excuse to be naughty. Prema unveiled Mila's face and lifted it by the chin for everyone to see the new bride. Another long mirror was placed before the newlyweds for their private eyes only. Irfaan gazed at her, grinning unabashedly through the mirror.

His cousins-in-law chirped behind him. "What did you see? Tell us, tell us."

He answered gleefully. "A full moon."

Then there was more joyous clamour. Mila lowered her head further, but Irfaan noticed a coy smile.

After several hours, it was nearly over. The last ritual was the exchange of the garlands. The couple now stood upon the podium, as the guests did on the grounds. Irfaan couldn't resist anymore. He reached out for Mila's hand from under her silk veil and pressed it. Mila didn't press it back. Something went awry within her. This new life, in a new house, all this experience, leaving the House of Chowdhury, her mother, Aunty Lutfun and Aunty Prema, Grandma, and her uncles, the orchard, her bedroom, even the green windows, the roof garden beckoned her. Everything beckoned her—memories—one too many. Where she grew up, her entire life suddenly stopped breathing. She was having difficulty breathing. Oh! Where was her breath, now? She should respond to those signals by pressing Irfaan's hand back.

Irfaan continued to signal. Her hands clasped in his, they walked towards the car. Her eyes were downcast; a strangeness numbed her. Suddenly, two strong arms held her. They nestled her against a man's chest. No less, but her own father. He began to cry. She cried; her father cried; a drop from pure delight to pure grief. There they were father and daughter united in separation. She clung to him, like a hanging bat on a wire. She was leaving them now to become someone's wife, a new becoming, a newness tore her in the gut, as though, as of this moment her past had died.

Prema came forward and extricated Mila from her father. She held her from behind and walked her towards the bridal car. Mila sniffled and didn't stop to see the expensive floral decoration over the car. A chauffeur opened the door of the passenger seat in the back of the car. Mrs Khan, her new mother-in-law, entered first, followed by Mila and then Irfaan. Irfaan's father took the front seat next to the driver. The car drove slowly through a milling crowd; a peacock danced in the rain.

homecoming

The day after the wedding, Nazmun Banu sat with their tea, at teatime with Prema and Lutfun in the orchard. Autumn leaves had covered much of the grounds.

"My Quasu is special in so many ways," Prema declared.

"Of course, he is," Lutfun answered.

"His teacher at school said that he is doing wonders with his studies. He's far ahead of the rest of the boys in his class."

"That's lovely. We all want the best for him."

Nazmun Banu yawned and looked around the orchard.

"Your brother Ashik said, we may now have enough money to send Quasu to an expensive English medium school. Our business is doing really well," Prema said.

"That's awesome news. But I hope you won't move out. The house feels a bit empty already, without Mila," Nazmun Banu said.

"Yes, how time flies. No? Mila was born just the other day. And now? It will be the same for Quasu too. He will grow up like slithering sands through our fingers," Lutfun said.

Lutfun didn't have any children. But she didn't miss much either with Quasu being around.

"What else does Quasu's teacher tell you?" Nazmun Banu asked.

"Oh, are you kidding me, sister?" Prema asked.

They were good at heart, but there was some rivalry between Prema and Nazmun Banu. The reason for it was unimaginably mundane. While Prema could marry Ashik by divorcing her ex-husband, Nazmun Banu couldn't. She couldn't move on. She couldn't, even if she wanted to, because in the eyes of her in-laws, she was the righteous wife, the family's elder, holy, and pure.

When Prema paused to rest from bragging about Quasu, which she had been doing often to almost everyone's disapproval, Lutfun chimed in. "Tea anyone?"

"No, no, Quasu would be home soon. I must get his fruit juice ready," Prema said.

She rose from her chair to go indoors, while Lutfun and Nazmun Banu rolled their eyes.

"Oh! She just wouldn't stop now, would she?" said Nazmun Banu. "Every time we are together, must she brag about how great Quasu is? My Quasu this, my Quasu that, he is the best, and what have we? As though we don't know what Quasu is. As though we don't love him enough."

"That's just her. Yes, I know it can be irritating. But you know what?" Lutfun asked.

"What?" Nazmun Banu answered.

"I have seen her other children from her ex coming around here and asking the maids if they could see her."

"Really? Gosh! What would our Amma say?"

"She looks the other way," Lutfun said.

"What a mess? Really! Say, how do you know?" Nazmun Banu asked.

"One day, Amma and I were sitting together under the neem tree. She saw them enter through the main gate and talk to the gateman. Amma didn't ask them to come inside or anything, but we overheard them asking about their mother."

"Hmm, how sad. I really feel sorry for those kids."

Nazmun Banu looked away at the orchard aimlessly and sighed. Lutfun was quiet too. After some time, she rose from her chair and ambled through the orchard. She looked at the plantain trees and the hanging wood-apples. A bunch of wood-apples hung over her. She reached out for one, twisted and plucked it. She tossed it up and down in the air a few times. As the sun downed leaving red streaks in the autumn sky, she returned to Nazmun Banu as she sat quietly amongst the circle of chairs; her shoulders slouched.

"Should we go in, now?" Lutfun asked.

Nazmun Banu looked up at Lutfun and asked. "Mila didn't call today, did she?"

"Not that I know. Why?" Lutfun asked.

"I wonder how she is in that new place with her in-laws."

"She will be back tomorrow after the walimah," Lutfun said.

"Yes, of course. She didn't mention a honeymoon yet," Nazmun Banu said.

"They only wedded yesterday."

"Yes."

"Have you decided what you are wearing for the walimah?" Nazmun Banu asked.

"Yes, my pink kanjivaram with the pearl and ruby necklace. What about you?"

"I'll wear my white kathan silk, with the diamonds."

Nazmun Banu rose and stood abreast of Lutfun. They walked towards the verandah to enter the house. The balustrade of the verandah was covered in green overhanging vines, trees, money plants, and rhododendrons like a delicate curtain. Lutfun decided that they needed some trimming done. As they entered the room, they saw Mrs Chowdhury sitting quietly by the window. Her walking stick was with her.

They didn't know where Prema had disappeared with Quasu. But the telephone suddenly rang in the hallway, breaking this cosmic silence of dusk.

"Oh! Who could that be?" Nazmun Banu hissed.

But before they could reach the phone, Prema had already come out of the dining room and had picked it up.

"Hello," she answered, organising her saree over her shoulder.

"Hello, this is Mila. Is that you Aunty Prema?"

"Yes, beta, it's me. How are you, love?"

"We're well. Sorry, I couldn't call you earlier today. We had to go to a feast given in our honor, the newlyweds."

"That's great. Enjoy every bit, Maa. How are your in-laws, Mr and Mrs Khan?"

"They're well. And so is Irfaan. Anything new there?" Mila asked.

"No, not particularly. The house feels empty now that you have gone. Some of the decorations are still there. Some have been taken down. The yard is a mess at the moment with wires everywhere."

"How is Quasu?" Mila asked.

"He is well, just missing you a lot. But he's really doing well in class. He's at the top of the world right now."

Lutfun and Nazmun Banu overheard this conversation from the other room. Lutfun suppressed a giggle, while Nazmun Banu blurted out. "Here we go again."

"Shh, keep your voice down, she'll hear us," Lutfun said.

Nazmun Banu continued to look at Prema until she finished her conversation, and the receiver was handed to her. Prema signaled them to come forward—first, Nazmun Banu, then Lutfun. The conversation went well over an hour. They talked about girly stuff, about the in-laws, parties, and the honeymoon. They were planning to go on a honeymoon soon. But they were still undecided whether it would be Cox's Bazaar or Rangamati. Then Mila let Lutfun in on a secret about the wedding night. Lutfun giggled and hid her face from the gazing Prema and Nazmun Banu, so they wouldn't hear her. They moved away.

"And then what happened?" Lutfun asked.

"He took me in his arms first. I lay there on his chest, listening to his heartbeat. He held me tight, then tighter, until we both had goosebumps all over us. He kissed me first on my forehead, nose, and lips. And then moved his lips up the jawbone line."

"And then? What? Tell me?" Lutfun asked.

"I'll tell you later after we come over."

"Yes, see you soon."

"See you tomorrow."

Mila hung up. It wasn't Lutfun's intention to smoke out what had happened on the wedding night, but Mila's spontaneity drew her into her own romance with her husband, Mila's Uncle Sheri. Why would anyone be so inclined to find out about such intimacies? But they were. Lutfun was just as eager to listen as Mila was eager to tell. Lutfun would have to wait until the walimah to listen to the rest of it.

The walimah celebrations usually took place one or two days after the wedding ceremony. This ceremony was hosted by the groom's family, after which the bridal couple returned to the bride's father's house and stayed there for a couple of days before they went back to the in-laws or to their own homes. However, Mila's case was different. They

247

decided to go on a honeymoon straight from her father's house after the walimah.

On the morning of the walimah, Mila's mother and aunts at the House of Chowdhury were making preparations. They were decorating Mila's room for the homecoming. Loads of garlands were brought in. Lutfun and Prema took them into Mila's bedroom. Prema walked up first and towards the wooden shutters. She opened them and a flurry of dust flew everywhere. Autumnal sun filmed through the dust particles. Lutfun looked at the bed and decided to put a fresh cover on. She walked up to the old Mahogany almirah and opened its ornate doors. Lutfun rummaged through the shelves. Accidentally, she opened the drawers and underneath tons of rubbish, she found some old pictures. They were mostly Mila's friends, but one friend Lutfun recognised. That was Rahim Ali, in his round spectacles from the war days. In this picture, he looked pretty much the same, except his curly hair was cut short. His complexion was fair, and his lips were thin with a cupid's bow. Rahim Ali was tall and muscular, Lutfun thought looking at the picture now. She had never really noticed him in Pretigram. He was a patient then.

She also found some letters. Rahim Ali had written numerous letters to Mila. Lutfun felt an urge to open them. She couldn't tell if they were ever in a relationship. Perhaps, it was unrequited. She opened one of many letters. Beautiful words which tried over and over to tie a bond; cajoled her to come closer. Words which flowed like a river, rain, and moon drops. Poetry, which expressed how they had sat in the rain. She, by his side. Her head lay on his chest. She held him tight, and he held her until a raindrop fell on her lips. He held her chin and licked it off her luscious lips. Romance was born. He carried her indoors. A flash of lightning clapped; a storm brewed. The words were magical, Lutfun thought and they sounded perfectly romantic.

"Hey, what're you doing there? Have you found some bedclothes or not?"

Prema's shrill voice brought Lutfun back to the present. She closed the drawer in a hurry and pulled out new bedclothes, neatly packed in a wrapper on one of the shelves. Nazmun Banu may have bought them some time ago and stuffed them in here. She gave them to Prema. But Prema saw her absent-mindedness.

"Everything okay?" she asked, as she pulled the bedclothes out of the wrapper, all at the same time.

"Yeah, sure," Lutfun said. "Nice bedclothes."

Prema held one end of it and Lutfun the other. They made the new bed together. Lutfun held a lump in her throat, wondering how far this relationship between Rahim Ali and Mila had progressed. Lutfun felt betrayed that Mila had not confided in her about these many letters. The bed was made in silence. They stretched the sheets out without a single crease and tucked them under the mattress. In the meantime, a maid entered the room with a hand full of rose garlands. Prema and Lutfun turned around and saw that it was Shimul. The three decorated the bed together. Some of the heavy garlands were laid across the mosquito net stand. The rest of the roses were spread evenly on the bed. Prema, Lutfun, and Shimul stood back to look at the decoration. The roses looked brilliant in the autumn sun which streamed through the open shutters. A light fragrance pervaded the air, as a prelude to the romance which was going to ensue tonight.

They left the room with the windows open for fresh air. Unless there was a strong wind, there was no reason to close the shutters. Let the room bask in the glow of the mellow autumn sun. As the trio walked out of the room, they found Nazmun Banu in the corridor. She had a few mango pickle jars in her hands. Nazmun Banu looked at them and peeked into the room through the narrow opening of the doors, as Prema was closing it. She smiled. Nazmun Banu liked what she saw. Then she also saw Shimul, who was also standing with them. She handed the pickle jars to the maid. Shimul took them and walked to the stairs to go up to the roof. Out on the roof, she put them down on the cemented floor on the roof's far end, in full sunlight.

The light shone like diamond glittering on the aluminium jar covers, as she lined them up on the edge of the roof next to each other. She squinted against the autumnal dazzle. She stopped to glance at the night-flowering jasmine hanging over the mossy walls. There were a few flower petals scattered on the roof. The stem of the shiuli, or rather jasmine, was a potential orange dye, she thought, which could be used to colour clothes. She sauntered towards the flowers and picked up two handfuls. She pouched them in her saree and ran downstairs. A gusty wind blew a strand of hair across her face.

The walimah was just two hours away. The members of the House of Chowdhury were getting dressed. Shimul rushed from one room to the next, running errands. Lutfun needed a hairpin to be put in place on her french knot.

Prema needed Shimul's help with the saree. Shimul sat
down on the floor and held the fall of the saree's pleats, as
Prema neatly pleated at the top and secured them by tucking
the edge inside the petticoat around the waist. Nazmun
Banu couldn't find her matching blouse and called out for
Shimul. Shimul flitted to her room and pulled it from under
the piles of sarees and jewellery boxes on the bed.

When they were ready, they came outside and found
their cars waiting under the porch. They entered their
respective cars. Comfortably seated, the cavalcade took off
towards the walimah venue—the Malibagh Ladies Centre.
Shimul saw them out and returned to her tiny room in the
servant wing, at the back of the house. She let out a sigh.

Shimul realised that the servants were either napping
now or cooking up bridal meals in the kitchen at the advent
of Mila and Irfaan's homecoming. She walked calmly up to
her room under the staircase and pulled a dented aluminium
pan sitting on a slat wall in the corner of the room. The pan
had the gatherings of shiuly flowers, which she had been
picking and saving here for a while now. She sat down on
the floor next to it and began to separate the saffron-
coloured stems off the white petals. Once they were all done,
she went to the kitchen to look for a mortar and pestle to
extract the pigmentations. She had a white saree, a gift from
Mrs Chowdhury a while back. She decided to colour the
saree in the pigmentation extracted from the shiuly stems.
This was the only time she was free before the bridal party
returned.

She walked over to her room; hardly any sunlight
entered this time of the day, except a trickle of ray through
an opening on the roof. In the dim light, she looked in the

direction of her belongings. They were her bedding and a battered trunk. She went over to the trunk, sat down, and opened it. The white saree was on top. She only had a couple of clothes, which she wore every day. She took out the saree and rubbed over it. The fabric felt smooth and new. It was a hundred percent cotton. She dropped the lid to the trunk and exited the room.

Back in the kitchen, she readied stems in the mortar and crushed it to extract the colour. She used a spoon to scoop the colour to transfer it into a pan. She added water to the crushed colour in the pan by pouring some from a terra cotta urn placed in the kitchen corner. A cold infusion of saffron was made in the pan. She unfolded the saree and doused it in, pressing it in the infusion. She moved the fabric around in the colour and then put a lid over the pan. She left the pan by the door, allowing the colour to seep through the fabric for a few hours.

She walked through the dark front yard feeling forlorn. She thought of her own wedding day. She thought about how it ended suddenly one day when her husband married for the second time. He had jilted her and hurt her feelings. She had stopped living, breathing. One day, she decided to leave him and come to Dhaka. She had found this employment in the House of Chowdhury through a friend's recommendation. She had decided that this was the life of freedom she wanted. People married because of social customs. But there was no other freedom than earning one's own keep. Trapped in a loveless, broken marriage was like a wheel locked to its spokes; tied up ruthlessly. The wedding party will be back soon. Shimul found this moment to reflect on her life as a maid. It was still freedom; she was free.

This was a silent house, at the moment. Except for Mrs Chowdhury, everyone had left. It gave Mrs Chowdhury an opportunity to ruminate. She sat by the window in an easy chair. Her eyes were closed. She was as old as this house—a repository of her values and traditions. Mila is growing up and getting married. The dramas played out over spanning generations. Tea gatherings in the orchard; the songs, the laughter, the romance, and also the grief—all tied up to give the house character. This was not just a house anymore; it breathed the living history of the Chowdhury family. It was meaningful to her. The House of Chowdhury was an extension of her memory.

beach

After the walimah ceremony the bridal party returned around midnight. Shimul opened the door and greeted them with a smile. Mila and Irfaan stood abreast at the entrance with the entire family cramming behind them. Mila was dressed in her walimah saree of pastel green of silver sequin beads with a necklace set in studded diamonds and rubies. She looked at Shimul and pulled a smile. Shimul thought, Mila looked glamorous—gleaming with happiness.

"How're you Shimul?" Mila asked.

"I'm Mila Apa. How're you?"

"I'm well, too."

Irfaan smiled at Shimul. She stood aside to let the family in. They walked through the doorway jamming it at times. Lutfun and Prema led the way to Mila's room where Mila would be sleeping with Irfaan. The rest of the family, including Mila's mother, Nazmun Banu retired into their own bedrooms with their spouses. Mila's father had a change of heart that night and decided to spend it with first wife, Nazmun Banu. She didn't mind.

Prema and Lutfun took the bridal couple to their room; sweet smells of flowers and garlands. The bed even had their names etched in flower petals. The couple stood quietly in front of the bed. Irfaan looked around. He was clearly happy.

"Who made this decoration?" he asked.

"We did," said Prema.

"It's beautiful," Mila said.

In the meantime, the melodic rain had started to pour. Prema and Lutfun left and closed the door behind them. Irfaan looked at Mila and held her hand. He smiled and pulled her towards him. Mila smiled back. She rested her head on his chest.

"Come with me to bed," Irfaan said.

"So soon?" Mila asked.

"How much longer? I can't wait," Irfaan asked.

Mila didn't say anything.

"Are you having second thoughts about me? Irfaan asked.

"And why would you ask me that?" Mila asked.

"Well, I meant to tell you. I must say, I was disappointed on the wedding night, when you didn't squeeze my hand back."

"Oh that! C'mon you can't hold that against me," Mila said.

"I'm not holding anything against you. But sure enough, it got me thinking. I just didn't get around to ask you."

"I see."

"Are you?' Irfaan asked again.

"What?"

"Umm, having a second thought about me."

"No, I don't think so," Mila answered.

"Then show it to me. Show me that you love me."

Irfaan demanded. Mila obeyed. She put her arms around his neck and gave him a peck at first. Irfaan stood quietly and let himself be wooed. She moved her lips slightly over his. Irfaan held her tight behind her back. Then he lifted her to the bed and placed her gently over the petals. She sat there looking at him. He sat down by her on the bed and started to take off her clothes; one layer after another of peeling. He took her jewellery off and put them on the bed. The saree and the blouse were next. He held her shoulders and rubbed his lips along its silky skin. Her shoulders were a delightful chocolate smoothie. He licked them and kissed them all at once.

His hands went roving round her body—exploring around her breasts, he cupped them; her nipples hardened. He kissed her on the lips. She kissed him back. They held each other in a tight embrace. They lay down on the bed, still clutching onto themselves. He continued to lick her body, her curves. They were oblivious of the rain. Regardless of the closed window shutters, its rising ferocity could be heard. As was their rising passion; it did not fall short in anyway. It wasn't until morning when they slept. They slept like well-fed babies in a crib—dead to the world.

The first person to wake up the next morning was Shimul. She rose, yawned, and walked over to the kitchen. She attended to the saree she had soaked for colour the previous night. It looked evenly saffroned from the shiuly flower stems in the infusion pan. The long, drenched fabric was coiled up. She pulled it like a rope and gave its length a tight squeeze to wring out the extra water. She doubled up the length and twisted it. She plonked the heavy, wet sari over her shoulder and took it to the roof. All the bedroom doors were closed. The sun had filtered through the leaves of the bamboo trees on the far side of the fence. The light had shone after a night's monsoon rain, issuing a new day of resplendent leaves.

Shimul off-loaded the saree from her shoulder and untwisted it. She put it on the clothesline stretching its breadth slowly across it. The saffron colour stirred a warmth inside her. It was an innocent pleasure, but it was immense. A red robin flew in and sat on the clothesline. She looked at it. Its curiosity piqued as it ogled back at her. It moved closer to the saree. Shimul shooed it away. She looked around for it, then turned to leave the roof.

On her way down the stairs, she heard people's voices. The house had woken up, already! Shimul stood behind the door and watched the family sit around the dining table. They were eating a hearty breakfast, a special feast for the returning newlyweds. She waited by the door for a while and hoped that nobody had summoned her. She quietly proceeded towards the kitchen. The family was chattering away as usual.

"How's your preparation for the honeymoon coming along?" Mrs Chowdhury asked.

She sipped tea, which Prema had just poured for her. It was white and sugary.

"We're thinking of going to Cox's Bazar," Irfaan said.

He took a bite from his omelette paratha wrap.

"Cox's Bazaar in this season won't be much fun," Ashik commented.

"Yes, we did think about that. Given our finances, this was the best we could afford," Irfaan answered.

"Our neighbour next door went to the Pataang Beach," Nazmun Banu said.

"You mean Pa Tong in Phuket Island in Thailand," Ekram corrected.

"Oh whatever, you always taunt me. When do you ever stop?" Nazmun Banu said.

Mila thought. Here we go again. But she didn't want a showdown in front of the new husband. Irfaan ogled at them like a red robin on Shimul's saree on the roof, but he soon looked away as though he hadn't noticed anything.

Good man; that was the sign of a well-bred man, Mila thought. When her parents continued to bicker over the correct pronunciation, Irfaan and Mila and the rest of them steadily ate the meal. At some point, Ekram thought enough was enough. He rose and excused himself saying that he had to go to the clinic. His patients would be waiting. Nazmun Banu knew that was a blatant lie. He was going to go over to his other wife or wives who were more educated and probably knew the correct pronunciation—was it her fault that she eloped upon his insistence? And did not get a proper education? Today, she didn't raise the issue because her son-in-law, Irfaan was here; he didn't know of her husband's multiple-marriages and the promiscuous Chowdhury bloodline.

Ekram rose and kissed a goodbye to Mrs Chowdhury saying that he may be back for dinner. He shook hands with Irfaan and gave Mila a kiss on her forehead. On his way out, he sang the same tune under his breath. A sense of calm descended. Apart from the clatter of cups and saucers, sips and crunch bites, there were no other sounds. No talks, no laughter. Mila finished first. She rose from her chair. Irfaan looked at her. She signalled him to join her in the orchard once he had finished. Irfaan quickly sipped his tea. They both rose and looked at Mrs Chowdhury and smiled.

"We'll be in the orchard, Daadi Amma," Mila said, kissing her on the cheek, too.

Mrs Chowdhury leaned back in the chair, nodded, and smiled back. The love birds walked briskly towards the open door leading to the orchard. The midday sun was up. They sat on a grassy patch in the shade of a guava tree to avoid the glare from a heightened sunlight. The fresh drenched grass effused an earthy sweet smell. They sat down next to each other but close enough for a touch to the shoulder. Mila squinted at the light. She looked morosely around her. Irfaan looked at her.

"What's up! Why the sadness?"

"No, just thinking about my parents. Does marriage come with an expiry date?"

Irfaan was surprised but his expression was neutral.

"Depends on the relationship, I think? Some marriages improve with time."

"How do you think we would fare?" Mila asked.

"How do I think we would fare?"

Irfaan repeated and then pondered for a while. He looked at Mila's downcast eyes and smiled. He extended an arm and pulled her towards him. Her face brightened like a summer's afternoon, as she broke into a giggle.

"Like this. This is how we would always be. Don't ever forget that."

He brought his lips down on hers and gave her a deep kiss. A pigeon flew over them and sat on a pomegranate tree over by the fence. They remained interlocked for some time. Mila's eyes were closed, Irfaan's eyes were open. He looked at her eyelids and realised that her eyes were naturally shaded. They were beautiful in light brown and long lashes. Mila pulled away from him after a while.

"About the honeymoon, I'm going to buy the tickets today and make a booking at hotel Saimon. What do you say?" Irfaan asked.

"Yes, absolutely. Is it over by the sea?"

"It is my jaan. You will be able to hear the roaring of the waves all day long and through the long nights, my love, the two days that we will be there," Irfaan said.

"Great, I can't wait. It's giving me goosebumps, already," Mila said.

Irfaan laughed. She laughed with him. Their laughter reached the top of the tree to a nesting cuckoo on a low branch. It ducked in its netted home as it beaked an insect into its baby's regurgitated mouth. Irfaan held up Mila's face by the chin and gazed tenderly into her eyes.

"You have beautiful eyes, Mila."

Mila smiled and gazed back into Irfaan's soft gaze.

Irfaan lowered her face and kissed her on the lids as she closed them. He kissed her on the cheek bones. He lifted his face and spoke gently. "Open your eyes."

"Why?" Mila whispered.

"Because, I want you to see me."

Mila opened them. She saw what she had already known. She saw love and more tender love into those eyes. As she continued to look at them, Irfaan rubbed her lips gently with his index. She opened them up for him. He lowered his head to touch them with his lips—light kisses. The kisses deepened. A crow swooped low over them at great speed; wings flapping energetically as it flew. But they held each other close, without a distraction. He held her face in his two palms and lifted his face to see her wet luscious lips and closed lids.

"Should we go inside?" he murmured.

"Hmm," she nodded.

He stood first then he extended his hand to pull her up as though he had pulled a fallen twig. A gentle breeze blew a strand of hair over her face. Irfaan glanced at her tranquil face and made no attempt to move the strand. He thought she looked beautiful with the wisp of hair dangling over her face in the gentle winds, like a tub of money-plant cluster tumbling over its edge.

"Come," he said.

They entered the house through the same door. In the dining room, nobody was here now or anywhere near. However, they heard a light wavering laughter from somewhere. They heard a man's and a woman's voice. It must be Aunty Lutfun and Uncle Sheri on the roof, Mila thought. Those two were so close and so much in love; no force in the world could break them. In a while, they heard footsteps coming rapidly down the stairs. It was them, indeed. Lutfun was in the front, and Sheri right behind her. Lutfun turned her head and laughed at Sheri, who was whispering humor into her ears. They stopped abruptly in the doorway when they saw Mila and Irfaan smiling at them from the middle of the dining room, by the broad, long dinner table. Lutfun and Sheri came inside.

"Hey, what's up?" asked Sheri.

"We're going to pack for our honeymoon," Mila answered.

Mila's voice crackled into pleasant modulation as she spoke.

"Good, good, all decided then, whereabouts?"

"We're thinking of going to Cox's Bazar."

"Yeah, I'll pay for your bridal suite at the hotel. Let me know when you make a booking. Also, make the reservation

ASAP, this wedding season, hotels get booked up really fast."

"Yes, we will do all that today. You don't need to pay for it though," Irfaan said politely.

"What, are you crazy? You're taking my niece on a honeymoon. Who else do you think should pay?"

Sheri winked at them, as he turned back to make his way upstairs into his bedroom. Lutfun grabbed a jug of water off the dining table and followed him.

Irfaan mumbled a thanks in gratitude and saw them disappear up the stairs. Mila and Irfaan walked along the passage to their bridal room downstairs. Mila's bedroom upstairs next to her parents was empty. She had been given a new room downstairs for the wedding. The phone in the passage rang like a siren. Shimul was coming to the dining room to clear the table. She picked it up.

Mila walked dreamily towards the window in her bedroom: she walked on the beach at stunning sundown, and moon drops sprinkled on the sand, she walked, her feet dug deep in the glossy moonbeam on the sand. Her thoughts drifted over the wonders of the ocean waves— curving and slapping on the shores—she whispered a prose poem, Beach she had read in an English Magazine.

"If I compare youth to a summer's beach, then I reflect on its rippled peach. The golden sand which time could never reach. It's pretty, pristine ripples preserved like the clenched newborn fist, saw billions of years come and go, but never touch the sands to bleach. However, sandcastles may break. Mandalas wiped off. Children play, past, present

263

and the future. Clearly time has moved on. But the beach remains without a blemish by the sea—carrier of bloody bodies, pirate histories, papyrus battles. Homer passes on. His Wine-Dark Sea remains just the same, remarkably old, and new. A new day is issued. A fresh face of youth. New creases appear on the skin, once which was smooth. Unchangeable, predictable, and unwrinkled, but time over time. Sands soak up human dramas played over it. I sit here on the lonely sand today. I sat here many moons ago. I shall continue to sit until I break my bones. Time will touch me. Time touched the great Ozymandias. Futile. But the sands proved more powerful than all. Time stands still at its edge without a stir."

There was a pounding on the door. Mila hadn't heard it, until about several minutes of moonlight walk. When she heard the pounding on the door, she tore herself from her thoughts and walked across the bedroom to open the door. Shimul stood on the other side, clearly distressed. She said that Mrs Chowdhury wanted to see her and Irfaan, at once. Not fully understanding the cause of the distress, Mila looked around the room for Irfaan. He was packing a small suitcase by the bed. He also looked at Shimul by now and came over to stand next to Mila. Shimul was in a frenzy. It took them a while to absorb the seriousness.

"Come, come at once," Shimul urged.

They moved from this somewhat petrified state to follow Shimul out of the door. They entered the dining room. Mrs Chowdhury sat on a highchair by the bay window, looking grim. She looked at them as they rushed in.

"What happened?" Mila asked

"Irfaan, your mother is in the hospital. Your father just called."

"What? Oh no!" Irfaan exclaimed.

"Yes, you need to go."

"Yes, yes of course."

"Forget the honeymoon, let's just go," Mila suggested.

"Yes, right. Let's just go."

They rushed back into their room. Irfaan paced up and down like a caged lion, trying to grasp the gravity of the situation.

"Okay, I'll get the car organised. Just leave everything and go."

Mila ran out of the bedroom to ask Shimul, to ask the driver to get the car out of the garage and park upfront. Mila and Irfaan came out of the bedroom. By now all the family had also gathered under the porch. As Mila came out, her vision rested momentarily on a regular vendor who sold a yoghurt drink called matha and homemade unsalted cheese and butter. Mila grew up seeing this man every day. Ashik, particularly, loved fresh yoghurt drinks; Sheri, loved his butter and cheese.

The man carried a pole across his two shoulders, two hanging baskets on each end. Each basket was covered with a tray. The tray had to be removed to get access to the drink which was stored in large clay pots inside the basket, and the butter and cheese in smaller bowls in the other basket.

The vendor stood by his paraphernalia, which he set on the ground. Mila smiled at him, and he smiled back. They entered the car. The family stood by the car looking rather morose. Shimul handed him a jar to pour yoghurt drink into it. The car slowly drove out, like a passing scene from a movie leaving all these people sliding in the background. Mila looked at Irfaan. He was very quiet and cold. Mila put a hand across the seat to squeeze his hand. Irfaan didn't respond. Not sure what to do next, she kept her hand loosely about him. Irfaan disengaged his hand from her. Mila looked at him surprised.

"Why do you look surprised?" Irfaan asked. "You never really wanted to go on this honeymoon, anyway. Now it's off. I hope you're happy."

"What? What're you saying?" Mila asked.

She felt as if a fog curtain had been lifted. This man sitting next to her was a perfect stranger— a new man.

"Do you remember the wedding night?" Irfaan continued. "Do you remember when I squeezed your hand on our way out, did you even bother to respond? Tell me, do you really love me, Mila? Or have your parents made you so cold that you don't even feel anything?"

Mila was astounded. Was this the man who kissed her so passionately just a couple hours ago back in the orchard? Was this the man who was prepared to die for her love? Mila said nothing. They were going because his mother was ill and perhaps in her dying bed. This was not the time to pick up a fight. Mila kept quiet. But Irfaan didn't.

266

"You smiled at the vendor, at a time like this. How can you even think of socialising? How was it even possible?

"I smiled at our vendor I grew up seeing every day, and you're taking an issue with that?"

Mila hissed in suppressed anger.

"Well, the penny had dropped for me. I saw you looking across the vendor and exchanging a smile when you should have expressed sorrow."

Oh! You mean, mean man, Mila fumed with anger. She never thought she could get so furious with anyone. But she said nothing and swallowed her anger. After a moment's silence when the car crossed the mosque down the narrow alley, she opened her mouth.

She said, "I'm sorry Irfaan, if I have hurt you. I know how you must be feeling right now with Maa being in the hospital."

Irfaan looked at her but said nothing. This confused Mila. Not fully able to comprehend the man she had married three days ago; this was a mere stranger pretending to be her husband. It was like a staged role. She felt hot and dizzy. She rolled down the window on her side and stared across the passing scenery. The car continued to go forward, while everything else reversed. She thought she had moved on from the frustrations of her parental problems. Now she wasn't so sure. She struggled to breathe. It appeared she had taken a step backwards by getting married. Was this a mistake? Was there any happiness at all in any relationships? Was marital bliss a myth? The car stopped with a hard brake. She jerked and woke up from her reverie.

They were at the hospital. It smelled of death, disease, and antiseptic. Cleaners worked endlessly to wipe these off the floor and the walls. But morbidity could not be wiped off anytime soon. It was nothing new to Mila and Irfaan. They knew their hospital only too well.

They made an egress from the car and entered through the emergency. The on duty doctors were their young colleagues who had just joined. Some even had come to their wedding, joking, and laughing on the bridal dais with the groom. Mila stumbled upon her slippers, but Irfaan paid no attention. She noticed that but she recovered on her own. She was determined to make this marriage work. She felt there was no place for a recurring marital disaster in her family—a precedent that her parents had established followed by her Uncle Ashik and her Aunty Prema. No way, she was going to let her marriage fail. That was her resolve. She realised at some point that perhaps it was just all bad luck. It ran in the family. But it would end with her. She would break this cycle of marital disharmony.

One doctor came forward and told them where Irfaan's mother was. Being a final year psychiatric student's mother, Mrs Khan also received special treatment from both Irfaan and Mila's friends. Mrs Khan suffered a heart attack but was stable now.

"Oh! Thank goodness," Mila uttered with a sigh of relief.

"However, we're not out of the woods yet," the duty doctor said. "She needs to be in observation for a couple of days more. It was all from the wedding stress, I'm guessing."

"Yes, I agree," Irfaan nodded.

They hurried towards the room where Mrs Khan was. The door was closed, but they quietly opened it and found her lying in bed. She was covered with a white blanket up to her neck. The white pillow had masses of her black curls, spread out like floating underwater weed. Mila walked up and stood by her side. Mrs Khan opened her eyes; Mila's fingers combed through her curls on the pillow. She looked at her and smiled. Mila smiled back.

"You'll be fine, Maa."

"I hope so. I feel so weak."

Mrs Khan's voice croaked as she tried to speak.

"Give Maa some water, Mila," Irfaan asked.

Mila inclined her head towards a water jug placed on a bedside table. She moved sideways and poured half a glass of water and held it to her lips for a sip. Irfaan stood at his mother's feet. Mrs Khan drank a quarter. She laid back on the pillow. Mila put the glass down on the table by the bed. Mrs Khan closed her eyes. She looked quite pale, observed Irfaan. They stood there like dummies for about ten minutes, until Irfaan said calmly. "Let's go."

Mila looked into his eyes. They were tender again. Mila smiled. Her cheeks dimpled. All was forgiven—not forgotten. She thought it was just a lover's tiff? Their very first one? Was it supposed to be romantic? That after they went home, and he'd pull her back into his arms? Her black head would crash against his chest under the ferocity of his regrets?

They walked abreast through the hospital's Dettol infused corridors. As students they hardly noticed it reek — a future gynaecologist, and a psychiatrist, they stepped outside the building and found their driver lighting a cigarette off a fire tipped rope, snaking down a tea stall's bamboo parapet. He was just about to inhale the first smoke, when he also noted them. He dropped the cigarette and crushed it under his feet, signalling that he was bringing the car over. Mila and Irfaan waited in the crowd. The air was laced with sweet smelling monsoon rain and jasmine from the hospital gardens. The dust had settled, but the mugginess was thick. Mila spotted the car and began to walk in the lead, Irfaan following closely.

Mila opened the car door and entered. She moved over to the far end of the seat to give Irfaan enough room to get in. Irfaan entered and closed the door.

"Where do you want to go?" the driver asked.

Mila looked at Irfaan. He was engrossed in thoughts. He said. "Home."

Meaning, at Mila's house, the driver understood and took them home. This surprised Mila. She would have thought Irfaan would have liked to go to his own house, since his father was alone, and Maa, in the hospital. But Irfaan chose to go to Mila's place instead, referring to it as 'home.'

No matter, home it was then. Although they didn't talk much, it gave Mila immense joy to think that Irfaan was starting to feel at home in the House of Chowdhury, regardless. On the brink of this joy, she looked at Irfaan and smiled sweetly; her angst slowly evaporating. She was able to feel comfortable again on her way home. Her heart felt lighter, and happier. Whatever lay ahead, in her own home, within the walls of her own bedroom, she could brave any battle. What Irfaan called 'home' causally, she couldn't call his 'home' her own. Her in-law's house remained a distant address shrouded in the mist of an unfamiliar territory, yet to be conquered.

In the car, Mila viewed the same scenery. But they didn't look as colourless—the resplendent undeterred greenery from the monsoon rains. Irfaan's mood swings taught her something new. She knew him a little better. When he called her home, home, that was uplifting. That made the vagaries of Irfaan's nature more tolerable.

Yes, she needed to express her emotions more. She loved him; she knew that much. But at times she felt lost. She felt cold and numb—unromantic. She felt no romance for Irfaan the way she felt for Rahim—an emotion she could not deny. Whether or not this was right or wrong wasn't so much an issue, as was the acceptance of this fact. Life threw its most powerful illusions, yet, regardless if it was right or not; did it not feel at times that life was almost eternal, as undying as the sun itself, or the cosmos, the gasses which gave birth to thousands of sparkling stars—life's building blocks, too? But people aged, died and melted like magic— they disappeared. Romance, parental love—life disappeared like mist as though the person had never existed, as though mothers and fathers never existed. But when people lived and thrived, the throbbing life felt infinite and inexhaustible. Only in death, this other reality struck; how powerful the

271

illusion called life was. The illusion that made people believe that it was invincible. When gasses ran out, stars blinked. Blackholes exist to galvanize them, even. But life's illusion beguiled the human psyche. Mila's fanciful mind wheeled on as did the motor on its motion. She felt her mind had left her body; a caged bird flown away.

"What's on your mind, my love?" Irfaan's question interrupted her thoughts.

"Oh! No, no nothing. I was worried about Maa," she lied.

"Really? You were that concerned about her?"

He asked, looking straight at her. She didn't respond. But she looked back plainly at his searching gaze. The black rounds weren't on his eyeliners, that Mila had seen in them earlier when his anger was showing. Mila dropped her gaze, and Irfaan looked away. He was up against a brittle glass-house of formidable love. Would it withstand a crisis? He thought. She didn't feel any romance for him the way he felt for her. Irfaan's abrupt question startled Mila. "When did the mind get back into the body?" Mila felt a chill but answered him boldly. "Is the mind a caged bird that its goings and comings can be tallied?"

"Not being in the present as often as you do, sends a message, for sure."

"Maybe, but I'm clueless."

Irfaan's lips curled into a cynical smile. At the gate of the House of Chowdhury, the car stopped.

A boy came running to open them. The car slow-paced through the gates and stood still under the porch. Shimul came and stood by the car. The driver made an egress and opened Mila's side of the door. Mila stepped out on the ground of the porch. Shimul looked at Mila and found her face was pale. But she kept quiet. What could have happened between now and then, she wondered? Or was it over already?

Her own marriage was over in just two days—a mere girl of fifteen. The henna hadn't even faded. Her mother-in-law had lashed out, saying how worthless this cheap girl without a dowry was, her son had married. A motorbike could easily be in their possession now and a new wristwatch if he had married elsewhere.

Her sharp tongue was enough to make Shimul cry, when her husband too had walked in, and added fuel to fire. He pulled a half-burnt wood out of the stove and landed it brutally on her young shoulder. Shimul, the new bride, couldn't endure it. Poverty was such a curse. She ran outside and kept running until she was at the bus stop to board a Dhaka bound bus. Henna was fresh on Mila's hands as well. In the end, all boiled down to perspective—a paradox of freedom which was also enslavement; the institution of marriage, regardless of class.

Shimul stood aside and let the couple enter. Mila went in first, followed by Irfaan. Mrs Chowdhury was the first person they found sitting in her chair by the bay window through which the dying sun was entering. She looked up. Her wrinkled face was concerning.

"How is she?" she asked.

"Better, now," Mila replied.

"That's good to know. Are visitors allowed?" she asked.

"I think so. Yeah."

Mila looked at Irfaan for confirmation. Irfaan nodded.

"That's good. I won't be able to go. I'm sure others would want to. Give her my best wishes the next time you visit her."

"Of course," Irfaan said.

They pulled up two dining chairs and sat down by Mrs Chowdhury. Shimul brought a tea tray. She poured them each a cup of tea. Mrs Chowdhury looked out of the window. She appeared to be pensive. As they sipped, a crow flew in and sat on the parapet of the window. He cawed a few times clinging to its edge, then flew away. The last blush of fading red brushed the isolated clouds, like islands of the sky sea.

chilies

Nazmun Banu bit on a green chili at lunch which brought tears to her eyes. She did not tolerate hot chilies well and usually stayed away from them. Today, however, she made an exception. Shimul had picked fresh, tender chilies from the vegetable garden and served them with lunch. Mila and Irfaan were also here at the table with the rest of the family. Irfaan told Mila that he wanted to be in this house until his mother returned from the hospital. They cancelled the honeymoon; however, he didn't feel like returning while Mrs Khan was still in the hospital. Although, his father, Mr Khan was alone in the house.

Today, Mr Khan was invited to lunch. In the absence of Mrs Khan, Mrs Chowdhury thought it was only civil to have him over for meals until his wife had fully recovered. Nazmun Banu poured herself several glasses of water. Mr Khan noticed it.

"Are you all right?" he asked.

"Oh! Yes, yes."

She managed to spit out the words, somehow, between glasses of water she poured and gulped, taking deep breaths, assuaging the burning off the palette. Mr Khan smiled and ate quietly. The fish fries were good.

"Please have another piece of fish," Mila insisted.

"They're great! Who cooked them?" Mr Khan asked.

"Our maid," Mila said.

275

"Ah, I see, do you not cook at all?" he asked lightheartedly as he ate a mouth full.

"No, not much," Mila answered.

"Strangely, I thought in great zamindari tradition ladies of the house knew how to cook and cook very well, too. The reputation of the house depended on the richness of cooking."

"Yes, that is a fairly well-established notion. One that my mother-in-law here could validate," Nazmun Banu replied curtly. "As for our Mila, she is an exception. She didn't because she had other interests."

Mila listened, as her mother defended her. Mrs Chowdhury, her aunties and uncles said nothing, but looked at Mr Khan and nodded politely with a smile.

"As per this great tradition, the ladies of the house also have other skills—cutting fish on the boti knife. Am I right?" Mr Khan asked.

Irfaan felt his father's comments were sharp and pernicious. He injected it. "I don't believe that's true at all. Why would noble ladies' slave in the kitchen when they had a whole village to work in the zamindari mansions?"

"You're missing the point. The point is those were the traditions, as it was also tradition to give expensive gifts to the groom's family when they got married," Mr Khan said.

"Why? The sky's the limit, no?" Irfaan asked.

"Never mind. To change the subject," Mr Khan said. "We had a maid in our mother's house once, who had saved up every single penny she'd ever earned to build a proper trousseau for her daughter over ten years. By the time the daughter got married, she was able to afford a respectable trousseau."

Mila knew that Mr Khan implied a dowry. Mila's rather light trousseau had not satisfied them. She was very quiet. There was also a lull at the table. The Chowdhurys had only retained the title and enjoyed the prestige; that they were wealthy once whose ancestors had owned huge villages for many generations; Mr Khan wondered where had all that wealth disappeared. He suspected they still had the wealth but stashed it away. He also suspected that Mila had not received her fair share.

Where was Mila's share? He wanted to know. He looked at the ceiling of this house and decided that perhaps this big house could fetch an inheritance for Mila and his son one day. However, the members of the House of Chowdhury remained silent—to insult, a guest was not something the nobles did. They couldn't stoop so low as to be uncivil and talk about crude money.

Mila's relatives ate away in silence without engaging. Mr Khan's veiled remarks concerned them. Even Irfaan cringed with shame. He was silent, his eyes downcast. Mila frowned and thought, 'what about my jewellery? Do they not count? They were antique diamonds and precious stones handed down over many generations. Besides, the dowry system wasn't even Islamic. In the Islamic tradition, it was the groom who paid all the money—not the other way round.'. She felt cross with Irfaan for not protesting enough. She felt she didn't know them at all.

Words once spat out, couldn't be taken back—like bitter aftertaste no matter how many rinses the tongue may have had. After lunch, Mila excused herself and rose from her chair. She walked absentmindedly towards the kitchen. Peeking, through the doorway, she saw Shimul sitting with a branch of a tree in her hand, whittling it down with a sharp knife.

"What're you making Shimul?" Mila asked.

"I'm trying to carve this into a door stopper. The doors bang too loudly in the strong winds."

As they were talking, they heard Lutfun summon Shimul to clear the table. She left the half-whittled branch on the floor. Mila stepped sideways to make way for her. She pondered. Would she be entirely wrong if she thought Shimul was freer than her? Thinking earlier in the car on her way home, Shimul probably had more freedom than her. After all, this was all about perspective. The young maid's failed marriage; her life of simplicity posed a formidable question to this paradox of enslavement. Mila sauntered through the orchard alone for a while. Then she decided to go inside. By now Mrs Chowdhury was sitting on her chair at the bay window. She had taken a paan leaf out of a paan-daani.

The betel leaves were neatly placed in an age-old silver casket which belonged to Mrs Chowdhury's mother. It was an ornate decoration piece of antique as everything was around the room. Every object in this room exuded aristocracy—including the elegant Mrs Chowdhury. Be it fallen, but aristocracy had its own flavour. It was in the air, the decorum, the behaviour, the mindset, and the language.

What would the upstarts understand? Those who had seen or been aristocratic, only they knew, what it meant to be a part of a seven-generation zamindari tradition? Why? Mrs Chowdhury's paternal house still stood in her village as a testament which even time could not tarnish.

Mila sat on an empty chair by her grandma. They were flanked by Mr Khan and her uncles. Irfaan wasn't here. Her aunties were busy helping Shimul clear the table. Mrs Chowdhury took bits and pieces of betel nuts out of the paan paraphernalia—the casket, and sliced the betel with a nutcracker. She handed some to Mr Khan.

The silver casket gleamed in the afternoon sun. Mr Khan looked at it and asked. "How old is that casket?"

"Old enough," Mrs Chowdhury replied.

"I love these intricate carvings on its body," Mila said.

"Yes, this was specially made by the village silverware jeweller for my mother—your great grandmother, Mila— Begum Noor—The Lady of Lights, she was called because of her kindness. Every Friday, after the Jumma prayers she hosted a feast in the village called the Noor Begum's Shinni. A cow would be slaughtered to feed the entire village at her behest. A lot of our wealth had been mismanaged badly and destroyed sadly, until the British Sahebs arrived. They took all our powers, and a big portion of our money in taxes, making us, zamindars, impoverished, and titular heads."

"Yes, yes, I know the history. How the British robbed from our nobles to restore the fallen nobility in England. They emptied the coffers of our zamindars to fill up theirs— sad, so sad," Mr Khan sighed. "They took and they took, until they milked them dry, until they were kicked out. But, by then, they had already taken massive amounts."

Admittedly, the zamindari wealth was reduced to a puny amount after the taxes were deducted by the British Raj. The seven generations of zamindars were made poor perhaps, but no one could strip away the title. In an odd way, Mila thought that Mrs Chowdhury still believed that they ruled. All those people who visited her from the village came in droves almost every day to be with her, just to spend some time so they could chat, laugh, and cry over the lost kingdoms.

Some villagers had come to Mila's wedding too. In their hearts, they still believed that they were Mrs Chowdhury's subjects. She was still their zamindar, to whom they owed an allegiance. No matter how cruel and exploitative some of these zamindars may have been, in the heart of it, they still preferred them over a foreign rule. People never respected the British. People thought of them as brigands who had invaded the land, taking the wealth to their own decrepit kingdom. The River Kali which had flooded Mr Chowdhury's village, Pretigram conveyed a powerful message. That human narrative was both evolving and unstoppable—fragile and prone to downfall.

Mr Khan looked outside at the greying clouds; rain, anytime now. The clouds drifted along until they eclipsed the sun, drizzling and bucketed down. Mila stood up and walked towards the staircase. She went to the roof. It lent an undeterred view of the rain. She looked at it unblinkingly; at its pattering on the hard concrete surface; the tiny ponding. She could stand here and watch them all day long—logged on to the etherised sky. She thought she should have been a poet, or a novelist, not a doctor. But it was her mother's wishes that she became one for better employment prospects. Albeit, our Creator was both a poet and a scientist.

Mila lost count of time, standing here in these enchanting rains. She heard a call from downstairs, Nazmun Banu, asking her to come and bid goodbye to Mr Khan. Mila turned around reluctantly. Her father-in-law, the honoured guest, was departing. She didn't feel too warm towards him. What had happened at the lunch table was uncalled for, discussion of property and wealth, seeking the truth about Mila's inheritance from this house, when her relatives still lived here? What was Mr Khan's interest, anyway? The nosy father-in-law was also greedy.

No matter, she was going to go downstairs and be polite; it behooved her to assume a flawless nature. To be the courteous little daughter of a noble house. She tiptoed slowly down the stairs. Not looking rushed at all, she appeared poised before him. All the members were present here. Her two uncles, her aunties, Irfaan, Mrs Chowdhury, even Quasu and Shimul. In their presence, Mr Khan looked at Mila and smiled. Mila smiled back. He mumbled a goodbye and said that he would soon see them both in his house.

Irfaan walked him to the waiting car under the porch. He opened its rear door, while the chauffeur stood in readiness by the door. Irfaan stood back, as the driver entered and started the car. It ambled through the rain. Mila waved goodbye, as did all her family. Irfaan walked back into the house with them. She walked to her bedroom with him following close behind. She went up to the round table

where her radio was. She turned it on and tuned it to
popular monsoon songs. The radio station played
captivating songs; Mila, staring out through her green
windows. She envisaged a courtesan's infinite beauty, as she
lay in her splendid garden—a scene from Herman Hesse's
Siddharta.

"Come here," Irfaan said lying in bed.

Mila didn't respond. She was lost in the music, the
magic, and the rain mist.

"Come here, my love," Irfaan cajoled.

Even after that Mila didn't respond. Irfaan climbed
down the bed and walked across the room to stand by her.
He looked at her stillness, absorbed in thoughts—the caged
bird's flight, dark as the heavy rain outside. Irfaan touched
the radio with his fingers tentatively. He picked it up and
dropped it on the mosaic floor.

Shimul heard a sound. It was coming from the direction of
Mila's bedroom. She rushed and stopped in front of Mila's
closed doors—all ears on them. There was complete silence
on the other side; an uncanny stillness, except for the rain's
steady streaming. Then she heard something. Scuffles. She
heard them now. Something was happening on the other
side of the door.

"Oh my! What have you done?"

Mila's shrill voice could be heard through the closed
door.

Calm prevailed, again.

"Do you think so? Do you even think that anything would replace this priceless antique piece? You bloody upstarts? Who do you think you are? You're nothing!" Mila screamed.

Her voice was fraught with anger and confusion.

"Why? Why? To get your attention. This is love," Irfaan yelled back.

"Love? What sort of love is this?" Mila asked.

"The deep sort."

"Why? What would you understand about antiques, anyway? Where was this "deep" love of yours hidden when we were dating?" Mila shouted. "Showing your true colours, now—you cannot win love by force. Get that? Why? You and your upstart family have no regard for old objects."

"Force? I can buy you hundreds of radios. Modern, new.—" Irfaan said.

"Do you think I care for new? This was memorabilia. This was priceless!"

Shimul heard everything she needed to hear. She heard sobs. Mila started to cry out loud. Shimul began to cry too on the other side of the door. There was no hierarchy in pain, in sobbing. Shimul moved away and ran upstairs to the roof where Mila was standing a while back. The rain poured. Pods of clouds had collected all their wistful tears to shed them together. There was nothing like the rain when one had to hide tears. Just dive straight into it. The world would never know.

Shimul wondered how Mila had reacted when she saw the broken pieces of the radio. Had she stood there like dark, smoky pod clouds? Maybe she did. Lost in her thoughts. She heard Mila's frantic calls. "Shimul, Shimul?"

She took a deep breath by the door. She heard Irfaan coaxing Mila.

"Do you ever regret saying that you love me?" he said.

"Perhaps you do. Why did you marry me, Irfaan? Why did you fall in love with me?"

"I don't know. It just happened."

"Was it even love?" Mila asked.

"I felt it. I don't know," he said. "When I was calling you just then, and you didn't come. You didn't even look at me, I felt terrible. I felt jealous of the radio. I felt compelled to do something."

"You were competing with this old radio?" Mila said.

"Yes, the songs, the radio had your complete attention. Please, please Mila, don't leave me."

Shimul knocked on the door. Mila asked her to enter. Shimul saw all the radio parts scatter on the floor.

"I'll collect the radio parts and take them to the antique dealer at the end of the alley, Shimul said."

Her words instilled some hope in Mila's heart, as Irfaan continued to look at her incredulously. Her emotional depth attracted him. Even now he felt like holding her in his arms.

"You're really amazing, Shimul," Irfaan said. "I wonder why your parents never sent you to school."

"My parents were poor. And we were five sisters growing up in the one-room thatched house. My father was suffering from TB; marrying me off meant one less mouth to feed."

"Yes, yes of course," Irfaan mumbled.

"Shimul, can you please clear this before Daadi Amma or anyone else sees it? They're probably taking a siesta," Mila said, controlling her emotions as her voice crackled.

"Yes, of course, I'll be right back."

Shimul disappeared through the open doorway. She returned with a brown, gunny sack. She collected them one by one, each tiny screw at a time with her nimble index and thumb—the wires, the knobs, and the many broken parts, bits, and pieces of nuts and bolts. The radio must be fixed, she thought. It was not just an antique piece. This was an emblem of what this family stood for. The rain looked dense and white. Shimul looked out of the window, as did Mila.

"Not now, Shimul. After the rain stops, I'll come with you too. We'll take a rickshaw," Mila said.

"Okay, Mila Apa. I'll just collect them for now and put them in my room. No one will know about it," she said.

Shimul knew how badly this would reflect on the groom; that the most revered guest of the house had done this. No one must know about it, of course, especially because this had happened so early in the marriage. However, Mila's heart had begun to turn. She was going to forgive him because he had apologized to the point of crying and begging. But her patience was wearing thin. A new sensation was slowly creeping inside her heart. Rahim Ali's image crept up. Oh! These memories! She wished she could kill them.

Mila calmed down and lay in bed. She turned on her right side with her back towards Irfaan, who was still standing by the window. He followed her to bed, and she felt his touch on her arm. Irfaan pulled her towards him.

"Are you still mad?" he asked.

"What do you expect? You broke my radio," Mila hissed.

"I'll buy you another."

"You're funny, you know. What could ever replace this?"

Irfaan was quiet. He held her in his strong arms and pulled her towards him. Mila struggled to get out. She said that she needed to go to the repair shop with Shimul.

"I'll come too," he said.

"No, you won't. I'll take a rickshaw, the only other person who can come is Shimul."

"Okay," Irfaan sighed.

Mila looked at his remorseful face and wondered. She was confused, 'who was this person?' But she said nothing. She got out of bed and slipped her feet into a pair of sandals set by the bed. She stood up with a jerk and fixed her loose anchal on her shoulder. Her handbag was in the almirah. She took the almirah key from the drawer of the mosaic table and opened it. She pulled her bag from the bottom shelf. She closed the almirah, locked it, and put the key in her bag, instead of the drawer. She looked at Irfaan who was simply staring at her. Irfaan felt that trust was beginning to fade between the two of them.

"Okay, see you soon," she said.

"Do you need money? Hang on, you'll need money to get this fixed," Irfaan said.

"I have money. I don't need any of yours."

"Don't be like that, please. I said I was sorry. Just take this."

He had climbed down from the bed and walked a few steps closer to his wife. He pulled his wallet from his trousers' pocket and tried to put it in Mila's palm by force. She struggled. He held her waist with an arm giving her no leeway. When Mila refused to hold the wallet, he opened her bag and dropped it inside, and snapped it back. Done. He released her. Mila glared at him. He looked back plainly and smiled. Unbelievable, Mila thought. She turned around and stalked towards the door. She opened it and stepped out and closed the door behind her.

When she was gone, Irfaan looked placid—a calm sea as though nothing had happened. As though he had it all under control. He smiled, while she raged—turbulent sea inside her.

Shimul was ready with a gunny sack. She held it tightly in her grip as they approached the front porch. The rain had abated. They walked towards the gate and waited by the roadside for a rickshaw. They saw one, Shimul hailed it to stop. It stopped. Holding on to the hood, they hopped on. Mila first, then Shimul. As they sat abreast on the rickshaw, Mila told the rickshaw-wallah where to go. To the antique dealers up the slip lane.

The rickshaw was in motion. It was slow. This slow movement triggered lazy thoughts in Mila's mind. She looped. Come to think of it, Mila pondered, she never felt any notable surge of romance in her heart for Irfaan. Love came, stayed for a few days, then it dissipated. She never felt overwhelmingly crazy to want him; to pine away, to miss, fear of losing, the palpitations, the fluttering, the breathlessness, the feelings of anguish or togetherness; soft blushes. To feel compelled to be in their company. She felt none of those emotions. What she felt was a necessity. That in this society, she needed to be coupled to look complete. This couldn't be defined as love? What was love anyway? She asked herself. She felt cold, she felt numb despite all her emotional maturity. Aunty Prema's and Uncle Ashik would have known love—and Irfaan, for all his professed love, oddly, how far would he go to show its intensity?

She thought of Irfaan. He must have laid down in bed by now—a calm face that knew no quarrels. A beautiful, sensible face. Perhaps, he had even picked up a book by now from Mila's shelf. He had a brilliant track record with impressive distinctions and scholarships. His scholarships still continued. Soon he would become a psychiatrist too, once the finals were over. What was he reading anyway? She sat beside Shimul, on the slow-paced rickshaw, looking at the rain occasionally. What book was he reading right now? Or, was he taking a siesta?

Shimul sat very still. "I hope they'll be able to fix it," she mumbled.

"It sure is a try," Mila said. "It is not enough to just put the parts back in. Even I could do it. The radio must work."

Shimul had no answers.

"Do you think Shimul would play songs again?" Mila asked.

"Who knows?" Shimul answered.

Mila almost wished that suffering gave Shimul a third eye; one which would enable her to see beyond. But a third-eye or not, Mila realised that their sufferings had broken a class barrier as far as the two of them were concerned. They were not the mistress and the maid, right now, but two women equal and united in suffering. While the maid had the courage to break through and start life anew, the mistress didn't. The mistress carried too much burden. She didn't want to hurt her mother; Nazmun Banu's dream to see her daughter happily married. Shimul had the freedom to choose. She had the courage to embark on it. Mila didn't.

The rickshaw ride was now minutes away from the shop. It pulled over at the shopfront. Mila opened the bag and brought out a purse to pay him. But the man said he wanted to wait until they were done. He would take them back, as they may not find another rickshaw in this impending rain.

"Very well, then," Mila mumbled. She climbed down, nodding to him, Shimul after her.   They both entered the shop. Behind the shop counter, a skinny, young man stood tinkering with wires, nuts, and bolts. Attaching them to a metallic piece of plate. His hair had a gleam from lavish use of hair oil. It was pasted flat on its skull like a skullcap. He looked at them without even a glimmer of a smile. Shimul was equally glum. She handed the bag of broken pieces over the counter. He took it and opened the bag.

"Are all the pieces here?" he asked.

"Yes, I think so," Mila replied. "Can you fix the radio?"

"Leave it with me and come back after ten days. I may have an answer for you, then. Also leave your address, just in case."

He said casually pushing a notepad and a pen towards them, looking into the bag with his mouth pursed.

"How much?" Mila asked, writing her address as the House of Chowdhury. There was just one in the neighbourhood.

"Advance payment of a hundred takas now and pay the rest later. Say, do you wish to play the radio?" he asked.

"Yes, of course, if that's still possible," Mila said.

"I'll see what I can do."

Mila opened her purse and handed him a one hundred taka note. He took it and shoved it through a half-open wooden drawer under the counter. He gave her an invoice. That was all the paperwork needed. Mila put it in her purse. She turned around, and Shimul too at the same time, as they both stepped out of the shop. Mila saw the rickshaw-wallah resting on the seat of the rickshaw. As soon as Mila hailed, he peddled his vehicle towards them.

Absent-mindedly, Shimul turned around and looked back into the shop and found the young radio mechanic gazing at her. She quickly turned away and followed Mila hastily into the rickshaw. The shopkeeper had smiled, Shimul thought, he had also winked at her, come to think of it. Shimul blinked. When they were gone, the shopkeeper grabbed the bag of radio pieces off the counter and took it to the far end of the shop. He shelved it by all the other orders of scrunched up brown paper bags and a few gunny sacks.

Mila jumped into the rickshaw and slid sideways on the seat to give Shimul space to get on. She gathered the saree's achaal in a bunch on her shoulder. However, she didn't realise that the long trail of the achaal had dropped into the spokes of the rickshaw's wheel. When the rickshaw began to move the achaal too began to wheel into it, until Mila started to feel some strain on her shoulder. By the time she realised it, most of the achaal had flowed into the wheel into a messy entanglement. Shimul saw it and asked the puller to stop by the side of the road. He looked back and saw the entanglement. He stopped the rickshaw immediately.

Shimul jumped out like a springboard and came around on Mila's side to aid her. Mila climbed down too and squatted on the road, trembling like a leaf. Shimul and the rickshaw-puller slowly unwound the achaal from the wheel by rotating it anti-clockwise to make it free. She felt relieved as she looked at the battered saree trail which was torn in many places. It was one of her favourite sarees; she felt wistful. She looked at Shimul and gave her a hug. Also, gave the rickshaw-puller a nod of approval. She stood up and found herself surrounded by curious passers-by, looking at this little street drama.

She climbed back up on the vehicle and sat carefully this time, tucking the crumpled and torn achaal into the saree's petticoat securely around the waist. She glanced at the motley crowd. And saw two hands waving in the crowd. She realised that it was Shuvo. She waved back and lip-synced to him to join her later for tea. He understood and nodded.

The rickshaw-puller brought them home at the sturdy iron gates of the house. She and Shimul were both quiet for the rest of the trip. She paid the man and got off. On second thoughts, she took more money out of the purse and gave him some tips for releasing the achaal. The last raindrops were just ebbing into slight drizzles. Shimul and Mila walked through the open pedestrian gate into the house. No sooner had they stepped in than they heard Quasu breaking into laughter. But they also saw Prema's other boy who stood by the gate, too afraid to go into the house. The moment he saw Mila, he shot out and disappeared next door.

It wasn't the best of days. Too many incidents had happened in one day. Mila walked across the yard thinking of all the affairs her father and her uncle had. How were the children affected? Did anyone even stop to think of them?

No—she didn't see herself any differently from Prema and her ex-husband's children. Being like this—this—'otherness,' caused insurmountable pain—an 'otherness' which wasn't exotic, or exceptional in anyway. But a sense of being an outsider in their own homes—of not belonging anywhere. They did not belong to their biological parents any more than the strays of the lane—who had split up, walked away, and had other children with their new partners.

Of course, they had been walled out. What did it really mean to be an 'outsider'? Or being walled out within one's own family? Such children waking up every morning to wet pillows; their mothers and fathers had parted because they chose other lovers. What their friends took for granted— security, warmth, and love of a family. The 'outsiders' didn't feel the same way with their new fathers or mothers. They felt deprived of full happiness without biological parents living under the same roof as a family, taken over by the half brothers and sisters who had more rights and biological parents.

Money could never buy happiness, Mila thought. She always knew this, but now she had the actual realisation. She had a big, extended family, who loved her dearly. But it did not compensate for a core family of her own. No one could understand this pain. Even the pullers who drove their rickshaws all day long, those who had no money, no power, who had lived practically in poverty all their lives, were happier than she could ever imagine. Her husband had added to that misery, now.

But she made a decision. She decided to not go down the same path as her Aunty Prema, Uncle Ashik, or her father, Ekram. Neither would she file for a divorce to make her mother Nazmun Banu sad. Irfaan was temperamental. But she can cope better because she thought she knew him now.

neighbour

Raja Hashem, Prema's ex-husband, was the closest neighbour to the House of Chowdhury. Living in such close proximity to a common boundary wall, which too had a narrow door cut out once for convenience, was now getting increasingly inconvenient both for the children as well as their mother, Prema. Her little boy continued to appear in the front yard of the House of Chowdhury to get a glimpse of the mother, as Prema continued to avoid him. It was hard for her too after all they were biologically connected; the resilient boy kept coming back. He would walk through the doorway and step into the yard like a ghost, loiter around without success. After a while, he would return home to the stepmother. He never had the courage to come inside.

The three children were much older now. Since the civil war and the birth of Quasu, the girls were in their early twenties. This marriage should have worked. Raja Hashem was a gentleman to the hilt. Yet, Prema found him too insipid, who read all day, knew no romance, and lectured morality. On the other hand, Ashik, well he had a bit of the devil in him, didn't he, which Prema found heroic?

Yes, Raja remarried. This time to a nice gentle girl without much physical beauty. He realised the shortcomings of a beautiful face—his fair wife had left him. He had come this close from falling into depression with the three small children, marrying for modesty, and values. His second wife, Shoma, Shoma Hashem possessed such virtues. She was religious, kind, and compassionate and loved his children dearly. Raja Hashem thought he found some peace

295

at last, in this quiet woman of faith who believed that her happiness depended on her husband's happiness. She was only too ready to please him and his children. Love wasn't factored into this marriage at all. She did her daily chores efficiently. And was loyal to him more than what was necessary to keep the family together. Happiness was elusive, anyway, Raja Hashem thought wisely. He opted for contentment instead of excitement.

The morning cuckoo bird's songs worked like a magic clock. Shoma woke up with a long yawn. Sunday, a weekend, she squinted at the radiant sun streaming through the window curtains dancing in the soft morning breeze. Raja Hashem was not in bed. She sat up and peaked at the verandah, where he usually read his morning newspaper; where she also brought him his morning tea. Today that chair was empty. Shoma found herself dithering between her chores and an urge to find her husband. She always had a big family to feed for breakfast, lunch, and dinner. Prema's three children were her responsibility now. The two girls, Payel and Douwel, and Liton, the boy. Today was no exception.

Shoma went into the kitchen, contemplating where her family went this morning. She took some flour in a bowl and sat down on a low stool. Her maid, a young girl, waited for instructions. She began to knead the flour, while she asked her maid to fry an omelette, and also to cook vegetable curry. Her young maid took water gourds, potatoes, onions, and eggplants for a curry. And eggs in a bowl.

She toiled in the kitchen all day long, feeding her family of five. After the chores, she was just too tired to think about anything else. Let alone think about philosophy or the purpose of life. Her only purpose was to complete this journey upon which she had now embarked. It was a clear mission which Allah had bestowed upon her. To save those motherless children and see them through life. Be their mother. Always be there for them. No other mission appeared greater than this to this plain, good-hearted pious woman. Yet, she was a stepmother, but she was so much more.

She heard them. She heard the children and her husband entering through the entrance. Quickly, wiping her hands in her saree, she rushed out of the kitchen to greet them.

"Where have you all been?" she asked.

"Oh! It's a long story," Payel answered.

"Can we have breakfast, Maa," Douwel asked.

"Yes, of course. I'll be back in five minutes with the chapatis."

The girls went to wash up, and Raja flopped down in his usual chair on the verandah with the newspaper. Everything was back to normal again. Everything fell in its slot.

When the children returned to the breakfast table, Shoma brought them hot chapatis straight off the stove with the maid's assistance. Raja Hashem was still outside reading his newspaper when Shoma called him to join them. He came in looking content, pulled a chair, and sat down with the family.

"So, where have you all been?" Shoma asked, tearing a bit of the chapati.

"We went walking down the alley all the way to Mosque Square," Liton answered.

"A morning walk? How nice," Shoma asked.

"Yes, it was going really well until we saw uncle on our way back," Liton said.

"Which uncle?" Shoma asked.

She looked at her husband and saw the radiance wan from the children's faces. Their jaws dropped, as they quietly ate. Shoma too ate in silence. The maid entered with a tea tray which she put down on the end of the table. The teapot was covered in an embroidered tea cozy of multi-coloured flowers.

Shoma rose from her chair. She saw a dead cockroach lying on the floor at the edge of the table's leg. She called out to the maid to broom it off and walked towards the end of the table to the tea tray. She poured tea for her husband and for herself; it splashed, and the spoons tinkled as she added sugar and milk from the pots. She came back to her chair and handed a cup on its saucer to her husband across the table and sat down with her own cup. As she sipped tea, she also looked around at all the glum faces.

"So? Who did you see and where?" Shoma asked.

"Uncle Ashik," Liton said. "We saw him on the roof of the House of Chowdhury. He was exercising in the fresh air."

"Keeping fit, hey? That's a good thing, right?' Shoma asked.

"I guess," Liton said.

"Was he alone?" she asked.

"No," Douwel replied. "Maa was with him. She saw us."

"What did she do then?"

"She just pretended not to notice us," Payel said.

"Really? And how do you know?"

"Because Liton waved at her. She saw. I saw, she saw. We all saw what she saw. But she quickly moved away."

Shoma was quiet and so were the children. The girls had finished breakfast and they got up from their chairs. They left abruptly without pushing back the chairs to the table. Shoma knew what was eating them. She put a lot of effort into this family to keep it going smoothly, and she managed very well most times; still, there were moments when she thought she was failing. Even with all of her "forty-thousand" kindness, and sacrifices, she couldn't take their mother's place, nor that of the ex-wife in Raja's heart. A raw pain gnawed through their lives, as they pined away to get a glimpse of the fair Prema, like a moth to candlelight they were drawn towards her regardless of being consumed by it.

With a sigh, she gulped the last mouthful of the tea. Raja put his hand across the table and held hers in a grip and squeezed it for a second, then he released it. He rose from his chair to return to his newspaper as she started to clear the table with the maid's aid.

At that moment, in the House of Chowdhury, Quasu was laughing. Mila walked towards him and found him on the verandah with her husband. Irfaan was telling him a joke, the reason for the delightful squealing. She stood quietly near the door right behind them, observing Irfaan's demeanor and his playful moment with her little cousin. She didn't fret; she only observed. Quasu saw her first.

"There's Mila Apa," he screamed.

Irfaan turned around and grinned.

"Ah, there you're, all good?" he asked.

"So far so good. Mila said looking somewhat distracted.

"Why this sullen look? Has anything happened?" he asked.

"No, nothing has happened, But thank you for asking," Mila said.

"It's the radio, isn't it? You told me yesterday that you would know after ten days if it will work again. I'll buy you a new one regardless, whether or not it works?" he said again.

He had a habit of repeating himself like a broken record, Mila figured. She flashed him an angry glance and thought you would never get it, would you? She turned around to go to her bedroom to get changed. The soaked, torn saree was lying on the floor since yesterday. It needed to be thrown away. She entered her bedroom, but Irfaan followed her, right behind. He closed the door. Before Mila could proceed any further, he grabbed her in his arms. He had a strong embrace. She buried her head in his chest.

"Do you have any idea, any idea at all how much I love you?" he whispered. "I was even ready to fight the rains to get your attention. You just seem to melt into nothingness at times, as though you're in some kind of warfare with the windmills fighting it for no apparent reason. As if I don't exist. While I, in flesh and blood, am here, waiting and waiting patiently so you would turn around, and look at me, instead of the rain and the radio. Look at me just once and come to me. Oh! My love, where do you go? Where do you lose yourself?"

For some reason, Mila's eyes became wet. She began to sob silently on Irfaan's distended chest. Irfaan felt her hot tears seep through his cotton shirt. He held her close, then closer. He lifted her face by the chin and looked into her wet eyes. They were large, brown eyes of ponded tears, meeting his tender looks. Her heart turned in a moment and she thought maybe, Irfaan's love for her was deep, that it was unfathomable. Maybe this was how people were supposed to love. She wouldn't know.

She felt his yearning for her. That must be it. He may have broken her antique radio, but it was still just an object. What could be more precious than this? His love, this true love. Mila forgave him in that instant. She touched his lips with her fingers. His lips trembled and seized hers demandingly. They kissed each other and made up.

Soon Quasu came and knocked on the door. Irfaan smiled and disengaged from her embrace, holding Mila with one hand, he turned sideways and extended a hand to open the door for him. He entered and asked if Irfaan wanted to play ball with him.

"Okay, okay, go outside now. Go already. I need to get changed," Mila said aloud laughingly.

"We're, we're. Come Quasu, let's go out, give your sister some privacy."

He mumbled regardless of what Quasu understood. They darted closing the door behind them again leaving Mila in the bedroom. Mila bolted the door and stood before the mirror by the window. She looked at herself. She picked up the torn saree from the floor. It had netted holes all over the achaal. There was no way this could be salvaged. Saree, the oldest dress in the world, a one piece untailored wrap, worn with a top called, a nivy, a word used to describe another piece of untailored cloth tied around the breasts in ancient India. Today, it evolved into this, but it still breathed the allurement of the ancient air.

Mila opened the almirah and pulled out another laundered saree from the stack. It was a navy peacock blue cotton with a running red border. She put it on the bed and unfolded it to check if it had a blouse. It sure did. Her mother Nazmun Banu was meticulous in keeping her things organized. On a monsoon blue evening, what could be more magical than a peacock blue saree? She stood in front of the mirror and wrapped it around her slim waist. She took lipstick from the mosaic table where the antique radio had been and dabbed some on her lips. Pressing her lips together, she plumped them up slightly. Opening the doors, she dashed out of the room.

Shimul was passing by. She looked at her transformation in awe but walked away silently. She thought about how quickly people forgot or forgave. Mila looked at her and instructed her to take the torn saree away and give it to a needy person. Shimul understood and she decided to keep it herself in her battered trunk which she hoped to give to her little sister when she went to visit them over her next holidays. She would sew the torn holes and colour it, the same way she had coloured her white saree, soaking it in the flowery water pigment of many shiuly stems.

Mila had perhaps forgiven Irfaan. But forgetting the incident was another matter. She suppressed the gnawing memory of sorrows and misgivings. For now, she was happy and was happy again to be just happy. Her heart fluttered. It danced like a peacock in stunning plumage. She floated in the memory of Hesse's Siddhartha—the enchanting blue garden of love where Siddhartha mated with his beloved. She walked towards the open door which led into the orchard of the House of Chowdhury. There they were—all three, Uncle Ashik, Uncle Sheri and Irfaan, sitting together and chatting. Her Aunty Prema and her mother had also joined them. Mila overheard a few words drifting in the air. War, property, and sales. Irfaan was telling her uncles about his experience of the war. That they had to board a launch to get away from Dacca/Dhaka. The launch owner was kind enough to feed them dal and rice, molasses, and dry rice—muri for breakfast each morning, which he, Irfaan, had to share with his servant boy upon her mother's instruction.

Irfaan was telling them that he and the boy ate from the same plate. The molasses mixed with dry rice was halved on the plate. This reminded Mila of her refugee days, as she noted the grimness on her two uncle's faces who continued to listen to Irfaan's story with rapt attention. He was saying how people fled leaving their children behind on the roadside, innumerable children who were lost from their parents.

"Say, Uncle Ashik, do you have any plans for this house?" Irfaan asked.

"No, not really. We are still living here, and the house is in Amma's name. When our father built the house he registered it in her name. Unless she agrees, we can't do anything," Ashik paused. "Besides, we like it—this sprawling house."

"Yes, it is. Come to think of it, I have been to the roof, but I have not been upstairs at all to your quarters," Irfaan said.

"Oh, there are five bedrooms upstairs. One is vacant at the moment. I and Sheri have two rooms, and Nazmun bhabi's room is beside Mila's maiden room which is empty since Mila has a new room downstairs. Across the hallway downstairs is Amma's living quarters. Her own sitting room for her guests and relatives from the village.

"It's a beautiful old house. I love the opulent balconies upstairs," Irfaan mused.

"Yes, it is beautiful, isn't it?" Sheri whispered.

All this time while they were chatting, Mila was well within earshot, but she didn't join them. She let Irfaan gel with her uncles in a male bonding kind of way. She didn't want to disrupt the process.

She busied herself organising the cushions on the heavy chairs of the living room. She came out into the orchard back and forth to fetch water from a shallow well under a guava tree. She took a pail of water and took it indoors and outdoors to water the money plants and the ever dry white lilies. She carried the bucket into the living room. These were potted plants of overhanging ferns of various families. They were set on corner tables and wall shelves. She took a tall vase, set on a centrepiece, and carried it out into the garden by the house, a narrow strip of flower bed closer to her bedroom window. Through the window, she saw Shimul making their bed. She called out to Shimul to hand her a pair of scissors, which she did through the windows. She selected some flowers and cut a few red shoe blacks in tall stems.

Mila sat down on a grassy patch, as she organised the flowers in the vase. She picked up the vase and the scissors and came indoors, feeling satisfied with the arrangement. She called out to Shimul again and asked her to take the scissors away to put them back where they were in her bedroom. Mila poured some pail water into the vase to fill it up to half a jar, enough to keep the flower stems moist.

The red, open flowers bowed slightly over the vase. Mila took it over to a corner table by the bay window in the living room, between two straight-backed chairs, and placed it in the middle. She looked out of the window and saw that dusk had crept in. The men of the house were still chatting in the orchard. She drew the heavy curtains across the window and lit a few shaded lamps. She came back and stood by the door, leading to the orchard, when Lutfun sauntered and stood by her. A silent orchard; a crow was cawing in the distant sky, looking like a black flying dot.

The male chatted about the war. Irfaan's mother wore a rag for a saree for days on end. The little boy, his servant companion, and he slept on the deck of the launch without pillows and blanket; cold and hungry. Irfaan often woke up in the middle of the night. One night, he tried to pull the corner of a blanket from a stranger sleeping next to him. It was rudely pulled away by the owner of the blanket. The little servant boy tried to edge his sleepy head on another man's pillow, but he too was rudely shunned. Stories—one too many, continued to be told and retold. Mila stood with Lutfun standing in the dining room's sliding door, listening in with arms folded. A scream startled them.

canary

"What was that?" Lutfun and Mila cried together and ran in the direction of the scream. They thought it sounded like Shimul. In the dark kitchen lit up by stove firelights, Shimul had been sitting on the floor dyeing yet another saree. Mila's torn saree from the incident of the rickshaw; no one else knew about this incident, except her. Mila and Lutfun were the first ones to respond to the cry. As they stepped out of the house into the front yard, they found some debris of bricks and cement on the edge of the kitchen. They also found Shimul lying here, under heaps of bricks.

"Oh my, what's the matter?" Mila cried out.

"Shimul, Shimul can you hear me?" Lutfun asked.

By now the men had come over too and stood around the debris. Irfaan was the first to remove a big chunk of a cement block off Shimul's knees. The others jumped in to rescue her from underneath. They were so engrossed in getting Shimul out that they had not noticed that the kitchen wall had collapsed altogether. A small portion fell over her. Shimul had fainted. Mila felt a pulse; the men pulled her out and quickly ushered her inside.

Her injuries were great. She had to be taken to the hospital. Sheri rushed into the dining room. On the wall of the dining room, the car key hung on a nail board. Sheri promptly grabbed them and returned to Mila's bedroom where Shimul lay in agony with her head in Mila's lap and Mila, gently caressing her forehead.

"I'm getting the car ready. She needs to go to the hospital immediately."

Sheri rushed out of the room, and promptly returned to Mila's room. Irfaan and Sheri lifted Shimul and carried her into the car, followed by Lutfun and Mila. Lutfun got into the car first, then Shimul's head was placed in her lap inside the car and feet on Mila's as she sat on the other end of the seat. Mila held Shimul's impaired knees gently. In the front, Sheri sat at the wheels and Irfaan beside him, Sheri driving them to the medical college emergency. They were all quiet in the car, but Irfaan was thinking of how this had happened. What may have caused it?

"What do you think happened here?" Irfaan asked.

He inclined his head towards Sheri.

"Hmm, I don't know. The old kitchen wall fell down, I guess. It is an old house, you know."

"But old houses usually have sound structural engineering, unlike new homes."

"Still, it happens sometimes. When we go home we need to check the walls. There maybe a few hairline cracks in the kitchen walls," Sheri said. "The house is in disrepair. It needs to be renovated. Such a big house, too. Someday the roof itself may give in. Sadly, the wall fell on our Shimul today. Thankfully, it was just a small portion of the kitchen wall, not the entire roof or something."

Irfaan sat thinking. Mila, who was sitting in the back, could see him from an angle. He looked absorbed. She was wondering what he maybe pondering. Was he thinking of a solution? The car pulled up at the hospital emergency. Sheri

parked the car and turned off the ignition. He came out and
rushed towards the emergency to find a stretcher. He
bumped into two ward boys, whom he asked to find a
stretcher trolley to bring outside. They brought it out to the
car followed by Sheri. Mila and Lutfun pulled Shimul out
gently and placed her on the stretcher. The boys then took
her into the emergency. Lutfun and Mila said they wanted to
stay overnight with Shimul. If the men wanted to leave, they
could.

Irfaan walked over and stood by Mila. He looked as
though he almost didn't want to leave, or leave Mila in the
hospital, rather. Mila looked at him and smiled. She said it
was okay because she was used to night shifts in the hospital
as a final year medical student which Irfaan knew better
than anyone present. But he lingered as though he almost
didn't wish her to do night duties anymore. As though he
didn't wish her to be a doctor.

"Go now. Go already you two. We will be fine," Mila
laughed.

"Of course, you will be," Sheri said. "Come, Irfaan let's
go now, the canary has opened our eyes to a fractured house
that needs proper investigation before the roof itself falls
through. Something needs to be done fast. So, come now.
We will come back and check on them later in the evening
when we bring them dinner."

Irfaan grabbed Mila's hand next to his and squeezed it
for a second before he let go. Her arm fell to her side. Lutfun
and Sheri saw that moment of endearment and smiled.
Irfaan took a step and stood abreast of Sheri, who was
standing by the car. Sheri walked over to the driver's seat,

opened the door, and entered. Irfaan did the same; he opened the door to the front passenger's seat. As Sheri started the car and drove away, Lutfun and Mila rushed towards the hospital.

Shimul had regained consciousness. But she was in pain. The emergency doctors suspected she may have multiple fractures throughout her body, which needed to be confirmed with proper tests and x-rays. In the meantime, she was put on pain relief and could barely talk. But she had opened her eyes enough to see that Mila and Lutfun were standing at her bedside looking concerned. She forced a smile but her eyes welled up as uncontrollable tears rolled down her cheeks. Mila wiped them off and whispered strength into Shimul to the effect that she was young and that she would be okay.

What if? What if she wasn't, okay? Would she become permanently paralyzed or wheel-chair bound? Thoughts were racing through Shimul's head. No one knew what uncertainty lay ahead, but she would have to be bed-bound for many days to come, for sure. As she lay in the hospital bed, Lutfun and Mila, sat erectly on two stools by her side.

This was the same hospital where Mrs Khan was also being treated. Mila and Lutfun sat here for a while. Mila looked at Lutfun and told her that she was going to see Mrs Khan. Lutfun nodded. Mila stood up and smiled at Shimul. She told her to be brave and that she would be right back. When she came out of the emergency, she walked towards the staircase to climb two levels up. By now, she had become quite tired of her stiff sitting for hours. She even yawned as she came up laboriously up those stairs and made it to the level. As she came closer to Mrs Khan's room, she heard voices that sounded like Mr Khan's. She stopped in front of the room to catch a breath. The door was ajar. She could clearly hear the conversation between Mr and Mrs Khan. He was telling Mrs Khan about Shimul's accident.

"Irfaan called a while ago just before I left home. There has been an accident in the Chowdhury house; a maid has been hurt. Apparently, she has been admitted to this hospital, too. Mila and Lutfun are here with her. Say, hasn't Mila come around to see you yet?" he asked.

"No, unless she came and went and hadn't disturbed me because I was asleep," she replied.

"Yes, I don't know. But about the House of Chowdhury, Mrs Chowdhury should get the will ready; and it should be in Mila's name, so Irfaan can start work on the house," he said.

"Start work?' What do you mean?" she asked.

"Well, it is an old, decrepit house. It could collapse any day. What happened must not be taken lightly. Irfaan knows a few fine builders who can demolish the house and build new apartments. Mila and Irfaan could have their own apartment. Mrs Chowdhury's days are numbered; she could go any day now. After she goes, Irfaan's share of the property is confirmed."

"All of it? What about her uncles?"

"Well, if Irfaan takes the responsibility of rebuilding it, he could claim at least one apartment. You don't know what those uncles could do, maybe exclude Mila. Didn't you see

311

how light her trousseau was? She practically brought nothing! What resell value would those semi-precious stone jewellery fetch? Cash-cash, that's what I'm saying."

"Maybe," she murmured. "But her uncles and her father are still the legal inheritors."

Mila was stunned. Her House of Chowdhury demolished, and flattened to the ground? And this was her own father-in-law hatching a conspiracy. He had already killed Daadi Amma. Was Irfaan in on it, too? Oh! This was happening all too fast; too early in the marriage. She felt dizzy. But she also thought perhaps she misunderstood them in her tired mind. Maybe, this was not what her father-in-law actually meant. No, she must be a good daughter and not make these wild accusations or a rubbish pile of misinterpretations. She must make her marriage work. She knocked on the door slightly and entered without waiting for an invitation. Mr Khan smiled at her and stood up from his chair, welcoming Mila.

"There you're finally. Come in, come in. How is the maid?" he asked.

"No, not good. Doctors think she may have multiple fractures," Mila said.

Looking at her depressed demeanour and the unceremonious blunt way in which she spat out her words, made Mr Khan wonder if Mila overheard anything. But he quickly squashed his doubts, saying. "Oh! Sad, So sad. But It's an old house. It will slowly give in, you know."

Mila heard it, but her attention was drawn to the doctors' chart lying on a table beside the bed. She walked around Mr Khan and picked it up. Glancing through the papers, she found a release letter, which said that Mrs Khan had been discharged.

"Oh! You've been discharged. When did the doctors give you this?" she asked.

"Just before he walked in," she said, pointing to her husband.

"Are you ready to go then?" Mila asked.

"Yes, nearly, I need to get changed and organise my stuff."

"Of course. I'll help," Mila said.

Looking around the room, Mila packed her belongings in a small black leather suitcase perched on a high table, by the hospital bed. She packed cups and saucers, clothes, all neatly into the suitcase. She asked Mr Khan to step out of the room, so Mrs Khan could get out of the hospital gown and back in saree. She took out a saree, a petticoat, and a matching blouse. Mr Khan gave them a private moment and took himself outside. Mila stood Mrs Khan up and asked her to take her gown off and put on the saree. It took her about fifteen minutes. Once she was ready to leave, Mila picked up her suitcase and slowly walked her out where Mr Khan was standing. He saw them and extended his hand to take the suitcase from Mila.

"I'll take you both to the lift. It's not far," Mila said.

Mrs Khan looked healthy. She walked them into the lift. A lift-man was sitting inside. Mila told him to go downstairs. Downstairs, they walked through the hospital.

Mila told them that she would take care of the bills. She saw them out at the entrance. She watched Mr Khan help his wife down the exit stairs outside of the hospital building and walk her down to the parking lot; it was well into the night. Mila was starting to feel hungry. Her Uncle Sheri hadn't come back with the dinner yet. Or maybe he had by now. She slowly walked back to Lutfun and Shimul.

Lutfun was still sitting on the stool and Shimul was in agony. Lutfun looked at Mila when she entered.

"Where were you?" she hissed.

"I went to see my mother-in-law. She has just been released."

"Oh, that's quite a coincidence," she said.

"Yes," she said quietly.

"Everything okay?" Lutfun asked.

"Yes. How is Shimul?" Mila asked.

"Doctors have come and gone. They don't say much. I think they must be waiting for the reports. Oh, yeah, your uncle was here with dinner. I haven't eaten yet. I was waiting for you."

Lutfun pointed at the dinner packets on the empty stool and put them on the floor for Mila to sit. Mila saw a large bag of stacked dinner containers. She took one out and opened it. It had curried beef in it. The other containers had rice, dal, vegetables, and fish. There were two dinner plates, and two flasks of tea and water bottles. Mila and Lutfun each pulled out a plate from underneath and served themselves some rice from the containers spread on a hospital bedside table. Mila plopped some gravy beef and dal on the rice. And Lutfun, fish, and dal.

They ate silently. Slowly mixing rice in and out of the yellow gravy and the dal, fingers moving through the rice. Small packs of mouthfuls one at a time. Lutfun finished first. She poured herself a cup of water attached to the flask bottle. She drank half a cup and used the rest to wash her soiled hand over the dinner plates, twisting and turning her fingers. She looked at Mila's long fingers as they negotiated through the rice.

Mila finished shortly. She stood up, picked up the two plates, and walked cautiously out of the ward, to not spill the soiled water from Lutfun's plate. She walked towards the hospital bathrooms. She turned back and saw Lutfun sitting, with one hand palming her cheek. Mila murmured. "I'll be right back."

When Mila had gone, Lutfun looked at the maid. Shimul was on pain relief, but she could not move much. Lutfun stood up and walked over to ask her if she needed anything. She whispered that she wanted a change of position on the side. Not knowing where the severe fractures were, Lutfun tried to roll her on her side by gently holding her waist. Shimul winced in pain.

"Imagine, if the entire roof had fallen on you," Lutfun said.

Lutfun shivered, even as she uttered those words. A sensation of fear went through Shimul too, as she looked at her; she blinked and closed her eyes. A small portion of the

315

wall had fallen on her legs. Her bones were probably all broken. Was she going to be out of a job now? How was she going to survive? Questions, one too many. Mila returned with clean plates. They still had some greasy yellow stains on them and a curry smell, the same as the fingernails. Lutfun put the plates back with containers inside the bag.

The night was long. Mila caught a glimpse of Shimul. She whispered to Lutfun that she was going to the doctors' rooms to check the X-Ray reports. Lutfun nodded. Mila's final year as a medical student gave her access to records and doctors. Her own father, Dr. Ekram Chowdhury, was also a renowned surgeon.

Lutfun moved uncomfortably on the hard stool. She sat erectly with her back straight up against the wall. Tensions were mounting driving her up the wall. She watched Shimul twist and turn and utter discomfort. But Lutfun only watched her, unable to give her any relief. Shimul began to utter nonsensical words. Lutfun understood a few words— 'your wishes will not be fulfilled'. Lutfun rose and walked closer to her. It was gibberish. Shimul opened her eyes. There were fears and anxieties in them. She cried out which Lutfun believed from sheer pain. But there was something else. She grabbed Lutfun's clothes and clutched them.

"Shimul, Shimul, what is it?" Lutfun asked calmly.

"My mother-in-law," she spat out.

"What about her?" Lutfun asked.

"When I — I— I," she stopped.

"Yes, what happened?" Lutfun asked.

" — left the village, she was screaming behind me and saying this."

"What did she say, Shimul?" Lutfun asked earnestly.

"That 'your wishes will never be fulfilled.'

"What nonsense, don't believe in such superstitions, Shimul, it's all baseless."

"No, her curse has come true, do you not see it?" she asked.

"See what though?" Lutfun looked confused.

"I had left my husband because he beat me," Shimul closed her eyes. "My mother-in-law had cursed me because my father couldn't afford a dowry. Bicycle, a new watch, and a radio. All they had asked for. He had promised them he would give them the dowry after the wedding. He couldn't. My mother-in-law was unhappy with me over the dowry. She cursed me—my wishes would never be fulfilled. Because my father had lied to them about the dowry. In one short month, my husband remarried."

"How do you know that you will not make a full recovery? Besides, as you said, they were torturing you," Lutfun asked.

"Even if I did make a full recovery, it wouldn't be the same," Shimul answered.

"May I ask what your wishes and dreams were?" Lutfun asked.

"I wanted freedom. Those were my wishes. Is that such a big ask?"

317

Shimul's eyes were damp through her eyelashes.

"Be strong Shimul, I think you will make it."

Lutfun consoled her as much as she could. And Shimul nodded. Lutfun returned to her seat. By now Mila had come back looking morose. It wasn't good news, Lutfun could tell by looking at her face. Mila walked up steadily and stood by Lutfun. Mila looked down at her and then at Shimul. She adjusted the drip of the near-empty saline bag; Shimul had been on intra-veinous saline since her arrival at the hospital. Mila signalled Lutfun to come outside. Lutfun followed Mila. Outside the room, they found a small verandah where they stood abreast; their tall shadows covering much of the narrow verandah's wall. Mila sighed. "Her legs would have to go."

"What? What do you mean?" Lutfun asked.

"They have to be amputated, but she'll live."

"When's the operation?"

"In the morning as soon as a theatre is available."

"Oh! This was exactly what she had also feared, Lutfun said.

"What do you mean?"

"She had a premonition. It was about some curse that her mother-in-law had put on her. About her dreams not coming true or something," she said.

"What premonition?"

"That she was going to lose her freedom," Lutfun said, biting a corner of her lips.

"Well, she will be handicapped."

There was silence. No one spoke. Lutfun asked Mila. "Are you superstitious?"

"Science cannot explain everything; 'there are more things in heaven and earth, Horatio, than are dreamt of in your philosophy,' remember Hamlet?"

"Yeah, I never read it, but I heard you recite those words when you were preparing for your stage presentation in school," Lutfun sighed.

"Shall we go in? I'll stay in the theatre until the operation is finished. You can go home with Uncle Sheri when he comes in the morning."

"Yeah, okay," Lutfun said.

This curse seemed almost too contrived to Mila. Maybe, Shimul went into a frenzy and came up with this ludicrous idea of the curse. Or it could be merely coincidental that perhaps the mother-in-law did curse her in those words, as it was also common to believe in the folklore tradition that curses exist. And they actually manifested. But Mila wasn't going to give it any quarter. She was going to work with the surgeons tomorrow and make sure that the operation was successful. That Shimul didn't lose those young legs.

It was well past midnight, and Mila and Lutfun were resting on the stool. They had both dozed off. Mila trembled and woke up. Shimul had startled her with a whine. She was whispering and murmuring in her sleep. Mila craned her neck and tried to listen.

"Leave a glass of water for the man's spirit in the room where he died. The souls of the dead stayed in the house for forty days. They get thirsty and they come back for water — why? The glass was half empty. I clearly put a full glass on that table there. Why was it half-empty? Who drank? Who drank the water? Did the water evaporate and leave a half-empty glass? But it was the middle of winter. No, no. That was not possible. He had come, the dead man's spirit had come, and he drank half a glass of water from that glass on the table."

Mila listened and tried to understand the gibberish. Then she remembered her grandfather. When Mr Chowdhury died, Shimul had kept a full glass of water in his room and continued to keep it throughout forty days. Because she believed that spirits lived in the house for forty days. Each morning, throughout those forty days, the glass was either half or full empty. A full glass of water every morning had visibly reduced in the glass, even Mila saw it; Mr Chowdhury's spirit drank it. That was how Shimul had explained it.

She had told everyone in the house, also, but no one had believed her. In their village, this was a custom that they did not cover the water pitcher, nor cover any pots or pans because the spirits of dead people came back for water for forty days. Mr Chowdhury's demise had surfaced all kinds of folklore beliefs; most of which the residents of the House of Chowdhury had dismissed as superstition.

Mila's thoughts rested on her grandfather. In his last days for about two years, he couldn't sleep. Mila knew because she would be up studying late for exams. She often came downstairs to take him back to bed. He would lie down for a short while sometimes, but more often he would be up instantly and start walking again. He walked and he walked, as though he was following a loop in time-space. He walked around the loop; he didn't go anywhere. At one point, he would get exhausted, and he would sit down for a moment, then he began to walk again, while everyone else slept at midnight. This he did every single night and only got some sleep at dawn.

However, he had been weakening over time. In the lead-up to his death, some days, he had to be spoon-fed and couldn't walk without assistance. Mrs Chowdhury tucked him comfortably under a rug and heavy cushions in his easy chair. One evening though, she had tucked him in his easy chair and had stepped out of the room, thinking he would stay there. But something mysterious had happened. He had regained strength suddenly, threw away his rug and stood up, and walked across the room to the door. He had stood there for a while, then he had flopped and had stress fractures in his legs. But, gradually recovered and could walk again in a few months.

Apart from his weakness and stress leg fracture, there didn't seem to be any fatal malady. The evening he died, a few months later this fall, he couldn't eat dinner. When Nazmun Banu went out to call a doctor, he did some extraordinary things in that short time, which he never, ever did. He embraced Mrs Chowdhury and made a throaty sound, some called it the death rattle, then he peacefully passed away. Naznum Banu had returned with the doctor

321

by now, who had proposed a number of causes for death, such as embolism, and stroke. However, such factors as the doctor suggested didn't quite add up, given his behaviour at death. He had the time to hug his wife and smile at her. It was mystifying.

Mila tried to make sense of the death over and over again in her mind without closure. The evening he passed away after two long years of random walking was an evening to remember. Mila looked at Lutfun who was snoring, sitting on the uncomfortable stool. They had all accepted her grandfather's death naturally. Allah had taken what was His. No reason to fret over it, fight with the Almighty or ask for answers. It was futile as there wouldn't be any answers. Submission to His will was the final.

However, Mila's restless, ever curious mind demanded answers. It rambled on. The world rotated on its axis; the sun set, and the moon rose. Those were the fixed parameters of physics as death was too—fixed. Mila loved her grandfather, growing up watching all his amazing feats. Walking miles both in health and in sickness, he had walked long distances; he literally walked to his death bed too, when the family walked him down to his bedroom from the dining table. Grandfather lay cold today, six feet under. One moment he was breathing—solid. Next, he vaporised into thin air. What lay beyond this illusory world of sense perception of sights and sounds was the question? Where did he go? What happened to the energy? Did it seep out of the body that we call soul? Or did the body not produce enough energy, resulting in death and a decomposed body—the end of it all? The answers perhaps could only be intuited.

Grandfather could intuit time. Or rather his end of time which was clear from hugging grandmother, smiling at her, and bidding her goodbye at the precise moment before he crossed over. Time could be internally intuited. But could he also intuit where he was going? Could he intuit space?

Space was an external element. Whatever form Grandfather was at the moment, outside of that vessel from which his soul flew away like a bird from its ribbed cage, his physical elements remained bound to the parameter of this reality of sense perception. The body slowly disintegrated into the soil, and bones turned into fossil fuel over time. In rain, the melted body parts fertilised more solidly into the ground, facilitating the production of food. The winds winged the dust made out of his body parts away to the distant lands. It spread.

Mila's thoughts were lucid. However, perhaps there was deeper magic out there, which eluded her. Which neither she nor Grandfather could intuit? She couldn't intuit the existence of heaven or hell. However, a vast cosmos lay out there, space, where perhaps the spirit flew. The spirit which sourced life from the undying elements of nature, energies, gasses which had once given his body consciousness—the lights, the sparkles, the movements. Mila combined the two realities in binary mode—the physical and the metaphysical were connected to form one complete universe. Life journeyed from one to another. Grandpa existed in various forms bound by binary oneness. There was no other reality outside of it, she intuited.

Shimul cried out in pain. She winced and groaned. Mila stood up and walked towards her. She went to the patient's bed and put a caring hand on her forehead. It was sweaty. Shimul opened her eyes; her tears rolled out.

black tongue

Mrs Chowdhury and Prema sat at the makeshift foldable table in the orchard with Quasu, waiting for the other members to join in. Quasu was drinking his orange juice and playing with a ball, throwing it in and out between two dry palm fronds hanging from the tree. Chapatis and omelette were for breakfast this morning. It was getting cold. Shimul usually serves it. Prema volunteered to do it this morning.

"I wonder how Shimul is today?" Mrs Chowdhury asked.

"I am not holding out too much hope," Prema said.

"Why? Is the operation not going to be successful?" Mrs Chowdhury asked.

"Hard to tell, Shimul is young, she may just pull through if she is lucky," Prema answered.

"I hope she does," Mrs Chowdhury sighed.

"So do I, so do I," Prema said.

Mrs Chowdhury gave her a sharp look thinking what Prema might be actually wishing. The bad blood still existed, although she had been given access into the house.

"Don't say anything bad, okay?" Mrs Chowdhury said.

"Why would I want to do that?" Prema asked, raising one of her arched eyebrows.

"I don't know. You seem to say and do things that turn out to be real sometimes."

"Such as," she said. "You can't just make up stuff like that, you know, just because I married your son. He too married me, let's not forget."

"Yeah, yeah I know. Let's not go there now, how you charmed my son so much younger than you," Mrs Chowdhury concluded.

" If any, I didn't fall for his money, aristocracy, or the successful business he owns now. He made money because of me, when I married him he was penniless."

Mrs Chowdhury listened quietly. She looked at her grandson Quasu and smiled at him. Prema knew if it hadn't been for Quasu, Mrs Chowdhury would never have accepted her. While they were there, the members of the family, mostly men, and Nazmun Banu without her husband, Ekram, came by and sat around the garden table for tea. They helped themselves to omelette and chapati; Prema stood up and lifted the tea cozy off the teapot placed on the edge of the table. She poured out the tea into all the cups and handed them around. She put the teapot back in its place within the tea cozy. The family sipped tea and ate breakfast in silence.

"Who made the tea?" Nazmun Banu asked.

"Why? I did." Prema answered.

"No, just wondering, since Shimul was the one who made it, usually."

"Is it not good enough for you?"

"She didn't say that now, did she?" Sheri asked defending Nazmun Banu.

"No, she didn't, but I know what she meant.'

"And what exactly did she mean?" Sheri asked.

"That, the tea isn't good."

"I neither said that nor meant it," Nazmun Banu retorted.

"Enough, quiet now," Mrs Chowdhury commanded.

"Tea is the least of our problems. What if something happened to Shimul? What if she could never work again?" Prema asked.

She flashed a glance at everyone around the table. Mrs Chowdhury's grips tightened around her cane. The family looked morose. Sheri frowned. Ashik put his cup down on the saucer with a noise. Irfaan looked away into the orchard with a deep frown. Nazmun Banu moved uncomfortably back and forth on the chair, unsure whether she wanted to sit straight up on its edge or recline. The fact remained that it was the partial collapse of the kitchen wall that had caused this terrible accident. It was neglectful of the Chowdhury family to have ignored it.

"Oh! How did this even happen?" Mrs Chowdhury asked.

"This was coming a long time now, Amma, we had been too occupied otherwise. Mila's wedding, this and that, the business, we just never gave the house enough attention.

I wouldn't be surprised now even if the entire wall collapsed," Nazmun Banu said.

"Well, something needs to be done about the house," Irfaan prompted.

"Yes, and we had some discussion too, Irfaan and I," Sheri said.

"What? What discussion did you two have? Selling it?" Mrs Chowdhury asked.

"That's one option, outright sale, the other is to demolish and build a flat for each of us," Irfaan added.

"Oh, and who is going to finance the new construction?" Prema asked.

"That we haven't considered yet, however, if we sold outright, we could all take our shares and move on, buy separate homes," Irfaan suggested.

"Hmm. The family would have to split up," Nazmun Banu grimaced.

It was undecided as to what they wanted to do. How were they going to fix this? They sat quietly, thinking away.

"Shimul could be our responsibility, even a burden," Prema said. "I have a bad feeling she may never recover."

"Oh! What a black tongue you have, Prema?" Nazmun Banu spat out.

The others listened but had not commented. Even Prema lowered her head with a wince at the sinister dig of her sister-in-law, but could not rule out the reality of the situation. The cat had got their tongue now.

"If Shimul becomes a burden along the line, then we must take care of her all her life," Mrs Chowdhury decreed. "Give her a life pension."

"Yes, but this house is not even liveable as it is. Something needs to be done," Irfaan persisted.

Irfaan's persistence made everyone stare at him for a while. To Mrs Chowdhury, it looked like his demeanor had spoken. In all her wisdom, she discerned an undercurrent of non-altruistic motives. Perhaps he was saying something which the others were missing. This newcomer into the family voiced a fresh idea but it was laced with self-profit. She kept her thoughts to herself thinking of Mila's relationship with him. Nothing must be allowed to come between Mila and Irfaan. For Nazmun Banu's sake, at least; she deserved her daughter's marital bliss.

What if she died suddenly? Mrs Chowdhury thought. Would her family start a war on inheritance over this house? Death was a near possibility, her husband died a while ago which still sat like a lump in her heart; she limped emotionally from time to time from that memory. Mila had been married off, what remained of her inheritance belonged to her son Ekram and then Nazmun Banu. Technically, Mila had no rights to this inheritance as of now, regardless of her new husband's ambitions and interest in the property. What if Irfaan divorced Mila on account of it? Mrs Chowdhury looked at Quasu; even he had more claims for being a boy. Girls got less, a one-third under the Sharia Law. But the primary inheritors were her own sons, Ekram, Ashik and Sheri in the event of her death.

She remembered talking to Mila once, some two years ago. Mila was explaining to her what had happened after death. That the body decomposed and degraded slowly into the soil; moths and insects fed on the carcass in the grave. Mrs Chowdhury had shivered at the time and had remembered her own morbid memories of childhood. She had told Mila how her own mother, Begum Noor, the zamindar's wife, had gone off on a tour of the village leaving her at home. She hadn't returned for seven days or so. Mrs Chowdhury, a young girl of seven, was wandering through the courtyard of the zamindar's palace. She had seen her mother's saree on the clothes line.

She had grabbed the saree and had smelled her mother. Even after the sari had been washed, she could still smell it. She remembered her mother sitting in one of the drawing rooms and putting fresh flowers in a tall, half-filled water vase. The gardener had just cut some fresh flowers and placed the gathering on a table before her chair, where she sat down to do the flower arrangements. Mrs Chowdhury, Raiza, the little girl looked at her then. She looked through the prism of her memories, now. That was another era, another reality. But her father was impulsive and quixotic. Like all the other lost zamindars, he cared less about her anxieties. He would leave her for weeks and sometimes even months when he went hunting.

Once, however, they too had accompanied him on one of his hunting trips. Raiza was seven. She was with her mother. They were passing through a dense forest at night in a palanquin. Her father was nowhere to be seen. He was on a horse behind them. But his horse was gone. Raiza looked through the drawn palanquin curtains. Just when the palanquin had also started to move. Raiza clung to her mother's saree asking her in a high-pitched voice, where her father was? Mother had held her tight to her chest; they heard the quickening of each other's heart beats, the trepidations, the fast palpitations. She still remembered how terrified her young mother of twenty years had been. In a quarter of an hour, the palanquin was parked near a lodge and her father had suddenly appeared.

"Oh, where were you?" her mother shrieked looking at him through the palanquin window.

"I was planning our next hunt with my men, and I ordered your palanquin bearers to carry you out of the forest. A rare breed of white tiger has been found near our hunting lodge, my next hunt," he grinned.

"What are we hunting on this trip?" my mother asked.

"Oh, the usual, horned animals and birds, gazelles, and deer."

Raiza felt faint. She felt she could smell clotted blood. She sat petrified. She felt like throwing up, thinking of her father's insatiable bloodlust. Raiza and her mother had descended through the palanquin door. Raiza looked at the forest; it looked blue. The feral tall trees wavered in the gentle winds. Somethings people never forgot. Memories could fuse the past into the present, as though the events had happened just yesterday. That lost era could be retrieved from the memory's undefined boundaries of time, past and the present pursuing each other like waves in proximity. The dead couldn't be brought back; they lived almost like imaginary creatures; those who had once lived, and danced to the nuanced tunes of life, and had loved once, now had become shadows in the repository of memories, a constant companion. Who knew where that reality had disappeared? Mrs Chowdhury ruminated and sighed heavily.

"Careful Quasu, look where you're kicking the ball. It nearly hit Daadi Amma. here," Prema screamed.

Mrs Chowdhury startled and came out of her reverie. Quasu had accidentally kicked his ball too close to her cane. Breakfast had finished. The men had risen from their seats and had gone to work. The sun was hot. Nazmun Banu and Prema were getting ready to clear the table. Rabeya, the other maid, came running after Quasu. She stopped near Mrs Chowdhury. Mrs Chowdhury stood up unsteadily with the help of the cane. The maid stood closely behind her to take her indoors.

Prema and Nazmun Banu cleared the table together. Prema gathered the plates and the saucers on top of the other. Nazmun Banu carried a leaning tower of teacups, balancing them carefully between the two palms. Prema, on the other hand, followed her with a pile of saucers and plates. A slight breeze blew over them causing some strands of hair to cover Prema's eyes. They took the dirty dishes into the kitchen. And walked carefully around the fallen wall. They tiptoed over the bricks, rocks, and broken cement patches. Inside the kitchen, they squatted and placed the soiled crockeries gently under a foot-tap.

"What a mess!" Prema said.

"Yeah, do you wish you were living next door at this moment?" Nazmun Banu asked,

"Gosh! Why on earth would I wish that? Because my ex-husband's kitchen wall is still standing?" Prema retorted.

"Yes, something like that."

Nazmun Banu laughed at her own dig. But it was a bad joke which they both knew. Tahera, who was sitting closeby gave them a dark look. They came out of the kitchen and went back to the orchard. The make-shift table needed to be folded away and the garden chairs neatly arranged.

"It's unimaginable how much work Shimul did alone," Nazmun Banu said.

"Yes, I am thankful that Tahera Maa, and Rabeya are okay," Prema replied. "If this had happened on Tahera Maa, just imagine, not only that one of us would have to take over the cooking duties, but Ashik would get really upset, too."

They were folding the table holding the edges from both ends. "Maa wouldn't have survived this at her age," Nazmun Banu said quietly.

"Do you see any new changes in Amma?" Prema asked suddenly.

"What do you mean?" Nazmun Banu asked.

"Hasn't she gone a bit too quiet off late?"

"Hmm, she always slips into her thoughts and looks morose, and sighs heavily thinking about her past, so I have also noticed. But she's also a creature of habit."

"I think," Prema said, holding one end of the folded table and standing up with Nazmun Banu. "She is thinking of losing this house and family. If they sell this place, it's going to affect her badly, I think."

"Yeah, now that you say it. It might actually happen," Nazmun Banu grimaced.

Quasu appeared from behind the mango tree with his ball and kicked it again towards them. It hit the folded table's legs and distracted the two sisters-in-law. They lifted the table off the ground and carried it indoors over the open doorway's threshold. They stood it down by the door, against the wall of the dining-room.

"In all honesty, I do believe that much of the tragedy occurs in this House of Chowdhury, because of their own folly. They aren't bad people, necessarily, but Bhadaima, soft in the head." Nazmun Banu reflected.

"Yes, this is not just a house though, it's so much more. Every brick of this house is encircled with love, laughter, and singing, a witness to so many dreams and dramas."

Nazmun Banu didn't speak. She let out a sharp sigh instead. She walked away from Prema, towards the bay window, looking outside at Quasu. The door leading to the orchard remained ajar at all times during the day. Prema found Nazmun Banu standing forlorn by the window. She joined her, as Quasu continued to kick his ball outside.

A heavy silence had fallen all around. There were some sounds of damp monsoon winds. However, another sound pierced through. It was the sound of the black landline phone ringing. Prema startled and turned around to pick it up fast-pacing, she picked up the handset and heard Mila on the other side.

"Hello, Mila? This is Aunty Prema," Prema said shakily.

"Aunty Prema, please let everyone know that Shimul will live but her leg has to be amputated."

"Oh! Is that good news or bad?"

"Well, you decide. She'll never walk again. Just let everyone know that. I have to go now."

Mila hung up. Prema stood near the phone somewhat rooted in the cold mosaic floor. Shimul was an amputee now, which meant disabled. Nazmun Banu came out of her room when she heard the ringing. She looked at Prema and Prema relayed to her what she had just heard. Nazmun Banu inclined her head to check if Mrs Chowdhury appeared in the passageway. She was there. Rabeya, the other maid, was by her side.

"Shimul will have to be our responsibility, now that she has lost her leg," Mrs Chowdhury said.

She solemnly turned around and walked away. Nazmun Banu looked pale. Both her and Prema looked at one another, when Nazmun Banu said softly. "I told ye' you have a black tongue."

Prema stood dumbfounded for a few quiet moments, then she looked away and ran to her room. Nazmun Banu now stood alone in the passageway by the black phone, tied up to her in-laws just like the phone's wires on the wall.

winds

In a month's time, Shimul was released from the hospital. She came back to the House of Chowdhury as a disabled. Nothing much had really changed around the house. The house was still there, breathing memories of many beating hearts. However, she noted that the debris from the fallen wall around the kitchen had been cleared; a new make-shift wall had been made out of thatched materials such as bamboo tied up in sturdy rope knots.

Shimul was driven back in the family car. The morning of her release, Sheri drove the car to the hospital and brought her home with Mila, and Lutfun. When they reached the House of Chowdhury, Lutfun and Mila helped her get out of the car but it wasn't easy. Even after a month's stay in the hospital, her leg was still in a heavily bandaged stump. There was a crutch by her side. Mila pulled her out and placed the crutch snugly under the armpit above the amputated leg. She stood on the other good leg and the crutch, and barely managed to push herself out of the car. With Mila's help she was out, but the crutch fell down. Lutfun quickly grabbed her and with Mila walked her to the maids' room, Shimul hobbling on the one leg and the crutch.

Upon her arrival, the members of the house came out and stood around the open space of the front yard. Prema, Ashik, Quasu, Nazmun Banu, even Ekram and Mrs Chowdhury too, with Rabeya behind her, had all come out of the house to greet Shimul. They stood there watching how Mila and Lutfun were helping Shimul gently into her room which the two maids, Rabeya and Shimul shared. Rabeya had taken over Shimul's chores now and Shimul was made to retire until she was able to walk again on the crutch. They lay her down on the thin mattress floor bed, blanketed by a hand-stitched cover. They left her to rest. Shimul felt groggy at first, then she fell off to sleep.

Shimul lay in bed at dawn; she saw something. Her companion, Rabeya, was fast asleep next to her. Folded up in the bundle of her own blanket, Shimul was awakened by a squeaking noise of the door hinge; it rattled in the hollow winds. Her leg was sore. But she was numbed by what she saw. She glimpsed a vision of a shape which danced in the pale light. It had extended an arm towards her, beckoning her. It asked her in a man's voice to accept a gift. She didn't think she was dreaming. She was certain of what she saw. It was a clear vision of a man offering her a red flower on a solitary stem with a single leaf; it had even touched her nose; it felt cold; she also felt a heavy weight descend on her body as though the spirit was laying on top of her. The apparition had come to say good morning with a flower, then it disappeared in a moment. She felt light again. She realised that it had left. In her young mind, she couldn't deny having seen this vision. Maybe, someone had passed away in the village, this—this spirit, had come to inform her of the passing.

The small ventilator in the room kept the air fresh. She was still coming to terms with the vision. Her mind drifted. She thought, as long as Mrs Chowdhury lived her future was secured. She would make sure as the head of family that Simul received her monthly payments. After her, it was either on Mila or Lutfun to bear Shimul's costs. But Shimul was also young. She mused, being permanently disabled now, she may also lose this pension.

She felt like going to the toilet. The maid's toilet was a bog, behind the neem tree in the front yard. An area which was unkempt and covered with hedges, spiky nettles and a rooty, ropey banyan tree: its tall, aerial roots hanging down.

Come to think of it, there was a man in her village aged twenty-five, who was called a tree-man because he was turning into a tree. Knotty roots had spread all over his hands, legs, and toes. She remembered him clearly. Was he still alive? This tree-man would have been eaten up by his own roots, surely, by now. Was it him? This apparition, she thought, but then, why would he come to her? She barely knew him. He was just famous for this rare condition, which was uncommon in her village. No one else had it. It was just him. What did the doctors say it was? A skin disease that all these root-like warts kept breaking out. If he could live with it, so could she with her disability.

But how was Rabeya going to take her to the bog across the front yard? She would probably either have to piggyback her or she would have to hobble on the crutch, balancing between her whole and half a leg.

As much as she preferred, Shimul couldn't go to the bog alone. But she also didn't want to wake up Rabeya. She slept peacefully. It was going to be morning soon. She could wait—what apparition could offer her a rose? It had to be a well-bred man. Her mind continued to look for a match and after man searches, she may have finally found one. It was— yes, it was, she was sure of it, it was Mr Chowdhury, whom they called Sahib. Sahib? Why would he offer her flowers when his beloved wife was still living? His own children were still alive. It was unnerving. Perhaps, he was trying to send a message through her. But she was no clairvoyant. Rabeya had just started to toss and turn in bed. She rubbed her eyes and opened them. She looked at Shimul and squinted at her. Shimul told her that she wanted to go, really badly. Rabeya rose and rolled out of bed. She squatted on the floor and rolled back her mattress and pushed it neatly against the wall.

"Stay here, I am coming in a minute," she said.

Shimul waited and Rabeya entered in a short while with a bedpan.

"Where on earth did you find this?" Shimul asked.

"I don't know. It was by the door. I had gone out to rinse my mouth when I found this by the door. I thought, if you couldn't walk on the crutch, I may have to piggyback you to the bog."

Shimul smiled. Rabeya could see her in the pale light as she brought the bedpan to her. She held her up gently by the waist, as Shimul groaned. Rabeya pushed it under her. And waited by her.

"It was really nice of Mila Apa to bring this bedpan," Rabeya said.

"How do you know it was her?" Shimul asked as she pressured herself into excreting.

"Who else would leave this?"

"I don't know," Shimul said thinking of the shape she saw in the room earlier on. "What do you think happens to souls after death?"

"I don't know. They go to hell or heaven," Rabeya replied.

"Really?" Shimul asked.

Rabeya nodded. "Why are you asking these weird questions?"

"I don't know. I think our shadow lives around us after we die."

"How can shadows live when there is no physical body?" Rabeya asked.

"Hmm, good question. Maybe the shadows are the real thing; not us."

"That's silly. Shadows exist because of us. They follow us. Without us, there is no shadow."

"True, but a different kind of shadow, soul shadow. Remember? After people die in the village, we usually leave a pitcher of water for the thirsty souls. They drink up the water, and it is evidenced from the receding of the water level. What do you think that is? After forty days, the water stops receding, which is when we know that the soul is gone."

"Yeah, I've also heard about that," Rabeya said straight-faced. "Anyway, Are you done?"

"Yes, I'm," Shimul replied in a small voice.

Rabeya gave her a wash and pulled the bedpan from under her and took it outside. Shimul lay quietly. She looked at Rabeya walking out of the room through the open door. She glanced up at the ceiling and thought what if this ceiling also fell down? She felt some trepidations and tears welling up and sliding down her temples. She heard some talks. It was Mila Apa and Irfaan Bhai constantly chattering about how this house needed to be demolished, sold, or fixed. And Mila Apa's continuous protest against any demolishing or selling. Fixing it was another issue. At any rate, she was telling him loud and clear that her family was quite capable of making these decisions. They didn't need to be shepherded by him. Why did Mila Apa protested so much? She probably had her good reasons, Shimul guessed.

At dawn, Mila had come out with the bedpan to pay Shimul a quick visit. Shimul was fast asleep. She had left the pan by the door and went back into the house. In the darkness, she felt eerie, creeping up through the slumbering passages of the house. She had not gone to bed but had stood by a window in the living room. She drew curtains apart and gazed out as the first ray of the sun pushed through the darkness. Her mind mulled over the conversation she had heard in the hospital between her mother-in-law and her father-in-law.

Her telltale heart was suggesting why Irfaan's parents had agreed to this wedding. It was not because their son had loved her, but because of the inheritance. The moment they had set foot into the house, that had always been their primary goal—this house. But Mila, growing up in the house never thought of it as an inheritance; except perhaps once, when she felt insecure on account of the colour of her skin being dark that she had poured out her anxieties to Aunty Lutfun on the roof, one evening. But that was a fleeting moment of insecurity. In the heart of it, she knew how much this house meant to her as it did to her family. She would never allow for this house to be subjected to her husband or his family's greed.

But how could Irfaan, who had given her so much love, allow himself to be so gullible? How could he allow himself to be pulled into his parents' conspiracy? How come he never objected to this disgusting idea of inheritance? Or was this all because of the colour of her skin? But when they first met, Irfaan was already in love before he even beheld this house. Oh! It was too confusing! She blinked her eyes and rubbed her forehead. Her thinking was getting muddled.

Morning had broken. She stood here, smelling a familiar body odor. She felt someone's warm breaths on her shoulders. She couldn't even turn around; she was in someone's strong arms; who else but her own husband's?

"How long have you been standing here?" Irfaan asked softly.

"I've lost count; I was checking on Shimul to leave Dada Bhai's bedpan by the door."

"I wanted you in bed. I waited and waited long," Irfaan whispered into her ears. "I can't be without you, you know."

Mila treated his advances with caution. She sighed and rested her head on his chest. No matter, she told herself. Maybe she was wrong. Maybe she had misjudged the conversation. But she had heard what she heard, and she told herself to believe that Irfaan wasn't a part of it. His intentions about the house were entirely altruistic. His parents still controlled him since he was unemployed. But it was up to Mila to tutor him out of the idea of inheritance. He had married into the House of Chowdhury, not to the house. He had married her.

"Should we go to your house today?" she asked.

"Yes, I think so. Maa has gone home. We should pack our bags and leave today."

Mila pulled herself away from him and rested her palms on his chest. She looked at him and the hair on his chest. She ran her fingers through it. She felt goosebumps pop up all over him. He looked at her and she looked at him. She didn't see any signs of treachery hiding in those eyes. He was either too naive or just too gullible to comprehend the hidden conspiracy laid by his father. Mila knew what she knew. She had heard what she heard in the hospital. She wasn't going to deny Mr Khan's propensity for greed. But Irfaan, she guessed, was being ensnared into it; he played the bait.

"Okay, enough said, let's go then," she said. "I'll pack the bags."

"Shouldn't we at least wait until everyone wakes up?" he suggested.

"No, there's no need for that. I'll call later."

"Okay, you're the boss."

They both walked up to Mila's bedroom. Mila in the front, and he, right behind her. They entered the bedroom and Irfaan closed the door. Mila crouched on the floor and looked under the bed for the suitcase which they had brought with them when they had arrived a while back. Shimul had put it under the bed since then. Mila pulled out the suitcase and clicked it open. Irfaan opened the almirah by turning the key. He took out a bunch of shirts and pants. Mila also walked up and down to the almirah and did the same, pulled out her sarees and her petticoats. They packed their two suitcases, sitting side by side on the floor.

It was a silent morning. Inside and outside until a crow cawed and sat down on the window parapet.

"The driver should be up by now," Mila said.

"Yes, why the rush, though?" Irfaan asked, inclining his neck towards Mila.

"Rush? What rush? The sooner we get out of here, the better, no?"

"Why?" Irfaan asked.

Mila kept quiet. When the suitcases were packed, she rose and gathered her saree's achal on her shoulder. She smiled at Irfaan and said. "Where do you see the rush? We're going home. Aren't you happy?"

She walked up to the door and opened it. Irfaan was quiet. He followed her through the passage out to the main entrance. She saw Rabeya in the front yard with the bedpan in her hand.

"Rabeya, please check if Shurjo is awake. He is an early riser, isn't he?"

"Okay, Mila Apa. I'll check."

Shurjo was the family chauffeur. His hut was on the edge of the courtyard. With the bedpan in her hand, she knocked on his door. Shurjo opened it, squinting.

"What's up?" he asked, coughing up a phlegm and then swallowing it.

"Quickly wash up and get the car out. Mila Apa wants to go somewhere. She is waiting with her suitcase under the porch."

"Oh really? This is sudden."

"Yes, everybody is still asleep. It is sudden."

"Anyway, I have to go. This bedpan needs to be cleaned. I'm going to the pond," Rabeya said.

"Okay, okay. You go on now."

Shurjo closed the door to get ready and Rabeya walked away. But she could hear the duo's faint conversation.

"I don't understand the suddenness of it, at all," Irfaan persisted.

"You will understand later," Mila said.

"Your uncles and I are supposed to discuss the property."

"It will have to be off, because we are leaving," she said.

"What? What do you mean?" Irfaan asked.

345

"This property will have to remain as it is. It will be renovated in time. The repairs will be underway soon, but never ever sold," she said.

"What? Who told you that?" Irfaan nearly yelled.

"No one. I know what my uncles would do. I know them better than you."

"Yes, that's why I'm here to help."

"Are you? Really? Are you really helping, Irfaan? This property is not for sale as long as Daadi Amma lives. Is that clear?" Mila said.

"And whose decision was it? I didn't hear anyone say anything," Irfaan said.

"You don't have to know everything. This is my house. These are my relatives."

"They're mine too, now," Irfaan said stubbornly.

Shimul had overheard the argument from her bed. She also heard the car revving up and stopping. There was silence. The car doors opened and closed with thud sounds. She heard the car starting and driving away. Shimul and Rabeya were the only two silent witnesses of this argument, although Shimul lay here mute and paralysed in a lonely world of apparitions and visions.

Shimul tried to turn to the side. She couldn't. If only Rabeya was here to help her turn over that would be great, she thought. Mila Apa and Irfaan Bhai left a while ago. Rabeya should be back soon. But Rabeya didn't return. What helplessness? No, she must learn to be independent. At the moment, she had no idea how. However, she was optimistic that her life would turn. The spirit had brought good tidings with a rose. Also, to bless her when it had sat on her body and had touched her nose.

A man had also arrived around mid-morning. No other but the mechanic from the antique radio repairs. He had come with a fully functional radio.

incandescence

The mechanic entered through the main gate. The residents of the House of Chowdhury had settled in the orchard for a late breakfast. This pale, young man wearing a creased, white cotton shirt and full black nylon pants was in the front yard looking lost. He carried a gunny bag. Rabeya found him and walked up to him.

"Are you lost? Did you enter the wrong house?" she asked.

"Hmm, I don't think so. Two women came to my shop with this broken radio. But no one came to pick it up. It's fixed now. I thought I would bring it back. This is the House of Chowdhury, right?"

"Yes, it is. Broken radio? When did Mila Apa's radio break? Anyway, she is not here at the moment. Is it even her radio?" she asked.

"A maid had come with her too. Can you call her? She'll know," he asked.

"Why though?" Rabeya asked.

"The other maid knows. Besides, some money is due on the radio."

"How much? You have to wait until Mila Apa returns for those dues to be paid," Rabeya said.

"Okay, here's the paperwork. But I want to leave it with the other maid because she was there."

He gave her the receipt which only mentioned an advance payment of 100 taka—500 taka was owing. The radio was fully repaired. And that was the total cost of the repair.

"Well, you have to leave it with me because she can't walk."

"What? Why? he asked.

"You see that wall, there? That's a new wall. The old one fell on her leg, and it had to be cut off."

"Oh! Anyway, where is she? May I at least see her? I want to give this bag to her personally," the young man persisted.

"I can't let you in, but I'll tell her."

"Okay, I'll go then, please let her know that I'll be back to see her. I'll take this back with me for now."

He pointed at the gunny bag which held Mila's radio.

His mouth was set, and his lips were pressed hard. He also had a frown. Rabeya looked at him and said, "Okay, maybe we'll see you around."

"By the way, how badly hurt is she?" he asked.

"It was really, really bad. She was in the hospital for many days."

"Oh! That's terrible," he said.

He walked away at a slow pace across the front yard. His head was crestfallen. When he turned around the bend to exit from the gate, he saw that Rabeya was still looking at him. After he went out of her sight, she took the receipt inside the main house to give it to one of the mistresses. But she didn't know about the radio incident at all, and that it was a secret.

Rabeya found Lutfun in the passageway on her way to the orchard. She called her out. "Lutfun Khala." Lutfun turned around. Rabeya walked up to her and told her that a man had come to give this receipt. Lutfun took it, and without looking at it, held it lightly. It was Rabeya's job now to lay breakfasts in the orchard. She took the breakfast out to the orchard, where the family had been waiting.

She walked back and entered their room. Shimul was struggling to sit up. Rabeya sat down by her side. She held her waist under both of her hands and pushed her right up against the wall. Shimul frowned and groaned. She sat up leaning against the wall with her heavy legs. Rabeya looked at her frowned face. It was visibly angst-ridden. Her disheveled hair was all over her temples stuck to her forehead from humidity. Rabeya moved back her hair with her four fingers and looked at her wary eyes.

"I got news for you," Rabeya said.

"What news? More bad news?"

"Depends on how you look at it."

"Tell me then, already."

"Okay. A man came a while ago looking for you. He said he was from the radio mechanic shop."

"Radio mechanic?" Shimul said, frowning.

350

"Yes. Do you know him?"

"Yes, I mean, no. What did he say?" Shimul asked.

"He wanted to speak to you."

"What did you say?" Shimul asked.

Her voice trembled as she spoke.

"I said you were sick, then he gave me a receipt. He held a gunny bag which he took back with him. He said he wanted to see you badly. Anyway, I gave the receipt to Lutfun Khala."

"What? Why didn't you come to me first?" Shimul said, clearly chagrined with deep frowns.

"I don't know." Rabeya said.

"Oh! What will I do now? I must get in touch with Mila Apa, somehow," Shimul said.

"How? She's gone to her in-laws. What is it anyway? Something important? Something I need to know?"

Rabeya opened her eyes really wide as she spoke.

"Tell Shurjo to come and speak to me. Tell him I would like to send a message to Mila Apa."

"Okay, okay, relax now, I will. But Lutfun Khala may have already read the receipt by now. What is this secret, Shimul? Why is this so important?"

"Call Shurjo now," Shimul said.

"Shurjo hasn't even returned yet. He drove Mila Apa and Irfaan Bhai to her in-laws," Rabeya grimaced.

Shimul closed her eyes. Her mouth was firm. She looked grim and thoughtful to Rabeya. She stood up and walked out of the dingy room. Shimul knew that Rabeya had left the room. She was still sitting up, leaning against the wall in one and a half legs. There was a sob stuck in her throat, she wanted to cry out loud. She thought she would do just that. She began to moan, and groan and cried so loudly that it could be heard all the way to the orchard where the family had gathered for breakfast.

Rabeya was unfolding the table on the orchard grounds when she also heard the cries. Lutfun was sitting in a chair with the receipt between her fingers. She was looking forlorn. Her mind was obviously elsewhere as Rabeya saw the folded receipt. The rest of the members was reading the morning newspaper, some ambling through the orchard. Mrs Chowdhury appeared in the doorway on her walking stick. She was negotiating the stairs. Shimul's cry startled both Lutfun and Mrs Chowdhury. Lutfun rose in a flash from her chair and walked a few steps towards Mrs Chowdhury.

"Here, Amma, let me help you," she said.

"What's with Shimul? Can you find out?"

Mrs Chowdhury murmured almost inaudibly. Lutfun helped her sit down first and then turned around to check on Shimul. In the meantime, Rabeya who was still here noticed that Lutfun unmindfully left the receipt in her chair. This was her chance to take it. When Mrs Chowdhury was looking up the mango tree to check if it had flowered,

Rabeya came around to the chair where Lutfun had been sitting, and quietly picked it up. She walked down the side garden by Mila's window, the narrow flower path leading into the maid's room.

Lutfun was already here and kneeling beside Shimul, when Rabeya entered the room. Both of them saw her. Rabeya went quietly behind the door and opened her trunk. Lutfun was too occupied with Shimul to notice what Rabeya was doing. Rabeya crouched and put the receipt in the trunk; she closed the lid and deftly latched it back. She turned her head at Shimul and found Shimul looking at Lutfun. From the corner of her eyes, Shimul saw what Rabeya did. Rabeya stood up, and with a slight nod at Shimul darted out.

Rabeya went into the kitchen to help Tahera, the cook, organize a tea tray. On her way to the orchard, she heard that Shimul had stopped wailing. Rabeya suppressed a giggle as she took the tray into the orchard. Rabeya thought it was a brilliant ruse to get Lutfun's attention. Pure luck! Lutfun may not have answered to her distress call, at all; it could have been anyone, even Prema. But it was Lutfun who had responded, and to boot, unmindfully left the receipt on the chair.

Shimul hoped that Lutfun Khala had not read it. But Shimul couldn't be sure. Even if she did, Lutfun Khala wasn't the type of person to share it with anyone. But she had to speak to Mila Apa about it. She wondered when Shurjo was going to return. She must send him back to Mila Apa's in-laws with this errand.

Rabeya entered the maid's room after a while.

"Do you think Lutfun Khala read it?" Shimul asked.

"I don't know. I couldn't be too sure," Rabeya answered.

"Hmm," Shimul said. "Let me know when Shurjo gets back."

"Why? No one had even noticed that the radio was missing, no?" Rabeya asked.

"Because they were busy with me."

Shimul thought Mila Apa had just been married. If the family knew that her marriage was already dwindling, then that would really hurt them. Shimul couldn't let that happen, especially after what Mila Apa had done for her in the hospital. She owed it to her. She waited patiently for Shurjo. She didn't have to wait that long, because Rabeya was back soon, with the news that the driver had returned. Shimul told Rabeya that before anyone in the house knew that he had returned, he must be sent immediately back to Mila Apa's in-laws with the receipt. Rabeya followed her instructions.

After breakfast, Lutfun was searching for what Rabeya had handed to her earlier. She had left unmindfully on the chair when she ran to attend to Shimul. She called Rabeya, who was with the driver asking him to leave immediately to Mila Apa's in -laws.

"Rabeya, Rabeya, can you come here for a second?" Lutfun called.

"In a minute," Rabeya answered.

A few minutes later she appeared, placid, faced before Lutfun. Lutfun looked at her and asked her,

"I can't seem to find the piece of paper you gave me. Do you know where it is?"

"No, Lutfun Khala, I don't. I gave it to you," she replied.

"Who was it from, again?" Lutfun asked.

"I don't know," Rabeya replied. "A man brought it this morning."

"Who was this man? Where did he come from? Oh! How could I lose it? What if it was important?"

Rabeya kept quiet, looking at Lutfun, wide eyed, gauging her frets, but she said nothing. After a while, she asked. "May I go?"

"Yes, yes, you may. If the man comes back, let me know this time. Don't just take a paper, ok?" Lutfun said.

"Okay."

Rabeya inclined her head slightly, and then she left. She pressed her lips and smiled after turning around. When she came out of the house in the front yard, Shurjo was already back. And was reversing the car into the garage. Rabeya walked towards the kitchen. She heard Shurjo turn off the ignition, and the car door shut.

Shurjo was now walking towards Shimul's room. As he came in front of her door, he coughed to let her know that he had finished the job. Shimul felt relaxed and asked him to enter. Shurjo stood on the door and squinted to look at her through the dark room.

"What did Mila Apa say?" Shimul asked.

"Well, she took it and asked me how I knew to give it to her and why I had come back to give it to her?"

"What did you say?"

"I told her that Rabeya asked me to bring it upon your instructions."

"And then?"

"She smiled and asked me to leave."

"Good."

"Ok, Shimul Bua, I'll go now. However, I don't think Mila Apa wants to stay in that house for long."

"Why not?"

"Because, when she took the paper, she whispered something. She said, "I miss them. I miss the house.""

"Yea, this house is also not the same without her. What is her in-law's house like?" Shimul asked.

"It's a flat and it's new."

Shurjo left Shimul when Rabeya entered with Shimul's breakfast of tea in a tin mug and two dry chapati on a tin plate. Rabeya placed the plate beside her and saw that Shimul turned her head towards the plate. Rabeya left. A silence descended in the room. She pushed herself to sit up against the wall. The wall had already a round, black head mark from her continuous leaning against it. She extended an arm and picked up the mug. She sipped the tea, tore a corner from the chapati to dunk it in. She looked at the stump on her half-leg, and wondered if she was ever going to be mobile again. Would she be able to go to the roof again in her limited capacity? Feed the birds, go to her village on holidays.

Unbeknownst tears flowed and some dropped into the mug of tea she held on her lap. She wished for Mila Apa to be here so she could discuss her future with her, although she could discuss it with anyone in the house, but Mila Apa was a professional. Her poverty was crippling as it is, now this had crippled her doubly over. She was young, and pretty, she could have a future, even fall in love again with the radio mechanic, maybe. Still, all she had now in her life was great despair.

She was angry for not being more careful. But how was she to know that a wall was going to collapse on her? No cosmic intervention had occurred to stop it. The sun rose and set everyday as did the moon. A tad of moonlight entered through the ventilator of her room each evening. Tides ebbed and flowed. Nothing had changed in the house, either. She could feel pulsing life throughout the day, just as at night too, as she lay awake in the slivered moonlight. Only her inside caved in. She was unable to retrieve it.

She heard Lutfun calling for Shurjo in the front yard, asking him to bring the car around. Another voice waved through. It was Prema's, giving instructions to Rabeya to pick fruits. "Guavas are quite ripe. Pluck some from the orchard, slice one, salt it, and serve Amma at high tea. We are going shopping. We won't be back until dusk."

Shimul wondered if Nazmun Banu was also with them because she had only just heard the two voices. Rabeya squealed. "You're all leaving together, there's no one else, in case something happened to Daadi Amma?" Mrs Chowdhury was left at the mercy of one maid, only, and old Tahera, who was the same age as Mrs Chowdhury. However, this wasn't the first time that she had been left alone to her reveries with the trusted maids, checking on her ever so often, Shimul thought, but she was well at that time and had always been with her. She loved the family, especially, Daadi Amma with her dear life? She had walked her up and down the corridor every evening when she was tired of sitting too long. She had given her a patient hearing, and made herself available when Daadi Amma talked about her glorious heydays.

The soft shutting sounds of the car doors; the engine's rasps; the gentle creaks of gravel on the driveway; the rusty squeaks of the main gate; the oceanic droning of the traffic, Shimul lay there, listening to all those familiar sounds, visualising every single detail etched on her mind. After some time Rabeya entered and found Shimul fast asleep. She stood at her foot, then she walked towards the corner where her trunk was. She had something in her hand, which only she knew what.

Her trunk was old and battered. It lacked the luster of new paint. In some places, paint had even peeled off. She turned her head towards Shimul and quietly opened the lid. She slid the object from her clutches into the corner of her trunk and shut it back. Rabeya took a sharp breath and pussy-footed out of the room. What she stashed away was just a shiny metal she'd found on the gravel after the car had left. She didn't know what it was. It was just an interesting object.

Rabeya was a foundling. She was left in a garbage bin on the roadside. Lutfun had picked her up and brought her home thinking that she probably was an illegitimate product of one of many lovers from the far end of the alley—a strange place, this alley. Rabeya knew better not to steal anything valuable from this house. She wouldn't dare. This house had let her breathe again, and had given her a new life.

Mila was making bed at her in-laws. After Shurjo left, she had read the receipt and felt a twist of pang thinking of her antique radio. Although it was repaired, she still felt anger towards Irfaan who had broken it needlessly, out of pure spite. She needed to settle the payments which meant she needed to go back to the alley where the shop was? As she started to make the bed, she heard the doorbell ring. Irfaan opened the door and let a visitor in. Afterwards, Irfaan came into the bedroom. He saw her making the bed. From the other end of the bed, he too pulled the ruffled sheet to help Mila. He tucked it under the mattress at the same time, as Mila also did from her own end. Irfaan looked at her a few times, but she made no eye contact. Irfaan noticed her grimness.

"Has anything happened, again?" Irfaan asked. "Has anyone died? Why the grim face?"

"No, I need to return to the alley to make a payment for the broken radio," Mila answered.

"How much is it?" he asked.

"Not much, the rest of the payment is due," she said.

"Oh, I see. Still, how much?" he insisted.

"What does it matter?" Mila hissed. "You've broken an antique; new parts have been put in. As far as I can tell."

"Isn't this better? Newer and more energy efficient transistor, better sound quality? It would have broken sooner or later, anyway, no?" he asked.

"You know what? I don't think you still get it. I'll go tomorrow back to the alley to settle the payment," she said.

"Okay, if you wish. But can we not have this conversation again? You have said it many times as I have said sorry. I am saying, sorry, again—sorry."

Irfaan put up both his hands together in a mock gesture and left the room. She sat down on the edge of the bed and realised that a sob was stuck in her throat. She tried to clear it by coughing a few times. But it didn't go away. She felt tear pricks, and tears rolling down her cheeks. Was Mila happy? She asked herself. Was this marriage even working? There were no answers other than the rolling tears. Perhaps that was her answer. No matter, there was no way Irfaan's family was going to put their dirty fangs into her ancestral home, not at least while Daadi Amma still lived. Mila wiped off her tears and arranged her saree over her shoulder. She walked towards the door and opened it. Her in-laws were sitting together with the visitor in the drawing room.

"Ah there you're Mila, please join us for tea," Mrs Khan said. " This is our dear friend, Mr Nazmul Haque," she said, introducing Mila to the visitor.

Mila greeted with a salaam, and he returned the salaam. Mr Haque rose from his seat and bade goodbye. Mr and Mrs Khan saw him out at the door. They opened it for him, as he left.

Mila felt Irfaan eyeing her. When Mila flashed a glance back at him, he pouted his lips to form a kiss. She felt a slight romance swell inside of her. She smiled and sat down with them on a three-seater beside Irfaan and his mother. She sat on the edge of the chair first, knotting and unknotting her fingers, and intermittently combing her hair with them. Irfaan rose and walked up to the tea table and poured her a cup of tea. He brought it to her.

"Oh, she can pour her own tea now, and for us, too. She needs to participate in the everyday affairs to feel included," said Mrs Khan.

"Yes, of course," Mila said. "I should start at the hospital soon. Also, my exams are coming up."

"When do you start?" asked Mr Khan.

"From next week," Mila answered gently.

"Good," Mr Khan said.

He rose to go into the bedroom. Mrs Khan and Irfaan sat quietly, sipping tea. Mila felt a chill. She felt cold.

"Do you know who that visitor was?" she asked. "He knows your father, Dr Ekram Chowdhury. And, he also knows something else, that had not been revealed to us at the time of the wedding— some vital information."

Irfaan hadn't heard all the conversation because he was in the bedroom after he had let the visitor in. He looked up at his mother plainly, not understanding the drift.

"Did you know that Dr Ekram married three times?" she asked.

Irfaan's mouth opened. And Mila's leg began to shake uncontrollably under her sari.

"What?" he rose from his chair.

"You didn't know, either," Mrs Khan said.

Irfaan neither affirmed nor negated. He only raised an eyebrow.

"Well, now you know that your father-in-law has married three times, the great zamindari family, huh?"

Irfaan looked at Mila, who was staring at Mrs Khan. Her eyes were wide open, and her mouth also fell apart. However, before she could verbalize anything Irfaan spat out. "Maa, how do you know Haque Uncle is telling the truth?"

"Why would he lie? Mila's family lied, if any," she said.

"We didn't lie. We just never said anything," Mila intervened.

"Is it true that your father married three times?" Mrs Khan asked.

"Yes, it is true."

Mila sat there tight-lipped. Not moving much and staring straight at her, she showed no remorse.

"I am not responsible for what my father does, and neither is my mother. What's there to tell? Who says things like this at weddings, anyway?" Mila asked.

Mrs Khan didn't answer her directly but changed the subject. She shrugged and said. "What's happened has happened, it cannot be changed? Are you able to cook tonight? Our maid has gone on leave," Mrs Khan asked.

"I have never cooked, but I can try."

"How come? I thought, you aristocratic girls knew how to cook, all the exotic and the fine cuisine, the classy meals."

"Some do, not all. I certainly do not."

A disquieting moment descended on the room. Mila held her teacup in her hand and looked away in the direction of a tree outside through an open window. A cuckoo flew chasing a raven. The raven turned around and ignored it. What was exactly expected of her in this house? The subtle pressures laid by the mother-in-law to cook, to get involved in the chores were not something she had signed up for. She didn't see Irfaan defending her much either. He simply sat there, listening, pretending, ignoring. Why couldn't Mrs Khan cook? This was her house after all. Why couldn't she ask Mila to help her, while she did the cooking? She was a better judge of her family's taste buds. Mila had loads of hospital work. The wedding had pushed her schedule back. There was Shimul's operation, too.

"Mila, Mila!" Both Irfaan and Mrs Khan screamed together.

Mila was startled and found that her full cup of hot tea had halved without drinking even a sip. The cup had tilted and the tea was rolling out on the saucer.

"Where is your mind, girl?" Mrs Khan yelled.

"Oh! I'm so sorry!"

Mila adjusted the cup on the saucer and rushed into her bedroom with the half-empty cup in her hand. Irfaan ran after her. Mila had barely opened the door, when Irfaan entered and closed it behind him.

"What's wrong? Don't tell me it's the radio again," he asked panting.

"No, it's not. Nothing. Just stop it, okay?" Mila said.

"What then is the matter? You have not told me about your father's marriages. Have I said anything? No, but you, on the other hand, have not forgiven me over the radio fiasco at all."

"What would you have done if I told you about Abba? Would you not have married me? She asked."

"I don't know but I am inclined to put you on pills," Irfaan said.

"Pills? What pills?"

"Anti-anxiety pills."

"I'm fine. I need to go home."

"This is your home."

"It doesn't feel like one," Mila answered.

"It's new, give it some time to take root."

"I couldn't be bothered cooking and cleaning. I'm not a cook. I didn't get married to cook in this house."

"No, and you won't have to. Just for a few days until the maid returns."

"Why can't your Maa cook? I could help her."

"I'll let her know that. For now, get changed and I'll take you back home. After all, home is where the heart is, right?" Irfaan said.

"Yeah, I guess."

Home was where the heart was. Irfaan left her in the bedroom, closing the door. He went to look for his mother. Mrs Khan was in the back verandah where she grew all her plants. She was attending to her ferns, where Irfaan found her.

"Maa, we need to talk."

"About what? Her?"

"Yes, she said she can help you in the kitchen."

"Okay, that's fine but she's also my daughter-in-law, my one and only, Bahu Rani, the Bride Queen of this house. Tell her to take some responsibilities. What have those aristocrats taught her? Her trousseau was nearly empty, too."

"C'mon, Maa that has nothing to do with anything. We did receive some furniture, bed, dressing table, an almirah not to mention a chest full of expensive jewellery, no? What were you expecting anyway? Loads of cash? A car? A fridge? A flat?"

His mother was quiet. She continued pruning the ferns. "I don't know, more silverware and gold-plated bowls, yes, a flat and a car, too—too much to ask from the nobles? What we have received is just ordinary furniture. The jewellery is hers to keep, she'll never sell any of it, God forbid, should our circumstances change. You father and I are both from peasant class, you know that, right? Our ancestry is not all that different from our maid. Your father was a good student, he did well in school, received scholarships, found a good job, a self-made man who gradually rose to what we are today."

Irfaan ignored her last comments saying that Mila had to go to her house, and that they were leaving shortly. Mrs Khan sighed and murmured that it was only a few hours that they had come from that house. What was in that house, anyway? The pruning punctured the tip of her finger which started to bleed. She screamed. Mila and Mr Khan came out at once.

"Mila, quick, get some Dettol and cotton buds from Maa's bathroom. They're in the first-aid box," Irfaan asked.

Mila rushed to fetch it and returned in a minute. She sat down by her and did a neat bandage on her fingertip.

"You need to have a lie down, Maa," she said.

Mila helped her up and then took her gently into the bedroom. Mrs Khan obeyed like a little girl. Mila put her in bed. Mrs Khan closed her eyes.

With the maid gone, and Mrs Khan indisposed, Mila didn't think it was wise to go anywhere. She came out and looked at Irfaan. He was sitting with Mr Khan, morosely, with his cheeks on his hand, resting on the arm of the chair.

"I'll see to it that dinner is cooked," Mila said.

She was on her way to the kitchen. Irfaan smiled and kissed her again through his silent pouts. Mila smiled back; all was right with the world. She looked around and found shelves of pots and pans and spice racks over a two-burner gas stove. She sensed Mr Khan following her to the kitchen. He stood at the open doorway, eyeing her; she felt uncomfortable under his scrutiny. He was wondering whether or not she could cook. Would she be able to cut a fish on the boti? Yes, that was a challenge, particularly, managing the boti. But she thought she had dissected insects, and human bodies. All she had to do was to follow the fish anatomy, and she should be okay. She turned around and looked at Mr Khan to ask almost, if he knew what she was meant to cook for dinner tonight. He nodded, walked to the fridge, and reappeared with a large plastic packet.

"What's in this?" she asked.

"Hilsa Fish."

He handed it to her and she opened the fish wrapped in it. She realised that it was a whole hilsa fish which he had bought in the morning from a vendor. It was her job to scale it, cut it, slice it and cook up a delicious meal. He came into the kitchen and looked behind the door. He found the boti there. She saw it and pulled the large, medieval implement towards her. It had a long wooden shaft on which one was

367

meant to be seated. As she was figuring out how to use this, she heard the front door-bell ring again. Mr Khan was turning around, when Irfaan had already opened it. Mila heard familiar voices. Her Aunty Lutfun's voice aired through like music to her ears.

"We thought we would give you a surprise visit," she said to Irfaan."

"They're here," Mila said.

 Mr Khan who was still standing in the kitchen space and dithering whether or not to greet them or stay here. Her excitement put a smile on his rigid lips. She bent over to leave the fish on the shaft and walked past him. She also heard a sigh from Mr Khan and a low grunt as she left him. She flew through the air nearly as she greeted her aunts and her mother. They hugged her and she hugged them back, and they all sat down in the drawing room.

"What's with you guys? Were you passing by, or something?" Mila asked.

"We went shopping, so we thought we'd drop in," Prema said. "Where is your mother-in-law?"

"She's asleep. She had a gash this morning pruning the ferns."

"Oh!"

They said together.

"She'll be okay," Mila replied.

Mr Khan had by now joined them and took a seat. He crossed his legs. There was an awkward silence in the room. Mila was fidgeting with the saree's anchal.

"I would have invited you all to have dinner with us tonight," said Mr Khan. "But our maid has gone on a vacation. I'm not sure how much Mila can manage with my wife being in bed."

"What's for dinner?" Nazmun Banu asked.

She knew cooking wasn't her daughter's forte.

"Mila was just about to scale a hilsa, when you dropped in," Mr Khan said.

Nazmun Banu shot a glance at all three. And Irfaan was just about to open his mouth to offer them tea, when both of them said. "Why don't I take the fish home and have it cleaned and cooked? Shurjo can bring it over before dinner."

It was a great suggestion, Mila thought. But when she looked at her father-in-law's grim expression, a slight scowl also appeared on her own forehead. He didn't spit it out exactly, but she read his mind, 'you have so spoiled her. She should have known how to do these things by now. Noble girls usually did.'

Instead, he said. "Sure, if you like. But Mila would have to learn, sooner or later. Sooner the better."

"Oh, yes, of course, these are still early days, plenty of time left to learn cooking," Lutfun said. "Come, Mila, get dressed and bring the fish. We'll get started soon. Irfaan? Are you coming with us, beta?"

She used a term of endearment which meant love. And hearing it, Irfaan had almost melted.

"Yes of course. I am," he said.

Mila stood up and rushed into the kitchen. She wrapped up the fish in its original cover and put it in a jute bag which she found hooked on the wall by the door. On her nimble feet, she went into her bedroom and back as fast as she could with her handbag. She reappeared in the drawing room in no time and stood behind the chair, her mother had been sitting.

She smiled. "Ready, shall we go, then?"

"Yes, just a second," Irfaan said.

He disappeared into the bedroom, too, to return momentarily.

"Okay, let's just go then," Prema said.

When they stood up, Mr Khan walked them over to the door. He could hear their high laughter ringing from the landing as they descended. He closed the door and sat down in the same chair with the same grim scowl with hands folded on his lap. The forlorn sun was nearly setting. He looked at the sun's crimson-yellow mix and a paling greyness of the sky behind the tall jujube tree. The room had darkened. But he did not get up to turn on the lights.

They were back in the House of Chowdhury. Shurjo drove them home safely and switched off the ignition under the porch. Nazmun Banu was first to get out, extricating herself from a really squishy spot in the car's backseat, squeezed between Lutfun, Prema, and Mila; Irfaan had taken the front seat beside Shurjo. Prema laughed over how they could all still fit in the car. That they were still slim. Her laughter reached the kitchen and Rabeya came out rushing to the porch where the car had been parked. Nazmun Banu handed her over the fish in the packet saying,"Here, give this to Tahera Maa, tell her to make a nice coconut curry for Mila's in-laws. They will take it back for dinner."

A light aroma of fresh coriander in dal was already drifting through the air. They entered the house, while Shurjo followed them with shopping bags through the main entrance. He placed the numerous bags on a chair in the passage. Mila's Uncle Sheri came down the stairs whistling a movie tune: Hridoy amar shundor o tobo pay... bokuler moto jhoria morite chaiy, O my beautiful heart desires to die like a falling bulletwood flower (bukul phool). The chattering of the women had reached his verandah upstairs.

He entered the dining room and found them sitting haphazardly on the sofa and on the sofa-arms, chatting about the colours and the prints of the sarees they had shopped. And how the skilful haggling halved the prices?

Sheri stood at the door amused, facing this small party of women; Irfaan, standing by the dinner table and listening with a smile.

"Oh, yeah, Prema, you really know how to bargain, girl," Lutfun said, followed by a peal of laughter.

"I have some good news."

371

Sheri coughed and interjected when he had an opportunity to cut in.

"What is it, brother?" Nazmun Banu asked.

"Well, we are about to establish a cheese factory. We have registered it under the name of Raiza Chowdhury Cheese & Company, the first cheese factory in Dhaka, ever.

"Oh my, how exciting!" Mila crooned.

"Really? Oh, that's marvellous, does Amma know?" Lutfun asked.

"Yes, of course, she was the first to know, as I needed her signature on one of the shareholder's forms."

"She's one of the shareholders? How much did she invest?" Irfaan asked.

"Oh! We used this house—her house, as collateral? That makes her a shareholder automatically," he said.

"Okay, so you are not going to sell it then, or demolish it to make new flats?" Irfaan asked.

"No, not at the moment; at the moment, we've shelved the idea, because of this new opportunity which all of us, brothers, think is a much wiser investment. What do you think, Irfaan?"

"Well, you didn't ask me, what does it matter now what I think or not think. It is an old house, and you know how cracked the ceiling is. You're lucky that Shimul survived or else there could've been a police and court case."

"Is that a threat, Irfaan?" Mila asked.

"No, it's not a threat, of course, but—."

"But what?" Mila asked.

Nazmun Banu was listening with interest. She interrupted the conversation saying that they should all sit down properly. Mila turned around saying that she wished to check on Daadi Amma. She raced through the corridor to her rooms at the end of it. Before going there, she went outside to find Shurjo, gave him some money, and instructions to go to the antique radio shop to bring back the radio, and give it to Shimul. Mila would pick it up from her and put it back where it belonged. Shurjo did as instructed.

Almost too many things had happened on the same day; it was hectic, Mila thought, on her way to Grandma's room. She had left in the morning for her in-laws, and events rolled on, one after another sandwiched between then and now. Her father, exposed! What if her family did decide to construct apartments? Mila's share wasn't guaranteed anyway. It was not going to be hers until her parents had passed away. Unless, her uncles, out of munificence, gave her a flat, too. Was Irfaan counting on that? What was his plan? Or did he want to coerce a flat out of them? She would, nonetheless, love a room on the roof amongst the garden. It put a faint smile on her lips. But those were her daydreams. She was not in the least concerned about properties at the moment. She entered Mrs Chowdhury's bedroom. Mrs Chowdhury saw her and smiled. Mila went over and gave her a hug, and kissed her on both cheeks.

"You look happy," she said. "Are you?"

"What?" Mila asked.

"Happy?" Mrs Chowdhury asked again.

Mila wasn't sure how to answer it. She kept quiet, her thin smile fading.

"Anyway; how're things?" she asked.

"Good, really good," Mila answered.

Mila thought her grandmother's sharp gauge had left her bare. Daadi Amma who had her own history of unhappiness and secrecy, Mila reminded herself. How much did Daadi Amma tell them, anyway, she wondered?

"Mila, I want to bequeath something to you," she said.

"What's that?" Mila asked.

"My personal journal."

"You kept a diary, why? I didn't know," Mila said.

"No one does."

She gave Mila her keys to the almirah and asked her to open it. The diary was in a built-in safe. Mila did as she was instructed. She found it here.

"Why would you give it to me?" Mila asked.

"Because only you would read it. It is a document of many events, some of which I have shared, and you have heard too as a child, but may not have fully understood what I was trying to say."

"Would I understand now?" Mila asked.

"Yes, I think you would. I think you have both the sharpness and the willingness, which none of the others do."

"Okay, if you say so," Mila said.

This reminded Mila of Rahim Ali. She felt romance for him once, but he was a distant memory, although the thought of him still stirred Mila's heart. At the time she felt it was true love, her dreaming, laughing, teen-ager days were over; she felt love for Irfaan too, newly wedded; early days, she had already started to feel that love fade. Who was she? She wondered. Another Madame Bovary? Another tragedy waiting to happen? She felt a chill up her spine. She shivered, as she sat on the edge of Mrs Chowdhury's bed.

"Do you have a cold?" Mrs Chowdhury asked.

"No, no cold, just a chill."

"When do you start work?"

"Next week."

Mila saw Mrs Chowdhury close her eyes as she often did, sinking yet again into one of her reveries. Mila looked at the diary in her hand and stood up to leave. Mrs Chowdhury heard the bed creak as Mila stood up. She opened her eyes.

"Leaving? So soon? Have you had dinner?" she asked.

"Yes, we have to go. My in-laws are waiting to have dinner with us."

"Oh okay, then. Come again."

"I will. Goodbye, Daadi Amma."

Mila bent over and gave her more kisses on both cheeks.

"Goodbye, love."

Mila left her in peace and walked out of the room. In the living room, her uncles, now Uncle Ashik had also joined, and her aunts were talking at the top of their voices, drowning in laughter and conversations. Mila didn't understand what they were talking about. That could be so interesting. They were talking about the cheese factory, she heard, as she drew closer. This was the family's second acquisition. The first was a successful pharmaceutical company. They decided to venture into something new and different this time. They felt optimistic about the fact that they could make Dhaka cheese famous.

Dinner was ready. Nazmun Banu had it packed up in containers for Mila and Irfaan to take it home. Shurjo was ready to take them back, his third visit to the same house in one day. Mila asked Irfaan to sit in the car, while she popped out to check on Shimul. Rabeya had the containers in her hand, which she handed over to Shurjo. He put them on the front seat next to his. Mila ran up to the maid's quarters and peeked through the door. Shimul was lying there alone.

Mila called. "Shimul, are you awake?"

"Yes, Mila Apa, I'm. I heard that you came," Shimul answered.

"How're you?"

"As best as I can be. But here's your radio."

Mila took the radio. "Okay, I'll get you a pair of better crutches from the hospital, soon. Maybe, next week when I resume my studies."

"Okay, Mila Apa, Be well."

"You too, Shimul. See you soon."

As Mila was about to leave, she noticed a letter in her hand. Shimul saw that Mila had seen it. She blushed and quickly dropped her gaze. 'What is it'? Mila's curiosity piqued.

"Shimul?" Mila asked.

"Yes, Mila Apa?"

"Good News?" Mila asked.

"Yes."

"Who is it, Shimul?" Mila asked.

"The radio mechanic."

"Really? Can you read? Or should I read it to you?" Mila asked.

"I read Bangla up to class five in our village school, Mila Apa."

"Good. Enjoy the letter, then."

Mila saw a shy smile appear on Shimul's pale lips. The atmosphere smelled of love. Shimul was in love with the radio mechanic.

Mila left Shimul and ran up to her bedroom to put the radio back. Outside her family was saying goodbye. They thought she was with Shimul. Mila put the radio back on the mosaic table in its original place. The mosaic table had a thick dust crust by now. She came out as soon as she could. Shurjo opened the backseat door for them to climb in, first Irfaan then Mila. They said goodbyes as Shurjo drove them out. A soft smile played on Mila's lips thinking how beautifully the tale of the antique radio had transpired for Shimul.

The evening moon shone an incandescent beauty. It was in contrast to its pale afternoon shadow phase. The legendary moon lady spun her threads as she sang her moon song. Just as well as she had threaded them since eternity through the phases of the moon. In broad daylight, it was but a shadow white moon. As the evening progressed the colour deepened to golden and then silver until it faded completely away at dawn; the moirai of eternal fate; she had spun all throughout over millions of years on an unbroken spinning machine since the Big Bang unveiled her and brought her out to light.

Shurjo pushed on the brakes gently in front of Mila's parents-in-law's apartment building. He came out of the car and opened the back door for Irfaan to make an egress, while Mila opened her side of it and promptly got out. They walked fast towards the building's entrance, with the dinner containers in her hands as Shurjo also left.

They knocked on the door for about ten minutes. Then, they heard a faint sound of a hard click of the metallic drop bolt. Mr Khan unbolted it and stood aside. His lips were pressed together. He let them through. Mrs Khan had been up too. She was seated in a chair facing the window in the living room. Her fingers were interlocked on her lap. It was past dinnertime, Mila grimaced at Mr Khan and rushed into the kitchen to organise dinner. She brought out plates and glasses and dished out the food on the dining table as fast as she could.

The four of them had a quiet dinner, sitting around the table taking seconds and thirds, scoops of rice and the fish curry. The spoon made a slight tingle as it came in contact with the bowl, now nearly empty, with bits and pieces of the fishy flesh and bones fallen in the bottom.

"When will you learn to cook like this?" Mrs Khan asked.

Mila ate away in silence and didn't really look at her. She didn't respond. What was there to say anyway? Mila finished before them and sat looking at them. When they finished, she asked if she could take the plates away and clear the table. They nodded. Mila pushed her chair behind her and stood up. She picked up everyone's plates including hers and piled them up, while the others stood up too, and left the cleaning up to her. Mila's lips twitched, and her eyes blinked. Her new role was unveiled before her. She was acutely aware of it but was unready to accept it. She never saw her mother or her aunts in this role, ever. Not even Aunty Prema, whom Daadi Amma accepted much later. Love, could love be so powerful to transform anyone so completely? She wondered, was her love that powerful?

Mrs Khan emerged from her bedroom and found Mila lingering at the table.

"Well? Are you just going to stand here all night? We were lucky to even have some dinner tonight."

Mila hurriedly took the plates and dropped a spoon on the floor, on her way to the kitchen. Irfaan picked it up after her. Mrs Khan looked at this, and nodded her head left to right in disapproval. Irfaan saw that but followed Mila into the kitchen anyway. In the kitchen, Mila was fighting back angry tears. She bit the corner of her lower lip, as she dumped the dirty dishes into the sink. Irfaan, dropping the spoon over her shoulder, gave her a peck on the nape; this slight touch made her happy, albeit, not exactly goosebumps sprung all over her body. Yes, she decided, love was powerful to change a person. This was enough to prevent a rift between her and her husband, and help her to adjust into this new role, and make her relatives happy. Her mother was happy.

Irfaan stood there trying to make light of the situation. He told her hospital jokes, of how a patient ate another patient's food as the other one slept. Some of them were funny, Mila laughed her head off as she did the dishes.

Later at night, Mila slept on Irfaan's arms in bed. Irfaan snored in sleep which Mila found disturbing sometimes. Unable to sleep tonight, she quietly raised her head off his arms and climbed down her side of the bed. She tiptoed into the bathroom and looked at her image in the mirror. She smiled, and then frowned and scowled, one after another. The moon was much smaller now, a silver half-dish; it peeped through the small bathroom window. Its light could be taken for granted, forever, there it was, shining hope to its onlookers. That was what the moon lady did best from her enchanting seat. She spun silver threads, of cause and consequences, and showered it on everyone, a beautiful folklore. Mila hadn't realised that it was already quite late before she could get some sleep. She came back to bed to a snoring husband. She lay down and closed her lids.

She woke up squinting and yawning to some seriously loud conversations in the morning. Irfaan wasn't in bed beside her. She got out of bed and rushed into the bathroom to make herself presentable; her in-laws were at breakfast. She bathed and wore a pink cotton saree. She combed her damp, dark hair and thought she looked beautiful. She came out of the bedroom with a fresh smile, this new, fresh morning.

Her in-laws were sitting around the dining table. They looked formidable and aloof, including her own husband.

"Finally, the princess has woken," her mother-in-law cried out.

"Oh! I'm sorry, I overslept, I didn't g-get much sleep at all," Mila said.

"I see," Mr Khan said. "What can we expect from the daughter of a three-timer?"

He looked at his wife and his lips curved into a sardonic smile.

"Mila ignored the touch of sarcasm and asked gently. "Can I get you something?"

"No, try to wake up early from now on," Mrs Khan said.

Saying so, both stood up and walked away. Irfaan was still sitting and Mila, standing on the door's threshold. Mila looked at Irfaan, who sat sipping his tea, silently. He looked up at her and gestured to her to sit beside him. She did not fully understand this cold greeting. He pushed a plate of toast and omelette towards her and poured her a cup of tea. While she ate her breakfast, he sat by her.

"What happened?" Mila whispered.

"The usual in-law stuff."

"What's that?" she asked.

"That's what's expected of a new bride. An ideal daughter-in-law would wake up at dawn before everyone, make chapati, cook vegetable curries and fry eggs, make tea, and serve hot breakfast to in-laws—you know."

"Oh! I see. Did you or did you not defend me, just then?" she asked.

"I couldn't. You were indefensible."

"How so?" she hissed.

"What could I have said in your father's favor which, even I knew of only yesterday? Or what could I have done to wake you up in the morning, when I knew you didn't get much sleep last night? You tell me," he asked.

"Oh! I don't know—anything. My father was not a three-timer. He married them legally under the Sharia Law."

But she didn't know that the subsequent two marriages were all illegal, even under the Sharia without his wives' consent. Regardless, there was nothing she or he could say

382

to change his parents' mindset, or the circumstance which her father had created. Sipping her tea, she overheard, Mr and Mrs Khan chatting from the verandah, "even my mother's maid, gave her daughter a better trousseau that she had been filling up over the years, silver plated tea set and what not." Mila finished her breakfast and went back into her bedroom and then into the bathroom. She stood before the vanity mirror in the bathroom. She heard Irfaan's voice. He called out for her. She came out immediately and found Irfaan standing and beaming with a letter in his hand.

"What is it?" Mila asked.

"I've got the job."

"Which one?" she asked.

"To teach at the medical college, junior lecturer in the department of psychiatry."

Mila clapped her hands and beamed back at Irfaan.

"How come you never told me that you applied?" she asked.

"I wanted to surprise you."

He walked towards her and gave her a tight hug and a deep kiss on her lips.

"Have you told Maa and Abba?" she asked.

"Of course, they were the first to know. Inform our relatives at the House of Chowdhury, too. Call them, now. Let's celebrate. Lunch is on me, we'll go somewhere nice."

Words tumbled out of Irfaan's mouth. Irfaan's shout, they were going out together for lunch. It was a Sunday, so they should all be able to make it, Mila hoped, and thought that the maid would be back by sun down.

Irfaan telephoned them himself. Mr and Mrs Khan were also excited and chuffed that their son had been blessed with such a good teaching position within the hospital. It was planned that the residents of the House of Chowdhury would meet up with Irfaan's family in a Chinese restaurant, The Bamboo Shoot, at the Dhanmondi Lakes.

Irfaan drove his family to the restaurant. They arrived first. He parked in a good spot. The restaurant was spacious, dimly lit, and wall to wall carpeted, decorated with dragon etched lamp shades; bamboo leaf dividers were placed along the four walls. The owner/cashier bowed and welcomed Irfaan and his family as they entered; a waiter led them to a round table with many chairs in the centre of this fairly large room. Once they were seated, he handed them a few neatly bound menu folders.

"We're waiting for our guests. We'll order after they arrive," Irfaan told the man.

"Yes, sure, not a problem,"

The man brought over a pile of the same menu folders and placed them in the table's centre. The family of four sat quietly, eyeing the surroundings. Irfaan and Mila sat next to each other with Mr and Mrs Khan.

"I'm thinking about the maid. The sooner she arrives, the better," Mrs Khan said. "So, you know, Mila, the maid has a habit of stealing food. One day, I caught her off guard drinking milk."

Mila said nothing. She was quietly praying for her family to arrive. What was taking them so long? She peered out of the glass window and saw their car parking. Her Uncle Ashik, in the driving seat. They were getting out of the car, one person at a time. Mila smiled and let out a sigh of relief. Irfaan noticed how her face brightened up. Mila rose from her chair to signal them where they were seated. They walked through the door and followed the same waiter to their table in the semi-darkness. A round of greetings ensued, cordial smiles were exchanged, and then they sat down in their respective chairs.

Lutfun sat next to Mila. Prema, Nazmun Banu, Ashik, Sheri, and Quasu sat down in a row around the table. Once they were comfortable, the waiter came back for the order. Irfaan and Mr Khan selected a large number of delectable foods—chicken corn soup, chowmein', fried rice, beef chili, sweet-sour prawn, and a bottle of small coke for everyone.

"Congrats!" Sheri looked at Irfaan across the table. "When do you start?"

"From Monday, week," Irfaan said.

"How nice?" Lutfun whispered to Mila. "How're you doing?"

"Happy," Mila smiled. "Yes, it was bound to happen sooner or later. But I didn't think it would happen so soon."

Mr Khan tapped on the table to get everyone's attention. Mila's uncles and aunties looked at him across the table. He told them that he was a proud father today. That his son had succeeded. They nodded in agreement, saying, 'yeah, yeah,' and smiled.

Irfaan looked at them gleaming with happiness. He looked at Mila and exchanged some soft stares of pupils dilating. Mrs Khan went on about her maid. That she still hadn't returned and, thanking them in the same monotone for the beautiful curry dinner they had sent over. Prema, Lutfun and Nazmun Banu listened and smiled politely to her monotonous conversation about the maid.

Three waiters served them. They brought hot food and placed them on the table. Mr Khan did the onus of asking the waiters to serve platefuls to his guests, first, and then his own family—Irfaan, Mila, and his wife. After the meal was served to everyone, Mr Khan was last to be served as a goodwill gesture.

"How's the cheese factory going?" Irfaan asked.

"Getting there," Sheri answered.

Mila twitched her lips with a mouthful of food. She asked for another scoop of fried rice by holding the plate out to Sheri to serve her. As they were eating, and drinking, talking, and laughing mirthfully, Irfaan suddenly rose to everyone's surprise. They looked at him. Irfaan pulled a box from under the table like a magician, and holding it towards Mila, he said, "This is my gift to you."

Looking at the box, Mila's eyes became large in awe. She took the gift, looked at it, and then opened it; out came a tiny radio from the box. Irfaan stood over her and grinned.

"Why? You?" That was all Mila could say.

She gasped and looked at everyone. Mrs Khan was very quiet. She hadn't even smiled while the others jubilated.

"Oh my, my, look at that Mila, how romantic?" Prema said.

Lutfun crooned, joining Prema and Ashik, and Sheri laughed with joy. Nazmun Banu nodded her head in approval; a lingering smile playing on her lips.

"Now when did you smuggle this in? Tell me," Mila asked. "How come none of us, me, Abba or Maa, knew."

"It's a secret."

Irfaan laughed and winked at Mila. But Mila wasn't convinced.

"When several waiters were serving around the table, I gave my car keys to one of them. I whispered to him to bring this from the car's boot."

Ah yes, Mila realised she was slightly distracted when the food had arrived and with all the conversations and congratulations. She hadn't noticed what was happening under the table, quite possible. Irfaan looked at her cheeks dimpling sweetly and gauged her happiness. But Mila swallowed the thought that this new object could never replace an antique; it felt like a bribe.

After lunch finished, a waiter handed them a few doggy bags to take home. The party broke up. They said goodbyes, hugs and kisses, which Mila received mostly from her aunts and uncles and walked towards their respective cars. By the time they came home, evening had set in, and her in-laws were tired. Mr and Mrs Khan went to their room, and Mila went into the kitchen to check if the maid was back. She looked around and found only the pots and the pans, but no maid. She let out a sigh and went into her bedroom.

Irfaan had changed into his pajamas and lay down in bed for a rest when Mila entered. He pulled her towards him. She came to him automatically. Under the sleeping suit, Mila saw his curly chest hair. She brushed it with her lips. He felt her hot sighs. He began to caress her under her clothes, as she did the same to him. Irfaan turned off the light and slipped under the blanket with her.

It was still evening. But no one seemed interested in dinner. Mila had come out of her bedroom to check if Mr and Mrs Khan wanted any dinner. But she realised that they hadn't even come out of their room since they returned. The leftover food brought from the restaurant was there on the table. But the family called it a night. Irfaan was still in bed. Mila went into the toilet. In her mind, the only thought which ravaged her was, what if she couldn't wake up early enough to please her in-laws. What if she overslept, again? At any rate, she came to bed, and found that Irfaan was already snoring. She lay down beside him, but she continued to fidget under the blanket turning over every two-seconds. It was very late, now and it woke up Irfaan. He turned around, and opened his groggy eyelids. He saw Mila and asked. "Do you want sleeping pills?"

"No, I think I'll be fine."

"I'll have to prescribe you some anti-anxiety pills," he said.

He didn't seem particularly concerned that Mila maybe suffering from anxiety on account of her in-law's annoyances and criticisms that she overslept every morning. This was the second time after coming to this house that he had suggested pills. Might as well, Mila thought, pills it was then; it had been just a few months into the marriage, and pills were already starting to make inroads.

The moon lady came out every evening, changing from white to glossy yellow and then white again before she departed. No caps in the number of human dramas she spun, sitting there at the weaving machine, threading eternal moirai, without intervening. Irfaan turned on the bed lamp and left her side. He walked towards a cabinet, placed in the corner of the room. He opened the doors of the cabinet and took out a bottle of pills.

Mila gazed at a number of medicine bottles in the cabinet which she never thought existed. She read a familiar bottle of anti-depressants. She wondered who took them? Was it Irfaan? Did he suffer from depression? But she dared not ask him now, at three 'o'clock in the morning. Irfaan handed her two pills, she took them like a submissive, untrained, non-medical wife. She didn't even ask him the name of the pills. She swallowed them with water which Irfaan handed to her. Irfaan turned off the bed lamp and lay down on one side with his back towards her.

In the morning, Mila was late as usual. But she felt calmer. She woke up and found Irfaan's side of the bed empty. She got out of bed, went into the bathroom, and took a leisurely shower. She dressed in a cotton, floral saree of many colours, red, pink, and mauve. She combed her long, wet hair in front of the vanity mirror and came back into the bedroom. She paused before the medicine cabinet in the corner. She opened it and found not just one bottle of anti-depressants but many. She closed the cabinet and went out of the bedroom.

Mr and Mrs Khan were sitting on the verandah with their cups of tea, reading newspapers. Irfaan was nowhere around. She wondered where he was. She went to the verandah and stood at the door.

"You're awake! Thank God, for the maid has arrived early this morning. Irfaan opened the door and went out for a jog. Anyway, yours and Irfaan's breakfast is on the table. Tell the maid to make you tea," Mrs Khan said.

She curved her lips and Mila saw her disdain. But said nothing. She walked away into the kitchen and saw the maid already making tea. As soon as Mila entered, she smiled at her brightly.

"How was your holiday?" Mila asked.

"It was very good. I went to my niece's wedding. Her in-laws are wonderful."

"Were they happy with the dowry?" Mila asked.

"Very happy. They got everything as promised—a motorbike, a wrist watch and some cash."

"Oh, that's great. I wish them happiness."

"Yeah. Here, your tea is ready. I'll bring it over to the table for you," she said.

"No, I'll take it here." Mila replied.

"You know, they'll eye you down and think badly of you if you ate before them. If you get hungry, eat when they are not looking," she said suddenly.

"What?"

Mila was trying to figure out what she meant. Then she remembered what Mrs Khan had told them the night before at the restaurant. But why would the maid tell her this? She was the maid, and Mila was the Bahu Rani. Why would Mila have to steal food?

"Don't worry about me. If you feel hungry, let me know, I'll give you food. You don't need to steal, okay," Mila said.

The maid ogled at her; she jerked her head with a small grunt and focussed on the task at hand. Mila didn't quite understand what the maid, or Mrs Khan were on about. Why would anyone have to steal food? When Irfaan came back, she needed to ask him. Just as well, the bell rang, and she rushed to open the door. There he was, all sweaty from his jog. He smiled at her and winked as usual. He disappeared into the bedroom and then into the bathroom for a shower. Mila sat down at the breakfast table.

The maid brought one more cup of tea to the table for Irfaan. Mila waited. Irfaan came out, refreshed and looking handsome in a striped white and black shirt and a pair of tight blue jeans. He sat down in a chair, next to Mila.

"Well, our honeymoon period is going to be over soon once I start work next week," he said.

"Yes, I shall start at the hospital too, starting next week," Mila said.

"You do that, life's going to be pretty hectic from then on," Irfaan said.

"Yeah, that's life, I guess."

They quietly ate the omelette and chapati which the maid had prepared. Mila suddenly realised that she had left her little radio in the car last night. She looked at Irfaan and found him engrossed. She thought she must not tell him that she had forgotten to bring the radio from the car. She hoped that Irfaan wouldn't notice it. He finished his tea and stood up. She stood up too, and asked the maid to clear the table, while she followed Irfaan to the verandah where his parents were seated. Mila thought now was the time to go downstairs and get the radio from the car. No one had to know. She went into the bedroom to look for the car keys. Rummaging through Irfaan's table drawers and the pant pockets that he had worn last night, she couldn't find them anywhere. The bedroom door opened suddenly, and Irfaan walked in.

"Looking for these."

He had the keys dangling from his index finger.

"How did you know?" Mila asked.

"Well, I didn't think I saw the radio anywhere this morning, when I opened the door for the maid," he answered. "Now you were going through my stuff and pant pockets, inside out, I guessed it. Am I right?"

"Why? Do you always have the keys on you when you go for a jog?"

"Of course, to let myself in."

"Good idea. Now give me the keys so I can go downstairs and get the radio from the car."

"Don't bother," he said.

"What? Why?" she asked.

He smiled at her panic state and said nothing.

"Why? Tell me," Mila asked again.

"Can you guess?"

"Guess what? No, I can't guess."

Beads of sweat had now appeared on Mila's forehead, which she knew Irfaan was looking at. Her breathing was short, and she sat down abruptly on the bed's edge. Irfaan had a vile smirk. She felt he gazed into her soul, as though she couldn't keep any secrets from him. He was reading her mind.

"I gave it away," he said.

"You did what?" she asked.

"I gave it to a boy on the street."

"You didn't, Oh! How could you?"

"I knew I couldn't win your heart with it, so I gave it away. What's the point?"

His intonation rose slightly as he ended the sentence; then he shrugged.

Mila had nothing to say. She simply stared at him and then started to cry.

"There, there, don't cry. These crocodile tears don't suit such a courageous and classy lady as yourself."

Mila stood up and decided to leave. She had enough of it. Irfaan didn't stop her. She packed a small suitcase of clothes and brushed past him, opened the door and stalked downstairs. She walked down the path and she knew full well that her in-laws were watching her from the verandah; but she was beyond care.

She took a rickshaw home. When she reached The House of Chowdhury, it was nearly midday. She let the rickshaw go at the main entrance, and stepped inside through the small, walk gate. She saw someone's tall shadow in the front yard. It was Rabeya with a bucket. As soon as she saw Mila, she startled and screamed. Her bucket fell down and some water flowed out into the grounds. She looked at Mila's grim face. It had a deep frown.

"Mila Apa?" she asked.

"Yes, Rabeya, how are you?"

"I'm well. Everyone is still in the orchard."

"Okay."

Mila walked inside the house through the open entrance and down the passageway towards the orchard. When she appeared on the doorstep, Nazmun Banu saw her first. She looked at her, and the suitcase; her jaw dropped. She knew this couldn't be a good thing. Prema and Lutfun followed her gaze and they too saw Mila. Mila stood there with the suitcase in her hand, and she started to cry.

The aunts rushed towards her and held her close; she cried out on their shoulders. "It's over, It's over. I tried. God knows I tried."

"Shh, tell us what happened?" they asked.

"I'll never go back to that house, ever. I'm so sorry, Amma! I tried my best."

Mila looked at Nazmun Banu through tear-stained eyes.

"Okay, it's okay. You don't have to tell me anything. Come and sit down, here," Mila's mother said.

Lutfun and Prema led her towards the orchard, and Nazmun Banu took her suitcase. This was completely opposite to the wedding day when they, the same aunts, had walked Mila in her bridal saree in a state of pure euphoria, down these passageways to the bridal dais, just a few months ago. Mila sat down in the chair and calmed down in her familiar surroundings. Quasu came and gave her a hug and offered her a bar of melted chocolate he had been holding; this made Mila smile. The fallen leaves in the orchard were sodden in a recent rain. In a few short months, her wedding was over.

Grief lay heavy like soaked bread in the House of
Chowdhury. The stale air of the house had dampened the
spirits of the residents. For a change of air, they decided to
go to their ancestral home in the village. There was also
good news that new Chowdhury land had emerged after
many years of being submerged in the River Kali. The Raiza
Chowdhury Cheese & Company was a success. Neither Mila
nor Irfaan's family, or even Irfaan himself tried to get in
touch in the last seven days.

Mrs Chowdhury decreed that the family needed a
vacation. They were going to go away for five days. On this
journey, they would also visit some historical hotspots and
put a claim on their rising land out of the river. A few Sufi
Dargahs were around the vicinity, they would pay homage
to one powerful Dargah. Shurjo was going to drive them in a
microbus which belonged to one of Sheri's childhood
friends, Ajmal Shah. All morning, Rabeya and Shurjo loaded
the microbus with several suitcases and Mrs Chowdhury's
wheelchair. They were ready to depart.

Mila saw Shimul standing near the microbus on her old
crutch. She finally got the hang of it. They exchanged a slight
smile and Mila climbed into the microbus. Mrs Chowdhury
sat in the front seat beside Shurjo, who helped her in. She
had her walking stick with her. Shurjo literally carried her
onto the seat beside him. When everyone was in the
microbus, he drove it out of the front yard, and stopped
momentarily at the main gate before merging into the
oncoming traffic on the thoroughfare. Rabeya stood by the
main gate and closed it after them.

As they were coming through the gate, Mila saw
someone enter. He had stopped to speak to Rabeya. Mila

even heard the word 'Shimul.' Mila tried to think who it was. Then she remembered. Ah! It was the mechanic from the shop. She smiled and felt happy for Shimul. At least something good had happened out of the radio tragedy. Who would have known that it would break up one couple and tie another; class hierarchy had nothing to do with it.

The journey ensued. The minibus had a radio attached, which Shurjo tuned to a station broadcasting a cacophony of cheap Bangla cinema songs. It was okay for the journey. Because this was what the journey required to uplift the mood with light artless music. Mila's uncles sat in the rear seat, and she sat with Nazmun Banu, Prema, and Lutfun in the middle row. About half an hour into the journey, Sheri asked Shurjo to stop at a tea stall. Shurjo slowed down and side-parked on a dirt path over uneven pebbles. While the women stayed in the car, Mila got out with her uncles. She also needed to go to the ladies. Sheri asked the chai-wallah where the bog was. He showed her plantain foliage behind the tea shack.

Mila had to go! She quickly disappeared behind the foliage and squatted on a grassy patch. There was some privacy here, Mila sighed. But there were also fire ants. She had barely sat down when she realised that she had stepped on a mound. She quickly stepped away and sat down in another place. A colony of fire ants dribbled out of the mound haphazardly and quickly formed a queue.

She had finished. Drawn by the fire ants, she stood up watching them. How resilient they were, these tiny creatures, humans wouldn't look all that different from the space above, she realised. They looked like little moving dots, too, maybe one dot slightly taller than the other, but dots, nevertheless. All of a sudden, she felt nauseous. She threw up over the mound. Being a doctor nearly, the first thing that came to her mind was pregnancy. She began to make a mental note of the first day of her last period. Yes, there was a match. She smiled shyly to herself. Another member to join the House of Chowdhury soon.

How was she going to break this news to Irfaan, she wondered? She would have to contact them at some stage when she began to show. Either she would, or her aunties would have to sooner or later tell the father of their firstborn. Would her in-laws be thrilled? Would this patch up the relationship? This was going to be the firstborn of his family. With the father suffering from depression and anxiety, what sort of an upbringing would that be? There were just too many questions crowding her head. She took a deep breath and decided to enjoy her motherhood. She inhaled some fresh country air and stepped out of the fire ant mound to join the party.

A smoky kettle was perpetually brewing tea over a stove in the tea shack. It was sooty black. A man of medium height made white sugary tea. Out of the black kettle, a man poured white, hot tea into each of the glasses and served them to the customers. Sheri ordered a glass for everyone including Shurjo. Shurjo also ordered a couple of samosas for himself which Sheri paid for.

Mila came out of the foliage organising her clothes and pulling down her saree. She also ordered tea and a couple of samosas like Shurjo. The samosas were handed to her by a tea boy in a half folded printed page, a torn page from a published book. She took it from the tea boy. And as she opened the wrap, she found a beautiful poem printed on the crumple of the half-fold page. She took her first bite, standing by the microbus, and read the poem. It was an unrequited love poem between two birds—one was a pigeon and the other was a dove. How lovely? Mila read smiling and sipping her tea. It was hot, but light, like a tea sherbet drink, only this was hot tea.

After they finished, the tea boy collected all the soiled glasses, but Mila kept the wrap of the poem. This was what happened to household books and old newspapers. They got sold to second-hand book sellers, and sometimes especially newspapers, sold them to peddlers or ferre-wallahs or to tea stalls. Torn pages from those books were used as paper wraps and bags; a poet's worst nightmare would be to find out that torn pages from his or her books were being used as street food wrapper. Samosas and hot chana were sold in their folds every minute, the fate of many books; as it was the fate of the one which Mila clasped now.

Back in the minibus. The journey resumed. It sped along the road in the hands of a competent driver energised after a much needed refection, Shurjo. Mila sat squashed between Lutfun and Prema. The minibus slowed down on an uneven gravel road. Just as well, Mila thought, this was the Sufi Durgah they were planning to visit. Every passing vehicle slowed down to pay respect to the Sufi. It was a powerful Durgah of this legendary Sufi, generally known as the Naked Fakir.

There were many stories that Mila had heard as a child about this Durgah. Vehicles that had not slowed down here in the past, either had fatal accidents or permanent damage to the passengers. Today, Shurjo made sure that he slowed down to minimum speed until he stopped the van, down by the road. Mrs Chowdhury gestured and asked the driver to stop.

She wished to get out of the minibus to pay homage. It was her wish to enter the Durgah. Mrs Chowdhury turned towards Mila and everyone in the backseats, asking them to accompany her inside. Shurjo helped Mrs Chowdhury out of the vehicle. Mila held on to her aunties as they hopped down, as did her two uncles, Ashik and Sheri. Ashik looked at Sheri and winked at him.

"Well, I've heard much about this Sufi."

"Me too. I heard that he stays naked most of the time," Sheri answered.

"We are not wearing a skullcap, I suppose he wouldn't mind, since he's nude himself," Ashik joked.

"I suppose not," Sheri laughed.

They walked towards the Durgah of the Naked Fakir, also respectfully called Pir Saheb. With Mrs Chowdhury and Shurjo in the lead, others followed them to the entrance, situated under the aerial roots, and a knotty banyan tree. There he was, the Pir, the Sufi himself, sitting naked in a lotus position with his eyes closed. But a skullcap was on his head. Ashik looked at Sheri thinking why the skullcap? When they appeared before him, he opened his eyes and winked at Sheri and Ashik. The men were puzzled. They remembered the skullcap conversation the brothers had at the entrance. They lowered their heads in shame before this enigmatic Naked Fakir.

"How did he know?" Ashik whispered.

"Shh, I don't know," Sheri responded.

The pir looked at Mila and asked her to come forward. Mila went closer and sat on a thick in-ground root. He looked at her, smiled, and nodded his head. He closed his eyes and appeared to have a vision. He opened them in a while, and he said:

"Where do you live, where do we live, where is our home? Under this tree, over the mountains and beyond, the sky, a time-rider. Dancing colours! This life is more surrealistic, this short life than death, death was natural, not the other way round. All will be well, go to the river. The river will wash away your pain. Now go! Must play the game. Once in it, can't leave the game— play it till the end. Someone is playing you. Something is playing us. We're all being played one way or the other. Dragonflies, Fireflies; air, water, fire, earth, hanging roots, all are in it—all are in the game— the river will tell you. The journey is all, not the destination. The journey is not as long as it appears. Appearance is nothing—nothing—listen to the river—."

He made no sense; not even in the slightest. As he went into a trance again, Mila looked at him mesmerised. She saw or rather felt she saw a fire emanating from him. A translucent light, a beacon of enlightenment in this madness. He had not opened his eyes again as long as they were there. He trembled in his skullcap. And would not speak to anyone. He spaced out. The Chowdhury family slowly retraced their steps back to the minibus. Ashik put some money into a donation box on their way out. They came back to the vehicle on the dirt road, where the van was parked. Shurjo helped Mrs Chowdhury back up in the front seat next to him, while the others returned to their respective seats. He drove them out on the main road. He was to take them as far as the river. The vehicle drove off fading into the distance until it disappeared over the horizon.

The story, this diary wasn't flawlessly written, told like the cinemas of the mind, was enigmatic. The Blue Café at Raven's Edge was now nearly empty. The staff was looking at her a bit oddly and thinking when she was leaving. She had come in fairly early, and it was nearly afternoon. They thought, maybe, Mila was waiting for someone. The staff kept looking outside for a car or a friend who might come for her. Then a car did stop. Mila looked at the car and waved at a teenager getting out and entering the café. She went straight to Mila's table.

"Here you are, mother dearest? I finally found you," she said.

"Why, were you looking for me?"

"It's late," she said.

"Oh! That's okay. I am still alive and well. I was coming home, anyway," Mila pulled a smile on her lips.

"Let's be off then, Naanjaan is waiting in the car," she said.

"Oh! Is Amma here, too?"

"Yes, of course, she is, and so are Prema and Lutfun Naani," she said.

"Who is driving?"

"Quasu," she answered.

"Why? Where is Shurjo?" Mila asked.

"Taking a nap, as usual," the young girl laughed.

"How did you find me here? I don't think I told anyone that I'd be down here."

"No, you didn't."

The girl kept quiet and lowered her head.

"Saima, I asked you a question. How did you find me?" Mila asked.

"Father apparently saw you and he followed you here."

"What? Why was he loitering around our house?"

"I don't know. You have to ask him. He had been coming around for some time, by the looks of it. Rabeya Bua saw him a few times. One day she even invited him in, but he had declined. Today too, he came by as usual which was when you were leaving. He saw you and followed you here, then he went back to the house, and told Rabeya Bua where you were," Saima said.

"I see. I have nothing to say to him."

"I do," Saima said.

"What could you possibly say to a sick man?" Mila asked.

"I don't know. He is still my father. How long can you keep me away from him? We would have to meet someday, ya? One day; I am sixteen, now. It's about time. Besides, he hasn't done anything to me!"

Mila looked at her fiery daughter. She knew she couldn't stop her. "Ya, you are right, there. He hasn't done anything to you. You two must meet. Let's go, can't keep Quasu, Amma, and Aunts waiting in the car."

Mila closed the diary. As she closed it, the last blank pages turned in the sudden gust of wind which passed through the café. Mila decided not to make the final entries of Mrs Chowdhury's passing. As they could never be scripted. What was there to write anyway? How had everyone grieved for her, this inheritor of a grand tradition? How had she died? No, Mila thought, the Pir Saheb finally made sense; her journey was more important than her destination, the death. Mila wished Mrs Chowdhury to be remembered for the great lady who she was, the tremendous willpower she had, and above all her intelligence.

Ultimately, her diary was about good and evil conflict. If anything, it was a reflection of Mrs Chowdhury's incandescent desire and continuous struggle to establish morality in her house to bring everyone, her rather amoral family to a path of righteousness, which only she was able to tread.

She may not have won the battle of the libido; unbeknownst to her, it was not winnable, this innate flaw of the blood couldn't be corrected anytime soon. But her suffering on account of it couldn't be undermined. She had known all along that only Mila had the empathy to understand her profound pain; she bequeathed the diary to her.

Some of the pages also spoke of Mila's story. How she never cared for a divorce settlement, after a year of separation from Irfaan, although there was a binding deed in place and Irfaan's family hadn't pursued it because Mila had never put any claim? The many blank pages stared out waiting to be filled. Whoever penned the future entries, the diary had to continue. Because life couldn't be silenced. Fresh episodes and new chapters had to be written by the future generation of children, children's children, the grandchildren and the great-grandchildren. The House of Chowdhury held them in a magical aura, an aura that could never be shaken. It carried mystery which charmed its inheritors throughout generations. Neither the house nor the diary could be parted with. Its enchantment was too powerful, just as powerful was the happiness leached out of its cold walls.

Still, Rahim Ali's many letters knocked on Mila's door, proving beyond any shadow of doubt of his love being enduring and pure. However, she had inherited her grandmother's morality and the willpower to subdue any illicit romance. Her love for him was just as pure but it had also ripened; marriage would have spoiled it. It was best this way, unsullied.

Mila and Saima left the café. Their lips were firmly set. The staff bade them goodbye politely. They looked at each other afterwards and said, "ditto," —a spitting image. The other nodded in agreement.

ABOUT THE AUTHOR

Multiple contests winner for short fiction,Mehreen Ahmed is an Australian novelist born in Bangladesh.Her historical fiction,The Pacifist,is a Drunken Druid's Editor's Choice and an audible bestseller.Gatherings,is nominated for the James Tait Black Prize for fiction.Her flash fiction have been nominated for 3xbotN,Pushcart.Included in The Best Asian Speculative Fiction Anthology,her works have also been shortlisted, finalist,and have received honorable mention.Critically acclaimed by Midwest Book Review,DD Magazine to name a few.She is a featured writer on Flash Fiction North and Connotation Press,a reader for The Welkin Prize,Five Minutes,a juror for KM Anthru International Prize.Her works have been translated into German,Greek and Bangla,reprinted,anthologised,and have made it to the top 10 read on Impspired magazine multiple times

Literary and Scholarly Publications

Cambridge University Press,University of Hawaii Press,Michigan State University Press,ISTE,Call-ej,University of Kent Press,The Sheaf:University of Saskatoon,Writer's Digest:Six Sentences,IceFloe Press,Litro Magazine,The BeZine,The Atherton Review:Academy Press,Ethel Zine Journal,Olney/Kiss Your Darlings Magazine,Alternate Route,Minison Project-Shakespear's sonnet reimagined,WordCityLit,Mōtus Audāx Press,KNOT Magazine,The Antonym,Insignia 2022 Best Asian Speculative Fiction Anthology,The Hennepin Review,Literary Heist,Alien Buddha Press,Rogue Agent Journal:Sundress Publications,October Hill Magazine,Synchronised Chaos,Perception Magazine:Syracuse University,Straylight Magazine:Wisconsin-Parkland University,The Talon Review:North Florida Univeristy,Oddball Magazine,Pine Cone Review,Noctivagant Press,Coin-Operated Press,Connotation Press,Door is A Jar,ELJ Scissors and Spackle,The Chamber Magazine,Flash Boulevard,Five Minutes,Quail Bell,Ponder Savant,Litterateur Rw,ShabdAaweg Review,Phenomenal Literature,Crêpe & Penn,Flash Frontier,Ellipsis Zine,Ginosko#24#29,Brown Bag,The Cabinet of Heed,Sequoyah Cherokee River Journal,Melbourne Culture Corner,Cogito Literary Journal,Breathe Everyone Magazine,Literati Magazine,Archer Literature,Active Muse,Dreaming in Fiction,Anti-Heroin Chic,Love in the time of Covid

Chronicle,Unpublished Platform,Wellington Street Review,Nailpolish Stories,Setu,Impspired Magazine,The Writers and Readers'Magazine,Solstice Literary Magazine,WINK,Mono,KREAXXXION Review,Thorn Literary Magazine.3 Moon Magazine,Merak Magazine,Sage Cigarettes,The Bombay Review,FlashBack Fiction,Down in the Dirt, CC&D,Nymphs,Portand Metrozine,Academy of Heart and Mind,Creativity Webzine,Mojave Heart,The Piker Press,Kitaab,Nthanda, CommuterLit,Angel City Review,Paper Djinn,FreeFlashFiction,Cafe Dissensus,Adelaide Literary Magazine,Scarlet Leaf Review,Terror House Magazine,The Punch Magazine,Furtive Dalliance,Flash Fiction North,Storyland Literary Review,Bridge House,Cosmic Teapot Publication.

Contest Wins

First Place,Academy of the Heart and Mind,May Flower contest,2022
One of the winners,Waterloo Festival,May 2020
Stream-of-Consciousness Challenge,Cabinet-of-Heed,Drawer Four,April,2020
Finalist,Adelaide Books NY for Fourth Adelaide Literary Award Contest,February,2020
Honourable Mention in the Weavers of Words contest,Unpublished Platform,March 2022
Nominated for the Publication of the Month,Spillwords Press April/May,2018